He Died Two Days Ago

John Posner

Author of *Forever is Too Long*

Books may be purchased at www.JohnPosnerBooks.com
Golden Echo Books

Development Editing: Peggie Ireland
Editing/Proofreading: Barb Wilson
Book Shepherd: Judith Briles, TheBookShepherd.com
Cover and Interior Design: Rebecca Finkel, F+P Graphic Design, FPGD.com

ISBN paperback: 979-8-9893354-5-9
ISBN hardback: 979-8-9893354-3-5
ISBN eBook: 979-8-9893354-4-2

LCCN: 2024910628

Sci-fi/Fantasy | Psycho Thrillers | Dystopian

Printed in USA

Content Warning

He Died Two Days Ago is speculative sci-fi novel that reveals a hidden alien possession of humans and the aliens' Machiavellian nature. Scenes of vengeance are involved. Some description of rape is included, but only at a high-level of detail. Alcohol use. Readers who may be sensitive to these elements, please take note.

Ephemeron One
40,000 Earth Years Ago

On a planet called Ephemeron, a baby cuddled in its mother's arms. The potential of a long life lay before it.

Two more of the mother's children sat around the table, one child approximately fifty years old, the other a little over 200 years of age. This oldest child, though technically a young adult, sat next to its betrothed. One hundred years hence, the oldest child and his betrothed would Fuse, creating a seed that would strive to find a safe place to grow and, in time, also be betrothed.

At the far end of the table sat the baby's father. Uncles and aunts of the children sat at the table. A wide selection of foodstuffs beckoned, though the table's occupants mostly picked weakly at the enticements. It would be one of their last meals together, but at this moment no one was sure which member would ever again be able to sit at the table.

From outside the home's walls clamored strained voices and great commotion. Motorized vehicles struggled to make their way through the chaotic city traffic. Hot, swirling winds mercilessly cut at all living things. The day's temperature soared especially hot under the sun's direct rays. Dust fought to stifle those that dared breathe.

Around the perimeter of the dining area, concave nooks pocketed the walls. In each nook, a statue of a different god was adorned with small tributes. On the space between the nooks, pictures of other gods cast their protections upon the family. This was common. A visitor could go into almost any Ephemeron home and at least one room would display as many religious icons.

"Our family is allotted one seat to escape this dying planet," said the father solemnly. "Our youngest has its whole life ahead. Should that not count for something?"

"But no one who is close to our family will be able to take care of it," said the mother, pulling her baby tighter.

"It would be the same challenge for the middle child," said an aunt. "He is only fifty years old. Still a young Ephemeral. How would it know how to stand up to others in the new world? It will not have family around to protect it. Do we believe the authorities will provide adequate care?"

The elders turned their gaze on the oldest child. "The betrothal would need to be annulled," said the father, speaking about the eldest child in third person. "But he has proven to have exemplary engineering capabilities. The new world will require such skills."

"We do not know if the child could be successful at continuing our lineage," noted an aunt. "It has not yet faced a Fusion."

An uncle came to the eldest child's defense. "But if it could produce a progeny, its potential long life would help save and expand our lineage."

"What of us elders?" asked one of the aunts. "We have proven ourselves. Any of us would be an excellent choice. We have hundreds of years left to our lives. We could Fuse multiple times before our deaths. Our lineage could be continued. One of us is a physician. One is a lawyer. One is a school principal. One is a builder. New Ephemeron will need all those skills."

"We are allotted one slot," reminded the father. "Some families are not given the chance to decide who goes. Other families are not allowed to send any. We are fortunate that we can choose who will go to New Ephemeron.

"The monarchy tells us that the planet is verdant, but harsh. Wild creatures abound. They say there are no sentient beings living there. Life will be dangerous and hard. Ephemerals will not be building a country. They will be building a world."

"A lawyer?" exclaimed an uncle disdainfully. "Why would such a harsh new world need lawyers?"

"Do you belittle my profession?" the lawyer responded; her tone defensive. "A world needs its rules. Lawyers are keepers of the laws and codes of our world. In New Ephemeron, these traditions will need to be remembered."

The uncle pressed his point of the lawyer's uselessness. "The king, his advisors, and priests will protect our customs and laws. They will bring the essential books of our history, our religion, and our rules. More importantly in the beginning, building a world will require strength and vision."

"Will they come back for the rest of the Ephemerals?" interrupted the eldest child. "Can't those left behind be saved at a later time?"

"They will not be able to come back for us," answered the mother, shaking her head.

The first uncle spoke. "I hear that they are allotting some spots for robots, declaring them as more essential than Ephemerals. I also hear two rockets are reserved exclusively for our gods and their priests. Statues, religious icons, sacred books, and offerings will be launched. Ephemeron has only one thousand rockets that can make the journey to New Ephemeron."

"Do not let your faith waver, my brother," said the father. "Our faith has protected and nurtured us."

"My dear brother, I have not lost faith, but Ephemeron is no longer graced by one faith. The religious divergence pulls us farther and farther apart."

"That view seems too harsh. The differences are more like accents. One faith believes one god is most superior over all the others, but they still give adoration to all our gods. Is that so far removed from how we practice the faith in this house? We know not all the gods have equivalent powers. We know some are more powerful than others."

"I worry that the 'accents,' as you call the differences, will someday spiral into a great fissure."

"We waste our time with such worries," retorted the father. "We must trust that those who settle New Ephemeron will preserve the faith. Our worries should be toward our immediate concerns. Our planet is dying, and we are besieged by unending battles with the Zorix."

"We raped the planet," observed an aunt. "It now lays waste to us. How could we not see what we were doing? How could we not have stopped ourselves? The war with the Zorix is the same Ephemeral sin repeated. We believed in our superiority, our divine right to more and more. For those who survive the journey to New Ephemeron, it will be a chance to cleanse the Ephemeral soul. My hope is that they find peace in its remoteness."

"My dear family," persisted the father, "we must still decide who will make the journey. Who will have the most valuable skills in the new world? Who will be best positioned to preserve our lineage?"

An aunt spoke. "I am a school administrator and though I have many years of teaching experience, I do not have the technical skills of an engineer or scientist. In time, the new world will need my skills. Education will be essential to its survival. But as our pioneers hew a new civilization, they will need those who can build and teach others how to build. I should not be selected to go."

"I have spent my life pursuing justice," said the lawyer. "Laws are a living testament to being civilized. I am saddened that such written traditions and deliberations will be lost. But, at this moment, my skills are not the most needed in the new world. I should not be selected to go."

The mother spoke to her sister, the physician. "Your skills will be needed from the very beginning. Your presence will be essential to the survival of Ephemerals."

The physician responded, "Do we know who else is traveling to the new world? Certainly, there will be other physicians. Medical tools and diagnostics will be limited. There will not be sophisticated hospitals. Medicine will be limited. I am a specialist. I think there are better choices than me."

"My baby and young child need me here," stated the mother. "I have lived a full life. There will be many travails for those of us left behind. My duty is to stay to protect and help our family."

"Nor will I leave," said the father. "The new world needs those young, strong, and brave of heart. It needs those who can carve civilization from nothing."

The other uncles and aunts had their turns at the fateful decision.

The eldest child listened as they spoke.

None said they would go. None said that they felt worthy enough to go.

He felt their gazes turn upon him. His doubts told him he should not be handed this burden. How could they ask him to carry on the family's lineage and honor? What if he failed them?

The teacher reached over and put her hand on the eldest child's arm. "We are all scared, my dear child. In this, you are not alone. You have proven yourself over hundreds of years. Yes, you are young for an Ephemeral, but we see our spirit in you. You are an accomplished engineer. The new world will need your skills. You can help build a new world. You can teach others. You are young enough to have many children. Accepting this trial is the best way to honor us and our faith."

"Then, if you choose me," said the eldest child, drawing himself up in his seat, "I will use the strengths I learned from each of you. I will make you proud of me. I will make our gods proud of me." He turned to his betrothed. "My dear, being separated from you will be my greatest pain."

In her sorrow, the betrothed's body turned pink. The limbs and antennae of the two young betrothed Ephemerals intertwined, stimulating shared memories and dashed dreams.

"Family, let us pray," said the father. All at the table held hands and bowed their heads.

In the following weeks, those chosen to be sent to New Ephemeron prepared themselves as best they could. In the chaos and heartbreak, Ephemeron was surrounded by its last gasps of life. The beauty of the world it had once been, was no more.

Underground water reservoirs that had fed the world's farms had dried up. With these underground water caverns depleted, the weight of the land above, collapsed, opening vast chasms that pocked Ephemeron like ugly dried cysts. Hurricanes and tornadoes whirled destruction, ever more often and violently. Weather patterns of the past were disrupted, engulfing regions with weather events to which they were not accustomed.

The world succumbed to the persistent rise of global temperatures that ensured the demise of the world's ice fields. Coastal cities became flooded and abandoned. Methane ocean vents spewed forth their toxicity. Lightning strikes would sometimes ignite the rising vapors, causing fireballs that danced over the oceans' surface.

The Ephemeron's monarchy scrambled to survive.

Not all the king's court would be taken to New Ephemeron. The hangers-on, the lazy, the ne'er-do-wells would be left behind. Those of accomplishment and capability would be approved.

Yet ironically, some of the court's members pressed the king for themselves to be left behind, not because of fear of the unknown or because of high morals, but because they recognized the last draconian remnants of power would fall into their hands. Why should they risk a perilous journey to an untamed land, when they could rule over the world where they stood? It mattered not that the planet was in its death throes.

Power was more enticing, even if it was reigning over the dying.

Seeing Ephemeron's growing weakness, their mortal enemy, the Zorix, had increased their assaults. The planet's encircling robotic guardians fended off most attacks, but inevitably a few missiles and energy blasts reached the surface, haphazardly and randomly killing Ephemerals trying to carry out their besieged lives.

From Ephemeron's two moons, retaliatory attacks were unleashed against the infidel Zorix. It was hard to understand this war. It took three months for interstellar hyper-missiles to traverse the distance between the belligerents. Each civilization deployed attack pods that tried to navigate through defenses that might get closer to the enemy to unleash energy blasts.

Still, little was accomplished by the war. It seemed to be more of a testament to psychological failure. At some time in the distant past, one species had felt slighted, as did the other. Nobody knew when the first slight occurred or if it was meant as perceived.

But after hundreds of years of animosity, pride was the war's commander.

An average Ephemeral lived equivalent to 1,200 Earth years. Ephemerals did not have genders, as one on Earth would imagine. Often, an Ephemeral would be referred to as an *it*, though in writings of its history and communications with other beings, a convenient gender nomenclature was sometimes adopted.

Two Ephemerals would reproduce through a process called *Fusion*. A complicated set of customs governed betrothals and the subsequent Fusions of Ephemerals. In some cases, especially regarding royalty or elites, betrothals would be ordained by the king. For more common betrothals, it might be arranged by families but often relented to the wishes of those who had found a special attraction to each other.

It was common for all betrothals and the subsequent Fusions to occur under the direction of priests who divined and calculated the auspices of Ephemeron's gods. Priests referenced complex charts to invoke the gods' blessings. Fusions rarely occurred as singular events.

About every 300 years, a mass Fusion occurred that mated the multitudes. Fusion was more similar to that of Earth's plants cross pollinating than a physical mating. A successful Fusion would produce a *seed*. Within five days, it would need to find a nest where it could rest and finally metamorphose into a young Ephemeral baby.

From time immemorial, three clans had dominated Ephemeron. A distinct custom of Ephemeron was how it chose its ruling monarchy. Every 1,000 years, a Selection process occurred to determine Ephemeron's ruling clan from which a monarch would ascend to become king over all Ephemeron.

1

*The henchmen's soulless faces
now surrealistically flickered strobe-like
across his consciousness.*

Planet Earth | Present Time, New York City

Earthling Nick Cowen should have died two days ago. He was shot seventeen times by six drug-fueled henchmen. It was on purpose, but it was a mistake. The assassins had gunned down the wrong target.

The thing of it was, Nick was now walking the streets stalking one of his killers, the man who always wore a NYC-emblazoned bucket hat.

In those seconds after Nick was shot, a hidden alien inside Nick's body saved him. The alien belonged to a race called Ephemerals. At least, that would be a reasonable earthly translation. The Ephemeral should have fled Nick's body to find a new host. But as blood drained into the dirt and death closed in, an emergency directive from Ephemeral Management ordered the Ephemeral to save Nick.

The Ephemeral took over physical control of Nick's body, standing him up, plugging the wounds, and staggering the unconscious body away from the scene. Its first concern was to save Nick's mind. Tidying up the rest would come later, which was why Nick would be out of commission for two days.

Being shot seventeen times was a crazy number. Nonetheless, with the alien's intervention, Nick lived.

After being shot, his first conscious moment was filled with the stench of garbage and searing pain. Not like the singular pain of when he had been shot during one of his army tours but a multiple-bullet-wound blanket of pain. Still, it was the putrid smell that always pervaded those first moments.

Nick fell in and out of consciousness numerous times over those two days. Images of the henchmen's soulless faces, having been lit by the muzzle flashes of gunfire, now surrealistically flickered strobe-like across his consciousness, searing themselves into his memory. The henchmen's flickering faces seemed to be canvassed against the olfactory rot, an unknown mixture of fetid food, mold, urine, and decaying tissue.

Nothing made sense. As Nick's mind retraced the gunfire, the fusillade of bullets, and now questioning this afterlife—for could it be anything else *but* the afterlife?

He thought God's judgment seemed cruel: sentenced to a loop of reliving his agonizing moment of death.

"Hello, Nick," a clear voice suddenly spoke *from inside his head.*

Adrenaline surged through Nick's veins. Nature's fight or flight response tore at him.

Had he gone insane? Was he losing his mind or was it already lost? Was he under deep sedation? Doctors did that sometimes to help traumatized victims recover, especially those with brain injuries. He hoped the doctors weren't seeing a flatline on a brain scan.

"You're going to be okay," repeated the calm voice, over and over. "Sorry I couldn't do a better job of it. You'll be hurting for quite a while. Try to rest."

One thing for sure: the voice was dead straight about the pain.

Sometimes he woke spontaneously, other times the disembodied voice would wake him, always promising the same thing, "You're going to be okay, Nick. Just rest."

It was an odd experience waking one time in the middle of darkness and another time in midday, never experiencing the transitional minutes of sunrise or sunset.

A crust of some sort hindered one eye from fully opening and pinned the other eye shut. He brushed his hand against his eyelids, picking at the crust. Dried blood as it turned out. More coagulation evidence was on his shirt and pants.

Efforts to lay eyes on his angelic lifesaver only revealed an alley of discarded wooden pallets, remnant steel beams, and that infernal-smelling mountain of trash. The nuanced smell of a small pile of rat skins rested a few feet away as if it might be a picky cat's favorite discard pile. He had no recollection of how he ended up sitting on cold pavement, propped against the unfriendliness of a rough-hewn brick wall.

Early on the second day, as Nick tried to push himself into a more comfortable position, a groan escaped his lips, though strangely he could feel his strength returning more rapidly than a human body could expect. Even his initial intense pain was sporadically relenting to tolerable moments.

The voice inside his head started to ask Nick how he felt. It told him he would be walking soon. The possibility seemed insane and impossible.

Yet, a mere two days after being shot seventeen times, Nick was stealing too-small-to-fit clothes off a backyard clothesline. His disheveled appearance was accentuated by an unconcealed belly gun holster and a mop of red hair intermingled with hardened blood clots. He transferred his folding tactical knife into a back pocket, pinned two bloodstained $20 bills to the clothesline, and discarded his bullet-riddled clothes in a dumpster.

Vengeance was on his mind.

He was lucky to have found his first target so easily. The man who always wore the NYC bucket hat had returned to the area on orders of the mob boss who wanted to know why gunfire had been reported but no body had been found. Bucket-hat man returned to crime scene, saw no body, wasn't going to ask if anybody had found a dead guy, and decided he had fulfilled his task. It was why bucket-hat man was hanging out near Ms. Tilley's, a local madam's house.

Nick had intended to return to his car, but spotted bucket-hat man parading his wise ass up and down the street like a wannabe rooster. He ducked into a nearby park and took up a spot that overlooked the street.

Bucket-hat man entered Ray's Bar, a place that helped to pre-fuel a man's libido and weaken a woman's hesitations. It was a popular area to hang out. A nearby back alley offered a wide variety of mind-changing drugs. Cops mostly left locals alone.

Though still swept by spasms of pain, there was no way Nick was letting bucket-hat man slip away. He would have to tough it out. Three hours later, when the bar was closing, bucket-hat man exited with some unlucky drunk woman under his arm.

Stealthily, Nick edged his way down from the park's woodsy protection. Bucket-hat man and his lady friend staggering their way toward her place. A cop car passed without slowing down.

Silently, Nick approached his target from behind, his tactical knife at the ready.

One hundred feet …

Fifty feet …

Twenty …

Two quick thrusts into bucket-hat man's vital organs and a slash across a carotid artery sent him collapsing to the ground.

Nick faded into the night.

The innocent intoxicated young woman never noticed Nick. She only noticed the fall of bucket-hat man. She thought he had fallen from having drunk too much.

Then she saw the blood spilling out and swirling around her best shoes. She screamed, but no one was there to help.

Bucket-hat man died that night and would later be buried in the ground like a dead person should be.

Nick, on the other hand, was a true dead man walking, with five more henchmen to hunt down.

2

"Are you saying you're an alien?"

Having dispatched with NYC bucket-hat man, Nick made his way back to his car, glad to see it was untouched.

Making himself ready for his long drive home, he ripped off the irritating belly holster. Nothing was worse than a tight seat belt, made even tighter over an ill-fitting belly holster.

Angry wounds pockmarked his body. Most oozed a clear liquid, blood serum, a good sign that the body was naturally flushing out bacteria. After having been shot twice before during different Army stints, he was familiar with the healing process. What was unreal was the speed of healing and the fact he knew several key organs had been hit if the wound placements were any indication.

"You said I would be okay," said Nick talking to himself. "Looks like you were right."

"Thanks for the compliment," answered the voice—again speaking clearly inside Nick's head—and startling Nick almost into the air.

"Fuck. Don't do that! Who are you? You can leave me alone. I'm fine now."

Annoyingly, the voice chuckled condescendingly. "Nick, you still need me. I did a quick patch-up on you, but you need more healing."

"How is it that you're in my head? Who are you?" Nick fruitlessly scanned the car's mirrors hoping he could catch a glimpse of … *what* … a prankster playing an elaborate trick?

"It's difficult to explain."

"I'm listening."

"Since you have a long drive back home, I'd suggest you get started. Explaining is going to take a while."

Nick didn't like being at this *thing's* mercy, but his alternatives were meager. He put the car into drive and headed west out of NYC. It would be a solid two and a half-hour drive back home.

"Are you saying you're an alien?"

His self-built house sat on a plot of twenty acres of mostly overgrown Pennsylvania woods that abutted a national forest and was ladened with a variety of camouflaged electronic reconnaissance gear designed to announce the approach of and ward off unintended visitors.

He drove a long while without saying anything, relishing the silence and fearful of the inescapable voice he would activate by speaking to it first.

"So, is this what they call the silent treatment?" inquired the voice.

Almost careening off the road, Nick cursed. "Can't you give me a warning?"

"Only by talking to you, but I guess that defeats the purpose."

"Smart ass," muttered Nick.

"Also, I can't read thoughts. You'll have to speak for me to hear you."

"Who are you? *What* are you?"

"I am an Ephemeral. Ephemerals can live deep inside a *being*, and one wouldn't know it. Ephemerals dwell in beings across the universe."

"Are you saying you're an alien?"

"That's what I'm saying."

"I'm trying to understand. I'm talking to an alien who is informing me he has possessed me for several years. Does that sum it up?"

"No, no. You're not really … possessed. It doesn't work like that. Our species can coexist in the same time and space as corporeal beings.

"I know this is upsetting for you, but we weren't supposed to meet this way. You were never supposed to hear my voice talking to you like this. When you got shot up, you should have died. Keeping you alive violated the usual rules, but there were special circumstances."

The deeper truth of why Nick was saved was left unmentioned.

"Do you have a name?"

"I do, but you can't pronounce it. No Earthling can."

"Certainly, you have a name; what is it?"

"What would you like to call me?" responded the Ephemeral.

Nick wasn't sure if the alien had told the truth about not being able to read minds. He hoped it was true because he was thinking of several choice insults.

"Then I'm naming you Mr. Voice."

Nick thought he caught the Ephemeral uttering a disdainful snort.

"Really?!" exclaimed the Ephemeral. "Is that the best you can do?"

"I kind of like it. Maybe in informal situations, I'll just call you *Voice*. Now, explain how it is that I didn't know you were inside of me."

"A crude similarity would be like saying you have a ghost living in a house. Like I said, it's a rough analogy."

"Most of the ghosts I've heard about cause problems."

"Sure, some ghosts like to stir things up. But other ghosts like to chill out, lay back, watch the happenings of the household. They're like voyeurs. Actually, ghosts give us a poor reputation if you want to know the truth. My species—Ephemerals—mostly stay away from all that spooky, woo-woo nonsense."

"Which are you? The voyeur or the one that stirs things up?"

"I'm regretting the analogy. Let's just say we are *harmless* to our hosts. Since we need a physical body to inhabit, it does us no good to destroy you or do things so dangerous that we are forced to find another body to inhabit."

With the Ephemeral dodging his question, it made Nick think Mr. Voice was the troublesome kind. "I may not have known you were inside me, but I wouldn't call that harmless."

"Would benign be a better word?"

Nick's anger flashed. At this moment he wished he could strangle Mr. Voice.

"Look, Nick, an Ephemeral was inside you for years and you didn't know. I saved your life and broke several rules in the process. That must count for something."

"All right, I'll give you that, but tell me, what were the special circumstances that made you break your rules and save my life?"

"It would be better to wait till later for that explanation. It's complicated."

"Hey, Voice, I deserve to know. I was shot up, stuck in a reeking alley, I'm in pain all day long, I stink, I'm starving, and I'm inhabited by an alien who is toying with my sanity. What's the deal?"

Nick waited a long time before Mr. Voice answered.

"I like you, Nick, but I'm not your true Ephemeral. I was inside you when the shooting happened. My Ephemeral friend and I had recently switched between you and your twin brother. We do it occasionally to make our lives more interesting. There is enough sameness between twins that residing in the other twin is similar enough to one's home to give comfort, but different enough to add spice. When you got shot, it was a mess. Management intervened. I was ordered to keep you alive."

Later, Nick would uncover a deeper story than an amusing swap.

Fighting self-doubts of insanity and the muddling drip of information released by Mr. Voice, Nick was simmering inside. It was more than getting shot, though that was certainly part of it. What really set Nick off was realizing the assassins had been trying to kill his twin brother, Tony. That was how the assassins had mistaken Nick's identity.

"You say, my brother has an Ephemeral inside him, too?"

"We're going to be a team for a little while longer," continued Mr. Voice. "I need to get you back on your feet and healthy, then we can try putting things back together. My Ephemeral friend and I will have to switch back."

"Oh, no. That's not going to happen," responded Nick. "Not after what I've gone through. You're staying. You saved my life, and now you're stuck with me. You're going to help me track down my assailants and avenge myself. You owe me that. Wouldn't you agree … Vince?"

"You're giving me a name?" asked the Ephemeral, pleasantly surprised. "That feels like progress. I like Vince. It has a nice ring."

"Well, Vince, it's time you help me hunt down my killers. I think I can make use of your troublesome nature."

"That's not really fair," responded Vince. "We're Ephemerals and we're pacificists. We inhabit species across the universe but we don't force anybody to do stuff."

"That sounds like a big lie," said Nick. "You can't tell me it makes no difference that a different Ephemeral inhabits one person or another."

"I told you; we simply coexist. We don't force you to do stuff. Your brother is a lot more emotional, though once you get riled, it can be a wild ride."

"Fuck you, Vince. The only thing that counts right now is my laser focus on raining vengeance on my killers."

"But you didn't die, Nick. They're not your killers."

"Vince, you're annoying. You kept me alive for a reason you're not telling me. Since you say you don't *control* what I do, then you are going to be along for the ride. I'm going to hunt down those assassins … and you're going to help me."

"I haven't received authorization for that."

"You saved me from dying, but now you're going to abandon me?"

"It's complicated."

"I'm sure it is, Vince. I'm sure it is, but I think you're stuck with me."

3

"Why do you inhabit us?"

A **single road led into Nick's rural homestead,** though two escape paths led off to the rear of the property. Fiercely tired, Nick stumbled across the rock path leading up to his house.

Making his way inside, he threw his belly-holstered gun on a table and made his way back to the bathroom. He stripped off the encumbrance of his ill-fitting clothes, kicking them off into a corner. Even knowing what he had gone through, the reflection he saw in the mirror was shocking. Seventeen angry and seeping red welts adorned his body. Wildly tousled red hair crowned a haggard man. A red scruffy beard framed his chin, highlighting penetrating cold gray eyes.

Though he was forty-five years old, Nick had taken care of his body. At six feet four and 235 pounds, his body was well-defined; or it *had* been prior to being shot. Stepping into the shower, he let the water run for a long time.

While standing in the shower, he wondered about Vince, though Nick never called out to the alien and hoped it wouldn't speak either. Exiting the shower, he wrapped himself in a robe and made his way to the kitchen. Opening the refrigerator, he grabbed a cold beer, and downed almost all of it in one long gulp. He chomped on a couple slices of leftover pizza, opened another beer, made his way back to the bed and crashed on top of the bed covers, only covered by his robe.

It was a solid twelve hours before he was able to pull himself awake.

With Nick's memory still seared with the faces of his would-be assassins, he opened his computer and applied a few search filters to help him identify the faces of the henchman. All had previously violated the law, resulting in the generation of mug shots. The federal pictures were in the public domain. Accessing the state-only mug shots was a simple hurdle.

Within a few hours, Nick had collected names, aliases, last known addresses, and a variety of background tidbits.

As a sergeant of an army special ops Green Beret squad, Nick had earned two Purple Hearts.

The first was a shot that hit his torso while saving two Afghan kids. The second took off two of his left-hand fingers. He didn't like leaving the army, but he thought two Purple Hearts were enough. Though his left hand was disfigured, his thumb and two primary fingers were okay. He was a right-handed dominant shooter but could shoot decently with his left.

Nick wasn't the type that looked for fights. He had avoided many, usually outmaneuvering drunk slob trying to throw his testosterone around. A quick knock to the groin or sharp jab to the larynx were effective methods to refocus a loser's attention. But being shot crossed the line.

They started it and he was going to finish it.

With his vengeance target list in hand, Nick went to a closet and tripped a hidden switch that popped open a sliding panel. He entered the safe's combination, drew out several bundles of cash and a handful of cash cards, and threw these in a backpack. Securing the hidden safe, he grabbed a few pieces of clothing and stuffed them inside the pack, swung it over his shoulder, then grabbed a zip bag that he had loaded with a hodgepodge of deadly instruments.

A couple years out of the service, he had joined a private mercenary group. They paid well for work that bordered on the illegal, but he kept his reservations to himself as long as he could until the work dipped too far to the dark side.

Nick cashed out and left most of the private soldiering behind. He would pick up an odd job here and there, which was what had dragged him into that tough area of NYC. He figured the screwed-up mess finding out about his Ephemeral was karma biting him in the ass.

"Vince, why do you inhabit us?"

"We live at an emotional level. We feed off sensations. We feel your anger, your sadness, your joy, even your love."

"We're talking together right now. That's a lot different than living at an emotional level."

"Talking with you is difficult for me," said Vince. "Also, I'm breaking a shitload of rules and prohibitions."

"Difficult? What does that mean?"

"Talking to you requires me to act in a physical realm. It is not how we normally operate. We can do it for a short time, but it drains us."

"Are you saying that talking to me makes you suffer? If so, keep talking."

"I saved your life. Remember? That should count for something," said Vince, his voice sounding pleading, perhaps indicating being hurt by the animosity.

"Your voice booms inside my head, and you've been inhabiting my body. You deserve to share my suffering."

"You've never been easy to please."

"How long can you act in the *physical realm,* as you call it?" asked Nick.

"Usually, not long. Your situation is unique. Ephemeral Management has stepped in. They instructed me to heal your body. I've had to access reserve energy stores to help you. The rules normally prohibit physical interactions."

"Damn, Vince. Maybe you do care."

"Don't push it, Nick. I'm here because somebody upstairs is allowing it to happen."

"Everything you say, Vince, raises more questions. I don't trust you. How did you people get here, anyway? Who are you? Are all humans possessed?"

"Have you heard of quantum entanglement? Your Einstein called it 'spooky action at a distance.' When two particles are quantumly connected, what happens to one instantly affects the other. It happens faster than the speed of light."

"I guess I've heard of it, but nothing goes faster than the speed of light."

"Well, that's not exactly true. At the subatomic level, particles are popping in and out of existence everywhere. There is no speed limit that prevents a particle from appearing on one edge of the universe one moment and then reappearing on the other side ninety-three billion light-years away."

"Ninety-three billion? I read that the universe is only thirteen billion years old."

"Sure, but it's expanding at an accelerating rate. Its diameter is now close to ninety-three billion light-years across. Some subatomic activities and certain forces are not always bound by the light speed limit."

"That still doesn't explain how you got here."

"When the universe first formed, some particles were quantum entangled. Some have remained entangled. When we can locate such entanglements, it's like having a thin rope that acts like a connector. We build on those old entanglements of the universe. It's why we are entangled with some but not others. It's how Ephemerals can seed themselves out to different worlds, out to different galaxies. I can't explain it all."

"You're populating other worlds?"

Vince's laugh rang in Nick's head. Nick wished he could squeeze his hands around Vince's neck to shut him up.

"Aren't you the curious fellow," chided Vince. "We're not populating worlds, Nick, just inhabiting some of the universe's beings—peacefully and unseen. We've extended ourselves across the universe. Humans are one of many intelligent life-forms. But back to your other question about possession …."

Vince paused before continuing. "We really dislike the word possession. It has all the wrong connotations. It is why we call our coexistence *dwelling* or *inhabiting*. But to answer your question; no, not all humans are inhabited."

"I'm feeling luckier every day."

"You should rest, Nick. You've been through a lot. Why have you packed two bags?"

"You can't read my thoughts, but you can see what I do?"

"I'm talking to you right now, so at this moment there is a physical connection. I have some awareness of your actions."

"My plan is simple. I'm going to hunt down those murderous bastards and kill 'em."

"Your body is still in bad shape. You should rest."

"I heard you, but I'm getting better. Are you going to stop helping me recover?"

"No, but maybe it's better if you lie low for a while."

"What about my twin brother, Tony? What is your friend saying about him?"

"That's harder to say. Your brother doesn't know he is inhabited so he doesn't speak with his Ephemeral. His emotions are running high. It seems your brother is in trouble right now."

"Why's that?"

"He can explain better. You'll need to talk to him directly."

"Vince, you're a bastard."

4

The explanation Vince had given him didn't ring true.
It was hard to put a finger on why.

The next morning, ignoring Vince's concerns, Nick made his way out to the county road. He went out the backdoor and followed a thin path covered over by moss and overgrown grasses. It snaked through woods of birch, black cherry, and sugar maple. It was over a mile to the road. He hitchhiked a ride into the city from a produce truck driver.

His bullet wounds hurt like hell, itched like fury, and burned constantly. It made no sense that he was alive, but he was, and thought that was certainly better than the alternative.

Bucket-hat man had been number one on Nick's hit list. Now that he had been eliminated, it was time to move down the list.

Assassin number two was a guy by the name of Morris Blecker who had grown up in South Wales, England. The hoodlum had lost his mother to an auto accident when he was only four years old. His dad was a drunkard who frequently took out his frustrations and wanton anger on his son. By the age of sixteen, Morris Blecker had been incarcerated multiple times, had been in numerous scraps with neighbors or anybody who mistakenly gave him a wrong look. He spent several years traveling the world on merchant ships, and along the way, became an even more hardened man. The hit job on Nick was a natural progression.

Nick's internet search pointed him to Philadelphia as a likely Blecker hangout.

Arriving in Philly by bus, he grabbed a cab to a used car lot, bargained for a silver 1995 Oldsmobile Cutlass Ciera, paid with cash, and used one of his false IDs to cover the paperwork.

When he finally located Morris Blecker, the cutthroat was spending his easy-earned assassin's money on a bender in a tough part of Philly, PA.

Nick spent an afternoon and night waiting for Blecker to return to his apartment but came away with nothing to show for his patience. He canvassed the area and found a little room to rent for cash overlooking the street. A shared bathroom was down the hallway.

Though it was the middle of summer, Nick wore a long-sleeved shirt, covering the bullet scars. One bullet had slashed across his scalp, but his Flyers cap shrouded most of it. The landlord noticed his bandaged hands but said nothing.

"Traveling a little light, aren't you?" asked the landlord, noticing this lodger carrying only the backpack and zip bag.

"I was supposed to meet a cousin of my brother's. He's a sailor, the kind who works the big freighters. I've been waiting for him since yesterday. His ship docked but he's not all that dependable. Is there a nearby place to eat?"

"Maxine's has decent food. It's down the block and around the corner. They stay open till midnight."

"Thanks," said Nick.

Entering his room and closing the door as quickly as he could, Nick tore off his shirt and pants. The bullet holes burned. He wished he could sink himself into a bathtub of ice. Instead, he pulled a bottle of water out of his pack and set up a watch station overlooking Blecker's place.

When he closed his eyes, images and memories raced through Nick's mind, compelling him to relive the moment bullets tore through him and the last second of consciousness before it all went black. There had been no wonderous white light that people had said would happen.

When he woke up after the shooting, the moments had been overwhelming. He had struggled to make sense of it all.

But thinking on things now, the explanation Vince had given him didn't ring true. It was hard to put a finger on *why*.

There was more to *why* Nick was alive and *why* Vince had to intervene.

Nick spent the next three days staking out Blecker's place.

The only time he left was when he visited Maxine's restaurant once a day, usually chowing down a big breakfast. Often, he would buy two cold-cut sandwiches to take back to the room to cover his lunch and dinner. At a nearby shop, he picked up a small thermos and cooler. Maxine was always willing to fill his thermos up with her strong black coffee.

One day walking back from the restaurant, Nick spotted Blecker exiting a car and entering the apartment complex.

"I've got you now," he muttered, racing back to his room. Throwing the sandwiches and thermos on the bed, he pulled his Glock 19 from the backpack, and grabbed a pair of binoculars hanging over the bedpost. Scanning the building across the street, Nick located his target on the third floor, far left window.

Blecker was pacing about, packing up items into a bag. It appeared he might be leaving again.

This was going to be a difficult kill. The neighborhood was busy most of the time and the long-time residents looked after each other with a care bordering on obsession.

Blecker probably wasn't likely a long-time resident, but that didn't mean the neighborhood would accept a killing in their midst. Nick figured it would be better to move his stakeout position to his car. That way, it would be easier for him to follow once Blecker left the apartment.

Nick packed up the backpack and zip bag, but then stopped by the landlord's door and knocked.

"Whatcha want, mister?" asked the landlord.

"I want to pay you for another week. I need to stay in the city a bit longer."

The money was the same green as before. Nick paid for his extra week and made his way to his temporary streetside home, the silver 1995 Oldsmobile Cutlass Ciera.

It was the most boring car he could find, and it drove him mad having to use it as a stakeout vehicle. He would have much preferred to be sitting in his restored 1996 Chevrolet Impala SS, in Dark Cherry, boasting the distinguished "muscle car" additions of a floor shift and tachometer.

Settling into his auto stakeout, Nick tried speaking to his resident alien.

"Who's helping you?" he asked, wondering if Vince was listening.

"Tony's Ephemeral is sharing some of his energy. There are a couple others."

"What's your friend's name? Oh wait, don't tell me. It's unpronounceable. Got it."

"Nick, you can't doubt everything I say. Our language is unpronounceable to you. That's the way it is. Since Tony isn't here, the naming honors fall on you."

"Well then, I pick … Paul, for Tony's Ephemeral. Any problem with that?"

"Not for me. You'll have to hash that out with Tony sometime. He's thinking about you, you know."

"I thought you couldn't read minds."

"We can't, but feelings for a twin brother are strong and unique. Emotions are telltale. Your brother needs your help. My fellow Ephemeral, Paul, as you have named him, communicated it to me."

Nick leaned back in his seat. "My brother and I are twins, but we had a falling-out years ago. Associating with his crime-friends has thrown his life sideways. It's weighed down his life. I didn't need to be part of that."

Nick couldn't escape the feeling that the Ephemeral was frequently playing with the truth. Ephemerals live in other beings, unseen, hidden away, only living off one's emotions by some magical entanglement. When necessary, Ephemerals could operate in the physical realm and, at times, can make educated guesses about what a human is physically doing.

Some things rang true. He had never been aware of Vince's presence prior to being shot. He lived after being shot seventeen times and his wounds were healing miraculously fast.

"Looks like life has taken an unexpected turn and thrown you two back together," offered Vince. "Maybe he will be able to help you as much as you will be able to help him."

Across the street, a door opened. Blecker walked out, got in his car, and drove off.

Nick started his Ciera and followed at a safe distance. He'd have to figure out a way to put a tracker on Blecker's car. Too many things could go wrong using a single tail. But the nearness of his second target set his trigger finger twitching.

Over the last few days, he had worked hard to limber up his fingers. The bandages would make things tougher, but his Glock was at the ready.

Blecker was going to die. Nick didn't care how.

Blecker drove into a liquor outlet. Nick pulled his car over in a nearby parking lot. A short while later, he exited, carrying a six-pack and a brown bag of liquor.

After driving down the street and pulling into a gas station. Blecker started filling his car and then walked into the storefront, apparently wanting an extra item. Nick saw his chance and steered his car into the pump behind Blecker's car.

Nick wasted no time. He got out of his car. His movements were casual. As Blecker finished his in-store purchase, Nick took the gas pump handle from Blecker's car and put it on the ground with it still pouring out gas, then went back to his car and waited.

When Blecker returned to his car, he smelled the gas, looked around, then noticed the pooling gas at his feet. Fear jumped across his face.

A gunshot from an Oldsmobile Ciera driving out of the station hit the pavement, creating a spark, and enveloping Blecker and the gas pumps in a raging inferno.

Nick later learned from the local TV news that Blecker hadn't died for three more agony-filled days.

Yeah, he and Blecker were even now.

5

"It may not have been all your fault,
but like you said, you loved the ride."

Later, **Nick dumped the Ciera** into a nearby reservoir, after cleaning it out and wiping it down.

Ducking into a nearby wooded area, he pulled out a change of clothes from his backpack. He discarded his Flyers cap and his old clothes in the first dumpster he came across. Making his way to the bus terminal, he bought a ticket to Memphis.

Nick's prior research had indicated assassin number three had a sister living in the area.

The bus route followed I-76 into Pittsburgh before switching over to I-70 to carry him west. Nick would have preferred to have been in his Impala SS driving the backcountry, but this section of the interstate system was one of the more scenic routes.

The bus passed miles of hardwood trees as it climbed up the eastern ridges of the Appalachians and then west across the Alleghenies before traversing the rolling hills of farmland and some of America's deepest heartland.

A woman had chosen to sit next to Nick, having sized him up as being a decent-enough guy. Within an hour, after listening to her seatmate mumble an incessant conversation with an invisible guy named *Vince*, she had moved to a different seat.

Nick was glad to see her move, as he had no choice. If he was going to communicate with Vince, it had to be verbal since Vince couldn't read thoughts.

And Nick had a lot more questions that he needed Vince to answer.

"So, Vince. Are you male or female? I suppose I should have asked that before naming you."

Vince laughed inside Nick's head again, which Nick found to be especially annoying.

"Sexually, we are like the plants of your world," explained Vince. "It's like we're both sexes simultaneously. When the time comes, two betrothed Ephemerals are merged. We call it Fusion, and an Ephemeral seed is produced."

Nick's phone rang. The screen ID said it was his brother. Nick had left a dozen messages, but all of them had gone to Tony's voicemail.

"Tony," said Nick harshly, "what have you got yourself into?"

"Oh, Nick. It's messed up."

"I can't say I'm surprised, but what the hell did you do? A few guys mixed me up for you and shot me."

Not asking if Nick was okay, Tony launched into his story. "It's a woman. I fell in love with Pierce Savage's girlfriend. He's a badass psychotic. She fell in love with me. We were going to skip town, elope; you know, get married."

"Jesus, Tony. They thought I was you. They really tried to do a number on me."

"Sorry, Nick."

"That's it? That's all you can say? Fuck you, Tony."

"What do you want me to say? How would anyone know you would cross paths with those guys? Wrong place, wrong time, huh?"

Nick almost hung up the phone. Did Tony even ask if he was okay? No. As usual, he was wrapped up in his own world. "I've been trying to get ahold of you for a week. They shot me, Tony. They shot me seventeen times," Nick hissed into his phone.

Dead silence. "Okay, brother, I know you're upset, but you don't have to step on my guilt like that. Where'd you get shot?"

"All over, brother. I'm serious. Seventeen times. You can count the bullet wounds. They were meant for you. We need to meet. Where are you?"

The last thing Nick wanted to do was meet his brother at this moment. It would be like opening an invitation to bad juju, but he didn't see a way to avoid it.

Inhabited by Vince and knowing his brother had a similar alien inhabitant changed the calculus. The way Nick looked at it, there was still the Ephemeral backstory to be revealed. Vince had said that normally Ephemerals leave a dying body, but "Ephemeral Management" ordered otherwise. What was so special about this situation? Tony was wrapped up in this mess, whether he knew it or not, and no way to put it all together with his brother hiding out hundreds of miles away. Despite the hard feelings of the last few years, Nick figured both their lives depended on it.

"We're north of Detroit, near Lake Huron. Where are you?"

"I'm on my way to Memphis, but I can jump off in Cincinnati. Can you meet me there? We gotta talk."

"It will take me several hours, but I can meet you. Oh, and I need to bring Sylvia. I can't leave her alone."

"Put her in the trunk," said Nick curtly—and only half joking.

"Nick, come on. She's going to be my wife," Tony protested.

"Somebody will be on the lookout for you and your girlfriend. You've got to keep her hidden away. Your gangster boss is seriously pissed, and that means you need to take precautions."

"Don't worry. We'll stay low. Do you need anything?"

"Yeah. A couple of changes of clothes, a wad of cash, and paid-up cash cards would help. I'll text you after I get to Cincy. One other thing. This might sound strange. Have you been hearing any voices lately?"

"Voices? What do you mean?"

"Never mind. Just get to Cincy as soon as you can."

It was hard for Nick to delay his plan to go to Memphis. He consoled himself by rationalizing it was only a temporary detour.

He took a deep breath, as he wondered how he and his brother had turned out so differently. They looked like twins, but their lives had taken on such different directions.

At least that's what Nick kept telling himself.

Racing across the interstate, as the bus turned from I-70 to I-74 toward Cincy, Nick looked again at his online research, though he had it mostly memorized.

While staking out Blecker, Nick had found more information on his Memphis target, Sammy NoName. A sister, Ellie, lived in the area. It seemed like a good bet to start. Until Tony's phone call diverted Nick to stop in Cincy, it was supposed to have been a straightforward plan. Take out Sammy NoName in Memphis, then hit NOLA and dispatch with Raul.

"How long has it been since you've seen your brother? Four, five years?" asked Vince. It still threw Nick off when Vince initiated a conversation. Maybe Vince needed to follow the old rule: speak when spoken to.

"Almost four years," said Nick after some thought. "He and I haven't been that close for some time. It always seemed he was never satisfied with anything he tried. After a while, life hung heavy on him. He found it easier and more exciting hanging with a criminal enterprise. You were inside him all those years, Vince. You know."

"You think you two are that different? You were a mercenary. That's not what most people would call an exemplary life."

"Well, aren't you the high and mighty. You're right. I have my sins, but I had boundaries. I walked away when the work went too far. Tony never had boundaries. Maybe you made it worse. Didn't you say that sometimes Ephemerals act like voyeurs, only watching, while others take pleasure in stirring things up. You and Paul enjoyed switching between my brother and me. Maybe that pushed him more than he could handle. How about you, Vince? Are you guiltless? Were you responsible for my brother's wanderlust? Did you play with his emotions?"

Nick was angry. He was angry because it could have been Vince's fault for ruining Tony's life. He was angry because he couldn't grab Vince by the neck and throttle him. He was angry because somebody shot him, and he was still hurting. He was angry because he no longer had a normal life.

"Well, Vince, be straight with me. Are you responsible for Tony's troubles?"

"I liked the excitement being inside Tony," conceded Vince, but ducking the question. "Maybe that fed into your brother's emotions and how he felt, but I never tried to steer him away from the things he wanted to do. I never pushed Tony to make the choices he did."

"You're guilty, Vince. Admit it. It may not have been all your fault, but like you said, you loved the ride. You knew at some level that fed back into Tony's personality. It was more pleasurable to him when he went on a bender. Then there is the whole matter of your Ephemeral partner, Paul. You two were trading places back and forth between Tony and me. I can understand it a lot better now. Some days I'd have odd feelings. I always thought it was just me, post-traumatic army shit, whatever.

"I pushed through those days. Kept them locked away. I guess I was stronger than Tony. I've put together a pretty good business for myself. I survived battles; I became tough. Tony could never quite keep his demons locked away. I think he succumbed to you. Admit your guilt, Vince. You owe me that. You owe Tony that."

Nick didn't know how much the Ephemerals' entanglements were responsible for Tony's life decisions, but Nick figured pressing Vince might make him reveal more about Ephemerals, their world, and what they really wanted from humans.

The bus's wheels whined on the pavement. Trees flashed by. Fenceposts hurtled into sight, then danced away into the distance. Vince said nothing. Nick waited. It was a long time. Neither said anything.

"I'm sorry, Nick. We're trying to make it right."

Nick said nothing. He wanted to throttle Vince's neck even more than before.

6

"How the hell did you get to Earth?"

Hours later, Nick arrived in Cincy. He checked into a nearby hotel and texted his brother the location.

Tony was still a couple hours away. Nick was hungry and needed a shower. Stripping off the clothes he had been wearing for too long, he let the shower run over him for a solid fifteen minutes. Drying himself, he looked at the bedraggled clothes on the floor and hoped Tony had thrown in the requested change of clothes.

Nick put on the one change of clothes he had. His belly grumbled, reminding him he needed some real food, not chips and soda. Leaving the hotel, he found a little diner close by, and picked a back booth to be isolated as possible.

Nick had more complaints to get off his chest with Vince.

"What do you know about the gangster boss?" asked Nick. "Tony said his name is Pearce Savage. What's he into?"

"He's got his hand in a lot of things: prostitution, shakedowns, chop-shops, drugs. He's not very particular. His girlfriend is Sylvia Vittorini, his gun moll. He's kept her in high fashion and jewels. When Pearce found out about the love affair with your brother, a hit was ordered for him."

"Does Pearce Savage have an Ephemeral?"

"He does. Since you can't pronounce his name either, let's call him Callum. He has been troublesome. Ephemeral Management has had numerous conversations with Callum. They need to tread lightly since he's from an important Ephemeral family. It often gets him a pass or a mild rebuke. It was bad luck all around when Callum ended up inside Pearce. They both run rough."

"Is Savage aware of his Ephemeral?"

"Not like you and me. There's never been direct contact that I'm aware of. But Callum pushes Pearce's buttons, and Pearce isn't the type to resist his urges. It plays out like an echo chamber."

"The more I hear, the less I think your species is as hands-off as you profess."

The waitress finally made her way to Nick's booth. He ordered a large breakfast: eggs, pancakes, orange juice, and undercooked bacon, even though it was midafternoon. The waitress had seen it many times before—the same order at the same time of day. She had automatically brought a coffee pot and Nick was pleased with that touch of anticipation.

Nick watched her walk off with his order. Though she was older, her calf muscles were well-formed. He was certain she had been an attractive young woman. The waitress' shoes looked orthopedic, likely chosen to help relieve her slightly uneven gait.

"Earlier, when you said Management 'betroths' two Ephemerals, what did you mean?" asked Nick.

"It's an arrangement for the reproduction of our species. Two Ephemerals are matched, then Fused. You would call it a mating. An Ephemeral seed is created. That seed must then find a living body to entangle with and inhabit. A Fusion is an Ephemeral-wide event that occurs once every 300 years or so."

"Just to be clear—your people have a worldwide Fusion that creates seedlings that then try to inseminate life-forms across the universe. What gives you the right?"

"Nick, it's how our species evolved."

"That's insanity. You say there are other life-forms across the universe?"

"Why would you think you are the only intelligent life-form across the entire universe?"

"Just … because."

"Well, now that I showed up in your life, it kind of changes things, doesn't it?"

"How many life-forms are there?"

"That depends how you measure it. If it's any type of life, even rudimentary, then billions. If it's intelligent life-forms, millions. The universe is a big place."

"How the hell did you get to Earth?"

"Like I told you, we use quantum entanglement to bridge the distances between life-forms."

"I really have no idea what that even means." Even to his own ears, Nick sounded impatient.

"Nick, we need a way to talk about Ephemeron and Ephemerals so you can understand. The sounds Ephemerals make to communicate with each other would seem like nonsense sounds to human ears. Our language is like the sound of insects. Think of translating the buzz of insects into human words. There is no way for a human voice to mimic those sounds.

"If I use a name for an Ephemeral, just go with the flow and accept it. There is no equivalent. I'm just making up names to help us both. When I reference time, like years or hours, I will convert them to approximate Earth time. When I describe Ephemerals, I'll try to use

Earthly descriptions. For instance, most Ephemerals have wings and generally six appendages. We can walk and stand upright on the back ones, but we can walk about on all six. I would just say arms, or hands or legs. We generally choose to fly if we travel any significant distance. I don't want to disturb you too much, but think of us as arthropods."

"Arthropods?"

"Insects with skeletal bodies."

"Jeez, you people sound ugly as sin … and even more disturbing to think about, especially since you're inside me, at least an entangled version of yourself."

"I could say the same thing about you. Have you looked at yourself in the mirror lately? Even by Earth standards I'm guessing you're smelling a bit ripe."

"You're a funny guy, Vince, but sure, your descriptive shorthand sounds workable. Now, tell me about your world."

"Ephemeron is governed by a monarchy, and dominated by three major clans. By law, a ruling clan is Selected every 1,000 years, and this establishes the Ephemeron kingdom. From this Selection process, a new king Ascends to the throne from the ruling clan. Our history has been marred by great pain and losses. From these tragedies, we depend on the kingdom to ensure peace and balance to our world.

"An Ephemeral's lifespan can extend almost 1,200 Earth-years. Like I mentioned, every 300 years or so, we biologically Fuse. This fusion creates a seed that can grow into a new Ephemeral. A new seed has approximately five days to find an entanglement. It has nothing to do with distance. A seed looking for entanglement is as likely to find a host a billion light-years away as a thousand.

"Ephemeron is at a crucial time. For the first time in almost 3,000 years, a Fusion and a Selection will be occurring in a major Conjunction.

We will be selecting a new ruling clan to rule our kingdom. The current king is old, so after the Selection, a new king will Ascend. The Fusion will create new alignments of power and privilege."

"I could use some entanglement to get over to Memphis. It sure would save me a backache of time and having to track down Sammy NoName." Nick knew he sounded flippant. It was intentional. He was going to need some time to consider Vince's revelations.

Before Vince could say anything about quantum entanglement not quite working the way Nick imagined, the waitress brought breakfast and refilled the coffee.

Nick downed his orange juice in one long gulp and dived into his food. He couldn't remember pancakes tasting so good. The bacon was undercooked like he liked, and he almost called the waitress back for an extra order of fried eggs. Maybe next time. Cleaning the plate, he dragged his fork through the remaining syrup for a last taste.

Nick was hitting the coffee again when his brother's text message came through. Tony was twenty minutes out. Nick flagged down the waitress for the check, threw down some cash, told her to keep the change, and left to meet his brother. He stopped at a corner market, bought a twelve-pack of beer, a cheap foam cooler, and a bag of ice.

It had been a little over four years since Nick had seen Tony … since their falling-out.

Thinking back, he realized it wasn't any one thing. Sometimes a family's baggage grows heavy, and it was easier not to bring it out into the open than trying to sort through the old attachments and misunderstandings. Distance hid the pains.

Arriving back at his motel room, Nick positioned himself behind the window curtain and scanned the parking lot for Tony's arrival.

Eventually, Tony drove up in a muddy white Jeep Compass, a vehicle that could be driven without attracting too much attention.

Nick watched for a few more minutes to ensure no one had tailed him into the parking lot.

Tony's appearance had changed; he wore a cheap cap, a plain T-shirt, and blue jeans, but his muscular physique indicated that he had been working out. His girlfriend Sylvia had her light brown hair in a ponytail that flipped out from a Chicago Cubs baseball cap, high-lighting her high cheekbones. Her T-shirt was snug, and her jeans accentuated her long legs. For supposedly trying to avoid detection by her former gangster-lover, Sylvia had not dressed inconspicuously. She carried a medium suitcase, while Tony carried two.

Nick opened the door as Tony approached. Exchanging glances, a pause held Nick and Tony apart. Four sour years hung in the air, then the brothers hugged.

Nick's face scrunched in pain, but he didn't make a sound. These days, his body was always sore; he wasn't fully healed from the gunshots.

Tony introduced Sylvia, and Nick almost introduced Vince.

Nick offered them beers, and the conversation drifted to Pearce Savage, who had put a bounty on Tony and Sylvia's heads. Tony and Sylvia related how they had been staying off the radar, holing up in a small cabin near Lake Huron in northern Michigan and hoping things would cool down.

"So, brother, you said you got shot up badly," said Tony. "Your hands look like they got whacked."

Without a word, Nick set his beer down, stood up, and with his bandaged hands, unbuttoned his shirt, showing them the bullet wounds that had left angry red sores across his torso and arms.

"Oh, my God," exclaimed Sylvia, stunned.

"Damn, brother. I thought you were exaggerating. I didn't know."

Then, reality struck Tony and Sylvia at the same time. How could Nick still be alive?

"This is going to be really hard to explain," said Nick. "For now, just accept the fact I received help from someone very special. He has unique capabilities, as you can imagine. For right now, I'm safe.

"The important thing is to lay out a plan against Pearce. He must be assuming you're dead so he is probably focusing his attention on finding Sylvia. But if he hears that you're alive or someone sees Sylvia, he'll be coming for you again. We got to get you two far away while I do what I have to do."

"You can't leave us hanging like that," exclaimed Tony. "What do you mean *someone special* helped you? Your body is covered with bullet scars. Did God Himself intervene?"

Nick sighed. "Like I said, this is going to be hard to explain. I promise, I'll fill you in later, but I can't go into it right now. You'll have to trust me. What I can tell you is that I've killed two of the henchmen who were after you but shot me instead."

Tony and Sylvia exchanged glances.

"Is that where you were headed? To get another one?" asked Tony.

Nick nodded. "Yes. Four more to go, plus the boss. Then you'll be safe, and I'll have my vengeance. Did you bring that change of clothes? Money?"

"Sure, Nick." Tony nodded toward a suitcase. "It has clothes, money, prepaid cards, burner phones, driver's licenses, and related fake ID cards. We guessed on your size," said Tony with a knowing smile.

Nick opened the suitcase. "Where'd you get all this, especially the fake licenses and IDs?"

"Sylvia and I have learned a few tricks working for Pearce Savage's organization. We skimmed off a few items here and there. When Sylvia and I started talking about eloping, we boosted our stash."

"Thanks, Tony. Don't worry about getting a room. I already took care of it for you. It's next door. Here's the key."

Nick was still shirtless; Tony and Sylvia kept staring at his wounds.

"Look, it's been a long day," said Nick, finally rebuttoning the shirt. "You're safe now. I need to crash and get some sleep, probably even another shower. Leave me a couple beers, and you take the rest. If you're hungry, there's a decent café a few blocks from here. We can get together tomorrow morning."

At the doorway, Tony gave a long look back at his brother, trying to fully understand the miracle that had saved his brother.

Sylvia had seen bullet wounds before. She had lived around tough guys most of her life, and she wasn't the timid type. Without fear, she walked over to Nick, put her hands on his shoulders, leaned in, and gave him a sweet kiss on his cheek. "Thanks for your help, Nick."

His shoulder wounds stung from the embrace, but it was a beautiful pain.

7

... he saw red blood staining the little girl's clothes.

With the door closed, Nick finished off his beer and popped another. "Well, Vince, who's going to talk first?" he asked now alone in his room. "Do you have anything to say? Did you talk with Paul?"

"He misses you. He thinks you're healing fine, and we should return to our rightful dwellings."

"What do you mean? You go back to Tony and Paul goes back into me?! That's not going to work. It's one thing if a human-host has no idea if an Ephemeral is inside, but it's a different situation once we're aware. You and I have a relationship, even if it is me wanting to strangle you."

"I made the same point to Paul. Also, Ephemeral Management remains involved. For the time being, it looks like you'll be getting your wish and Paul will have to remain inside Tony. There's a lot happening on Ephemeron. We're closing in on our reproductive time. It will be transpiring across the universe, not just Earth. Management wants to keep things calm leading up to Fusion."

"What are we going to do about my brother? If Paul suddenly announces himself to Tony, Tony will have a mental breakdown. I almost had one myself. And what about Sylvia? Does she have an Ephemeral inside?"

"Nobody thinks it's a good idea to let Tony know. Paul will have to adjust to his new dwelling and stay in the background. It shouldn't be that big of a problem for him. Ephemerals live for 1,200 years. Humans rarely live past 100. We change dwellings many times in our lives."

"And Sylvia?"

"No Ephemeral is inside her. That's being discussed."

"Being discussed? I thought an Ephemeral-seed must canvass the universe in search of its special, quantum-one-and-only. It sounds to me like someone is identifying Sylvia as a target. Who's doing this discussing?"

"Management. There are gray areas around the rules as you might imagine. Callum's family is involved."

"Callum? Isn't he the Ephemeral inside Pearce Savage? I get the connection between Pearce and Sylvia—jilted love and all that. But you said Pearce doesn't know about his Ephemeral, Callum. How are Callum and his family involved?"

"They're worried about their social standing. Callum has been a problem for a long time. Callum's family has a distinguished position within the Ephemeral world. His family has served the king well, so there has been forgiveness for his antics. The upcoming Conjunction of Selection and Fusion heightens the scrutiny. Callum's persistent troublemaking puts their position at risk. Inciting Pearce Savage has caused unneeded difficulties. It has reflected badly on the family. Callum's family is pulling every string they can. If they can somehow betroth Callum to the proper Ephemeral and direct the seed to establish its quantum connection inside the correct host, the family believes it will give Callum a new opportunity. It will give him a clean slate and a chance to turn his life around. The family will remain protected."

"I'm getting a headache. You people are crazier than we are," said Nick.

"If you didn't want to know, you shouldn't have asked."

"I'm getting that idea."

"I have some questions," said Vince. "What's your plan? What are you going to do with Tony and Sylvia? Until you kill Pearce, they'll never be safe."

"I know. Hopefully they see it the same way. If they want to run and hide, I can't stop them. But staying with me puts them in the crossfire, too. One thing you must promise me."

"What's that, Nick?"

"There can be no way Tony finds out about you, Paul, or anything about the Ephemerals. That includes Sylvia."

"Nick, I gotta be truthful with you. I can only make that promise for myself. I promise I won't divulge anything to them. I can make the best case to Paul and Management, but Callum remains a wild card. There could be ploys I'm not aware of."

"You ask about my plan? Hell. You, your cronies, and your deceptions have made this thing a lot more complicated."

"Yeah. I can see that. The whole save-your-life-thing tends to do that." Vince purposely chuckled inside Nick's head.

Vince's satire didn't go over well. One day, thought Nick, he was going to reach out and touch Vince in a way he wouldn't forget.

Nick slept fitfully that night. Images of his time in Afghanistan haunted him. A cacophony of voices and gunfire were relived.

A young boy, dirt-covered and eyes wide with fear, hunkered next to the remnant of a stone wall. Holding protectively close in his arms was a girl, probably the boy's younger sister. A mixed fusillade of rifles and automatic weapons slammed randomly across the battle scene. Chips of the stone wall splintered off, showering the boy and his sister. An upended wooden bucket lay on the ground beside them, its precious water lost to the sands.

"Corporal, how soon till chopper support gets here?" yelled Nick. "This area was supposed to have been cleared. They're flanking us."

"Three minutes out, Sergeant," yelled the corporal.

"Davison, Lawson. Take a position left behind that wall. Keep them from flanking us. We'll give you cover fire."

With the platoon giving cover fire to the two men, the little sister broke free from her brother's grasp, crazed fear powering her senseless dash into greater danger.

"Fuck!" said Nick to himself. With almost as little regard for his own safety, Sergeant Nick Cowen yelled for his own cover fire, leaped over the low-slung rock wall, ran toward the child, and scooped her up, then used a baseball slide to the wall where the boy was positioned. Nick pulled the boy close.

Bullets seemed to be raining from everywhere. Afghan fighters were yelling amongst themselves, now turning their full firepower on the stone wall barely shielding Nick and the two innocent children. The moments seemed like forever, then he heard the thump-thump of the arriving helicopter break across the bedlam. Fifty-caliber machine gun fire blasted from the chopper's four guns, raking across the enemy's position, and sending them fleeing into the hillsides.

"Sergeant, you could have been killed. Why did you do that?"

"The kids are innocents," was all Nick said. The deep brown eyes of the children spoke all the thanks that could be said. Then, he saw red blood staining the little girl's clothes. But it wasn't coming from her. The blood

was coming from Nick. He hadn't felt the shot, but the pain was now announcing itself.

"Medic!" yelled the corporal.

Rudely, the early morning sun raked across Nick's eyelids. He had forgotten to pull the nightshades. Burying his head under the covers helped, but couldn't put him back asleep.

A short time later, a knock came through the other side of the door that connected Nick's and Tony's rooms. Nick stumbled out of bed, went to the door, and said he would come over in fifteen minutes.

For breakfast, Nick led them to the café's back booth. He was glad it was a different waitress. All three of them ordered and then engaged in a bit of small talk.

Tony spoke first. "Nick, we can't be running from Pearce for all our lives."

It was the best thing Nick could have heard. "That's my thinking, too," he responded. "Hunting Pearce will be just as dangerous as running, but at least you'll be fighting back."

"I've been fighting my whole life," said Sylvia. "I thought Pearce was going to be my ticket out, but it was just more of the same hell. Pearce loves only himself; he cares only for himself. I want out." Her dark brown eyes were hard as stone.

"We need to force Pearce to make mistakes," said Nick. "We need to get into his head. Sammy NoName is in Memphis. I was going after him when you called."

"He deserves to die," responded Tony. "He is a hard man. Not even the other guys on Pearce's gang like hanging out with him."

"After that, I was going to head down to New Orleans. I suspect Raul is hanging out there. Do you remember him?"

"We remember him," said Sylvia, as she gave a quick head-bob alert to Nick and Tony that the waitress was approaching with their orders. They fell silent as she served their plates.

"Would you be up for doing a little reconnaissance in NOLA before I get there?" asked Nick. "You'll need to be careful. He knows your faces, even though he thinks Tony is dead."

"Once the news of Sammy NoName's death gets back to Pearce, he'll go ballistic," warned Sylvia. "I know him. He's paranoid on a good day. Finding out his henchmen are being knocked off one by one will make him crazy."

"Nick, Sylvia and I saw your bullet wounds. How can you be alive? You need to tell us what's going on. Tell us what happened."

"I can't right now," answered Nick. "I will, I promise. Besides, this is not the right place for that conversation."

"That raises even more questions," said Tony.

"I know. Give me a little more time. Right now, I need to get hold of a car."

After breakfast and a little driving around, they found a used car dealership. It looked like it had seen better days. Tony and Sylvia stayed in the Jeep.

On the search for plain, functional, and cheap, Nick approached the lot.

"Hello, sir," greeted a hefty older salesman. He had a ruddy complexion and was sweating bullets despite having been sitting inside. His horizontally-striped shirt accentuated his belly and was soaked with his sweat. Nick noticed that a simple fan twirled inside.

"Hi," answered Nick with a friendly nod.

"Can I help you? We have some fine used cars for a decent price."

Nick danced the sales dance, talking about specific models and comfort, though he didn't care. He talked about favorite cars, though he didn't care too much about that either. He was quick to pass over several cars with obvious rust. One car had a bad stench and had likely been a victim of flood waters.

While Nick pretended to be interested in examining the engines of the cars, it was just a smokescreen to keep the salesman occupied. The salesman was sweating profusely and constantly wiping his brow with a very damp handkerchief. Nick asked for the keys to a car and started it up, but claimed that it didn't sound quite right. He then requested the keys to another car, prolonging the stalling dance.

Eventually, after taking several test drives, the salesman pushed back, wondering out loud if Nick was really interested in getting into a car. Nick assured him that he was ready to buy. They discussed vague numbers on one car, then on a second, and then on two more.

Nick told the salesman that the numbers were too high. He then revealed that he had cash and pulled out a roll from his pocket.

The salesman's eyes popped. He hadn't sold a car all day and the last month had been lean. The salesman knew he was playing with a sharp customer. No sense drawing out the pain. Make a sale, even if it was going to be skinny.

They settled on a deal. Nick paid cash, using a fake ID, and drove off in an unremarkable 2011 silver Honda Accord.

Later, back at the motel, Tony and Sylvia were preparing to head off to NOLA to locate Sammy NoName.

"Are you doing okay, Tony?" asked Sylvia. "All the stuff you told me that's happened between you and your brother … you should let it go. He's sticking his neck out to help us. He's standing by you, his brother. We're all in this together."

"I know."

On another day, Sylvia might have pressed Tony harder, but figured now wasn't that moment. There would be time for that once Nick caught up with them in NOLA.

A few minutes later in the parking lot, Tony and Sylvia were tossing their suitcases into the Jeep. Nick joined them.

"You two take care of yourselves," cautioned Nick. "Your job is reconnaissance. Use disguises like we talked about. Nothing more. I'll do the wet work."

Sylvia gave Nick a big hug.

"You watch out for my brother," said Nick, turning to his brother, "You take care of this fine lady."

"We'll be okay," asserted Sylvia.

Tony stepped forward, almost hesitantly. "Be safe, brother." They shared a hug.

Sylvia noticed Nick grimace.

8

"I like the voodoo option," said Vince.

Sylvia had been especially helpful by providing phone numbers for Sammy NoName and Raul. She had them in her contact list from working with Pearce.

Nick was ready to put that information to work.

New Orleans was a solid twelve hours away—Memphis, a solid eight.

Driving his silver Honda through the night, stopping only for gas and one thirty-minute rest, Nick rolled into Memphis in the early afternoon. He had given a lot of thought on how to kill Sammy. Bullet to the brain would be quick and easy, but if Nick was recognized, it could give Sammy time to react. Maybe an explosive device would work. But of course, there were complications with that.

In the end, his zip bag held the most tempting answer. He had packed dried mushroom powder made from the *conocybe filaris* mushroom that was noted for its amatoxin danger. It was a relatively common mushroom of North America that grew in wet areas around dead logs and was extremely toxic. The mushroom's toxin was not destroyed by cooking.

But no matter what method he used, he first needed to locate Sammy.

Nick set himself up in a hotel room, then using the phone number from Sylvia, he did some old-school tech sleuthing.

Using one method, he created a phone-message link. If Sammy clicked, it would give away Sammy's location and a variety of other details. Nick sent the nefarious link with a simple story for a 25% discount to a famous Memphis BBQ joint.

After he launched that, Nick tried using a Site:domain search across various social media platforms that came up zip. Finally he tried an Intex:phone# search that produced some promising leads on the owner of the phone.

Then, Nick got lucky. Sammy NoName clicked on the BBQ text link. Nick was now tracking Sammy in real time. The new technology to follow someone was so much easier than the old days.

Over the next few days, Nick carefully tracked Sammy's habits. Mostly Sammy spent his days sleeping and his nights carousing. He visited his sister once, but mostly he liked hitting the gentlemen's clubs and a couple of favorite bars.

Today, he ducked into JoJo's Bar. If Sammy followed his usual pattern, he would be there for a couple hours.

Nick called a local pizzeria, ordered a small smoked brisket pizza to be delivered to JoJo's Bar in the name of a "Michael Jones." He added extra for delivery and tip. Now it was a matter of waiting.

He pulled a glass bottle of ground *conocybe filaris* mushroom powder from his pocket.

Nick, seeing the pizza delivery vehicle slowing down, jumped out of his car and calmly interrupted the delivery person to ask if there was a pizza delivery for Michael Jones. Nick explained he was an old friend and wanted to surprise him. Nick offered the kid $20 to let him make the delivery in person. The kid gave him the pizza.

As the kid walked away, he opened the lid, sprinkling the toxic mushroom powder lightly over the pizza. It wouldn't take much. Supposedly, it added a smoky flavor, though Nick knew of no one who had ever risked a taste. He walked to the doorway of JoJo's Bar and asked a guy if he would be willing to make a surprise delivery to his friend in the bar. Nick gave Sammy's name, description, and offered the man $20.

"Who should I say it's from?" asked the man.

"Tell him it's from Pearce. And he needs to be back at business by Friday." Nick held out the money.

"I know the guy you're talking about. I'll give it to him." Carrying the pizza, the man took a couple steps toward JoJo's front door, then looked back. Nick had vanished.

Nick had read that *conocybe filaris* mushroom effects were brutal. Symptoms began about six hours after ingestion: nausea, vomiting, diarrhea. Most people thought they've eaten some bad food or maybe they thought they were coming down with the flu.

After twelve to forty-eight hours, symptoms seem to resolve.

But here's the kicker that Nick really appreciated: two to three days after ingestion, a relapse occurs, causing liver and kidney failure. If the poisoning was not immediately recognized and treated, there was a better than 50% chance of dying. If not dead, a liver transplant would soon be Sammy's most critical need.

Nick needed to catch up with Tony and Sylvia. They had spotted Raul in New Orleans. He turned his silver Honda onto I-55 south.

"You've messed up my mind," said Nick, speaking aloud to Vince while he was driving. "I know you said Ephemerals can't read our minds, but having you inside me screws with my head. I can't help but think you're always watching me."

"You're kind of a special case, Nick."

"You really haven't explained that. Why am I so special?"

"It's because of Paul."

"Your Ephemeral friend? The one that was supposed to be inside me, but you two were trading between Tony and me?"

"Yes. When Paul and I switch between you two, it creates extra complexities with our quantum entanglements. Normally, it's not that much of a problem for our computer systems to manage, but if you had died, that would have caused special scrutiny. Like I told you before, Management wants to keep things calm. The Conjunction is soon. Families are positioning themselves. Nobody wants undue attention."

Nick had heard bullshit before. There was probably a bit of truth in what Vince was telling him, but it certainly wasn't the whole truth.

"Vince, you make it sound so sanitary. Your species is messing with the universe. How many wars have you started with your emotional … entanglements? I wouldn't be surprised to find out that an Ephemeral was inside Hitler. Just a little emotional tweak here; a little emotional tweak there. And boom, we had a world war on our hands."

"Nick, Nick, you're embellishing things."

"Am I? I don't think you want to face the truth. You're sitting inside people feeding off another life-form. You admit that sometimes you want more excitement. Your species is not innocent."

"You have free will. We can't override your decisions. We're along for the ride."

"You're lying to yourself."

"Can we change the topic?"

"You can try, but I'm not letting you off that easy. Someday, you people will face the consequences … Vince." Nick spat out the word *Vince*.

"What's your plan for Raul? I was impressed by your method for dispatching with Sammy NoName. You had been planning the poisoning, right?"

"I brought the mushroom powder, but I didn't know who I was going to use it on."

"And Raul?"

"I've been thinking about that. Again, it will be a matter of opportunity. It is New Orleans. His death should have a related theme. You know, voodoo, alligators, snakes, death by fear. Random street crime isn't as fancy, but it gets the job done."

"I like the voodoo option," said Vince.

"You would. See? You're unsatisfied with 'normal' vengeance. You want me to hype it up. You need your shot of adrenalin. Hmm, I think I understand my brother a lot more now. You pushed him over the edge. He had always tried so hard in life, but he always came up a little bit short. You pushed him because you weren't satisfied with a regular working guy. I don't know your Ephemeral friend, Paul, who was inside me, but he seems a lot more balanced than you. Maybe Ephemeral Paul will help my brother find his way back."

"How are you going to deal with Pearce Savage, the big boss? Management is wondering."

"That's a load of crap. They're just as titillated by this mess."

"Nick, can't you trust me by now? I saved your life. I broke rules, big time."

"Trust you? No." It was Nick's turn to laugh. He wondered if that bothered Vince. He hoped so. He continued, "Tell me more about this reproduction-Fusion thing that's going to happen."

"When the moment happens, two Ephemerals reproduce by fusing together. It takes about one Earth day to consummate. If the Fusion is successful, an Ephemeral seed is born. That seed must find a living host to dwell in. By Earth time, the seed has about five days to find a host. It can be anywhere in the universe. If it can find a host to connect to, the seed entangles itself."

"So … what if the Ephemeral seed connects to an insect? Can that happen? What happens then?"

"It can happen," said Vince. Nick thought he heard distress in Vince's voice. "We lose ten percent to poor matchups."

Nick roared with laughter. "I love it. I'm picturing one of you bastards stuck inside an ant. That'd be appropriate. What happens then? You said Ephemerals live for a thousand-plus years. How long does an ant live? I don't know. A few months? Longer? What if they get squashed? No time to jump ship with a big foot slamming down."

"That feels insensitive," responded Vince.

Nick laughed again. "It's only my *feelings*, Vince. You feed off feelings, don't you? You should be rolling in this shit."

"We feel the loss," said Vince. "The two Ephemerals who gave birth to the seed are always connected to their seed. These emotions extend across the universe. We know the realities. But it still hurts."

Nick responded with another callous remark—something about an Ephemeral's surprise of being entangled to an unemotional ant.

The route south to New Orleans was different than his bus ride across the Alleghenies. I-55 had its trees, but the roadside hardwood lusciousness had disappeared.

Nick missed the heavy road-lined trees of Pennsylvania. He was entering a new world. The bayou beckoned.

New Orleans, often called NOLA, was a city surrounded by the mighty Mississippi River and Lake Pontchartrain. It was also a city of unique culture, food, more food, drink, and people that were beautiful, daring, and sometimes dangerous.

9

The smell of gumbo permeated her hair.

Sylvia **had remembered Raul raving** about the food in NOLA's famous French Market. So, it wasn't all luck that she and Tony had spotted Raul chowing on char-broiled oysters, crab claws, and pickled green beans. He didn't seem nervous, and he wasn't looking over his shoulder. It seemed he felt safe. Maybe it was because he felt he was home.

As Nick's Honda Accord sped toward New Orleans, Nick imagined several methods of killing Raul. When he thought back to the moment when he was being shot, his blood boiled, pushing his rage to make the killing more than a simple execution.

He knew he was feeling the weight of the recent days. His emotions were winning out. It was a bad sign. He knew getting emotionally involved could lead to mistakes. Driving all night didn't help.

At least he had been able to take the bandages off his hands, though they still hurt a lot and were stiff. He moved his fingers often to keep them from stiffening up. His other wounds were mostly red welts now. He didn't know if Vince was still helping the healing. His battle experience told him that Vince was helping, but he knew his body was working overtime, too. It was why he was always tired.

One thing Vince had learned from the army was that guys would blow off steam on each other. At times, they could be merciless to each other. It was part of the toughening.

Nick wondered how tough Vince was. His heartless attitude toward Vince was as much a technique to find out more about Ephemerals and break down Vince's lies as it was to vent his anger at his own powerlessness.

He felt for Vince, a little bit. He even felt momentary sympathy for the fragile Ephemeral seed that was faced with the hurdle of quantum-jumping across the universe only to find itself imprisoned inside an emotionless ant, and then suddenly being squashed into oblivion. Still, Nick wanted to throttle Vince's neck … and somehow figure out a way to get this damn Ephemeral out of his head.

Finally arriving in New Orleans, he rolled up to the French Royal Hotel. It was one of those places that is described as having "good bones." Its best days were in the past, but there was still pride in the place. The frontside street was cobblestoned, narrow, and clean. Its outside walls were whitewashed. Iron balconies adorned its presence.

Nick texted his brother, announcing his arrival. At least Tony had the foresight to pick a place with nearby parking. Nick's room was 204, while Tony and Sylvia had 206. Tony texted that he and Sylvia were on their way back from their reconnaissance.

Nick walked through the hotel's inner courtyard. A fountain welcomed clients, though no water was running. Dirt-infused old bricks supported creeping ivy and small bushes adorned the perimeter. A clay mustiness hung in the air. Four wrought-iron colonial-style tables and matching chairs beckoned.

At one table, an older, semi-distinguished looking man and a younger woman sipped cooling beverages. It was likely this beverage was not their first of the first of the day. They seemed to be enjoying each other's company. Her hair was a bit tousled. Her hand was high up on the man's thigh, and one of her breasts seemed to be escaping its clothing confines.

Nick walked up the stairs to room 204, and unlocked it with a brass key. He liked the old-time touch. The bed was prepped with tightly stretched cover and sheets. A small balcony, with a small wrought-iron table and two chairs, overlooked the street.

He threw his luggage down, striped, and headed for the shower. The bathroom's white marble exuded a sense of purity. Nick wanted that feeling, though he knew there was nothing pure in what he was doing.

There were dark days ahead. More men would need to die.

Knowing his brother and Sylvia would be returning soon, he kept the shower short. The warm waters helped to ease some of his physical pain. He stared at his hands. What he had gone through was real; he knew that. But there were days when he couldn't make sense out of it.

Exiting the shower's cleansing waters and wrapping himself in a towel, he dropped onto the bed, falling quickly into a dead asleep.

Whether asleep for five minutes or five hours, he had no idea, though in reality it was barely fifteen minutes before the phone indecently rang him awake.

"Yeah?"

"Brother, were you sleeping?"

"Yeah. I'm checked in. Room 204."

"We're parking our car now. We'll be up shortly."

"Sure. See you soon." Nick forced himself off the bed, dug into his luggage and found a change of clothes that likely would make him look like a tourist. For what he needed to do … looking inconspicuous was the perfect look.

Nick remembered earlier trips to NOLA. On a previous visit, he promised himself that the next time he was in town, he'd find time to drop in on his favorite fine clothier. It was a promise he wouldn't be able to keep.

A knock on the door interrupted his daydream. The door's spyhole let him see that Tony and Sylvia were in the hallway.

As he opened the door, he noticed Tony smelled like gumbo and a hint of fried chicken. It made Nick realize he was hungry. Sylvia hadn't found a way to minimize her stunning looks. It seemed the NOLA atmosphere had infused her with an extra dash of spice. She wore a medium-gray, soft cotton, body-conforming dress. It accentuated her breasts and her hips, making her look tall. White sunglasses made her stand out. Tony's eyes were bloodshot red. Behind the sunglasses, Sylvia likely had the same condition.

Though they had scored big by locating Raul, Nick knew the dangers these two were toying with. They were acting like they were big-time detective sleuths now. He had seen it too often—casualties due to overconfidence.

Sylvia gave Nick her usual big hug and a kiss on the cheek. He was tempted to hold onto her for a long time. The smell of gumbo permeated her hair.

Now he really was hungry.

"A creole crab-pot with cornbread is calling me," said Nick, stepping back. Realizing Nick had caught the lingering scent of lunch on Sylvia, the three broke into a small, synchronized chortle.

"We just ate," said Sylvia. Nick gave them a disappointed look. "I need some food. Let's go find a restaurant."

As he devoured his crab-pot, Nick looked up. "Tell me about Raul. Besides seeing him at the French Market, do you know where else he hangs out? Has he met with anyone?"

"We were able to tail him to a small hotel," said Tony. "When we first saw him at the market, he seemed very casual. We caught sight of him later in the parking lot near his hotel. He got a phone call, and after that, he started looking around very nervously. We made sure he didn't see us. He moved his car after that call, parking it farther away inside a covered parking lot. We caught sight of him a couple times after that, and he acted really nervous, was always looking over his shoulder. Yesterday, we followed him west on the Earhart Express. We dropped off after crossing Causeway Blvd. I was worried he might spot us."

Nick told them they had done a good job. He knew they wanted to hear his story of survival or, at least, they thought they wanted to hear the story. Reality would surely hit Tony and Sylvia hard. Tony would find out he was *inhabited*, and Sylvia would find out she was next in line.

Nick said he needed to sleep, that his body was still healing, and promised to meet them the next morning. He knew it was a poor excuse, but it was the best he had.

10

"Better that your hands are dirty than being dead."

Back in his hotel room, he figured it would be easy to fall asleep, but his thoughts sparred with each other. He sat on the edge of the bed.

"Vince, you there?"

"I'm here," answered Vince.

"Who is Callum betrothed to?"

"Paul."

"Does Paul know this?"

"Of course."

"Are they compatible?" asked Nick.

"In this case, compatibility is of secondary importance. It's about status."

"Doesn't Ephemeral Management worry that they will create a bad seed?"

There was a pause before Vince answered. "That's on its mind, yes."

"Who are you betrothed to?"

"It was Paul. Things have changed."

"Holy shit. Do you have any feelings about that? What changed?"

"Paul and I had been betrothed for the last couple hundred years. With our sharing of twins, it made us very close. Paul's family has a royal bloodline. It makes his standing exceptionally desirable. If Callum's family can manipulate a Fusion between Callum and Paul, it would raise their standing and heighten their family status."

"What does your family have to say about it? You were in line to Fuse with Paul. Now you're kicked aside. Your family must have had a special status over the last two hundred years for you and Paul's betrothal to be on the books. Callum has been a thorn in his family's side. It sounds like someone is getting paid off."

Vince didn't respond.

"Vince, you need to fight back. Haven't you learned anything from me?"

Vince remained quiet.

"Well, isn't this a watershed moment," chided Nick. "You don't know how to fight back, do you? The last couple weeks inside me has merely been another little joyride. You are vicariously living out your poor-assed wishes through me. Time for you to find out what the hell is really happening in Ephemeral-land and shiv the bastards."

"I suppose," said Vince weakly.

Nick laughed, then sarcastically mimicked Vince in a feeble voice, "I suppose."

"What does Paul think?" continued Nick.

"He is conflicted. He wants to follow his family's wishes. He wants to support the ways of our culture. But he wants to be with me, not Callum. Paul's preference may not matter."

"Oh, Lord. You two are so sad. I'm going to help you, Vince."

"How can you do that?"

"I'm going to help you grow a pair."

"I'm sorry, what? Grow a pair?"

"It's a phrase that humans sometimes use. Like, grow a pair of balls. It means toughen up. Fight back. Stand up for yourself."

"Ephemerals don't do a lot of that. Our species is dependent on cooperation and acquiescence."

"That's the last time you say that to me. You keep asking me about my plan for vengeance. Now, I want to hear *your* plan for vengeance. Think about it, Vince, because I'll be asking for details"

One of the hard realities of returning from Afghanistan was that Nick's sleep was rarely peaceful and sometimes barely restful. Whether they would be classified as dreams or nightmares, they were inescapable.

A small group of teenage Afghan girls had gleefully exited their one-room school, a cave with built-up mud walls that formed an entrance. Some held precious pieces of paper with their day's drawings. And with only two textbooks to share among them, a couple girls held open the books so the other girls could take one last peek.

From a distant hillside, Nick and his platoon were surveilling the area. A group of five Afghan men approached on motorbikes. They all carried rifles, a common sight, but none were automatics. It was impossible to know if they were Taliban, but their arrival by motorbikes was a warning sign.

The Afghan men stopped in front of the young girls. One man barked a command and held out his hand. The two girls with the books tried hiding them behind themselves, but the man barked another order. One girl produced a book, placing it in the man's hand. Flipping quickly through its pages, a scowl crossed his face and with a quick swipe, he slapped the book across the girl's face, sending her sprawling to the ground. Then the man ripped the book apart, sending pages flying.

Nick cursed under his breath, powerless to intervene.

Six months later while in a firefight with Taliban soldiers, Nick caught sight of the same man at the end of his rifle-scope. Nick had always had an excellent memory for faces.

It was a cold kill that had been too long coming.

Awakening in the hotel the next morning, night sweats saturated his shirt. The rumpled sheets looked like a tractor had run through the bedding. The coverlet laid strewn on the floor.

Sitting on the bed, the images of the young Afghan girls hung in his memory, and he could feel his blood boil all over again.

He went to the bathroom, opening and closing his hands to loosen the stiffness, popped several pain pills, and stood a long time under the hot shower. Later, standing in the hallway, Nick knocked on the door of room 206. Sylvia opened the door looking like a housemaid ready to go to work. She wore a white T-shirt underneath a medium-blue, below-the-knee, bib overall, and a black bandana imprinted with pale white flowers that hid most of her hair. Sylvia gave him a big smile, proud of her disguise.

"Good morning, Nick." She gave him a big hug. He glanced her up and down, sizing up her transformation. "You should see your brother," she said, inviting him in and noting he carried his zip bag.

Tony stepped forward, wearing dark blue jeans, a black belt, and a dark gray collared shirt. An insignia of a large oil company graced his left shoulder. A pair of brown gloves and safety glasses sat on a nearby table.

"Nice," said Nick, nodding in approval.

At breakfast, it was decided all three would ride together in Nick's car. They guessed Raul must have gotten a message that three of his fellow hitmen had run into a streak of bad luck. It was likely the reason he was suddenly looking over his shoulder. Raul wouldn't know Nick's car, and he wouldn't be looking for three people.

Didn't everybody think Tony was dead, anyway?

They rolled by Raul's place toward the parking garage where Raul stored his car. Nick pulled to the side, reached into his zip bag, and pulled out a small black box. He flipped the power switch while at the same time he checked his phone app. The signal was green.

"Here's the tracker," he said, handing it to Sylvia. "Put this underneath the passenger's side if you can, near the rear seats. Do it like we practiced. Wiggle it to make sure it is stable. It needs to be on the steel chassis."

"I've got it, Nick. I'll meet you on the other side of the building at the stairway exit." She slipped the tracker into her purse. The brothers watched her until she ducked into the garage entrance. Nick drove the car slowly around the block. Ten minutes later, Sylvia came out.

Now, it was stakeout time. They had to wait until Raul woke up and decided to grace them with his presence.

As they waited in the car, Sylvia asked, "Nick, how come I never saw you before?"

Nick wasn't sure how much Tony had said about their backstory. "I was in the army for a while, and now, I've got a business to run. I was busy."

Sylvia looked at Tony. "You told me your brother didn't care. He's here now for you. It sure seems like he cares."

The car felt like it quickly got a lot smaller.

She turned to Nick. "Busy doesn't seem to be an answer for not seeing your twin brother in … how many years now? Four? Five? More?"

"Hey, honey, let's leave it be," implored Tony. "We don't need this now."

"Really, Tony? When do you think that perfect moment is going to be? That goes for both of you," she said, making sure she gave Tony and Nick equal stares.

Neither brother said a word.

"Give it up," she persisted. "What happened? I know you two were close at one time in your lives."

"Nick was always the favored brother," said Tony. "Day after day, you see your brother getting all the special treatment, the extra love, the parental accolades. It didn't matter how much I tried or what I accomplished; it was never enough. After a while, I just thought, fuck it. I don't care anymore; I'll make my own path."

"Oh, Tony. You had the same chances," responded Nick. "You have the same chip on your shoulder you've always had. You made choices in life and they weren't always good ones. You didn't want to make the sacrifices of life. You wanted easy gratification."

"See what I mean?" snapped Tony. "I didn't do enough; it was always my fault. Nick, you know our parents favored you more. It went on the whole time; and you enjoyed it. All three of you pushed me away. What did you expect to happen?"

"Nick," said Vince's voice, sounding like a reprimand.

"What?" Nick responded automatically to the unexpected voice in his head.

Tony shot a glance back toward Sylvia. She shrugged her shoulders and flicked her palms up in bewilderment.

"Are you okay?" asked Sylvia, noting Nick's sudden shudder.

"Yeah. Yeah. It's … um, some post-traumatic stuff. It jumps out at me occasionally." He waved a hand in dismissal. "It's nothing; don't worry about it."

He wiped his brow. "It's hot in here. Let's go over to that café across the street and get something cold to drink. I have my tracking app."

Sitting in the café, Nick thought it was very unfair. In public, Vince could say whatever he wanted, and Nick had to stay silent. Did

Vince realize how hard it was to maintain a human conversation while an alien simultaneously carried on its own chatter inside Nick's head?

Almost on cue, Vince spoke again. "Remember, yesterday you were blaming me for your brother's troubles? Maybe it wasn't all my fault. Maybe you could try harder seeing his side."

Nick was ready to explode. His brother was dragging out a bunch of childhood guilt shit. Sylvia was pressing them to *share their feelings* to clear years of bad blood. Vince was an alien inside his head getting in on the fun, pressing the psychodrama button.

He was about to say to hell with subtlety.

With the turmoil bubbling inside, Nick envisioned himself, standing up, telling Tony and Sylvia to hang tight. He saw himself walking out the door over to Raul's place, knocking on the bastard's door and blasting the fucker into oblivion. It made more sense by the moment.

Then the GPS app beeped.

Fuck. Raul is in motion.

Returning to the car, Nick handed his phone to Tony to help monitor Raul's route.

"Tell me where Raul is going. I'll need to hang back, so he doesn't see us. We could lose him temporarily. I'll need to know where he turns, if he takes a freeway entrance, exit. That kind of stuff."

Tony shot him a testy glance, implying *brother … I know how to navigate. Chill out.*

Raul headed west, making his way toward the Cypress-Tupelo swamp. Nick followed from more than a mile behind. Eventually, Raul exited into a remote section off the roadway. Watching the GPS tracker, Tony warned that Raul's vehicle had stopped.

Nick slowed their approach. They saw Raul uncover a swamp boat with a camouflage design imprinted into the hull.

Nick edged closer.

With Raul busy hauling out the boat and getting it prepped, Nick and Sylvia exited the car. Nick had his 9mm in hand.

As Nick and Sylvia slipped through the surrounding foliage, Tony waited. Halfway to Raul, Nick told Sylvia to "hang tight" and snuck in closer to Raul. Tony steered the car forward.

Exiting the car, he kept the sun's rays shining from behind and in Raul's eyes. Tony could see Raul squinting trying to see who was approaching. Tony's voice was calm, pleasant, evidencing a northern accent.

"Excuse me, sir. I've lost my way. I'm looking for the Broussard's place. Do you know it?" Tony continued his approach as he spoke.

Raul raised his hand over his cap's brim, still trying to discern the man's face. Tony made sure his shadow didn't cast itself over Raul's eyes. Twenty yards and closing, then he saw Raul freeze with a stunned expression.

"Hi, Raul. I hear you've been looking for me. I have a beef to square with you."

The man Raul and his fellow assassins had killed was alive!

Raul had left his gun in his car. Caught off guard, he pulled his knife.

"I'm going to cut you up, sucker. The gators are going to feed well tonight. I don't know how you lived. I should send your head to Mr. Savage. C'mon, boy. Come get me." Raul crouched, wiggling his fingers, taunting Tony to bring it on.

A shot from the bushes hit Raul's right shoulder, knocking him to the deck. The knife dropped onto the wooden boards.

Tony raced forward as Raul reached for the knife with his left arm. Tony kicked up under his chin, throwing Raul backwards and landing on his back.

Nick closed in and picked up the knife. Tony stood over Raul.

Raul looked across the twins' faces. His eyes widened, unable to comprehend what he saw. As fear spilled across his face, he vainly tried to push himself upright with his left arm. Pain seared through his right shoulder. Blood flowed across the wood planks and dripped into the water. Two nearby alligators stirred.

Nick stripped open his shirt. The red welts of the bullet wounds glared down on Raul.

"Hell is waiting for you, Raul," said Nick.

Raul had nowhere to go.

Tony grabbed a rope from the swamp boat. He cut off a couple lengths, flipping Raul over onto his stomach, eliciting a belch of pain as he hog-tied Raul on the dock.

Helpless, Raul pleaded, saying he would disappear and promising they would never see him again.

"You're a piece of shit, Raul," said Tony, pulling him toward the dock's edge.

Nick reached out and held Tony back. "It's my vengeance, brother," said Nick. He reached down and flipped Raul into the bayou waters.

Nick and Tony watched Raul struggle, kicking his tied legs like some hobbled animal, bobbing and grasping for air. They watched water spilling into Raul's mouth. They watched him fruitlessly kick his tied legs again and again as he spit and gasped. The two gators, attracted by the churning water and blood, hit him almost simultaneously, tearing him apart, so each got his fair share.

Raul's last shrieks bubbled from under the gore-filled waters of justice. Flies descended onto the sweet smell of the blood-stained dock to suck up their portion. Experience had taught Nick that Raul's bones would take about three weeks to dissolve inside the gators' stomachs.

Nick untied the swamp boat and set it adrift.

For the first half of their return to the French Royal Hotel, it was mostly a quiet ride.

At last Nick spoke. "I shouldn't have dragged you two into this mess."

"We're not innocents," answered Sylvia. "We never did wet work for Pearce Savage, but we associated with him. We supported his criminal activities. Our hands aren't clean."

"Better that your hands are dirty than being dead."

"Brother, how did you survive? You can't keep putting us off. What is going on? When you pulled off your shirt in front of Raul to show him the bullet wounds, they are nothing like they were a week ago. They're healing … not like any bullet wounds I've ever seen."

"You won't believe what I tell you. I can hardly believe it myself."

"We're listening."

"I can't tell you right now. I will; I promise. Just not now."

"Damn you, Nick," exploded Tony. "You're fucking shutting me out again. Just like always."

"Fuck you, Tony!" shot back Nick.

"BOYS! BOYS!" interrupted Sylvia. "We're in this together now … whatever *this* is. Nick, you owe us something. No matter what it is, you have got to let us inside. The only reason I can figure that you're not telling us is because you think it affects us. Well, if that's true, then you really do owe us an explanation."

"I know," muttered Nick. "I know."

He desperately wanted to talk to Vince. It was confusing—needing to talk to Vince while simultaneously wanting nothing to do with the damn alien.

"Who's the next target?" asked Tony, trying to accommodate Sylvia's reprimand.

"It's a guy by the name of Mandla Shinga. He sometimes hangs out in the north Texas area."

"Zulu," said Sylvia. "That's his nickname, Zulu. His father has Zulu heritage. His mother is Comanche. He grew up in Dallas."

"I met him a couple times," said Tony. "He was in and out of juvenile detention multiple times by the age of 16. Did some adult hard time, too. He was proud of all the time he did. Zulu told me that a cousin of his father's lived in the Philly area so to feed his wanderlust and to stay ahead of Texas law, he headed northeast. It wasn't long before he met Pearce Savage. Pearce valued the young man's lack of restraint and gave the kid respect. The kid was willing to stand up to any man. Pearce groomed him and gave him the street name Zulu."

Back in room 204 of the French Royal Hotel, Nick waited for Vince to say something. In fact, he was surprised that Vince had not said anything on the way back from Raul's misfortune.

"I'm waiting," said Nick. "Talk to me."

"You're not going to like it," said Vince. "Pearce Savage is not the only danger Tony faces. A rebellion is simmering across Ephemeron. The approaching Fusion will chart the Ephemeral path for the next 300 years. Your observation about stomping on an ant had more insight than you imagined. It is that risk of dying a sudden death that propels an Ephemeral to find an intelligent, longer-living life-form. As the life-form grows old, it gives us time to prepare to leave and find a new dwelling. Using your analogy of the ant, an Ephemeral would have little forewarning of the ant's death.

"The Ephemeral would be suddenly disentangled from its host and cast into the universe. An Ephemeral has only a few hours to establish a new entanglement and set into its new dwelling. But the same thing goes for the situation where the dwelling, such as a human, meets a sudden death. There is the same chaos for the Ephemeral and only hours to live."

"Hours to live? I thought you had five days."

"A newborn seed has five days to entangle, but an Ephemeral who is looking for a new entanglement only has a few hours," explained Vince.

"How does that put Tony in greater danger?" asked Nick.

"Paul is the highest ranked prince in Ephemeron's ruling clan. His father is Ephemeron's ruling monarch. Paul's Fusion will have great bearing on how the clan powers will be aligned. Of course, his clan wants to retain its kingship. Killing Tony will throw Paul out of entanglement. If he can't find a new dwelling to entangle with, he will die. It will be a sign of his clan's weakness. An alliance of the other two clans would be enough to establish the next 1,000-year dynasty."

"The other day, you told me of Ephemeron's grand tradition of its kingdoms, how you Select the next monarchy, and the splendid Fusion of Ephemerals. You made it sound like beautiful chess play. Now, I get the sense that it was all bullshit. It sounds like you have a pitched battle on your hands."

"Perhaps it would be better to describe it as noble competition."

"Is it just you lying to yourself, Vince? Or is this a common quality of Ephemerals? Playing with a prince's life and my brother's life is more than a mere dalliance. Treachery comes to mind."

Nick grabbed the nearby bottle of bourbon and poured a hefty portion into a large glass. He drank half in one gulp. Vince's bombshell revelation coursed through his head. He doubted the bourbon would have the effect he wanted.

"You want to know how I see it?" asked Nick perfunctorily, though it wouldn't matter how Vince responded. Nick would be finishing his assessment.

"I think it is all about power. It does not matter that there have been thousands of Selections of an Ephemeral kingdom. Callum's clan is willing to go to any length to be the next monarchy. They used Callum to stir up Pearce Savage, just to order the hit on Tony. If everything had gone to plan, my brother would have been shot and then you, Vince, would have been scrambling for a new entanglement to save your life. I wouldn't be surprised if there was a glitch planned for interrupting that, too. You would have died. And with that, the only remaining suitor for Paul would be Callum.

"But they didn't know you and Paul had exchanged places between Tony and me. When the hit went down on Tony, they unwittingly shot me. It looked like there was an assassination against Paul, against the royal family. The shit hit the fan. Ephemeron Management stepped in and ordered you to help keep me alive. They needed to know what the hell was going on. Your story about saving me for some noble cause was a lie. The way I see it, Ephemeron is on the edge of tearing itself apart."

Finishing off the rest of his bourbon, Nick poured himself another drink.

"I told you. Ephemeron has learned hard lessons from its past. We were a warring culture, but it only ended in death for others and ourselves. We have peacefully Selected many kingdoms and we will elevate a thousand more." Vince's voice rang with the sound of false sincerity.

"Anything else I need to know that I don't want to hear?" growled Nick.

"There is one more thing that you will need to do."

"You're along for the ride, Vince … not to tell me what to do."

"There's an extra person you need to kill."

"You're crazy. Do it yourself."

Vince chuckled, not trying very hard to contain himself. He knew it bothered Nick when he laughed.

"If it makes you feel any better, you're not the only person in the universe we're recruiting," revealed Vince.

"A lot of people on Earth believe we're the only intelligent life-form in the universe. Obviously, having you in my head proves otherwise. But I'm wondering. Since Ephemerals inhabit others across the universe, how many different intelligent life-forms are out there?"

"That's really hard to say—millions, for sure."

"Seriously, Vince? Are you playing with me? I'm not in the mood. Millions of intelligent lifeforms?"

"Definitely."

Nick did a quick calculation in his head. "If you want an extra kill or two from me, then multiplying that number times millions more, tallies to a goddamn big number. Is your Ephemeron subterfuge dragging in other life-forms?"

"I can't say."

"Can't or won't say?" pressed Nick.

"Can't."

"I'm stuck with you, Vince, but I don't trust you."

Nick looked at his empty glass, wondering how he could protect Tony and Sylvia. At this point, he cared little for himself.

Were Vince and Paul the naïve good guys trying to help? Had it really been luck that Pearce Savage's men had hit the wrong target? Maybe everything that had occurred was an elaborate ruse and Paul, the monarchy's favored prince, was truly the target.

Maybe saving Nick was planned all along; one small step in a universe-spanning plot.

11

The next morning, Nick threw his gear into his car, while Tony and Sylvia put their stuff in theirs. It would be a solid day's drive to the Dallas area. It might have been inefficient, but there would be value in having two vehicles.

For Nick, it meant another opportunity to talk to Vince on the long drive. Nick had initially thought it would be best that Tony should never find out about Ephemeral Paul. Now, he realized he had made a mistake. Tony and Sylvia would surely press him again on how he survived the gunshots.

He had said he would tell them more later, but now was caught in a web of his own creation. How could he tell them why he had not died and protect his brother from finding out he was inhabited by an alien and that Sylvia was a future target? Details always messed up lies and deception.

Regardless of whether Vince was telling the truth, a partial truth, or simply himself being clueless of an unfolding Ephemeron plot, Tony and Sylvia needed to know about the Ephemerals.

Nick had a fair sense of what Tony's reaction would be. It would not be a pretty sight.

Each vehicle rolled out onto I-10 west from NOLA. Later they would head north on I-49 and east on I-20. Nick kept a wide distance back.

He thought of the story of the three blind men touching an elephant for the first time. One touched the legs, one the ears, and one the trunk. Each presented a perfect description of what the elephant was, but none really knew.

Maybe Nick was one of those blind men when he assumed Vince was one of the good guys and Callum was one of the bad guys. He was stuck inside an alien's game without being able to stand outside. Was he a small cog in the Ephemerals' machinations or an important linchpin? Despite increasing misgivings, there was little choice but to keep his head down and persevere.

Nick didn't know of any easy way to explain the Ephemeral reality to Tony and Sylvia, but he figured it was a wild card that could upset the Ephemeral Gamemaster's careful orchestration.

Nick found himself staring at his hands. They were stiff and ached, especially his left. Idly, he wondered if Vince had the power to restore his two lost fingers.

Letting his legs guide the car, he removed his hands from the steering wheel, opening and closing them to cut through their rigidity. His body was healing.

Vince had to have been helping the wounds heal faster than normal. That much Nick could believe, but it reminded him of other things Vince said. Vince had said he had to borrow energy from other Ephemerals. Maybe Vince was lying, or maybe it was embellishment. Nick had to find a way to crack open Vince's tale.

"Vince," called Nick.

"I'm here. You seem deep in thought. What's on your mind?"

"I know I said we can never let Tony know about Paul, but I don't see how it can be avoided. You said Paul was from a royal family, right?"

"Yes, that's right."

"How about your and Callum's families? Are they royal bloodlines?"

"No. But our families have served the kingdom for a long time. Our families have special status. Why the curiosity? Shouldn't you be focusing on your next target?"

"There's not much I can do driving down the road except think. You're the one that brought up the idea of me doing some wet work for you. If there's a royal bloodline at risk, why does it need to involve me?"

"Nick, I should correct myself. I admit there are many *positionings* circling about Ephemeron, but this tumult happens every time a Selection or Fusion approaches. It's not a direct challenge to the kingdom. It's a normal competition for power and status. A limited number of royalty slots may be bestowed on those who provide exceptional service. Some disagreement is expected."

"*Tumult* is an odd word for you to use, Vince. It's not just the Fusion and Selection that is approaching, but also a change to your world's monarchy. Besides me, are there any more Earthlings that you want to help you with your dirty work?"

"I can't say," said Vince.

"Can't? Or *won't* say?"

"I can't say."

Nick knew he had hit several soft spots, and he planned to hit those spots again and again.

Why did the Ephemerals need Nick to kill someone? Were there other Earthlings being recruited for the same? What palace conspiracies were brewing?

Ephemerals were vulnerable, and there was desperation in Vince's voice. Ephemerals lived off others' emotions, but it made Nick think that their dependency was also their weakness.

Though he was an outsider to the Ephemeral world, Nick realized he was not completely powerless. Ephemerals, if Vince was speaking truthfully, could not force a human to act; nor could they read minds. They could screw with someone's feelings and make a person feel like they were going crazy, but if a person was strong enough, a human could resist.

A human who was in control of himself was less valuable to an Ephemeral.

Tony and Sylvia were cruising down I-20, two miles ahead.

"How did he live?" asked Sylvia. "You saw the bullet holes. Nobody could survive that." She was so locked in thought that she saw nothing, though the roadside swept by. Her dark brown eyes stared straight ahead, and her jaw was set tight.

"I don't know. He mentioned he had a special friend."

"That doesn't make sense. No *special friend* could save someone from seventeen bullet wounds unless it was God himself."

They drove for miles, both thinking about Nick.

"At one point, he asked me a strange question," said Tony, breaking the silence. "He asked me if I ever heard voices."

"Have you?"

"Not exactly. Sometimes in my life I find it hard to know who I am. I feel like I can't control myself."

"There are always voices in people's heads," Sylvia insisted. "I don't think he meant those kinds of voices. You're his twin. Has he ever said anything to you about hearing voices?"

"No. We need to ask him what he meant. He needs to tell us about his miraculous friend."

12

The ability to harness quantum entanglement
had transformed the Ephemeral species ....

The biggest lesson from Ephemeron One was that an intelligent civilization could kill a planet. In the planet's waning time, not all inhabitants of Ephemeron One were able to leave. The privileged, the connected, the smartest and brightest, and those of special talents were selected. Various types of robots had high precedence.

A few Ephemerals found illicit ways to board the escaping spaceships. In the end, those remaining on Ephemeron One were left to struggle against an environmental debacle, then perish. No one came back to ferry them to New Ephemeron.

The pioneering survivors of New Ephemeron thought of themselves as blessed and true believers. These keepers of the faith located onto a distant planet, intending to populate and create a dreamed-of nirvana. With the most advanced technology and a thousand ships, they left all their possessions behind except for the essential tools to create a new homeland. They pictured a world where their dreams and hopes could come true. Ephemerals immersed themselves in conquering the planet's untouched resources.

Building and manufacturing skills were rewarded. Education and skilled trades were revered. Newer technologies sprung forth. Ephemeron

One's kingdom survived on New Ephemeron—now simply called Ephemeron.

Across legions of time, Ephemerals constructed their new civilization. Their species grew and flourished. Though their history' told of old and distant battles with the Zorix, that enemy never again appeared.

This cosmic isolation might have continued except for the Ephemeral's momentous breakthrough. It was the accidental discovery of how to manipulate quantum entanglement (QE) that cracked open the universe.

Many intelligent civilizations across the cosmos understood the scientific property that a single subatomic particle could be "entangled" with another particle. In such experiments, a scientist could touch one entangled particle, then that touch would instantly impact the outcome of the other particle. The effect occurred faster than the speed of light, regardless of distance across the universe.

Scientists of many civilizations continued their research advancing to the point of entangling and managing groups of atoms. Theoretically, scientists knew that much larger quantities of particles could be entangled.

When Ephemeral scientists chanced upon their deeper understanding of quantum entanglement, they unleashed an inconceivable power. Ephemerals used this power to seed their offspring across the universe. Where the habitat was hospitable, they cast more Ephemeral seeds to invade and to dwell inside others. It was in this way that Ephemeron established a presence on many planets.

In a sense, Ephemerals live a life of duality. All Ephemerals physically live on Ephemeron. They use QE to project themselves across the universe. Both their physical existence on Ephemeron and their projected essence are living entities. Physically, Ephemerals sit at their Entanglement Stations, often referred to as "E-stations," which project the essence of themselves. It is this quantum projection that is entangled to another life-form.

An Ephemeral spends its time at its E-station pulling and pushing levers, twirling dials, all to manage a projection that is living inside a distant life-form.

On that faraway world, an unsuspecting host was living its life, surreptitiously entangled to an Ephemeral who was cohabitating with them inside their bodies. The innocent life-form was not only unaware that an Ephemeral alien essence lived inside, but that the entangled projection was governed by a distant computer-screen operator. E-station manipulations were considered by Ephemerals as simply an optimization of entanglement, allowing for a more efficient harvesting of emotional energy.

Vince had described to Nick that these entanglements were peaceful habitations.

He just left out a few details, that's all.

For an entangled human—or another world's entangled species—it would not begin to imagine that some of life's turmoil might have been due to an embedded alien's influence. Humans would live, thinking they had been cursed by fates, a random genetic aberration, or hexed by an unlucky star presiding over their birth. Humans would never know that their life and psyche had been *influenced*.

A human would never know … except if one was shot seventeen times and lived.

Nick was not supposed to know an Ephemeral lived inside. He was not supposed to know of Ephemeral intrigues. And certainly, Tony and Sylvia weren't supposed to find out.

Sometimes shit happens, even for Ephemerals.

The ability to harness quantum entanglement had transformed the Ephemeral species from strong pioneering survivors that shaped the wilderness of New Ephemeron into E-station puppeteers. It was an evolutionary transformation that turned Ephemerals into desk jockeys with watchful supervisors, and supervisors of supervisors, accompanied by Management's insatiable need for data, questioning how many new life-forms were inhabited last month.

Ephemeral Upper Management scrutinized daily data charts that coldly aggregated the emotional ups and downs of each entangled world. Slickly designed reports were routinely sent to the advisors of Ephemeron's king, hoping to titillate His Highness with intriguing stories that described the emotional ups and downs of the entangled hosts.

More Management directives were dispatched, setting new production goals. More efficient entanglements equaled more energy harvested. The emotional traumas of others became cold numerical outputs.

Like most intelligent life-forms, humans looked up to the heavens with wonderment and dreams. Humans might indulge themselves with afternoons of escapist entertainment, watching movies and reading fantasy books that unfurled stories of scary invading aliens, but the vast majority of those who looked up to the heavens on crystal-clear star-filled nights believed that advanced aliens had surely evolved to overcome the psychological sins that humans struggled against: ambition; greed; intransigence; and the need to dominate.

Nor would human starwatchers have imagined that Ephemeron's E-stations were as important to keep its citizens busy and happy as much as harvesting Ephemeron's energy requirements. A cynic might conclude entanglements served a more prurient set of domestic desires.

Titillation? Tune to E-Station channel #10. Want to be a voyeur? Try channel #15. Want mindless entertainment? Channels 17 and 23 were Ephemeral favorites. Feeding off the emotional disruptions of others was just the way Ephemerals lived.

Learning how to efficiently and passively manipulate the innocent inhabitants of the universe became a basic requirement for moving up the Ephemeral corporate ladder.

Entanglement indoctrination started early for Ephemeral children, who were encouraged to manipulate life-forms using cleverly programmed computer games. The games taught the children how to encourage or suppress emotional displays.

Of course, the games had the added benefit of acting like bits of crack cocaine to keep the children busy. It would have been innocent enough … if it had stayed a game.

A critical piece of Ephemerals' entanglement conquests was the use of a projection of themselves. If Ephemerals' corporeal bodies had been directly entangled with another life-form's physical existence, then the acts of one would instantly impact the other, and vice versa. Because entanglement runs bidirectionally, both species would be doomed by each other's random daily activities.

When Ephemeral scientists found a mechanism to generate an Ephemeral "essence," or projection, they realized this projection could be entangled with another life-form.

Other critical scientific advances followed. Scientists learned to adjust the entanglements to act as one-way energy pipes, allowing emotional energy to flow from a host back to Ephemeron for harvesting. Though the entanglement pipes technically support bidirectional effects, this aspect remained hidden to the host, similar to a one-way mirror. An Ephemeral at its E-station could see and manipulate the entanglement, but the host would have no idea of the connection.

Throughout most of Tony's life, he may not have heard Ephemeral voices in his head, but his life had been negatively impacted by the Ephemeral entanglement. Vince and Paul—or whatever their real unpronounceable names were—bounced back and forth over the years inside, controlling the computer levers and knobs that toyed with Tony's and Nick's minds while sitting millions of light-years away.

Vince and Paul would admit that Nick was not as much fun since his emotional ups and downs were not as extreme. Yet, switching back and forth between the twins was an amusing delight. It was supposed to have continued that way.

But Callum, as usual, pulled one of his stunts, needling Pearce Savage's psychotic ego till it exploded and he ordered the bombastic killing of Tony.

When Pearce's henchmen mistakenly hit Nick instead of Tony, Ephemeron was thrown into turmoil. It appeared to be an assassination attempt against Paul, who was Ephemeral royalty and was supposed to be inside Nick. That's what the official Ephemeral tracking documents showed; that Paul was supposed to be inside Nick.

So, because Paul and Vince had surreptitiously switched places, the bullets that struck Nick looked like an attempted hit on Paul, Ephemeron's crown prince.

Management immediately intervened, knowing an Ephemeron had only a few hours to find entanglement with a new host. If Nick had died, Paul would have been at risk.

Emergency protocols kicked in, bypassing the non-interference principles. Ephemeron Management ordered Vince to save Nick.

Management needed to understand the situation. More critically, the Ephemeral Royal House wanted answers. There would be repercussions.

Callum professed innocence. How was he to know Pearce Savage would order the hit on Tony? After all, feeding off the emotions of others was the daily business of Ephemerals.

He pointed to the Ephemeron computer algorithms that had predicted Pearce Savage would order a severe beating of Tony, not his execution and said he was just following the E-Station's computer guidance.

Did he secretly suspect that Pearce would order Tony's killing? Perhaps. An Ephemeral, after dwelling in a host for a time, got to know that life-form.

Regardless of the exact reason that spurred Pearce Savage to send six henchmen to kill Tony, a prince had been put in jeopardy. Somebody needed to be punished.

The problem? An Ephemeral didn't have the capability to kill a human.

And despite Callum's history of bad behavior, he was protected by his family's elite status and the analyses of the E-station computer algorithms. It was the perfect defense, even if there was suspicion that Callum was partially to blame. Dangerous political ramifications encircled all.

Ephemeron royalty demanded a plan of retribution.

In Nick, they had stumbled on their weapon of choice. Nick wanted to kill Pearce Savage as much as did Ephemeron royalty. But Nick's involvement created problems. It meant a human would be a necessary partner.

The fact that Ephemeron royalty couldn't control Nick meant that they would be along for the ride as passengers on Nick's vengeance train. It meant Nick could dig into an Ephemeron world they didn't want to reveal. It meant the upcoming Selection and Fusion could be upset by unforeseen variables, putting a 1,000-year monarchial rule on the line.

Vince certainly glossed over some of the details he had told Nick, but a few items were accurate. If an Ephemeral lost his entanglement with another life-form, it was true that there were only a few hours to find another entanglement.

Normally, an Ephemeral could scramble successfully. Fighting to stay alive was substantial motivation in and of itself, but Ephemeron Management maintained a running list of potential entanglement targets.

A computer ran the unattached Ephemeral's profile against the potential list and determined if a new entanglement could be established. It was true that a Fusion occurred approximately every 300 years. It was true that a new Ephemeral seed must be implanted within five days or it died. It was true that there was an Ephemeral kingdom and that Selection of a ruling clan occurred every 1,000 years, followed by a king's Ascension.

But Vince lied about a couple items.

He lied about breaking rules to talk to Nick. In fact, it was a direct order from Management.

He lied when he minimized the conflict ongoing on Ephemeron.

He omitted the mention of a rebel insurrection.

He failed to mention anything of Overlord Draxis and his megalomania.

He failed to mention that an idea was taking hold in the minds of Ephemeron's population. And physical manipulation of other beings, not merely passive entanglement, was their God-given right.

Vince also failed to mention that Ephemeron's long-held religious customs were fracturing under the weight of political self-interests.

Other lies and truths intermingled.

13

"You better brace yourselves.
First off, you're not going to believe a word I say."

Stopping for an interstate break at a roadside restaurant, Nick, Tony, and Sylvia ate a quick lunch of sandwiches and sodas. Sylvia remembered that Zulu had talked about his childhood in the historical part of south Dallas.

Nick also had spent days investigating Mandla Shinga, aka "Zulu." He agreed that that was a good place to start. It was a sketchy lead, but the best they had.

Sylvia searched for nearby hotels and found a mid-tier hotel named the Daphne. It was a hotel on the south side of downtown Dallas, north of I-30. It seemed like a place where they could stay under the radar.

Hours later, Tony and Sylvia pulled into the parking lot of the Daphne. They received room 206—the same room number they had had in NOLA.

Nick decided he didn't want to check in at the same time, so he stopped at a local bar to kill an hour.

At the Daphne front desk, Sylvia asked the clerk, "Why do you have ghost references around the lobby?"

"Some people think the hotel is haunted," the receptionist replied calmly. "Rooms 316 and 318 generate the most comments from our customers. We don't normally put customers at that end of the hall."

"You keep rooms intentionally empty? How do you stay in business?" continued Sylvia.

"Some customers specifically ask for those rooms. We get to charge more for them. There's usually a waiting list."

"Have you seen a ghost?" asked Tony, amused.

"It's not like on TV. But, yes, I have. For instance, you can look down the hallway and you notice that something seems to be warping the air. It's not always the shape of a person, but sometimes it is. It's like looking through distorted glass. Every employee who has been here for a while has seen or heard something. The most unnerving experience is hearing footsteps inside the room that you're sleeping in. It always freaks me out."

Rethinking their choice of hotel, Tony and Sylvia looked at each other, but it had been a long day and they were tired.

"Does much haunting happen on the second floor?" asked Tony.

"I've been here three years. Second-floor sightings are uncommon. You should be safe. Some customers will hang out in the lounge, waiting for one of the third-floor residents to spin the latest tale. It can get quite lively. We have a happy hour from 4-6 p.m., Monday through Friday. Basic drinks, wine, and beer are half price, and we set out a few appetizers. Sorry, they're closing happy hour now. You can try it tomorrow.

"Here's your key cards," the receptionist continued. "Do you need someone to help you with your bags? The elevator is around to the left. We serve breakfast between seven and nine a.m. It's twelve dollars for the buffet. There is some limited a la carte available. Is there anything else I can help you with?"

"Is there a place to pick up some cold beer?" asked Sylvia.

The receptionist pointed a direction over her shoulder. "Go to the end of the block, turn right. Jelly's Liquors is a few doors down. He's open until two a.m."

They declined portage assistance and thanked the talkative receptionist before making their way to room 206. With time to kill before Nick checked in, they stretched their legs with a walk to Jelly's. Having noticed a refrigerator in the hotel room, they picked up a twelve-pack. Sylvia handed a bottle of bourbon to Tony, saying Nick would be needing that, though she really meant all of them could use a shot.

Tony finished up paying for the beer and liquor. As he walked toward the door, Sylvia caught Tony's attention, motioning him to come over to her. She was looking out the iron-barred window. Speaking quietly, she murmured, "Tony, do you see the green Thunderbird sitting across the street? Look carefully at the driver. Who does that look like to you?"

"Jesus. It's Zulu. I hope he doesn't come in here. That would be messy."

The car wasn't moving. Two rounds of lights completed, then a skinny man approached. He stopped at Zulu's car, bending toward the window. It was a quick, subtle exchange. Sylvia snapped a couple photos.

Jelly was eyeing his two customers. They had seemed like regular customers, but their actions were making him nervous. He stepped closer toward his undershelf shotgun.

At the next green light, Zulu drove through it.

Jelly's two customers left.

Nick arrived at the Daphne Hotel about a half-hour later. The receptionist greeted him with the same ghost-haunting backstory, happy hour info, and breakfast details.

Nick wondered what the receptionist would say if she found out an alien was dwelling inside his body and another one could soon be lurking within hers. She gave him a key card to Room 204. Once in his room, he texted Tony and Sylvia that he had arrived and would be over shortly.

Minutes later, he knocked on room door 206. Sylvia handed Nick a cold beer. He readily accepted it even though he had already lingered at a bar and had a head start.

"We caught a break," said Tony. "Sylvia spotted Zulu. He drives a green Thunderbird. It looked like he was purchasing drugs; money and a little packet were exchanged. Sylvia has a photo."

Sylvia pulled out her phone and zoomed in on Zulu's face. She handed it to Nick.

"Yeah, that's one of the guys who shot me. I remember the face." Nick resized the photo to normal. He didn't see what he was looking for. He slid to the next photo. The second shot had what he wanted; the license number for the car. He zoomed in. "We can track him down with this," he said, showing the picture of the license plate to Sylvia and Tony. Nick took a long draw of beer.

"Have any ideas in mind?" asked Tony, referring to how Nick might kill Zulu.

"Several, but opportunity will dictate terms, like always." Nick plopped himself into a chair. He had no problem hunting down Pearce Savage's henchmen. That was justified payback.

At the moment, Nick's thoughts were consumed by Vince's suggestion that Nick kill an extra person. Even though Vince hadn't specified who, it was triggering warning bells.

"Nick," said Tony, breaking into Nick's musings. "Why didn't you die? You said you had a special friend. No one could live through what you went through. You need to tell us what happened."

Nick wasn't finished with his first beer, but he already needed another. He eyed the unopened bottle of whiskey.

He knew he had to have this conversation. In his mind, he had run scenario after scenario about how he would talk about his failed death. He always arrived at one option: tell Tony and Sylvia the whole truth.

"You better brace yourselves. First off, you're not going to believe a word I say. You will think I am insane. But I ask you to remember one thing: seventeen bullet wounds. You saw them."

"We know, Nick," said Sylvia. "It's why we're asking."

Nick laughed. "I'm glad you saw the wounds days ago, when they were worse. They are only red scars now." Nick pulled up his shirt.

Tony and Sylvia stared, as they had before. They looked at each other, again facing the proof, but barely comprehending. Nick pulled his shirt down, poured a whiskey for himself and similar shots for both Tony and Sylvia. He took a deep breath.

"An alien lives inside me, and he is the one who saved me. He has been living inside me for years. I had no idea until I was shot."

"An alien!? What do you mean?" asked Tony, the disbelief clear on his face.

"An alien from another planet. It has been living inside me. It saved me. It's how I survived."

Sylvia downed more than half her whiskey.

Tony scrutinized his brother, his twin. "You're not joking. How is that possible?" Tony took a slug of liquor.

"I know this makes no sense. Believe me, if I hadn't lived through it, I wouldn't believe it either. How do you think I feel? I never knew it was inside me. I only know that I am alive. You saw the bullet wounds last week. You see them today. Humans don't heal that fast. Humans don't live after being shot seventeen times."

"People are shot all the time. Why haven't others lived to tell an alien tale?" wondered Sylvia.

"It's complicated."

"How do you know it lives inside you? Does it talk to you?" joshed Tony, making light of the matter.

"It does talk to me and I can talk to it. Since the shooting, we talk almost every day."

Sylvia finished her whiskey and poured herself another. She topped off Tony's glass. Nick held out his glass.

"What do you talk about?" questioned Tony.

"I think this might be a long night." Nick took a swig. "Maybe it's best if I start from the beginning."

Nick restated it all. The first night laying in the alley. His fears he was going insane. He described the persistent voice of Vince nagging him, even the repartee he had with the alien before naming it Vince. He retold them the stories of Ephemeron and Ephemerals that Vince had revealed. He told them everything as best he could.

He saw the panic in his brother's eyes when Nick said an alien dwelled inside him, too.

Sylvia's eyes widened large when she heard she might soon be an alien host.

Vince's voice chimed inside Nick's head. "You're doing a good job, Nick. I couldn't have done it better myself. What do you Earthlings say—rip the bandage off quick."

"Vince, you need Paul to speak to Tony," said Nick.

"Brother, what did you say?" asked Tony, confused. "Did you just talk to … uh, this Vince alien?"

"I did. I've told you everything I can. I'm telling Vince that the alien inside you—his name is Paul—needs to talk to you. You need to know it's real."

"That's such a funny name for an alien," observed Sylvia, with whiskey coursing through her veins. "Couldn't it have been something more alien-sounding—like Monstro?"

"Shit, Sylvia," exclaimed Tony. "I don't need an alien possession by an alien named Monstro. If I'm going to be possessed, Paul sounds just fine."

They laughed hysterically, covering their fear.

Sylvia kept offering names for Tony's alien. *Kraken. Medusa. Malevolento.* Each name made her laugh harder. Though her humor was driven by alcohol, Nick found it amusing.

Tony squirmed. He was already conjuring images of the monsters. In most scenes, they were devouring him or finding painful ways to inflict pain.

"Hi, Tony," spoke Paul suddenly inside of Tony's head. Tony shot up straight in his chair, frozen stiff.

"I'm not going to hurt you," said Paul calmly. "Everything your brother told you is true. We are Ephemerals. We are like spirits. We mean you no harm."

Sylvia noticed Tony's rigidity and his face turning ashen. "Tony? What's happening? Tell me," Sylvia said, concern washing away her chuckles.

"The thing is talking to me," said Tony, his voice trembling. "He's fucking talking to me right now. I can hear him in my head like it's another person talking to me."

"It's going to be okay," soothed Nick. "I had to go through the same thing. It's freaking crazy to hear that voice. I'm here for you. You don't have to go through this alone like I did."

Tony's face contorted. His eyes darted around the room, as if scanning the room would somehow reveal who was speaking inside his head. Finally, full of frustration, he jumped up, ready to fight.

"What do you want from me?" spat Tony, his voice trembling.

"It's what we can do for each other," said Paul, speaking calmly. "I can help protect you. You can help my family; I am on your side. I know this is overwhelming for you. Nick will help guide you. I will help you. I've never hurt you. I'm not going to hurt you now."

"It's in my head," exclaimed Tony, dropping his glass to the floor and grabbing his head with his hands. "It's in my head, just like you said."

Sylvia grabbed at Tony's arm, trying to calm him, but he thrust her hand away.

"It spoke to me. How can this be?" Tony again grabbed at his head, trying to fight against the impossibility that had come true.

"Fuck off, Paul. Leave me alone. I will never talk to you," challenged Tony as he breathed heavily like he was gasping for sanity.

"It's going to be okay, brother," said Nick. "It's crazy. I know. I went through it. I'm here for you."

Tony grabbed Sylvia into his arms, squeezing her tight to him and closing his eyes as if that would ward off the untouchable and unseen alien. He loosened his hold, but still held onto her.

"I don't hear him," said Tony, finally opening his eyes and casting a desperate look toward Nick. "I think he's gone. He knows I don't want anything to do with him. I told him. You heard me." Tony's eyes were wide and bulging. "You heard me, didn't you? I told it to get away from me."

"Sure, Tony, we heard you," said Sylvia, trying to console her lover. Nick noticed the warble in her voice, figuring she was fighting her own fears.

Tony collapsed onto the couch, burying his head in his hands.

"Tony," said Paul softly.

"No. No. No. Go away. I told you. Go away." Tony repeatedly slapped his head, then looked pleading to Nick and Sylvia. "What am I going to do? It's talking to me again."

"Tony, I'm not going to hurt you," continued Paul, trying to be soothing.

"What do you want from me? My brother says you have been inside us for years. How can that be?"

"It's difficult to explain. Think of us like spirits. We simply use the energy from your emotions."

"For what?" questioned Tony.

"To live," answered Paul.

"Nick," said Sylvia. "What is going on? Can you hear what Tony's alien is saying?"

"Sylvia, I can only hear when Vince speaks inside my head."

"What are we going to do?"

"The good news is that Tony is talking to his alien. That's the first step. We let him—them—be alone together. Let Tony and Paul talk it out as long as they want."

"All night?"

"If that's what it takes."

Sylvia paced back and forth, her nerves showing. "Nick, you said that this could happen to me. How likely is that? When would that happen? Can I stop it?" She crossed her arms tight and pulled them close to her chest.

"I don't know, Sylvia. I don't know."

"What have we gotten into? If these aliens have been living inside us and we've never known, how can we fight them? This is some messed-up shit."

"I don't know, Sylvia. I don't know."

"Tony is already lost. Look at him."

"My alien has never hurt me. I'm not defending it. Every day I want to wring its neck, but the only thing it has done to me is heal my body."

"And drive you almost insane with a voice in your head that you can't control."

"Yes."

Sylvia grabbed a cold beer, covered in condensation, twisted off the cap and deftly flicked it perfectly into a nearby trash can. She took a long swig.

"Nick, there's something bigger going on. Something they're not telling us. I don't trust them."

"That seems like a reasonable starting point. I don't trust them either. Vince has told me stuff. But I agree. There's something bigger going on."

"I doubt I'll sleep a wink tonight. I'm sure Tony will be awake pacing. Why don't you go back to your room, Nick, and try to get some sleep. I'll call if anything goes off the rails … at least, more than it already has." She flicked a nervous glance at Tony.

"Sounds like a plan," Nick agreed, knocking back the last of his drink. At the doorway, he looked back. His brother was now sitting in a corner of the room, seemingly arguing with Paul.

Nick gave Sylvia a wink. "Stay strong."

"Wait up, you lug," she commanded lightly as she went over to give him a big hug and a kiss on his cheek. "I'll be fine, Nick."

"I'm counting on it," said Nick, exiting the room.

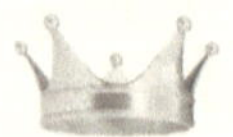

That night, Tony's mind would fight against the impossibility that had come true. He would lash out, challenging the untouchable and unseen Paul. He would tell Paul he would ignore him and never, ever talk to him and commanded him to go the fuck away.

And during those moments when Paul had to retreat to his E-station to revitalize himself, Tony would think he had succeeded in chasing Paul away.

Later, upon Paul's return, Tony would pepper Paul with questions. In this way, Tony and Paul would intermittently talk all night long … about Ephemeron, about Ephemerals, about Paul.

Nick had told Sylvia to let them be.

Later, out of desperation, Sylvia moved herself to the bedroom to catch a few fitful moments of sleep.

Zulu would be graced with an extra day of life.

14

"You've been spinning as many lies as truths."

The next day really dawned as a new day for Tony because he had stayed up all night, witnessing the sky's darkness slowly melding with the first hints of the sun's distant approach.

As Nick and Sylvia also slept poorly, the new morning weighed like a surreal confusion. Belatedly, in the early afternoon, they found a nearby café that served all-day breakfasts. The afternoon breakfast made Tony feel slightly better. He ate, barely speaking.

Nick had seen it before in the war. A soldier sees his first major battle and lives. A soldier is always different after that.

Tony had spent the night battling his mind, adjusting to something beyond his control. Paul wasn't going away. Tony had never even heard of quantum entanglement before last night. Certainly, if he had come across the phrase within an online internet search, it would have meant nothing. He would have kept scrolling.

Now, his life was being completely reshaped by aliens who could cultivate a vast power of the universe. Though only a single person, how Tony felt must have been the same way past civilizations must have felt when they were overcome by a previously unknown enemy wielding unimaginable power.

Paul declared that he was peaceful and said he was sorry that Tony had to find out about the entanglement. It was an accident that the Ephemerals' existence was exposed. The explanations did little to calm Tony's torment nor quiet his demons.

"Paul said Ephemerals can't read our minds. Do you believe that?" asked Tony.

"I think so. It seems Vince has had questions about me and my plans that would have been stupid questions if he had already known the answer. Any conversation I've ever had with him has been verbal. But they are very adept at reading emotions. If I am thinking of something that provokes me, Vince knows that. I suppose they can sometimes guess what's going on."

"Do they hear us as we speak? Like, right now?" asked Tony.

"I expect so," answered Nick. "If they're listening."

Sylvia pulled a pen and piece of paper from her purse. She wrote, *We will have to write secrets*, and then showed it to both men. They nodded.

"Did Paul tell you about their Fusion?" asked Nick.

"He said Fusion is a time when Ephemerals reproduce. He was supposed to Fuse with Vince, but that's now uncertain. Paul may have to Fuse with Callum."

Sylvia thrust herself into the conversation. "Nick, your body is mostly healed. You don't need Vince helping you to recover. How do we end their entanglements? We have to set you and Tony free."

"Ain't that the truth, honey," said the waitress, having approached and overhearing their conversation. She held a pot of coffee and smiled at them. They laughed.

"More coffee?"

The three nodded. "Yes, ma'am, please," said Nick.

After the waitress's departure, Sylvia asked, "have you found anything more about Zulu?"

"I have an address where the car is registered. The car belongs to a Koko Shinga. Her age is a little older than Mandla's, so maybe she's a sister. She lives in the Eagle Ford area. It's twenty minutes west of here. I'm going to canvass the area on my own, but for now I want you two to stay near the hotel."

"That's not going to happen," Tony objected. "You can't leave me alone with Paul." Sylvia slapped him across the arm, reminding him she was part of the situation.

"He shot me so I'm the one that has to do this," said Nick. "Besides, it'll give me some personal time with Vince. I need to talk to him. Tony, you could do the same with Paul. Paul could help shed some light on Ephemeron. Ask him if he misses me."

"I think he does," responded Tony, holding his coffee cup in both hands. "Paul kept saying he wished things were back to normal. Isn't that hilarious? I want the same damn thing. *Back to normal* would mean aliens would be living inside us, merrily trading places with each other whenever they wanted and we would have no idea."

"Push him to talk," encouraged Nick. "I don't trust either of them, but you gotta make Paul trust you. I can't help but think they need us for some reason. Use your charm, brother. Get Paul to open up. He's royalty. He probably knows a bunch of secrets."

"Vince is probably listening to you right now," cautioned Sylvia.

Taking Sylvia's cue, Nick asked, "Vince, are you there?"

Nick shrugged his shoulders. "He's not responding." After several more calls to Vince and no answer, Tony tried calling to Paul. Again, no answer from the Ephemerals.

Nick took a sip of coffee, figuring that with no response from the aliens it was safe to talk. "Seems like there are limits to their eavesdropping.

Vince said he had to borrow energy to help me and that it's draining for Ephemerals to operate in our physical world."

"What do they want from us?" asked Tony. "Talking to us costs them energy. Why would they bother with that? Why not go back to the way things were? Be silent and reap the energy off our emotions. They don't have to respond to us, but they do. Why?"

"Good questions, brother."

"We shouldn't waste the whole day," interrupted Sylvia. "We should be tracking down Zulu."

"You can't go with me," said Nick. "It's going to be hard enough to stay out of sight, but three of us together is tempting fate."

"We're in this together," pushed Tony.

"Agreed, but we need to be smart. Sometimes it's better to be safe than try to go for the big score. I'm sorry, but today I need to track down Zulu by myself."

Indifferent to Tony's and Sylvia's protestations, Nick refused their company. Within a half-hour, Nick was heading west on I-30 as he drove his uninspiring silver car close to the speed limit.

Vince had said that he was no longer betrothed to Paul. But Paul had told Tony the betrothal with Callum was uncertain. Nick figured that meant factions were battling behind the scenes.

"Vince?"

"Yes, Nick?"

"Why didn't you answer when I called earlier?"

"I was resting."

"You said Paul is royalty. It might have been fun for you and Paul to jump back and forth across a couple human twins, but something like that must have been approved at some level. After I was shot, you told me you broke rules to save me. But it was really Ephemeron Management that ordered you to save me. There's more going on that you're not telling me. The way I figure it, the Ephemeron kingdom is in the middle of a shitstorm."

"That's empty speculation."

"I hardly think that. You've been spinning as many lies as truths."

"That's not fair. I saved your life."

"Vince, you can stop pulling out that card. I bet nobody knows who they can trust. By the way, how old is the king?"

"Nick, you're inventing conspiracies."

Nick sensed Vince's weakness. Apparently, the emotional entanglement pipeline could run both ways. "You didn't answer me. How old is the king?"

"Closing in on 1,200 years old."

"Who is the heir apparent? Is it the oldest seed?"

"No, most of the time it is a younger seed."

"Like Paul, for instance?"

"Yes. Paul is under consideration."

"Who called off the betrothal of you and Paul?"

"It wasn't exactly specified. But such matters flow from the king's wishes."

Nick was trying to put it together in his head.

Paul seemed to be the prize. If Vince's betrothal was being held up, then at least two factions were fighting behind the scenes.

One faction was backing Vince. Another was backing Callum.

"Vince, you tell me I'm imagining an unreasonable plot, but you're at more risk than me. I've mostly healed from my wounds. I don't think I need you anymore. You might be able to play with a voice in my head and provoke my emotions. Maybe you could drive me to insanity, but it's you who needs me. And I think Paul needs Tony, which means you two need to work with us. It's to everyone's benefit."

"Paul and I could set up a double entanglement at a local level."

"What does that mean?"

"It means I am entangled with you. Paul is entangled with Tony, but Paul and I can set up an extra, localized entanglement with each other. It would solve the communication problem. All five of us could communicate together. It only works at short distance. It would work within a room."

"How can all five of us speak together? Sylvia isn't entangled."

"If we all were within the radius of the double-entanglement, she would be part of the conversation. There is one major downside."

"What's that?" asked Nick.

"A double entanglement depletes our energy levels even faster. It's dangerous."

"You said that others were helping you."

"I was telling you the truth, but it takes great resources for us to operate at a physical level in another world. It's a huge strain. The supplemental energy resources I've been receiving are limited."

To Nick, Vince's answer seemed evasive. What he didn't know was that it was a spot-on guess. While it was true that Vince had been receiving extra energy from others to maintain those physical connections, some Ephemerals were no longer donating their energy to him.

Ephemerals were taking sides.

"Besides you and Paul liking each other, what does it matter whether you Fuse with Paul or whether Callum does?"

"If my family can prevail with the king, I will Fuse with Paul. This will show that our family is an important ally to the king. It will change the direction of Ephemeron. If Callum's family prevails, a very different kingdom will emerge. Nick, I'm growing tired. I feel sick."

"All right, Vince. No more questions for a while. I'll let you get your beauty sleep. But think long and hard. The five of us working together is your best chance for survival, Paul's best chance to be king, and the best chance for you two to Fuse. I'm betting your family will see it the same way."

Vince was unable to answer. Light-years away on Ephemeron, he had collapsed from the demands of his Earthly interactions.

Nick wasn't sure about the royal family seeing it the same way as he did, but figured that the kingdom was primarily interested in survival. Vince was right that Nick was playing a dangerous game.

Nick had just made a pitch to Vince to ally the five of them together. But he wasn't sure it was Vince's family that he should be backing. Maybe Vince and his family were the bad guys and Callum's family the good guys.

Nick turned off interstate I-30, donned a Dallas Cowboys cap, tilting it low over his face. Slouching in the driver seat, he rolled his car slowly by Koko Shinga's address. A Pagoda Green Thunderbird sat out front.

Parking down the block, he adjusted his mirrors so he could watch the car.

15

"That was so weird," said Sylvia.
"I spoke to an alien through my boyfriend."

In his room at the Daphne Hotel, Tony was suffocating in a soup of paranoia. He raided the hotel's business printer tray, removing half its blank paper. He took it to the room and became insistent that he and Sylvia should write everything down instead of speaking.

Finally, Sylvia had had enough. "You have to talk to him, Tony."

Tony tried to shush her, but Sylvia was having none of it. "He can't hear me, so I'm not writing down another damn thing. Ask Paul who he wants to Fuse with," she demanded.

Initially, Tony refused, but she kept pushing.

"Okay, okay," relented Tony.

And so, the strange dialogue commenced, with Sylvia prompting most questions, Tony repeating them to Paul, and then Tony restating them back to Sylvia.

Tony: Who do you want to Fuse with?

Paul: Vince. We have always been close friends. We were betrothed for many years.

Tony: Did Callum push Pearce Savage to have me killed?

Paul: Officially, no. Unofficially, yes.

Tony: How would that have helped Callum if I had died?

Paul: Vince would have been left without a corporeal body to live in. He would have had to find a new entanglement, and that would have weakened or killed Vince and undermined Vince's family. But the plan went haywire. Vince and I were exchanging bodies between you and Nick. When Pearce Savage's henchmen mistakenly shot Nick, Management thought it was an attack on me. All hell broke loose. Emergency procedures kicked in to save Nick, because they thought that would save me. Once the confusion lifted, everybody was under the spotlight. The kingdom is almost 1,000 years old. It needs a renewal. Humans would say it needs new blood. My family needs a strong ally.

Tony: Why did the king put your betrothal to Vince on hold?

Paul: I don't know. Either Callum's family or Vince's family can save the kingdom or bring it down as the Fusion arrives, depending on how alliances develop. Most of my royal family has become soft. They frolic their days away in fun, palace intrigue, and their personal pursuits. They are satisfied with the energy we passively reap from our hosts. The Callum family wants Ephemeron to press for more aggressive entanglements. The king is wary of Callum's family.

Tony: What does that mean—more aggressive entanglements?

Paul: Callum's family wants to physically control other life-forms.

Tony: Isn't that impossible? Haven't you been saying physical interactions exhaust you?

Paul: It has always been that way, but Overlord Draxis, the head of Callum's clan, claims research has opened up the possibility of physical control.

Tony: What about Vince's family? What do they want?

Paul: Ephemeron has always been anxious about other life-forms. You would say we are xenophobic. Vince's family is wary about other life-forms but doesn't want to be seen as weak and unable to keep up.

Tony: Will it even matter? If any life-forms, especially humans, find out Ephemerals are trying to control them or harvest them for energy needs, everyone will fight back. The Ephemeron civilization will be exposed. Your world will become the most hunted in the universe.

Paul: We feed off emotions, remember? If you tear yourselves apart trying to get back at us, it only provides us with more energy and makes us stronger. And to make a small point, you don't have the technology to touch us.

Paul's voice wavered, trailing off: I'm sorry, Tony. I can't do this anymore. I am very tired. I must rest now.

Tony called Paul's name multiple times. There was no answer.

On Ephemeron, Paul was being infused with special regenerative fluids. He would be in a deep slumber for hours.

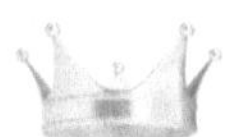

"That was so weird," said Sylvia. "I spoke to an alien through my boyfriend. The Daphne Hotel's claim to ghostly hauntings has got nothing on us. Hey, let's go check out the third floor where the ghosts hang out," she said, trying to add levity to the moment.

"I pass," said Tony.

Sylvia went to the refrigerator. There were far fewer beers remaining than she expected. "We need to go back to Jelly's. We're low on supplies. Want one?"

"Not now. Thanks, honey." Tony pulled out a joint and lit it up.

"Tony, what the hell are you doing? Somebody is going to report that smell. Put it out. We don't need to call attention to ourselves," she scolded.

Tony took two more big inhales, then stubbed the joint out. He opened up the window and increased the speed on the room's fan. A few minutes later, they were walking the street to Jelly's.

Jelly recognized them. This time he kept a keen eye on them.

Sylvia put a twelve-pack of beer and a bottle of premium whiskey on the counter.

Sylvia again went to the barred-up street window to look out as Tony waited for the total.

"That'll be $95.25 with tax," said Jelly, smiling at the profitable sale.

Tony placed a hundred-dollar bill on the counter. "How much for a pepperoni stick?" Two dozen sat in a jar.

"You can have two and we'll call it even," said Jelly. Tony grabbed two and added them to the bag, then walked the goodies to where Sylvia was standing.

"Have you seen Zulu again?" asked Tony.

"No. But I see his dealer. Don't eyeball him when we leave. We gotta be cool. We're just customers needing booze. He's probably seen a thousand customers from the Daphne."

Tony's phone vibrated. Nick was texting from the hotel.

Sylvia and Tony exited Jelly's, noting the dealer's shade-covered spot he called his office. They felt the dealer's gaze scan over them as they made their way back to the Daphne.

Moments later, Sylvia knocked on Nick's door.

"Hi, brother," she said, giving him a one-armed hug, as her other arm held Tony's bag of junk food. Tony carried the twelve-pack and the whiskey.

Sylvia wasted no time, tearing open the twelve-pack and popping open a beer. "We talked to Paul. He had some interesting things to say. Did you find Zulu?"

Tony popped a beer. Nick declined.

"I tailed Zulu to a local hangout and I put a tracker on his car. The app will record the car's movements. We'll be able to see where he goes and where he spends the most time. What did Paul say?"

"Are they listening to us?" worried Tony.

"Vince, are you around?" called Nick.

No answer.

"Vince, are you there?"

No answer.

"You try it with Paul," he said to Tony.

"Paul, are you there?"

No answer.

"Paul?"

No answer.

"We should try to figure out how long they need to rest," said Nick. "We can use that to our advantage. So, what did Paul say?"

"There are three main factions on Ephemeron. There's the existing kingdom. Paul is part of that royal bloodline. It appears he is the heir apparent, provided their clan wins the world's next Selection for monarchy. The king is old. Most of the family are lazy bastards and are more interested in indulging themselves.

"The kingdom is weak, and it needs allies. Another faction is Vince's family. They had been the favored ally to the kingdom, but Vince's family is under political pressure. The attack was meant to disrupt the betrothal between Vince and Paul by attacking me, but by a quirk of fate, the plan went sideways because they had switched between our bodies.

"Another faction is Callum's family. They are an aggressive clan, and are looking to expand the Ephemeral capability to physically control life-forms across the universe."

Nick gave Tony a quizzical look.

"Okay, okay," said Tony. "I'm paraphrasing. There's more, but that's the gist of it."

"You left out the part about me," said Sylvia, slapping Tony across the shoulder.

"Not only have I have been approved for entanglement, perhaps with Callum the bad boy Ephemeral … or, I could be implanted with the seed of Paul and Vince, or the seed of Paul and Callum. What kind of fucking choice is any of that? Ephemerals can simply implant their seed in us, and we don't even know it happened. Can I simply say *no*? I doubt it. Can I do anything to disrupt their fucking insane plans? It doesn't seem so. And if I can't prevent an entanglement, how do I pick *my favorite*?" asked Sylvia sarcastically and with added air quotes.

"Perhaps I'll have a beer after all," remarked Nick. Tony threw him one. "You know, Vince gave me pretty much the same story. That helps us to keep them honest." Nick popped open the beer and took a swig.

"Look, none of us have much say in anything that is happening to us," said Nick. "But for some reason they seem to need us. We don't know all the whys. It's more than the failed hit by Pearce Savage's henchmen.

"Sylvia, what you said earlier gave me an idea. You were right. I don't need Vince to heal me anymore. My own body can take care of the rest. So, why are they interacting with us, communicating with us? We know that it is exhausting if they spend time even talking to us. Vince says too much physical activity can damage an Ephemeral. We know Paul and Vince want to Fuse. I tried threatening Vince. Whether that will have any effect, we'll have to see. We don't have a lot of cards to play against them. If those two want to Fuse to create the new

Ephemeron Kingdom, so be it. But I told him I didn't need to work with him anymore.

"If they expect us to be part of their grand plan, then they need to bring us inside the tent. The upcoming Selection establishes the next Ephemeron kingdom and sets the stage of alliances with the following Fusion. I gave a pitch to Vince that the five of us need to work together. I'm betting Vince's family will think the same way. If Paul is the heir apparent, he will press the king to ally with Vince's family.

"And there's another wrinkle," continued Nick. "Vince told me he and Paul can create a double entanglement. Vince will still be inside me and Paul inside Tony, but it will allow all of us to speak and hear each other if we're in the same room. But it exhausts Ephemerals even faster."

"I'll be able to speak with them, too?" asked Sylvia.

"Yes, you too."

"I keep asking myself: why do they remain here? Why us? Why are humans so important?" wondered Sylvia.

"It's a good question," said Nick. "For some reason, it looks like they're stuck with us. I think it's our job to poison the waters. If both Vince's and Callum's families are looking to expand their interactions with other life-forms, it doesn't matter if one family is the nicer alien. I don't like them hanging out inside me. Let's help them find a new planet."

"There's another problem," added Tony. "Paul said that Callum's family has been researching how to physically manipulate life-forms, not just use passive entanglement. Some guy by the name of Overlord Draxis is leading the charge. He's the head of their clan."

"Damn. If they can do that, we're screwed," exclaimed Nick. "Every life-form they inhabit will be screwed. As much as I distrust half of what Vince and Paul tell us, I get the sense they want to put Humpty-

Dumpty back together and be on their way. The upcoming Selection of a new monarchy is magnifying the madness."

"We need to be careful," urged Tony. "Do we know when Vince or Paul will recover? They could hear what we say."

"We'll have to work on that problem, though I don't know that much of what we're discussing is all that secret. In the meantime, I'm going to finish my job hunting down the bastards that shot me. Killing Pearce Savage is in our interest and our Ephemeral friends' interest. We need to leverage that. Time to go shopping."

As they exited through the Daphne lobby, the talkative receptionist called out, "Have the ghosts been bothering you? Some customers have reported strange happenings the last couple nights."

"I've heard a few voices," said Tony.

The receptionist looked startled. She had asked the question as a mindless joke.

"Me too," said Nick.

"Really?"

"Definitely," added Tony. "The voice was as clear as day. His name is Paul. It's damn unnerving, I can tell you that."

They left the hotel receptionist dumbfounded and with a worried expression on her face. Nobody had ever reported hearing voices from rooms 204 and 206.

16

With Tony behind the wheel, they took the Jeep to a hunting supply store. Nick picked out a tactical compound bow, an adjustable triple-stack sight, and a dozen 400-gram arrows with razor-sharp, fixed broadhead tips. He included helical-shaped vanes, and a mongoose release. He picked up some lightweight camo clothing and a few other essentials.

"That's a nice setup you got there," commented the salesclerk, as he totaled up the sale.

"I thought I'd treat myself," answered Nick. "I'm looking to hunt some wild hog."

"You might try Lewisville Lake. There are some spots that allow bow hunting for that. Those feral bastards do a lot of damage. If you're bow-hunting hogs, some of the ranchers will let you hunt on their property."

"Thanks, sir. I was thinking along the same lines."

In the Jeep driving back to the hotel, Tony wondered, "Are you planning to kill Zulu with a bow and arrow?"

"It depends where he leads us. If not him, there's another henchman on the waiting list plus Savage himself. The tracking device on his car will give us a pattern of who he visits and where he goes."

Returning from their shopping spree, they passed the hotel receptionist. "Were you guys kidding me?" she asked. "Did you really hear voices? You said his name is Paul?"

"No kidding, ma'am," said Tony. "He told me his name was Paul."

The receptionist looked at Nick and Sylvia.

"I heard voices, too," said Nick. "But my voice called itself Vince. This hotel is one weird place, that's for sure."

"I didn't hear anything," said Sylvia and shrugged her shoulders.

The receptionist grabbed her phone as they passed through the lobby. She was calling the manager again. Resignation was on her mind.

Nick dropped his stuff in room 204, and then walked through the door to room 206; Sylvia had thoughtfully left it ajar. Tony and Sylvia had already popped beer tops. Nick grabbed one from the refrigerator.

"Tony, let's check if they're back with us," said Nick. "Hey, Vince, are you back with us?"

"I'm here."

"Paul, are you there?" asked Tony.

"I'm here."

"Why don't you two try that double-entanglement thing?" suggested Nick. "We're as close together as you could want."

"Give us a minute," said Vince.

"They're working on it," explained Nick.

Narrow light-green auras pulsed from around Nick and Tony. The two auras throbbed at different tempos, and it seemed that the auras grew stronger. Inside each aura, other currents of multitudinous colors randomly emerged. The auras altered again and again until the two auras vibrated in perfect rhythm.

Then the auras expanded, even touching Sylvia. A flash blasted through the room. A colorless, but evident distortion of the air encircled them. The distortion pulsed slowly, like the inhalation and exhalation of deep breaths.

"Can you hear me now," asked Vince.

"I can hear Vince," said Tony.

"So can I," said Sylvia. "Sweet Jesus. I'm talking to a space alien. The checkout counter tabloids will pay me big bucks for this story."

"Tabloids?" asked Paul.

"Never mind about that," said Nick. "What have you two decided? Are the five of us going to work together, or did you simply want us to see a fancy parlor trick?"

"We want you to help us," said Paul. "Ephemeron is on the edge of war with itself and with worlds across the universe. Overlord Draxis is winning over the public's sentiment. He tells Ephemerals it is the gods' blessings and our destiny to control those we inhabit. The Overlord promises our people a path to great rewards and riches."

"Fuck, no," said Sylvia. "I'm not helping you to inhabit anyone, especially me."

"Overlord Draxis is depending on that reaction from you," said Paul. "I suppose you want me to explain."

Hearing no objections, Paul continued.

"Callum's clan is known as the Xermegans. It is ruled by Overlord Draxis. Callum is one of his sons. Of course, you know Ephemerals have no gender, so you have to bear with me on how I speak of these matters. The names and descriptions I use are loose interpretations to your language. Vince's family is known as the Vimegans. It is ruled by Commander Vaaruv. My family is known as the Omegans. Its ruler, my father, is King Boolong. The Omegans have ruled over Ephemeron for almost 5,000 years.

"Selection is a worldwide time of voting. Each voter must decide their first choice and preferred second choice for Ephemeron's ruling clan. If no clan receives half of the first-choice vote, the second-choice votes are added. Whoever has the most first- and second-choice votes together is Selected as the ruling clan. It is common that voters vote their first choice for their own clan, so it is rare for a clan to be Selected by only first-choice votes.

"The Omegan clan has survived through four Selections because they have been more tolerant of differing religious customs as long as an Ephemeral gives loyalty to the Omegan's reigning authority. The Xermegan and Vimegan clans have been less tolerant of each other's customs, so their second-choice votes favor the Omegan clan.

"But Overlord Draxis's strong words have gained favor among the people. He says that the Omegan clan has grown lazy and self-indulgent. The Overlord tells the people they deserve more. People already live easy lives, untouched by war, so they feel invulnerable. Rumor speculates that the Vimegans or the Xermegans will rise to become the next kingship. The rulers of the Vimegan and Xermegan clans tell their people that non-interference with other worlds is a sign of weakness. They say that the Ephemeral ability to entangle ourselves in other life-forms gives us the right to exercise a greater influence. I say the words *greater influence* as a kindly interpretation. The Xermegans believe influence means exerting physical control over the life-forms we inhabit. They do not hide their intent.

"My family—the Omegans—is saddled by internal strife, rebellious lords, and self-indulgence. The reaping of energy from life-forms from across the universe has been an indulgent and easy existence. We have harnessed energy from others for millennia without others knowing. The Xermegan and Vimegan clans are in a blood feud. If one of those two clans can gain the alliance of enough Omegan voters, they can rule Ephemeron."

Nick wanted to wring Vince's neck more than ever.

Paul just earned his place on his strangle list as well. Callum, too, was a dead man.

"Why Earth? Why humans?" asked Nick.

Paul let slip a light chuckle. "Consider it bad luck. Our scientists studied many worlds and many scenarios. Ephemeron's analysis showed that humanity was the best first target for Ephemerals to exert their physical control over an intelligent life-form. Our algorithms are blessed by our gods. I'm just a prince, not a scientist, nor a high priest, but the priests tell us that expansion upon Earth has been ordained. Ephemerals are a religious people."

"Fuck," Sylvia and Tony said at the same time.

"Look at yourselves," added Vince. "You don't have the technology to stop us. Your species is exceptionally emotional."

"There has to be other civilizations that have similar technology and are also emotional," countered Nick.

"True, but humans have always shown a fondness for mob behavior. At this point in time, your technology is the perfect tool to rapidly spread whatever message, fears, or passions we want you to spread. Your social media is a powerful tool. It will be used against you."

"You're asking for help?" said Sylvia, stunned. "Fuck you. Fuck you a thousand times. Fuck your world. You say you need and want our help, then you tell us your gods have ordained that you take over all humanity. Jesus. I thought I wanted to hear what you and Vince had to say, but now I wish I had never heard a word. You people are bat-shit crazy."

In his mind, Tony imagined the coming days with Paul's voice ringing in his head about humanity's upcoming servitude and eventual demise. He saw his limbs manipulated like a marionette: controlling where he went; what he did; who he met and talked to.

He saw himself going insane.

Paul spoke again. "This is why we need your help. What I've told you *IS INSANE*. I believe that. Vince believes it, too. We want Ephemeron to abandon this idea of domination. It is a perverted and vile idea brought about by our rulers' egotistic interpretation of our gods' intentions. Ephemerals have become slaves to computer algorithms blessed by high priestesses that secretly sin in the night. We are a religious people, but nefarious rulers are using religion as their tool to control and lead our people into a certain destruction they cannot imagine. We need your help to stop them. If I become king, I will lead the Ephemeron people back to the true path."

The aura surrounding the three humans flickered.

Paul's voice became distorted, like on a crackling phone line. "Vince and I can't maintain this double-entanglement any longer. We have to rest. One last thing. If we are reading Zulu's emotions correctly, he enjoys fishing."

"Zulu is inhabited?" asked Nick, surprised.

"Yes. And if you get him—"

A green flash engulfed the room, leaving silence.

"Are they gone?" asked Tony, shivering.

The brave fighting words of the other day had abandoned him. At that moment, he wanted to flee.

Reaching into his shirt's breast pocket, a marijuana joint stood upright within easy reach, but his trembling fingers fumbled with this cigarette-sized object. He had a hard time lighting it.

Sylvia told him to do it near the window. When he tried to respond to her, she rapped him hard on the head.

He pushed himself up and toward the window, sweat permeating his shirt.

As he saw his reflection in the window, his face looked drawn. Fear-filled eyes stared back at himself. Unable to calm down, he trembled harder, nearly vibrating.

Tony had worried about going mad, but as he stared at himself, he wondered if he had already entered insanity.

17

"Life is to be lived outside,
not in the dark room of one's fears."

That night, lying in bed alone and not drunk enough to mollify the demons that stood at the edge of his mind's horizon, Nick worried about his brother.

Finding out about the alien possession had flipped Tony over the edge. It was too much, too fast. He needed to get a grip on himself.

Nick had seen it many times while they were growing up; Tony was the chance-taker and he always had pushed the envelope. He was lucky to have Sylvia; she was a scrapper and stood up to everything. Tony needed to find that fire for himself again. Even as a kid, Tony needed the edge, the adrenaline rush.

In Nick's mind, taking Sylvia from Pearce Savage was part of that risky pattern.

Sure, Nick believed his brother was truly head-over-heels for Sylvia, and she saw something in him she could love.

Still, he wasn't going to spend a lot of time trying to psychoanalyze his twin's behavior. He was going to protect his brother—and Sylvia—as best he could. The hardest fight he had on his hands wasn't with Pearce Savage or his henchmen, nor was it the extra person Vince wanted him to kill.

Nick's hardest fight was going to be restoring Tony to the man he had been, the man he could be. He knew, at some point, Tony would need to be that brother again.

Their lives would depend on it.

After two days of following Zulu's movements, Nick trailed him to a bait and tackle shop, followed by a stop at a boat rental shop. Zulu even made a stop at the same hunting store Nick had visited.

Tracking Zulu's movements on his phone's screen sent prickling premonitions through Nick's body. The sword of vengeance would soon fall.

The next morning, Nick, Tony, and Sylvia caught breakfast at their favorite café.

"You children are here early," said their favorite waitress. "Coffee?"

She poured their cups. Finishing up Tony's, she quizzed him with her waitress's insight.

"What's with you, child? You look like you've seen a ghost. Are you staying in that Daphne place?"

Tony looked at his coffee, not responding. He grabbed the cup handle and brought it shakily to his lips. He never looked up.

The waitress looked over him like a knowing mother, then glanced at his friends.

"He's had a tragic loss," explained Sylvia. "A good friend of his died."

"Oh, my dear child, I'm so sorry to hear that. I can't tell you how to feel, but I know what it's like to lose someone close. I've lost two of my sons to violence. I was afraid to go outside after that. I thought I could sit in my room, and I would be safe. My life turned inward and became a very dark place of fear and dread. The Lord finally saved me. Child, I don't know if you believe, but a couple prayers asking for help wouldn't hurt. Life is to be lived outside, not in the dark room of one's fears."

The woman cast an almost apologetic glance toward Nick and Sylvia for having rambled on. Sylvia mouthed the words *thank you.* Nick raised his cup in salute.

Tony sighed deeply and Sylvia punched him in the arm. He cracked a small smile.

The waitress's words hung across the table: *Life is to be lived outside, not in the dark room of one's fears.*

"I won't let you down," declared Tony quietly. "It's just so hard. Paul's voice is like a tumor inside my brain that I want to rip out."

"I know the feeling, brother. Vince saved me, but I thought having him in my head would make me kill myself. I'm here for you and I know you, brother. You can survive this; you gotta fight back."

"I never know if he's listening to us. It makes things worse. If I never knew he existed, my life would be my life. They're voyeurs and we're their victims."

Sylvia scuffed up his hair. "There's my Tony, throwing out the big words."

"Stop," said Tony, pushing Sylvia's hand away.

She smiled at Nick, telling him without words that Tony's energetic rejection of her hand was a good sign.

In his mind, Tony was telling himself to fight back, to get off his weak ass. He had promised to take care of Sylvia and he was going to fight hard to keep that promise. Sylvia had saved his life and he owed her.

He owed his brother, too. For all their years of estrangement, it was his brother that stood by him now. Tony took a deep breath. He thought of the waitress's words. As he exhaled, a prayer slipped his lips.

"I have to be on my own today," said Nick.

"You can't leave us here," protested Tony.

Sylvia flashed Nick a displeased look.

"Extra faces will increase the risk," responded Nick.

"That's the same mumbo-jumbo you said before, brother. We have to do this together."

"We are, Tony. Call it my sixth sense, okay? I'm going after Zulu on my own today, but I need you two to research Tubby Vaughn, And to be honest, you need to get ahold of yourself.

"Pearce Savage is surrounded by a hundred more men. Killing off a handful of his henchmen may be my vengeance, but it's not the end of our task. If Savage stays alive, you and Sylvia will forever be looking over your shoulders. Tony, I need you back, brother. I can't do it without you."

Perhaps Nick's words were empty pleasantries, but for Tony, they meant something.

The words cut through the impotent darkness: *Nick needed him.*

After breakfast, Nick drove off in his silver-gray car. He could barely remember the auto's model name. If left to its own devices, it was likely to outlive the cockroaches of Earth. Durability would earn a 10-star rating, but the rest … don't ask.

Nick pulled up the tracking app on his phone, just in time to notice Shinga's Pagoda Green Thunderbird was on the move, driving north. The tracking app made his job so much easier than the old days. Death's prickly anticipation coursed across Nick's skin.

The Thunderbird dropped off the I-35 Express onto Stemmons Freeway. Leaving a safe gap, Nick hung back as Zulu wound his way to a boat launch on a small lake. Finally, the tracking app showed that the car had stopped.

Nick drove forward slowly, wanting to catch a glimpse of his target. It was indeed Zulu driving the car, towing a small boat trailer hitched to the Thunderbird.

As Zulu backed the rig into the lake via the boat ramp, Nick donned his Dallas Cowboy cap, pulled it low, and reached into his zip bag. Zulu, still focused on getting the trailer aligned with the boat ramp so he could drop it onto the lake's waters, wasn't paying attention to his surroundings. That would cost him.

Nick pulled out his Glock and fitted a silencer on the barrel. Slipping the 9mm into the back of his pants, Nick pulled up as Zulu was preparing to slip the boat into the lake's waters.

"Hey, friend. Sorry, I'm a bit lost. Can you help me? I'm looking for the Appleton residence. Do you know them?" Nick approached as he exited the car, calling it all out.

"No. Never heard of them," said Zulu, his tone belligerent. "I just fish here." His attention was focused on the boat trailer, and he ignored Nick's presence.

"Do you know the best way back to Stemmons Highway?" asked Nick, keeping up the distraction, walking closer. He was twenty-five feet away. Nonchalantly he reached behind his back, still walking closer.

Fifteen feet.

Zulu nonchalantly looked up.

Eight feet.

Zulu's eyes widened and his mouth dropped open in shock. The man he'd shot was standing in front of him!

Not possible ....

Zulu didn't understand.

He had heard his fellow henchmen had mysteriously died. Take care, they had said. Nobody said that Tony was still alive.

It couldn't be ....

We shot the hell out of him, thought Zulu. Nor had anybody said that Tony had a twin. Zulu stood frozen with the impossibility approaching him.

Nick pulled out his Glock and slapped three quick shots into Zulu, sending him sprawling. For insurance, he sent another slug into Zulu's brain, then bent down and rolled Zulu under the trailer rig.

He picked up his shell casings, and pulled the tracker loose from underneath the Thunderbird. Picking up a nearby tree branch, he swept away his tracks back to the car.

Nick knew it was a thin coverup, but he would soon be gone. It was not a well-traveled area. Maybe a bobcat would get to Zulu before his body got too ripe. Scavengers were sure to descend to strip the bones. Given the remote location, it was hard to say if a person would stumble on it any sooner.

As he drove away, heading toward the city, Nick looked back at his bow gear. It would have to wait for another time.

"Vince, are you around?" asked Nick.

"I felt it," said Vince. "You killed him, didn't you?"

"Yeah. Paul said an Ephemeral inhabited Zulu. How does that help ... us?"

"It was an older brother of Callum's. He was the second son of Overlord Draxis."

"Oh, this is sweet," said Nick, but meaning the complete opposite. "You knew this all along. You could have said something."

"Sorry, Nick. As you might say ... it was on a need-to-know basis. Before, we weren't working this closely together."

"Yeah, right. Paul mentioned the Ephemeral inside Zulu but failed to mention its significance. Not telling me that detail is *not us working together.*"

"As you recall, we were in a double entanglement. Paul told you everything he could in the time we had, so give him a break. Besides, what difference does it make? You want us off your planet. I know that. You know that, so let's be honest. Killing Zulu served you as much as it served us. The Ephemeral inside Zulu was a sleeper agent for Overlord Draxis.

"Because the Ephemeral didn't know Zulu was about to die, he had no time to prepare for another entanglement. It's chaos on Ephemeron right now. The Overlord's brother only has a couple hours to find a new entanglement and there's been a system problem getting him reentangled. They may have found one for him, but it's probably on the planet Reevin. That's a nasty place, for sure. A bunch of ground-hugging reptiles. Reasonably intelligent for sluggards, but god, they're gross. I guess not too far from your ant analogy."

Nick roared with laughter. "Damn! *THAT IS SWEET!*" He chuckled a lot after that and hoped Vince found it to be unnerving.

"Vince, how do I know when you can hear me?" asked Nick.

"Like always. You call my name. I answer, or not."

"Yeah. Yeah. I know. We talk, or you do the double entanglement thing, and then you're tired. Sometimes I can't reach you. Nobody knows when you're coming back online. Same for Paul."

"It's hard to give a precise number. When you were first shot, I received extra energy that my Ephemeron friends donated. I still am getting some from my family and some from Paul's family, but not as much as before. Normally, it takes me a couple hours to recover from one of our conversations. After a double entanglement, we both need to rest for several hours."

"I'm worried about my brother," lamented Nick. "Finding out about Paul has sent him over the edge. He can't process it. When we were growing up, he was fearless—a real daredevil. I need to get my old brother back; I'm going to need him for these next jobs."

"I don't know if I can help you with that one," said Vince. "I'll talk to Paul. Maybe it's just a matter of time before your brother gets used to it. Who's your next target?"

"I'm going to St. Paul. Sylvia's information and my research points to Tubby Vaughn being there. By now, Savage's henchmen are looking over their shoulders, so each job will get tougher. I'm sure it's driving them nuts. Sylvia has disappeared, too. That must worry Savage. She knows too much."

"You'll need to make a side stop in Denver," said Vince.

"That's not on my itinerary. What's in Denver?"

Vince didn't answer.

Zulu's death had ejected one of Overlord Draxis's sleeper agents, forcing it to scramble for a new entanglement.

Vince had been pulled away by the ensuing complications swirling on Ephemeron.

18

"People must understand that Alborix,
The Most Supreme, has spoken directly to me."

On **Ephemeron,** Overlord Draxis conferred with Artemesia, the Xermegan clan's High Priestess. Overlord Draxis had prayed the Divine prayers and fasted for thirty days. The voice of the god Most Supreme, Alborix, had spoken to him. The Overlord's visions showed him an enlightened future where Ephemerals would no longer hide passively behind their E-stations.

In Overlord Draxis's mind, he perceived Ephemeron's citizens as lazy and weak. They did not fully grasp how the Most Supreme god graced their daily lives.

Did Ephemerals truly not understand that the next Selection could be the blessing of a new age? If the Xermegans rose to be Ephemeron's new monarchy, Overlord Draxis would become its king and Ephemeron would embark on a great conquest of the universe's inferior life-forms. The Overlord needed a sign from the gods that the people could see, so that they would believe. The sign needed to anoint the path of the Xermegan clan to kingship over all Ephemeron.

Yet, many Ephemerals were satisfied with an ordinary life of going to work at their E-Stations and easily reaping emotional energies from other life-forms. Millenia ago, pioneering Ephemerals had fought to survive as they carved out a new civilization. Their reproductive cycle was fraught with difficulty. But Ephemerals had endured.

After discovering how to harness the bounties of entanglement, their existence had become an easier life. Their numbers had grown. Ephemerals had spread out, seeding themselves across the universe. They felt safe, and their lives felt predictable. They felt privileged as they reaped the whirlwind of the universe's emotions. It was a time of plenty.

"When people see, they believe," said Overlord Draxis to the High Priestess. "The festivities must show our people that the Xermegan clan deserves to be the kingdom's new monarchy."

"Your Lordship, I suggest three days of grand ceremonies with religious processions, music, dancing, special food, and extra energy packets. It will be a worldwide event that will bring all Ephemerals together. We can tie it in with the annual Crystal Moon Hunt."

"People must understand that Alborix, The Most Supreme, has spoken directly to me."

"The festivities will bring all Ephemerals together. We will invite the other clans and we will show our generosity. No one will be turned away. Your name will be admired and Ephemerals will feel united. Our many gods will be put on display and honored. Of course, the honor of our Most Supreme god will be woven into each celebration, procession, and each day's many gifts. The Xermegan clan will shine."

"The Omegan clan has ruled over Ephemeron for almost 5,000 years, leaving the scraps to the Xermegan and Vimegan clans," complained Overlord Draxis.

"The Omegan clan has played both sides," responded the High Priestess. "The Omegans honor the gods but embrace the ambiguous religious debates as long as an Ephemeral citizen follows the dictates and laws of Omegan authority. Clans vote for their clan leader with their first-choice votes, but when adding in Ephemerals' second-choice votes, it favors the Omegan clan."

"I know this, but it is a profound weakness," snarled the Overlord. "The history of Ephemeron has always been blessed by its many gods, but the gods are not equal. Cannot others see that? Alborix reigns over all the other gods and therefore Alborix deserves special respect. The Xermegan clan knows this."

"Your Lordship, you are right to feel frustrated, but look at what you have accomplished," the Priestess soothed. "People are listening to your words. You are capturing their imagination. Our mastery of QE has blessed Ephemeron with an unmatched power. Physical manipulation of the universe's other species will allow us to create more emotional chaos in their worlds. It will reap Ephemeron magnitudes more energy. Ephemerals will spend half the time at their E-stations. Ephemerals will be freed to indulge their most fervent passions."

"High Priestess, your suggestions please me. Make it happen. We are Alborix's dutiful servants."

"I will make the arrangements as you wish, Overlord Draxis. This will show your great benevolence. It will elevate the Xermegan clan and Your Lordship."

Overlord Draxis believed the grand festivities would charm other Ephemerals to cast their votes for the Xermegan clan, putting one more piece of Overlord Draxis's stratagem into place.

"One other thing, High Priestess. Have all the arrangements been made for the upcoming gathering of our scientists?"

"Yes, Your Lordship. The Great Hall has been readied."

"My expectations are high. The Chief Scientist needs to provide me with good news. You may go now."

The High Priestess bowed respectfully, then exited to arrange the celebrations.

The warrior Xermegan High Priestess had been born into the Omegan clan. Over many years, Overlord Draxis had cultivated the young Ephemeral's conversion to the Xermegan clan, bringing her ever closer to his ideas, guiding her steps to reach the position of the High Priestess of the Xermegan clan.

Overlord Draxis pointed out the Omegan king's waning days, emphasizing that the young Omegan had many hundreds of years to live. The Overlord tempted her with power and authority. He filled her mind with self-righteousness. The successful transformation of this Omegan into his faithful Xermegan servant brought a smile to Overlord Draxis.

But all was not as perfect as Overlord Draxis perceived.

A Vimegan spy, Meerlex, had positioned herself as the High Priestess's devoted aide. Standing in the Overlord's chamber as attendant to the High Priestess, Meerlex overheard all that had been said. To reach this trusted position, she had appeared to betray her Vimegan clan. Her service to the Xermegan High Priestess was well-known and infamously publicized as one of the worst forms of treason. That Artemesia, the Xermegan High Priestess herself was a convert to the Vimegan clan, made Meerlex's service to the High Priestess a treachery built on treachery.

Meerlex lived in shame, but her deeds were the great sacrifice she had sworn. Only two Vimegans knew of her task of loyalty and stealth.

Meerlex had risen to the position of the High Priestess's attendant by enduring many torturous humiliations. Yet, no matter how much indignity was thrown her way, Meerlex refused to condemn her assailants. Many times, she had felt lost, almost not remembering who she really was and why she was enduring these pains and great loneliness. There were days when all was black, when her status would be unexpectedly demoted and Meerlex was assigned to a position that she had previously arisen from, not knowing it was a secret loyalty test.

Finally, a dim light broke through. Meerlex was assigned a position within the High Priestess's enclave. It was a lowly position, doing dull work. But that pale light was like a beam of the sun breaking through the clouds and shining into her soul. The gods had noticed her innumerable sacrifices of love for her Vimegan clan. From these fires that tested her loyalty, the Vimegan spy had climbed to the right hand of the Xermegan High Priestess.

The Vimegan spy was always faced with one hard question: *is this the time to risk everything, all the sacrifices, to contact her handler?* Rarely did she ever do so. Certainly, other spies met with their handlers. But the right-hand attendant to the Xermegan High Priestess was a spy of most extraordinary value. In the many years of her servitude, she had contacted her handler only twice.

In her bed this coming night, she could not fall asleep. Perspiration soaked her night clothes. She imagined ferocious Xermegan guards storming into her room and ripping her from the bed, snapping tight cuffs on her and constraining her wings tight against her body, then bumping her mercilessly down flights of steps and across stone thresholds. They would fling her into an enforcement vehicle, unconcerned of her ragdoll jostling, as the vehicle's driver raced to inquisition's headquarters. It would be a nightmarish ordeal that she had not experienced for a long time. But in this coming night, her terror would not be due to a mere nightmare, but due to what she had vowed to do.

She breathed deep, trying to slow her breathing, telling herself this moment would pass. Coldly, she tried to calculate her situation. There was no meeting planned with her handler. It was not yet the time. But, in her bones she felt the day was approaching.

Tonight, her fears were terrors conjured by her mind. If her suspicion was true, Draxis would soon reveal details that could not be ignored. She would need to reach out to her handler, risking the revelation of her existence—risking everything. Was this not the moment she had worked for? To reveal the secrets of the Overlord's grand plan and cause its disruption by the Vimegan clan? Her importance might never be known, trapped in the bowels of the most secret of files. To Vimegan citizenry, she would die in infamy and shame—an unsung hero to the cause.

Meerlex was unaware that her brave efforts were more than taking a stand on Ephemeron, but were also creating tangles across the distant reaches of space.

These tangles would soon be touching Nick, Tony, and Sylvia.

In the far corner of the Daphne's bar area, Tony and Sylvia sat waiting for Nick to return from his confrontation with Zulu. Sylvia was on her phone, tracking down leads about Tubby Vaughn. Tony scrolled through mindless clickbait links.

"Tony," called Paul's voice, shattering the ghostly Daphne peace. "Tony, answer me."

"What!?" exclaimed Tony, startled. "Leave me alone!"

"You need to get a grip. Pearce is looking to kill you and Sylvia. Your brother needs you to be strong."

"Stop. Get away from me!" Tony exclaimed harshly.

"Tony, what is going on," asked Sylvia.

"He's torturing me," said Tony. "He's in my mind. Why can't he let me go?"

"Really, Tony? Is the whole thing only about you? Nick is out there fighting. Pearce is trying to kill us. Ephemerals want to impregnate me. I love you, but we … *I* … need you to fight back. If we have to babysit you, we will all be at greater risk."

"He's in my head. He talks to me. I can't control it. Nobody is in your head speaking to you … telling you what you should do, what you should think." Tony clutched his head in his hands.

"Is he doing that, Tony? Is he really telling you what to do?"

"Some creature is inside me. Isn't that enough?"

"A creature is inside Nick. He carries on. He is fighting back. He's your brother. He's your twin. You need to fight, too, Tony." Sylvia was insistent.

Tony rocked back and forth, torn by loyalty and fear.

A waiter approached their table. He noticed Tony's unsettled demeanor. Sweating. Hands shaking. Rocking back and forth. Looking like he wanted to curl into a ball.

"Can I get you anything?" he asked.

"Two double-shots of bourbon on the rocks," said Sylvia.

A few minutes later, the waiter brought the drinks. Tony grabbed his, almost before the glass hit the table and killed the drink in one swig.

"Bring another," directed Sylvia.

As the waiter headed for the bar, she spoke again. "Do you love me, Tony?" she asked. She knew she had to push him.

"You know I do. I am willing to do anything for you. Fuck Pearce; I will kill the guy. Sylvia, I would do anything to protect you."

Sylvia let Tony's words sink in. She knew he loved her. She knew he would sacrifice himself for her. But she didn't know if he could again be the Tony she had fallen in love with. Would her love be enough to restore his spirit? Could she help rekindle his fire? Could he rekindle the fire?

The waiter soon returned, bringing a double shot of whiskey.

Tony inspected the drink. He picked it up, holding it up to the light. The bourbon's beautiful amber hue beckoned.

His mind bounced among Sylvia, Paul, his brother, and fear. He studied the liquid for a few moments, twisting the glass. Analyzing it. Searching for an answer that was not in a bottle, but hidden deep within himself.

After a few minutes, he downed the glass.

With the courage of four-plus shots, Tony steeled himself against demons known and imagined, telling himself he would stand by his brother, and would fight for Sylvia. He would try to make peace with his scrambled mind

Nick entered the hotel's lobby. The talkative receptionist greeted his return.

"Hello, sir. Welcome to the Daphne, hotel of ghosts and strange occurrences," said the receptionist, parroting the standard welcoming patter.

"I heard more voices last night," said Nick, playing with her mind. "Can't you people shut them up?"

The hotel receptionist's response faltered. "We'll … uh, we'll do our best, sir. I'll talk to maintenance."

Nick restrained a chuckle as he noticed her confusion. She was a receptionist at a hotel haunted with ghosts, but it was just a job to tell an invented story. It wasn't supposed to be real.

Entering the bar, Nick caught sight of Tony and Sylvia in the far corner. He steered himself to them and sat on one of the old wrought-iron chairs, ordered a beer, and noted the empty whiskey shot glasses. His brother's glassy eyes confirmed Nick's assumptions.

Sylvia appeared rock-steady, but certainly had downed a couple.

"Did you get Zulu?" asked Tony, his voice thick.

"Yeah, I got him," answered Nick.

"I bet he was surprised by an arrow sticking through his body," said Tony fawning courage.

"I shot him with my Glock," said Nick. "It was the moment."

"Oh," said Tony, stumbling to rectify truth with his imaginings. "Who's next?"

"That's difficult to answer, brother. For now, our plan is to go to St. Paul, but the Ephemerals say they have other plans for us. They want us to make a stop in Colorado."

"What do they want from us?" muttered Tony, his voice strained. "I thought that we were supposed to be working together. But now they give us instructions and we follow them blindly like they are our lords. They always want more from us." His face flushed red. Sweat beads glistened on his forehead.

"Vince had to break off our conversation before he could tell me more details, but killing a human when an Ephemeral is inside causes major problems. Ephemerals have a hard time managing such a moment. When a host unexpectedly dies, an Ephemeral must scramble for another entanglement—or apparently also face imminent death."

"How can you trust them?" asked Sylvia. "Ephemerals are asking you to kill innocents."

"I don't know that they're innocent. Zulu wasn't. Still, it's a good point. If Paul and Vince want us to trust them, then they will need to prove themselves by doing some of their own dirty work."

"If Zulu is dead, it'll only be a matter of time before they find the body," said Sylvia.

"I'm hoping it will take a while before anybody finds the body. The area was remote. One other thing, I'll be leaving early in the morning. It would be best if we don't check out at the same time."

"We're not going to Colorado, are we?" asked Tony, his voice colored by a tremor of continuing doubt.

"I want to say no. In any case, the first few hours north will be the same route. But first, I'm going to get some rest. The wounds are healing, but my body is tired."

With that, Nick rose from his seat. He knew Tony wanted to talk with him more.

Nick didn't want to leave his brother in the lurch, but at some point, Tony would need to find the peace he was looking for, and he hoped Sylvia could help.

19

The early morning alarm jarred Nick awake.

Mental replays of Pearce Savage's henchmen—some would call them nightmares—had kept Nick tossing and turning for most of the night, only finally falling asleep for a scant hour or two.

Nick gathered his stuff—there really wasn't much to pack—and was in the lobby in less than fifteen minutes. On the way out, he told the hotel's receptionist he had been called to meet a sales client in Santa Fe.

"Did you really hear voices in room 204?" she asked.

"Definitely, ma'am. It said its name was Vince and it's happened almost every night. You should talk to your manager. It might be a good idea to warn people about that room. It's haunted."

"Yes, yes. The manager will want to know," she agreed although she had already briefed her boss. He had told her to verify the hearing-voices story, though she had no idea how she was going to accomplish that feat. He wanted to raise the room rate and put out some new advertising. The manager imagined the Daphne becoming a ghostly legend.

Driving north out of Dallas, Nick remained intrigued as to why it was so hard for Ephemerals to communicate with their hosts. Both Vince and Paul talked about all the energy it took out of them and double entanglement drained their resources even faster.

Nick had spent a little time learning about quantum entanglement, reading articles online. After a few paragraphs, the articles often took a turn into mathematics and physics concepts he had never heard of. But he found one article of particular interest. It talked about resource usage. He couldn't put it into scientific words, but intuitively, it made sense.

A part of the article said that manipulation of either side of the entanglement would affect the other side. Did that mean that humans could cause impacts on Ephemeron? Could there be a way for humanity to fight back … to poison the well so Ephemerals would look to another world to invade? Could humanity rid itself completely of these invaders?

Nick was just a man with a gun and skills that on Earth were powerful, but in comparison to these aliens, horribly inadequate. With the heart to fight back and his wits, he just didn't know if it would be enough.

One thing Nick did grasp: the aliens were more like humans than he imagined.

They sought power, schemed and connived, misused people's trust and beliefs to further their egoistic goals, were willing to murder, and could be ruthless. They saw themselves as superior. Deep in their psyches, he guessed they lived surrounded by uncertainty, wanting and needing approval, just like humans. They sought a godly intervention that would magically bail them out or, at least, give them a heavenly sign.

It made Nick wonder if Ephemerals thought about heaven or hell. Vince and Paul had said Ephemerals were a religious people. He wondered if God had a favorite between Ephemerals and humans. Would it make any difference to Nick's struggle against them?

Vince had said Ephemerals sit quietly inside their E-stations as they harvested emotional energy to power Ephemeron. Nick figured the connections had to be fragile. Why else would an Ephemeron need to spend most of a day at an E-Station finagling the optimization of the entanglement?

"Nick," came Vince's voice. The unexpected voice startled Nick. The Honda slightly swerved.

"What do you want, Vince?"

"You'll need the details for the Denver target. Maybe you can pull over somewhere and I can tell them to you."

"I'm not going to Denver," answered Nick. "I'm going after Tubby Vaughn. I'm going to St. Paul."

"That wasn't our agreement," Vince resisted.

"What agreement, Vince? Is it the one where we should work together? But it seems to me you want us to follow you down a one-way street. I don't know this human you want me to kill. He had no part in shooting me. You, Paul, and your families are the ones that want his death. It is a *he,* isn't it? I don't see you helping us."

"I told you about Zulu going fishing at Lewisville Lake."

"That's not really accurate. You said you had a feeling. Hell, I put a tracker on his car. You didn't reveal anything special. I'll tell you what I know. You and Paul and your families are in a bind. The Omegan clan is on the verge of losing a monarchy and being persecuted by Callum's family for the next 1,000 years.

"And here's a big kicker: Paul is trapped inside Tony, who at this moment, is teetering on a tightrope to insanity. Somehow, I think you may enjoy feeding off humanity's wild emotions, but insanity may be problematic. Maybe I'll just shoot myself in the head. I won't give you any warning, of course. Then, you'll be scrambling for a new host. Perhaps you will land inside one of those Reevin reptiles, or a beady-brained rodent. Maybe Tony will be put into a psychiatric hospital and live out his days in a drug-induced stupor. That should be a wonderful emotional experience for Paul. Am I missing anything?"

"What do you want from me, Nick?"

"Are you and Paul physically living on Ephemeron?"

"Yes."

"How often do you see each other?"

"Our E-stations are in the same building. We often have lunch at the same table, but Watchers are always nearby. They watch us closely, even though we have special privileges because of our standing. Still, our movements are monitored. We have friends who are helping us."

"E-Stations? Explain that."

"You might call them computer stations. They are like pods that we report to each day. In them, we become tuned to our hosts. This tuning must be maintained to optimize the entanglement. Once properly connected, we reap the energy from our hosts. Some Ephemerals are satisfied with reporting to their pod, tuning-in, and reaping the energy that is harvested. It doesn't matter to them if their hosts are overly emotional or not. Other Ephemerals spend their time always trying to maximize the emotional connection. They receive plaudits and occasional public recognition. For performing superlative work, they are able to earn rewards for their families."

"That seems like a woeful life."

"When we are in our pods, we physically feel the emotions of our host. We don't feel a direct translation, like *happiness gives us happiness*, or *fear gives us fear*. It's more like an energy coursing through our bodies."

"You're in the pods all day reaping this energy?" asked Nick.

"Ephemerals have evolved so that our bodies can directly consume this emotional energy. The excess is channeled to storage banks. Some Ephemerals may sit in their pods for more than a day at a time. Everything else is secondary or meaningless, depending how you want to describe it."

"Addiction comes to mind. If you don't stay at your E-station, how do you stay entangled?"

"We are still entangled with our host even if we leave the pods. The E-stations use an automatic setting that maintains the entanglement. But stepping away from an E-station lessens how much energy we can harvest. It's like the system runs at fifty-percent efficiency. If I go home, I am still entangled with you. When I return to my E-station, I go through a process that recalibrates our connection and reoptimizes it."

"Is there any pattern between an Ephemeral sitting in its E-station and a human's life? I mean if it's Ephemeral work time, does that coincide with day or night for a human?"

"Not really. Our world turns faster than yours. As long as I put in my required hours, there's no set time for me to be in my pod, though it makes sense to be at my E-station while you are awake to maximize the energy harvest. Some Ephemerals do their minimal hours. Others can't get enough of the energy surges."

"Why does Ephemeron need to tap into the emotions of other life-forms to produce energy? Can't Ephemerals use their own resources to produce energy?"

"Energy isn't just energy. As an example, there are different types of sound: high-pitched, low-pitched."

"Yeah?"

"Well, it turns out that energy harvested from emotions has a different taste than energy generated by harvesting the rays of the sun or generating energy from some mechanical source."

"A different *taste?*"

"Yes. Ephemerals have become tuned to it."

"Like I said, it sounds like an addiction."

"Nick, would you say that you are addicted to water?"

"No."

"But you need water to live. Emotional energy is like the same thing for us."

"Water is a natural resource. We're not harvesting it off living beings."

"We can debate this issue, but do you have something else to ask? I can't maintain this physical connection a lot longer."

"Why is it that you need my help? And the help of Tony and Sylvia … of humans?"

"Ephemeron has been stable for many millennia. Previously, our people had to endure great losses and hardships. We failed to take care of our planet and were forced to relocate to another world. At one time in our history, we had tried to conquer other worlds, though our technology was crude, using spaceships and kinetic weapons. It was fruitless. It chastised our people."

"Stop right there," interrupted Nick. "Your planet and your people had a sad history. Well, you know what—same with Earth, same with humans, and I imagine the same for many others. So what? This doesn't tell me *why* you need our help. What is so important about involving us in your scheming?"

"Quantum entanglement has turned into a temptation for conquest. The Xermegan clan tells Ephemerals that conquest is our God-given right. Paul and I, and our friends see the direction. Some of us are resisting."

"Vince, you make no sense. How can you physically manipulate humans if it makes you so tired?"

"Overlord Draxis says that physical manipulation would be accomplished via modified E-Stations. We would remain unseen—hidden—but have greater influence on your emotions and desires."

"You have this perfect setup mooching off the universe. Why would you need to muck that up? Why do you need to physically control others? How does that help you?"

"It would dramatically increase the energy output that could be reaped from humans or any other life-form. As emotional as you may think humans are, can you not imagine what it would be like if Ephemerals had a greater influence on your minds?

"I will give you a simple example—a barroom fight. We urge a person to bad-mouth another, to insult their mother, their race … anything to stir up the moment. Passions will boil and likely, a full brawl will ensue. More examples are easily conceived—some gruesome, some deviously manipulative. Even as I have told you this, I can feel your emotions rise. Paul and my friends see the horror of this path. The leaders have told the people that our past hardships were the gods' punishment, our survival was the gods' forgiveness, and our future will be the gods' new blessings. For many Ephemerals, it is an attractive story and not easy to resist."

"Vince, you are not filling me with much confidence. It sounds to me the greatest powers of your world have sharpened their swords and are already committed to a war."

"The leaders of the Xermegan and Vimegan clans have a mutual hatred that is born of ego. That is their weakness. Neither can let the other win. If they battle each other, the people will see the carnage. The people will recoil at the horror. They will reject this belligerent path. Humanity's conquest will become a forgotten whim."

Nick doubted the rosy scenario where Ephemerals would become aghast at the internecine bloodshed. He wondered if Ephemerals even had blood. What color was it? These were aliens. Their blood had to be something nasty, like bile green, or a thick blue.

"So, Vince, how is your band of merry men going to upend these evil plans?"

"I don't understand you. What is this reference to a band of merry men?"

"It's a childhood fable. The true good king is off in another land fighting great battles. While he is away, his cheating low-life brother and a black-hearted sheriff terrorize and steal from the kingdom's citizenry. So, a guy by the name of Robin Hood leads a revolt against the power-hungry brother and his lowlife lackeys. Robin Hood's supporters are referred to as his band of merry men. It is a children's story, with a moral for us all. The small and righteous fighting and prevailing against evil."

"You are mocking us."

"From what you've told me, there's not much else to go on. How do you expect to stop two powerful clans on the edge of war?"

"That will have to wait for another time," said Vince. "My energy is starting to run out. We must talk about one more thing before it does."

"You were more talkative today," noted Nick.

"I received extra energy from those friends you mock. It also helped that you were so emotional today. That gave me an extra spurt. Do you think it was something I said?"

"Very funny, Vince. What else did you want to say?"

"Hear me out. You need to make that stop in Denver. The man is named Shelton Robertson. He is a billionaire that has secretly funded several international terrorist organizations. His syndicate even controls Pearce Savage, though Pearce thinks he commands his criminal enterprises. Pearce is a small gangster in Shelton's eyes. Shelton is truly a man behind the curtain. Your government has suspected him for years. Nothing has been enough to prove the connections. You can look up everything I am telling you."

"I've heard the name. I've read the stories. What does he have to do with Ephemeron?"

"He is inhabited by an Ephemeral who is a powerful sister to Overlord Draxis. This sister and the Xermegan High Priestess are to be betrothed at the upcoming Fusion. The High Priestess was born into the Omegan clan. If she and the Overlord's sister Fuse, it gives the appearance of a marriage of the two clans. It will bolster the strength of the Xermegan clan and raise the standing of Overlord Draxis."

"If Shelton is a billionaire, he will have the best protection guarding him. Even if I could get to him, how does that really help the fight on Ephemeron?"

"Shelton won't know it's coming. The Overlord's sister will be thrown out of entanglement and forced to scramble for a new one. Our group has plans to ensure her death when she tries to escape. Assume there will be an unexpected interference with finding a new entanglement. We are doing our part to resist. You may not like it, but you're going to have to trust us."

Nick wondered how much time humanity had. Selection and Fusion events were to take place soon, but he just didn't know what *soon* meant.

He tried calling out to Vince, but there was no answer.

Vince had retreated to his E-station pod where a devoted attendant replenished him with special liquids and an intravenous energy shot.

*The Chief Scientist was like a beaten animal, afraid,
willing to do anything to appease its master.*

On **Ephemeron,** the best Xermegan clan scientists had gathered in the great hall of Overlord Draxis's famed palace. An invitation to attend was a grand honor and considered a mark of special status.

These scientists knew why they were in attendance. The Overlord's plans and wishes were clear. Ephemeron's scientists were tasked with expanding QE capabilities to physically control other life-forms. Many precious resources had been spent researching and testing this new power. Within recent years, a breakthrough had teased the possibility of being able to physically control other life-forms. More resources were thrown at the problem and Overlord Draxis's favored scientists.

Today, those scientists sat at the Overlord's long, polished reddish-orange table. Its complex grain patterns exuded strength and power.

"Chief Scientist," spoke the Overlord. "Tell me of your team's progress."

"Yes, sir, thank you," said the Chief, feigning outward confidence, but shuddering inside. "We have achieved the capability for physical manipulation of life-forms within our labs."

"Are you referring to the early tests using drogs?" interrupted the Overlord.

"Yes, sir. Each pair was separated across the whole width of our planet. Other studies placed them apart in labs on our most distant moon, Eglan."

"I already know of these preliminary studies," interrupted the Overlord. "What you are describing is nothing new. These are entanglements of a few hundred thousand miles. They are drogs, low-intelligence creatures. What is something new you can tell me?"

"Yes, of course, sir. I was simply giving some background. We have made additional inroads since the drog tests. You have heard of the planet Twikker. It is millions of light-years from us. Its top-level life-forms have minimal technology, but they are emotional creatures. We've had entanglements with them for centuries. They are a great energy resource for us. Our newest efforts have shown we can actively and physically manipulate them, causing more disturbances on their planet. It has increased our energy harvest from them by twenty-five percent."

At the table, a gifted prodigy was seated alongside the Chief Scientist. She had seen all the data, and she knew the Chief was lying.

The research team's pilot manipulation of the Twikkers was rudimentary and fragile. The energy output increase from Twikker manipulation was no more than two percent, at best. Only one day showed a twenty-five percent spike. Most technicians assumed it was a measurement anomaly. Worse still, many times the attempt to physically manipulate Twikkers caused a negative energy drain on Ephemeron.

The prodigy knew better than to contradict the Chief, but wondered if the consequences of his lies would also fall upon the staff's heads. She said a silent prayer that she would not be killed in the inevitable purge.

"That is very good work, Chief. The Twikkers have always been a dependable energy source. I wish I could watch their turmoil as we manipulate them."

The Chief Scientist gulped, wondering if the Overlord was actually asking to view the manipulations. Trepidation filled his mind and his lies stuck in his throat, but he was afraid to tell the truth.

The Overlord could see the sweat on the Chief Scientist's brow and the heightened glistening on his wings. The Overlord laughed. "I know I can't see their agony. It is wishful thinking. But maybe someday. What do you think, Chief?"

"Yes, sir, maybe someday." Relief flooded through the Chief Scientist, though he felt an urgent need to evacuate his colon. In the days to come, he would need to push his group harder.

In a corner of the room, the High Priestess and her closest aide sat quietly, observing those gathered. The High Priestess noticed the Chief Scientist's tense expression, a couple times swallowing hard. He constantly played with the edges of his computer tablet. His vibrating wings were evident. Did his obvious nervousness mean anything important?

At the same time, Meerlex, the Vimegan spy, was fixating on the Chief Scientist's protégé. The spy had a peculiar advantage in her assessment.

Meerlex had previously met the young data scientist years before. As she worked her way up the ladder of trust, the spy was assigned to clean the scientists's lab and equipment. Often the prodigy worked late into the night. Sometimes the two Ephemerals had brief conversations. Those memories gave the spy insight into the prodigy's temperament and inclinations.

The Vimegan spy remembered that the prodigy often tapped her fingers while she was thinking, but when she was nervous or under pressure, the tapping became rapid. It was a small thing. While the Chief Scientist had spoken, the prodigy's fingers tapped more vigorously. Meerlex knew something was amiss.

The Overlord pressed the Chief Scientist. "The Selection is in six months. Fusion is soon after that. Our demonstration project on Earth will show the Ephemeron people the righteousness of our ways. Chief, our Ephemeral agents have been pre-positioned on Earth. Do they know what they must do?"

"Yes, Your Lordship. The ten sleeper agents were entangled with humans and are awaiting their code words. The plan has been refined with our most sophisticated analyses. Even as a pilot project, it will have pronounced impacts on Earth, creating and magnifying humans' emotional outbursts. Unfortunately, one of our members had to be pulled from their human entanglement. It was your youngest brother. He had been dwelling in a human named Zulu, but Zulu unexpectedly died."

"How could this happen?" stormed the Overlord, enraged. "I recognize the name Zulu. Isn't he part of the Pearce Savage crew? How did he die?"

"He was shot. Murdered."

"Why? Who did it?"

"We're not sure, Lord. Our entanglements don't give us that insight."

"My sister Maxxerna is the leader of the infiltration squad. Has she been informed?"

"Yes, Lord. We reached out to her, but she doesn't know why Zulu was murdered. There is no need to worry. As you know, your sister dwells inside Shelton Robertson, a wealthy man. He is protected by skilled bodyguards. The loss of Zulu was unwelcome, but it won't hold up our plans, sir."

The Chief Scientist prayed silently to the Supreme god, asking for deliverance from the Overlord's wrath. He asked the Supreme god to safeguard the remaining entanglements of the Overlord's agents with the humans.

Most fervently of all, he hoped the Overlord would not discover his lies.

Among the billions of entreaties crisscrossing the universe, the Chief Scientist hoped the Most Supreme god, Alborix, would note his earnest pleadings for a breakthrough. He had no wish to be tortured for his failures.

"My plan must succeed," restated Draxis. "Our enhanced entanglements with the Earthlings will demonstrate Ephemeron's power. It will demonstrate the power of our Xermegan scientists and the Xermegan clan. Our domination of humans will be the sign our people need. It will propel our family to the Ascendancy of the Kingdom. The Xermegan clan will rule over Ephemeron for the next 1,000 years—and for 10,000 years after that. Show me the plans again. How will we turn Earth into a bloodbath?"

"We have entangled ourselves with influencers," explained the Chief Scientist. "These are humans who have large social followings or great political influence. Human technology captures what these important people say and amplifies it across the world. In many instances, we twist their original words into something else that boost the outpouring of peoples's emotions. It matters not what is the truth of the matter. Our intent is to inflame. We take both sides. We have entangled our most aggressive Ephemerals within these humans. When our agents receive their code words, it will begin a great turmoil."

Not only did the Chief Scientist's protégé know he was lying, but she was horrified when she heard him speak. The Chief Scientist was like a beaten animal, afraid, willing to do anything to appease its master. The team's research had always been a technical investigation of what quantum entanglement might provide.

Instead, the Overlord's power-hungry plan demanded that QE would be bent to the will of his depraved politics. Driving the insanity were the Overlord's promises of unlimited energy and his self-administered blessings of the gods.

Nurturing Overlord Draxis's folly, the scientists deluded themselves by telling themselves that physical manipulations of other life-forms would be properly supervised by authorities and managed by policy. That there would be ethical boundaries. That there would be limits.

The protégé asked herself how she could have missed seeing the stark truth.

For the Overlord, the advanced research into QE was no more than a stark grab for power and dominance, and his only allegiance was to success. The Chief Scientist was a mere tool and a weak man. If the Chief Scientist succeeded, he would be lauded. If not, he would die miserably and publicly. Then the next Chief Scientist would be selected and would know the consequences of failure. Each Chief Scientist knew, once selected, they lived inside a caged wheel running endlessly to nowhere, *hoping* to find the brass ring of success … and deliverance.

The protégé wondered if there was a way she could survive when the lie was uncovered. She stole a glance at the High Priestess and her aide, the Vimegan spy.

The aide's eyes caught the protégé's glance, enough to communicate caution about the Chief Scientist's words. The protégé then quickly averted her eyes.

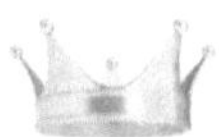

Across Ephemeron, in a building housing thousands of E-stations, the Ephemeral workers from Shift One entered the lunchroom. Before even gathering their plates, they stood rigidly and respectfully, waiting for the invocation to begin. Their insect wings exuded a respectful hum.

The selected ministerial designee of the day stood in front of its coworkers and led them in a prayer to the Ephemeron gods. It was an inclusive prayer. It did not pit clan factions against each other. It had been approved by the Omegan monarchy. The high ceiling of the room, with its skylight, helped frame the benediction. Upon the prayer's completion, the E-station workers selected from the multiple food offerings, a supplement to their E-station energy harvest, then sat with favored coworkers.

Vince and Paul shared a table with several coworkers. Many of the table conversations were the usual stories about the funny tweaks of emotional outbursts the Ephemerals had caused on other worlds.

The Ephemerals, especially the young ones, exchanged tidbits of how to better upend another life-form's day. They compared how much emotional energy they harvested, and wondered about year-end bonuses. Some feigned minimal success, though knowing they had reaped an impressive harvest and would be rewarded by their superiors. Ephemeron Watchers wandered amongst the tables. Occasionally, the Watchers would make small talk with the workers.

Vince and Paul sat slightly apart from each other at one table, engaging their fellow workers in trite conversation. With a time-limit allotted to consume their meal before returning to work, it left only a small slice of time for Vince and Paul to speak together.

They had developed a method to avoid the Watchers. In some instances, they used trusted confidants to exchange messages. It was imperfect and convoluted. Those receiving messages could not be seen making a beeline from Vince to Paul, or back. Conversations had to be guarded from those who might overhear.

It was not uncommon for messages to take multiple days to traverse from one to another. In rare situations, Vince and Paul would meet in the courtyard. It was a delicate dance. The Watchers paid special attention to Vince and Paul, two ultra-privileged Ephemerals. But not meeting would have triggered as many questions as meeting too often.

Yet there were weaknesses in the Watchers' procedures. While they spent much time eyeballing Vince and Paul, and reporting to their superiors lengthy mundane updates, this fortuitously kept the Watchers from recognizing the movements of other rebel coworkers.

Rebels had been drawn to the opposition for a multitude of reasons. Some joined because they believed the politicization of the Ephemeron gods was a transgression that must be corrected. Others thought that Overlord Draxis's plan for physical manipulations and emotional destruction of other life-forms was an ethical travesty. Others were young and robust, rebelling because they were young. And others feared that the evil manipulations of a few self-serving officials would lead to the eventual destruction of their Ephemeron civilization.

On this day, Vince and Paul stole a few minutes to meet in the courtyard.

"Will Nick kill Shelton Robertson?" asked Paul.

"He is resisting. He thinks we are trying to use him as a pawn. He won't be easily swayed," responded Vince.

"Nick must see the threat Robertson is. His funding of terrorists will bring great misery. Robertson's temperament is the perfect foil for manipulation by his entanglement with Draxis's sister. Maybe if Nick sees the proof, he'll help us."

"He sees no point for himself; he is only focused on retribution. Our targets are not part of his plan. He doubts half of what we tell him. We see him as a ruthless and willing killer, but he apparently has some sort of principles."

"He is an odd man to figure out, and I was inside him for decades," agreed Paul.

"What about his twin, Tony?"

"He's a basket case, huddling in self-pity and paralyzed in fear. At this rate, it is only a matter of time before he does something stupid."

"If Nick knew Robertson was being manipulated by an Ephemeral, he would object to that," offered Vince.

"Maybe we can give him a recording."

"Neither you nor I have access to the Overlord's inner sanctum."

"For the moment, let's suppose we had a recording. We could use double-entanglement to share it," offered Paul.

"Well, it's empty speculation," countered Vince. "We have no way to make a recording of the Overlord's private plannings. We'll have to find another way to convince Nick to go after Robertson." Noticing approaching visitors, he quietly warned Paul. "Beware. Watchers approach. As usual, they are wondering what we're talking about."

"We say that we're talking about the upcoming Selection and Fusion, of course," said Paul confidently. "What else is anybody talking about? If they ask for more, we say the same thing that everybody wonders about. Which clan will be Selected for the next monarchial rule? Will you and I Fuse, or will it be Callum and you? We tell them everything about nothing. They just need something to report so they look like they're doing their job."

The Watchers circled in, trying to eavesdrop, straining for glimpses of words or phrases to report to their superiors.

Vince and Paul dispersed.

21

"In truth, I sold my body and my soul.
I'm not selling myself anymore."

On Earth, it was morning. Tony and Sylvia were checking out of the Daphne Hotel. A different hotel attendant was at the desk, but it was evident on her face she had heard the recent stories regarding rooms 204 and 206. She tried to keep the checkout professional, and her training had taught her not to pry. It was Sylvia that disrupted the illusion.

Sylvia leaned across the hotel checkout countertop to accentuate her message.

"When we checked in, the other receptionist told us that a couple rooms on the third floor were haunted, but said nothing about the second floor. We've been staying in room 206. Last night I heard voices. It was clear as day. The ghost said his name was Paul. The voice said some crazy shit about impregnating me … impregnating women … inhabiting humans. It was horrifying. I couldn't sleep all night. People should be warned about those rooms. Voices seem to be coming from room 204, too."

Stunned by Sylvia's stark revelation, the hotel receptionist did her best to follow her training, staying calm as possible, acknowledging the customer's complaint, and saying that she would personally report the matter to the manager. The receptionist apologized for the unexpected haunting, though she did mention the fact that the Daphne Hotel was known for such activity. The receptionist gave Sylvia a twenty-five percent discount on her bill.

Tony and Sylvia had barely checked out when the attendant called the manager confirming the stories of voices from room 204 and 206. Moments later, the manager was logging into his computer, increasing the room rates and adding a new marketing release. He didn't really care if the stories were true. It was enough that two receptionists would attest. He made a note to himself not to sleep in those rooms.

With Tony and Sylvia behind Nick, Sylvia was driving, barely pushing the speed limit. "You never told Nick about growing up in Denver," said Tony.

"I never got the chance. Besides, how do you blurt out half your traumas to someone you've just met? My uncle is a bastard and a rapist. He's a rich son-of-a-bitch, too. His money has always bought him respect and protection."

"You were young, honey. You didn't know."

"Didn't I? Somehow, I knew it was wrong. I just didn't stand up for myself. Dad had died in the car accident. Mom spent months recovering from her injuries. It was Uncle Shelton that offered to help us, his brother's family. He paid Mom's bills, hired extra nursing help. It seemed so magnanimous. The other kids my age knew my story and they felt sorry for me. Uncle Shelton made me revere him for helping us out. He twisted my thoughts. He treated me so special and showered me with gifts. I believed I owed him. He raped me off and on for years."

"Sylvia, you ran away. You were strong. You gave up all the privileges. You became tough and found your way in the world. You lived on the edge of survival. You have become the strongest woman I have ever known."

"I prostituted myself, Tony."

"No. That's not what you did. You always told me you never did that."

"I was lying to you and to myself," said Sylvia, growing in anger from her memories about Uncle Shelton. "Becoming Pearce Savage's girlfriend was virtually the same thing."

"Pearce grew to respect you. He gave you control of many of his day-to-day operations. You made money for him."

"In truth, I sold my body and my soul. I'm not selling myself anymore. That's not how I want to be cared for. It's why I love you, Tony. You are a wild guy, but you have never tried to own me."

"Remember how you saved me?" asked Tony, smiling.

"That's hard to forget," said Sylvia, her eyes dilating as she remembered. "You just passed out. Marco and I looked around for you, but there you were, free-falling, upside-down, limp as a ragdoll. We were skydiving from the plane at 120 miles an hour. I was lucky I didn't kill myself crashing into you. It was nuts; all instinct and a huge rush of adrenaline. I kept telling myself: *focus, focus.*

"I flipped you upright, pulled your parachute's backup release and up and away you went. Of course, your chute was slowing you down, but it seemed like you took off like a rocket upward. I didn't know if I was going to fly into you when I pulled my chute, but there was no time. Fuck, I can still feel the jerk of that parachute. I'm getting a rush talking about it. The tape showed I pulled my chute around 2,500 feet."

"I love that sport," said Tony, caught up in memories.

"Me too. It's been too long since we last jumped."

"I used to feel so brave," said Tony, his voice faltering a bit.

"What are you saying?"

Agitation and weakness bent Tony's thoughts. "I used to be brave. I lived on the edge because I had no fear. I did crazy things. Now, I have an alien's voice in my head, and I'm a basket case. I can't live this way. How do I get it out of me? We can't do anything to them. They sit billions of miles away, feeding off us.

"If Nick had died, I would know none of this. They would have lived silently inside me, reaping my emotions. Hell, if I was unaware, it would be a lot better for them. I would have stayed the crazy Tony, living wild, daredeviling my way through life."

"Tony, don't say that about your brother. You know you don't mean that."

"Of course, I don't. Not really. But life has turned to shit. I can't do anything to fight back. I can't protect my brother. And I can't protect you."

More miles of the interstate passed by. The scenery was dry and nondescript.

Sylvia began to chuckle, and the chuckles gave way to laughing. She tried to hold back, but her laughter kept bursting forth.

"You wonder why I'm laughing?" she asked, turning her head to Tony, eyes not on the road. "I'm thinking about the stupid fucking hotel receptionist. They tell their customers that bullshit story of hauntings, then we tell them we're hearing voices and a guy named Paul wants to impregnate me. I can still see the receptionist's face in my mind. She was calling the manager before we got out the door. It's sick, I know. I'm the last one that should be laughing but I can't help myself."

"I understand, honey. We're naked and vulnerable. Sometimes gallows humor is all we've got to keep us sane."

"Tony," called Paul's voice. "You need to go to Denver."

Tony jumped. "Jesus. I hate it when you do that. Can't you give me a warning?"

Sylvia looked over.

Tony pointed to his head, silently mouthing, "It's Paul."

There was no double-entanglement so Tony had to relay the conversation back and forth. It was cumbersome as usual, but they made it work.

Tony spoke first. "My brother is going to St. Paul. We need to catch up with him. My brother also said I should ignore you."

Paul's voice was agitated. "No, you need to go to Denver. Shelton Robertson is inhabited by an Ephemeral. Robertson is part of the Ephemeral plan to tear Earth apart. There are only a few days before millions of dollars will be committed. Robertson secretly helps fund terrorists. It is part of Overlord Draxis's plan to provoke your world's antagonisms. Draxis doesn't care what chaos is unleashed, only that emotions are stirred. Your brother doesn't understand the danger Shelton Robertson poses. You must go to Denver."

Tony was almost ready to again tell Paul to go to hell, but suddenly caught himself as the name Shelton Robinson registered in his mind. Shelton Robertson was the uncle who had raped Sylvia.

This was the same man Overlord Draxis was going to manipulate to fuck up humanity.

"What?" asked Sylvia, wondering why Tony had stopped sharing Paul's words.

"Tony, what's going on? Sylvia needs to hear this, too. You need to convince her and your brother. Tony? Are you hearing this? You can't shut down." Paul's voice was filled with urgency.

"Tell me what's going on," insisted Sylvia.

"I can't," muttered Tony, like he had fallen into a trance. His mind felt overloaded, like it would explode. Paul was beseeching him from one side. Sylvia was pummeling him from the other side.

"Tony, tell me," Sylvia demanded. "Tell me!"

"Will both of you shut up!" snapped Tony. Sweat poured down his face. He reached forward and turned all the air vents toward him, adjusted the air conditioner to its lowest temperature, and cranked up the fan.

"It's your uncle," he related to Sylvia, who was trying to understand what Tony was explaining.

"What about that piece of shit?"

"Paul is saying your uncle is part of the Ephemeral plot to fuck up humanity. Apparently, Uncle Shelton is a willing co-conspirator. He's inhabited by an Ephemeral, but Overlord Draxis is calling the shots."

"Tony, is Sylvia Shelton Robertson's niece?" Paul sounded hesitant.

Tony shook his head. "For being the super intelligent aliens, it seems you're missing some vital pieces of information. Yes, Sylvia is his niece. But before you get any grand ideas, you should know there is very bad blood between them. She'd probably kill him on sight."

"That's the idea. Go to Denver and kill Robertson." Now Paul sounded gleeful.

Tony had been talking with Paul, but he was receiving a simultaneous earful from Sylvia spewing a tirade about her shit uncle who she just learned was turning traitor in a plot to rape the world.

Paul kept talking. "Killing Robertson ejects his Ephemeral, who must scramble for a new entanglement. The rebel resistance will ensure there will be problems acquiring a new entanglement.

"You need to call Nick," urged Sylvia. "We have to stop him and meet up with him."

"I don't think me telling my brother that he has to go to Denver will be enough to convince him," replied Tony.

Sylvia was insistent. "Ask him if Vince has mentioned Shelton Robertson. Then tell your brother he's my bad-blood uncle and I want to kill him myself. Hell, just call him. I'll tell him myself."

Relenting, Tony called Nick's phone. "Well, hello travelers," answered Nick. "Where are you?"

"Coming up on Wichita," said Tony. "Where are you?"

"I'm south of Salina."

"What are you doing over there?"

"I was going to stop to stretch and grab a bite to eat," said Nick, without explaining why he had gone straight north and failed to take I-335 northeast out of Wichita.

Overhearing Sylvia shouting something about killing Robertson, he continued, "Don't tell me Paul convinced you two into thinking going to Denver was a good idea."

"Well, Nick, I don't know how good an idea it is, but we have to go. I can't explain it on the phone. It's too complicated. But Vince told you about Robertson?"

"He mentioned Robertson funds terrorists. That's a problem for the FBI, not us."

"He's Sylvia's uncle. A lot of unresolved wounds and hostility. Stay in Salina. We're not that far behind."

Sylvia was yelling in the background. "He's a fucking piece of shit!"

Vince had done his best trying to tempt Nick to go to Denver.

Nick believed most of what Vince had been telling him about Robertson; that he was a front-man for Overlord Draxis's plans for Earth. He couldn't help but wonder how he could get close to such a guy who obviously would have grade-A protection.

Against his better judgment, Nick let himself be convinced to leave his planned route and head straight north, closer to Denver. But he still planned to stop in Salina.

He was surprised Sylvia was so outraged at hearing Robertson's name. The woman was practically shrieking through the phone. Had he hurt her? It sounded like it.

Nick had been juggling a sliver of ethics by saying no to Vince. After all, he didn't know this Shelton character and had no reason to eliminate him. Nick wanted to finish off Tubby Vaughn, but thinking Robertson had hurt Sylvia steamed Nick's blood.

Driving into a Salina gas station, Nick went in to relieve himself, pick up some car snacks, and also to get a recommendation for food. Both the station attendant and a nearby customer recommended Blake's Cafe. He even got a little lowdown on the feisty waitress Eileen, the flirty waitress Janis, and a couple menu recommendations.

The store's patrons all attested that Blake's restaurant was a "pretty damn friendly place."

Nick needed to kill time. An online search popped up suggestions to a few nature trails running near the Smoky Hill River.

He thought it would be a nice way to stretch his legs and think.

*... both the young and the wise came to the same understanding:
action was the only true path.*

On Ephemeron, the meeting of the Overlord's premier scientists was an opportunity that Meerlex, the Vimegan spy, could not ignore.

During the meeting, Overlord Draxis's detailed plans for expanding the control over humanity was described. Many times, Meerlex had watched or heard of transgressions against her clan but could say nothing. Many times, she had helped facilitate the pain that befell them. It was this sacrifice of her treasonous pains that opened the way into the enemy's inner sanctum. Overlord Draxis's plan against humanity would now force her hand.

At all costs, his plan must fail.

It wasn't that Meerlex particularly cared for humans. In fact, it mattered not at all that humans were targeted. If Draxis's plan was to target the planet Reevin, it would be an equivalent travesty. For Meerlex, destroying an entire planet's most intelligent species by turning them into emotional slaves was crossing an inviolate ethical boundary, even for Ephemerals.

In Ephemeron's history, its populace had been forced to abandon one planet because of greed and hubris. For a time, Ephemeron's leaders had learned the hard lesson of waging intergalactic war and its inevitable futility. But technical mastery of quantum entanglement redefined the equation, allowing Ephemerals to remain hidden, safe, and triumphant across the universe.

On New Ephemeron, existence seemed peaceful, and domination of other species seemed justified to average Ephemerals, who believed they didn't really hurt anybody. They simply lived silently within other beings. Yes, sometimes Ephemerals sparked the emotions of the alien species they inhabited, resulting in outbursts and angst. But it was merely harvesting psychological currents. What could be wrong with that?

Overlord Draxis was a new breed of Ephemeral who had never felt the actual pains of Ephemeron's past. He was supremely self-confident, having been raised privileged on the backs of the many who had fled the original dying Ephemeron and built New Ephemeron.

Overlord Draxis was unrestrained and egotistical. He thought of the monarchy as weak. He was incensed by what he perceived was a timid nd lazy populace. When his god, Alborix, told Draxis to subjugate humanity, any self-doubts were easily cast aside. That Draxis's narcissistic imagination was the voice he heard, was a minor detail not worth questioning.

The meeting of the Overlord's premier scientists was a moment that the Vimegan spy would not be able to ignore.

In upcoming days, Meerlex would go into a bookshop, and using a special coded phrase, she would tell the manager she was "looking for a special print edition of *The Golden History of Ephemeron One*."

The manager would respond with a specific response. "That is an unusual book. I don't think we have a copy."

The Vimegan spy would answer, "I was hoping to give it as a gift, if it is not too expensive."

The manager would give his final response. "I will have to submit a special edition search. If you stop by in a few days, I can tell you more." The code phrase meant that a predetermined message would be passed on.

Meerlex would only know that if the message was properly received, a dead-drop marking would show up on a city bench. Meerlex would respond with a marking at a different site that would indicate to her handler that a package would be ready for pickup at a preset destination.

Before leaving, Meerlex browsed the bookstore's aisles, finding an interesting speculative fiction that told a story where all Ephemerals had the same nightly dream except for two young Ephemeral lovers, who would be the hope and salvation of their world because they could dream differently. She paid for the book, thanked the manager, and said she would be back later.

In truth, it was unlikely that Meerlex would return. If anybody ever asked, she would simply say she had decided on a different gift.

Meerlex had sacrificed so much, but she could not know if her moment of redemption would come to fruition. She could not guarantee how her clandestine case agent would use the information from the package. It would take only one chatty Ephemeral to destroy her years of sacrifice and subterfuge.

Meerlex could not know, even if her information stayed secure, whether the Vimegan leadership would use it wisely. They would certainly not ask her—a supposed traitor to the Vimegan clan. Along with her deep loyalty to the Vimegan clan, Meerlex's hopes had been recently buoyed upon hearing the High Priestess and Overlord Draxis discuss the rise of a resistance movement. Other Ephemerals were fighting the same fight for Ephemeron's soul.

Many of the rebels thought of the regular populace as sheep, mindless of individualism, mindless in their ability to stand upright and say no.

The rebels thought of themselves as patriots. They huddled in secret gatherings, most times not knowing another's name and not wanting to know. Calling oneself *Mr. X* or *Ms. Z* would suffice.

Often rebels argued among themselves, engaging in philosophical conversations, debating the "true path." Among the young ones, this dialectic repartee was to be expected. They were testing the world, themselves, their ideas.

But somehow in the end, both the young and the wise came to the same understanding: action was the only true path. All the rest was merely talk and chest-thumping.

Plans of sabotage and resistance were drawn up and cells were formed. Nobody knew all.

The singular thread was their fear of an upcoming tyranny. Most really didn't know what they were saying when they said they were willing to die. None had truly faced a bloody battlefield. In the rebels' clandestine gatherings, surrounded by themselves, their innocence made them feel invincible.

These were the dedicated silent Ephemeral allies that would be fighting alongside the Vimegan spy.

This night, the sky of Ephemeron's capital city was streaked with fast-moving thin gray clouds. Friends gathered in their local gathering spots. All talk was speculation, hopes, and imagination of who would be Fused with whom and which clan would Ascend.

Watchers of the three clans milled about, especially crowded venues: taking notes; sitting amongst fellow Ephemerals, taking more notes; and if needed, inventing notes to impress their superiors.

Religious advisers walked amongst all, bestowing their gracious blessings. Stopping at a table, a gentle question might be asked: "Do you know of the god Alborix?"

Though Alborix was one of the many Ephemeron gods, asking in this way was a test because this was the god that the Xermegan clan revered as the supreme god.

Hesitation marked anyone who answered slowly. The Xermegan Watchers would make note of the hesitation. But enthusiasm also marked the responders; Watchers of the Vimegan and Omegan clans made their notations of a different sort.

At another table, another holy man would ask if the Ephemeral knew of a different god. Again, it was the same test, essentially used to determine the allegiance of the one who answered. Enthusiasm marked the respondent. Hesitation similarly earned a mark.

It was not difficult for an Ephemeral to be placed on both the *Loyal* list for one clan and the *Disloyal* list for another. On a different day, the sycophant Watchers would report opposite findings. Using the computer algorithms that each clan analyzed, mostly everybody was labeled potentially disloyal … or potentially loyal, depending on the day's report from the Watchers.

Rebel Ephemerals learned the public language of non-committal.

Those rebels having private conversations always had an eye on who was nearby and how close they were. Upon a waiter's approach, the topic would smoothly shift to a frivolous topic of the day, perhaps a jest that made fun of a table friend's laggard academic performance.

As the waiter would drift away and the Watchers trained their ears on others, the conversation returned to plans of disruption and their passion for a new world. Despite the risks, the rebel Ephemerals still publicly met. They drank with cheer and embellishment. Being in the open was the best subterfuge. It made things look like they were harmless.

This night, in one restaurant's courtyard, an Ephemeral singer with a rich and vibrant voice was backed by musicians utilizing a rhythm that humans would recognize as a Brazilian-like melody.

At a table tucked off to the side of the courtyard, Mr. Coco, one of the rebel leaders, spoke in hushed tones. "We know the location of three sleeper agent Ephemerals and the humans they are inhabiting. Should we reveal our hand now? Is this our chance to disrupt Overlord's mad vision? If sleeper agents start dying, perhaps the others will panic and reveal themselves. Hopefully, we will be able to identify the others later."

Another rebel at the table added her perspective. "Commander Vaaruv has also told his people that passive entanglement with other life-forms is a sign of weakness. He says that it is time for Ephemerals to announce themselves across the universe. He insists Ephemerals' actions will be peaceful and that other life-forms will adjust to our cohabitation within them.

"His Vimegan data scientists have published studies which state that a quarter of those that discover that Ephemerals inhabit them will meekly accept it. Eventually more than half will accept the inhabitation. And their Vimegan research shows that over ten percent of those not inhabited by an Ephemeral will volunteer to be inhabited."

"Because Commander Vaaruv couches his ambitions in more peaceful terms, does this make Vimegan leadership any better?" asked another. "For over 200 years, Commander Vaaruv and Overlord Draxis have been locked in a deathly struggle against each other. Commander Vaaruv cannot afford to look weak. He fears the upcoming Selection will vault Overlord Draxis to the throne. Commander Vaaruv will do anything to prevent that."

Mr. Coco spoke. "They are all lies. We have already argued this. Both Overlord Draxis and Commander Vaaruv are tyrants. They manipulate with fear, money, and authority. Each insists that the gods are on their side and on the side of those who are loyal to their clans. They direct secret funds to those who echo their words, and they cause hardships for those who oppose them. We made a choice which devil to fight. Again, I ask: do we take action at this moment, or not?

"Draxis's plan has already been set in motion. If we can disrupt it and shame him with his failure, Ephemerals will turn away from him. They will have second thoughts. His plan's failure will make Ephemerals question his excessive pride. With his humiliation, Ephemerals will again turn toward the Omegan monarchy. It will continue its indolent rule, but Ephemeron will avoid the misery of being hunted by hordes of life-forms."

"But Ephemeron is safe," countered one of the rebels. "Our planet is remote. It makes no difference if we are hated by the universe. Alien lifeforms cannot reach us. If our people feel safe, what concern is it that others feel ill will toward Ephemerals? Ideology is important only if it lessens a person's pain."

Mr. Coco sipped on his inebriating drink, called The Blossom. It was a popular drink across Ephemeron. Many versions were offered. Bartenders filled each blossom with a mix of Ephemeron liquors. Some regions were noted for a spicier accent. Another region concocted a version that premiered a complex sour note. All versions used a fresh flower blossom from the Qualance plant. The Qualance blossom generated moving rings of sparkling color, vertically rising up and falling down around the bloom. The wild version of a Qualance blossom was preferred because it exuded a scentless waft of calming psycho-active vapor.

Mr. Coco spoke. "Entanglement works in both directions. Alien lifeforms may be unaware of our presence inside them. They may not yet have the mastery of utilizing quantum entanglement. But if we make ourselves known to them, they will awaken. They will fight back, all of them. Their hate and fear of us will drive them relentlessly. They will find a way to master entanglement. They will come after us. Ephemeron's peace exists because we are unknown."

"I received communication from Vince," reported a rebel. "Vince reports little progress convincing Nick to help us. So far, the human is refusing to kill Shelton Robertson. He doesn't see it as his fight."

When the Ephemeral used the name "Vince," it generated a little smile on a couple of the Ephemerals' faces. They had gotten used to referring to their compatriots as Vince and Paul. It was entertaining, since the names were so impossibly different from their real Ephemeral names.

"We may have caught a lucky break," said another. "Paul reported that the woman, Sylvia, is the niece of Shelton Robertson. Paul is not inside her, so he didn't fully understand everything. It seems Robertson abused his niece. She wants revenge on him. Nick has become her protector, along with his brother Tony. Maybe this will influence Nick's decision."

"Abused? How?" asked Mr. Coco.

"Paul said it was a sexual abuse."

"Humans are so unlike us, said one Ephemeral. "What is sex? Two Ephemerals Fuse to create an Ephemeral seed that we send into the universe. I don't understand this concept of sexual abuse."

"Maybe it's like a misuse of power," conjectured another. "Overlord Draxis intimidates those under him, spreading fear into their lives. Same with Commander Vaaruv. Maybe it's like that."

"Aren't we fighting the same fight against oppression?" asked Mr. Coco. "We know Draxis has forced conscription on some Ephemerals to work the deep crystal mines. We don't understand the humans' sexual ways, but we can understand freedom and liberty." A couple of Ephemerals nodded as they thought through Mr. Coco's words.

Mr. Coco inhaled the ether of his Qualance blossom, took a sip, then continued.

"We need Paul to stir Tony's passions. Make Tony feel like killing Robertson serves Sylvia's vengeance. At the same time, we need Vince to work on Nick. If Nick sees Robertson as a threat to Sylvia, he will intervene."

"Watchers are asking questions," cautioned a rebel. "Management is asking questions. Vince and Paul are frequently exhausted. Their physical connections with the humans are draining. Paul is doing his best to cover up their interactions by saying it is no more than a fun dalliance of an heir-apparent prince. I'm not sure how long we can maintain the deception. It's getting harder and harder to unobtrusively divert extra energy to them. It puts Vince and Paul at risk of being bumped out of their entanglements that would leave us scrambling to find another way to defeat Overlord Draxis's plans.

"Does anybody have anything else?" asked Mr. Coco.

Another rebel spoke. "The Head of Vimegan Intelligence had an hour-long meeting with Sub-Commander Vre. The head of Vimegan Intelligence carried a strong, locked satchel. When he came out after their meeting, it appeared thinner, like something had been removed. We are keeping an eye out for any hints."

"Yes, that is significant," responded Mr. Coco. "Those two are very close friends. They have Fused twice together. Evan's father always treated Vre as his son. When they were young, Evan and Vre always got into trouble together. Sub-Commander Vre is loyal to his boss, so the meeting that you described between Vre and Evan is likely proper. Let us not imagine specters where they don't exist." Mr. Coco was doing his best to temper undue speculations. "Still, it is worth noting any changes in Sub-commander Vre's habits."

"Watchers!" hissed an Ephemeral rebel in a low and resolute whisper, holding the glass in front of his lips so as not to be seen warning the others. The others followed his cue, changing the conversation to topics of everyday life.

23

"You'll want to kill him and run at the same time—
but you can't. There has to be fire in your eyes."

Nick was completing his second circuit walking along the Smoky Hill River trail when he received a text from his brother. Tony and Sylvia were entering the city limits, and promising to save him a seat at Blake's Café.

Driving up to the café, Nick spotted their white Jeep in the parking lot. Most of the lunch crowd had left. It was a rural community where *the work* was never finished; there was always more to do than could be done. It was a community where high personal work ethic was valued, combined with a neighborliness borne of knowing the hard struggle against nature's whims.

"Well, we know what we want," said Tony to Nick, purposely pressing him for a quick answer before Nick had a chance to look at the menu. He added, "If you could hurry up and make a choice, that would be nice."

Sliding in on the open side of the booth, Nick gave his twin brother a smirk. He was hungry and had planned to have eaten and well on his way by now. It lifted his spirit to see his brother trying to make light of the moment, but Nick read a heavy sternness on Sylvia's face. Her prior hysterical outburst from the car and the name *Shelton Robertson* had wormed around in his mind over the last hour.

A waitress came to the booth.

Seeing the redheaded twins, the waitress took a double take. A pleasant smile crossed her face but then, just as quickly, a more direct nature surfaced.

"I hope you're not fancy city folk that need a lot of time to figure out what you want to eat," she said. "I have a whole bunch of other customers to take care of and my feet are killing me." Nick pegged her for Eileen, the feisty one that the gas station attendant warned about.

When he walked into the diner, Nick had sized up the place. Only a couple tables and booths held any patrons, so it didn't seem Eileen was that swamped. Still, he figured it was best to keep his mouth shut and order.

"I'll have the breaded pork tenderloin and a sweet tea," said Nick.

"What do you want on it?"

"Onion, pickles, lettuce, and mustard. Potato salad as my side. As an extra side, can I have tomato slices?"

"Your pleasure is my pleasure, dearie," said Eileen with a sweet inflection that left Nick to guess what she exactly meant by *pleasure*. "Now, how about you two?"

"How's the fried chicken?" asked Tony, feeling a bit slighted that Nick got the waitress's sweet attention.

"Well, the chicken is dead. It's been double-dipped in special spices, and … get a load of this …," she paused for effect, "… then it's fried."

Tony, not having received advance warning of Eileen's quirky tableside manner, looked confused.

"Honey," said Eileen, noting the uncertainty on Tony's face, "It's the best damn fried chicken for a hundred miles. Is that what you want?"

"That sounds good," answered Tony. "Green beans and a Mr. Pibb to drink."

"How about you, dear?" she asked Sylvia, who seemed to be warming up to the old biddy.

"I'll have the brisket salad with blue cheese dressing and a Coke."

Eileen went off to bark the orders and grab the drinks. Her feet really did hurt. She had been working at Blake's Café for over twenty years. Blake was a fair boss. He had helped out a couple times when she had ended up in bed for some illness or another. Eileen had an older cantankerous sister in Albuquerque, who lived off a disability check, but moving down there would be a harder life than staying at Blake's.

"While we have a few moments before our waitress returns, can one of you clue me in?" demanded Nick. "What is this thing about Shelton Robertson? Your phone call was over the top."

"He's my uncle," said Sylvia without a drop of fondness in her voice. "He's a bastard. My dad was his brother, but Dad died. Uncle Shelton helped us out, but then he started raping me. I want to stick a dagger in his heart." Tony nudged her on the leg. The waitress was approaching with the drinks. Sylvia held her tongue but was raging inside.

Eileen told them their food would be ready in a few minutes, then left to again rest her feet.

"Vince told me there's an Ephemeral inside your uncle," said Nick. "It's a sister to someone named Overlord Draxis who apparently wants to fulfill the Ephemerals' newfound desires to be the universe's puppet-masters, starting with humans. Vince also said your uncle is funding terrorists and is a criminal bigger than Pearce Savage. I believe only half of what Vince tells me. It sounded like made-up bullshit to get me to do Ephemeral dirty work. They should be knocking off their own people."

"Paul basically told me the same thing," said Tony. "But he had no idea Sylvia was Robertson's niece. That's why my call with you was so fucked up. Sylvia and Paul were blasting me from two sides: one from two feet away and the other yelling at me from inside my head. Sylvia was hearing about her uncle's involvement and Paul was warning about humanity only having a few weeks before Robertson unleashes his traitorous acts. I couldn't take it."

Tony exhaled mightily. His woeful gray eyes met Sylvia's fierce gaze. "Sorry, Sylvia."

"We have to kill the bastard," said Sylvia resolutely. "I'll do it myself. I can get close to him. I can pretend like I'm like the lost child needing to get back home to Daddy. Then I'll jam a butter knife through his throat."

Tony again nudged Sylvia's leg. The waitress was returning with the plates. No one needed to overhear the murderous talk. Sylvia having buried so much for so long, and now on the edge of telling of her pain, was again cut short.

"Here's your *friiied* chicken, young man," drawled Eileen. "Brisket salad for you, young lady, with blue cheese dressing. And for the big guy, the biggest and best tenderloin sandwich in Kansas. Potato salad and tomato slices on the side. Does anybody need anything else, maybe a refill?" They declined.

Blake Café's country fried pork tenderloin was a sight to behold. It was huge. The bun looked like it had been improperly miniaturized. Nick grabbed the monster, took a huge bite, and felt like he was in heaven.

Tony and Sylvia sat nibbling at their food, no doubt lost in their internal troubles.

Nick knew Sylvia wanted him to say the magic words: *let's go kill Shelton Robertson.* But it wasn't that simple. And even if the guy deserved it, and if Nick was convinced to get involved, he wasn't sure how this would play out. Killing a billionaire often made the authorities take extra notice.

Add in the shadow of Overlord Draxis spreading his quantum tentacles of domination, it didn't make for good odds.

"You need to eat something," Nick coaxed. "Sylvia, I know you're angry; I know you're hurting. I'm not going to pretend I know how you feel or that I can understand what you went through. I can't. But you have to know, I want to help you; I want to help you both. As weak as it may sound to you now, you need to get some food in your stomachs. Sooner or later, you'll crash, then you'll be no good to yourselves or to me. And, if you don't eat, our salty waitress is sure to come back to ask why. We don't need her spreading stories of the strange interstate visitors that ordered meals but never touched a bite."

With the waitress returning to rest her feet, Sylvia said quietly but with an evident edge to her voice, "I'm more than angry; I'm seething. I know you're right, Nick, that we have to think this thing through, but it's a lot to take in. I've spent years trying to bury those memories. What are Paul and Vince doing on their side? Are they just leaving it for us to do the dirty work against my uncle? Maybe some interstellar cooperation could take down a couple cosmic shitholes."

"They likely can't do much directly against your uncle, only the escaping Ephemeral if your uncle dies."

In between mouthfuls, the three threw ideas back and forth. No one said the words, "let's suppose Nick agrees to this." The words were unspoken, but Nick wasn't saying no, so Sylvia and Tony were assuming he was agreeing.

"Sylvia, would you really want to be bait?" challenged Nick. "Why would Shelton even bite? You have rejected and ignored him for years. Have you ever told him to fuck off? Have you ever told him how much you hate him? He might remember that," added Nick pointedly.

Sylvia squirmed and squeezed her fists open and shut. She admitted to herself that she had told her uncle those things. Shelton had even once tried to reach out to her through Pearce Savage relaying a message of reconciliation. Her response had been very clear. Pearce should tell Shelton to stick it and spin.

Nick saw the answers on her face. So did Tony.

"Can we make it look like an accidental meeting?" asked Tony. "If we could get an idea where Shelton will be, we could put Sylvia there, too. It could be a surprise encounter; tense, awkward, not friendly. Maybe Sylvia could play with that." He sucked down the last of his Mr. Pibb.

"That could give us an opening," affirmed Nick, mulling over his brother's worthy idea.

"I can do that," said Sylvia bravely, even though, she was simply saying the words. She hoped she would be brave enough to meet Shelton face-to-face without immediately attacking him.

"Want a refill on that Mr. Pibb?" called Eileen from a counter stool, doing her best to rest her feet.

"Sure," answered Tony.

Nick gave his brother a look—*dummy, we don't need her coming over again.*

"What!?" responded Tony, pushing back. "She sees my glass is empty. You don't want me to appear odd, do you?"

"Here you are, honey," said Eileen bringing a fresh, full glass of Mr. Pibb. "Anybody else want a refill?" The others declined. Eileen returned to her perch at the counter.

"How do we find out where he'll be?" asked Sylvia, continuing to fidget.

"From what Vince said, Robertson will be hosting a charity event. I assume there's been a splashy marketing announcement. Time and place should be easy to determine, but what will be harder is getting us into that space. You know I hate this kind of plan. It's all improvisation. It will be dangerous.

"Sylvia, it will be hard to see him. You will need to dig deep. You'll want to kill him and run at the same time, but you can't. There has to be fire in your eyes. Somehow, you have to hang in there, hold his gaze. He's going to be examining your face, picturing you as young and vulnerable. But he'll know how much you said you hate him. At the same time, he still desires you. If you don't run away, he will be pulled to you, thinking he can conquer you again. Your emotions will show through. Your emotions will make it true in his mind."

Nick didn't ask Sylvia if she could do it. He didn't ask if she was prepared. None of them, not even Sylvia, knew if she could do it. If Sylvia fell apart under the moment, it would be the most human of reactions.

Nick pulled out his phone and started an online search: *Shelton Robertson* and *upcoming charity event*. His internet searched identified news articles pointing to Colorado's Mile High Stadium in five days.

Five days was easily enough time to get there from Salina, Kansas, but the problem was penetrating the facility's privacy measures and Shelton's own protective ring. Also, what method could he use? The hunting bow was still in his car. That was out, though the visuals in Nick's mind were dramatic.

Nick visualized himself walking to a balcony's edge with people glamorously milling about, entertained by this man with a bow and arrows slung over his shoulder and dressed in a tuxedo, sharing a slight smile at everyone he passed. He envisioned the fashionably dressed attendees parting like waters.

He visualized what the balcony crowd would think: *what incredible entertainment.*

At the balcony's railing, he would scan for his target, Shelton Robertson. Sylvia would be standing below a few feet from her abuser, capturing her uncle's attention. Shelton's protective agents would see Shelton's gaze fixate on the stunning woman. It would divert the bodyguard's attention to Sylvia as the agent sized her up.

Nick, having his window of opportunity, would notch his bow with an arrow, aim, and fire a hog-killing, razor-tipped arrow through the human pig, Shelton Robertson. Imagining the scene, he felt a surge of retribution course through his blood.

"Nick? Nick? What are you thinking about? You seem lost in space," said Tony.

"Oh, sorry. Just running things over in my mind."

"Did you come up with an idea?" continued Tony.

"Thallium," said Nick.

"Thallium? What's that? How would that work?" asked Tony.

"It could be slipped into his drink. A very small amount would profoundly mess him up. He'll experience severe abdominal pain, cramping, vomiting, and diarrhea during the first six hours. A couple days later, other symptoms will develop such as intense nervous system pain. He'll likely have difficulty walking and experience severe muscle cramps throughout his body; his major organs will eventually fail. Such poisonings in the US are very rare, so even his doctors are unlikely to understand what's happening."

"It might not kill him?" asked Sylvia, not liking the idea Robertson might live.

"It will likely kill him, but if it doesn't, his remaining life will be a torture. Thallium is tasteless and odorless; it's highly toxic to even touch it."

"Do you expect me to slip it in his drink?" asked Sylvia. "I hate him, but I'm not looking to commit suicide. What if the thallium touches me?"

"I'm working on some ideas."

"But will it be enough to expel the Ephemeral?" asked Tony, now more thoughtful than he had been in days.

"Not sure, but it sure won't help the Ephemeral's cause or Overlord Draxis's plan. Robertson will be out of commission. Since he's apparently important to the Overlord's plans, this could be enough to help Vince and Paul to advance their plans on Ephemeron."

"What are their plans?" pressed Tony. "They've never really said beyond wanting us to get rid of Robertson."

"It's a good question, brother. Try to press Paul. I'll work on Vince. In the meantime, you two hit the road. Get us a couple rooms in Denver. I'll catch up later. I need to do some online research." He raised a hand toward Eileen for the check.

24

Over time, he learned that his power was greater
when he became more than a throne of retribution.

Despite all the unknowns that would spiral from Nick's decision to go to Denver, for Vince and Paul, it felt like a first victory. For the Ephemeral rebels, it was enough to keep them hopeful into the next day and believe that the many foreboding days ahead would be worth the fight.

Inside a war, it isn't easy to understand whether one battle is the key turning point. Surely many generals have been left crestfallen at losses, or when faced with a worse scenario; when a battle was won but had little meaning. And, if a general couldn't determine a battle's true impact, how could a frontline soldier know?

Maybe those soldiers would never know because they would die in a few days in another day's battle. Maybe they would never know because only future historians would be able to understand the moment's significance.

Because of their entanglements, Vince and Paul were privy to the evolving plan to kill Sylvia's uncle. A few others were also part of the unfolding, hidden machinations to decide who would be the future ruler of Ephemeron. Vimegan clan's sub-commander Vre and Vimegan's spymaster were charting their clandestine involvement.

And there was the old king, perceived as weak and vulnerable, though in fact, greatly aware of the many threads of subterfuge crisscrossing his kingdom.

This day, King Boolong, ruler of the Omegan clan and king of all Ephemeron, endured listening to his advisors tell of the citizenry's growing disdain for the kingdom's self-indulgent Omegan royalty. He had heard this complaint many times. Patiently, he nodded to their revelations and repetitions.

Patience was a hard lesson that he had had to learn. As a young king, he hastily reacted against disobedience. He had wanted to ensure there was no doubt he was king and that he would exercise his powers. Violators faced consequences.

Over time, he learned that his power was greater when he became more than a throne of retribution.

The king swept away the prattling complaints of his advisors. He was interested in the report of his spies. With the approach of the Ascension, King Boolong expected the positionings, the plots, and clandestine manipulations. It was an Ephemeral competition that had repeated itself for many millennia. Yet, King Boolong knew the upcoming Selection was different than what had ever occurred. The provocative words of Overlord Draxis and Commander Vaaruv had taken hold. Ephemerals embraced the idea that they had Divine Rights over life-forms across the universe.

The words of the two warlords entranced Ephemerals with tantalizing dreams and obscured the many years of peace and prosperity that the king had brought upon his people. The citizenry's wavering appreciation for their king was the disfigured crown he was willing to wear. As often before, his enemies underestimated him.

Given his age, King Boolong would be handing off his authority to a young Omegan prince. Whether that authority would be as the new king over all of Ephemeron, or whether it would be simply over the Omegan clan, only Ephemeron's upcoming Selection would reveal. When King Boolong suspended the betrothal between Vince and heir-apparent Paul, it was whispered that the king did it out of necessity to appease Overlord Draxis.

The king endured these perceptions of weakness. He used the betrothal suspension as bait for Draxis to feel emboldened and to be reckless. The king knew about the involvement of Paul and Vince with the humans. He knew of Ephemeron's underground rebellion that had grown and taken hold. To his own ends, King Boolong intended to leverage these crosscurrents of passions and desires. It would serve the king's grander plan to ensure that his clan would retain the monarchy.

King Boolong understood that a particularly delicate negotiation with Commander Vaaruv of the Vimegan clan would be needed. Even though both the Vimegan and the Xermegan clans had been championing the idea of actively manipulating other life-forms, the king thought the concept flawed. Throughout Ephemeron's history, each time it had militarized its engagements with other species, drastic repercussions had befallen Ephemerals.

The king's advisors, learning of the king's desire to set up a meeting with Commander Vaaruv, cautioned against it, saying the differences between Vaaruv and Draxis were nothing more than minor differences. The Vimegan clan merely couched their aspirations to physically manipulate other life-forms within a "cooperative" framework, while the Xermegan clan unashamedly promoted the subjugation of alien species.

But for King Boolong, it was enough of a difference to chance a rapprochement with Commander Vaaruv. There was a long history of hatred and jealously between Commander Vaaruv and Overlord Draxis. King Boolong had intentionally and surreptitiously emboldened

Draxis, calculating that as Draxis became more powerful, it would stoke Commander Vaaruv's concerns. As Draxis grew stronger, Vaaruv would appear to grow weaker. King Boolong intended to dangle a partnership between the Vimegan and Omegan clans.

Several choice rewards could be bestowed on a loyal ally. Of course, the king knew Commander Vaaruv also wanted to be king of Ephemeron, but King Boolong understood that the Vimegan clan was facing the greater jeopardy at the upcoming Selection, which would chart each clan's position for the next 1,000 years.

If Vaaruv felt at enough risk, then his best option would be to ally with the Omegan clan, or at least to tell his followers to vote their second choice for the Omegan clan. In exchange, King Boolong would respond with favorable allotments upon the Vimegan clan. There would be promises of several elevations to royal status for the Vimegan clan.

Perhaps the greatest enticement the king could offer would be a promise to provide greater support to the public devotional renewal of the many founding gods of Ephemeron, which the Vimegan clan had never abandoned.

The differences and animosity between the Vimegan and Xermegan clans revolved most upon this singular religious issue: Was there one singular god over all gods, as Xermegan Overlord Draxis was promoting? Or was Ephemeron's pantheon of multiple gods still to remain Ephemeron's custom?

A negotiation between the king and the commander was fraught with missteps. Each would be exposing their egos. Each would feel they deserved the kingdom and Selection by Ephemeron's citizenry. It was a negotiation that would set the structure of power for the next 1,000 years.

Cloaked behind the veil of a private dinner invitation, the negotiation would take place in-person between King Boolong and

Commander Vaaruv. The king knew such an invitation would not remain a secret, even though the invitation was hand-carried personally to the commander. The commander would surely let it be known.

Such news would spread through the official hallways and out to the streets, then winding like a gossip-worm into the ears of Draxis's advisors, who would warn about the implications.

Along this circuitous pathway of whispers and conjectures, the announcement of the king's dinner invitation to Commander Vaaruv reached the ears of sub-commander Vre and the head of Vimegan Intelligence. In a routine electronic conversation between the two, a particular phrase was uttered indicating that a *chance* quick meeting was needed.

As the only two Ephemerals to know of the Vimegan spy embedded within Overlord Draxis's sanctum, each had to prepare for what the other would say. There was no guarantee that each would see the answers the same way.

There would be little time in the staged meeting to reconcile differences. They could only rest on the foundation of their lifelong friendship to carry them through that moment.

There were hard questions to answer.

Do we divulge to Commander Vaaruv that we have a spy inside Draxis's chambers?

If we tell him, why have we not told him before this moment?

How much do we divulge about the spy?

Do we risk a catastrophic leak of the spy's existence?

If we don't tell the commander about the spy, what information can we reveal to him?

If we provide especially sensitive details of Draxis's plans, how do we explain its source?

Perhaps he will not ask how we obtained the information but hoping he will not ask is not how espionage is won ....

The upcoming thought-filled nights of Sub-commander Vre and the head of Vimegan Intelligence were to be restless hours of analysis and deep qualms.

The *chance* meeting between the two spymasters happened at a fashionable and popular Foxcovvy shop. Foxcovvy was a favorite beverage of Ephemerals, drunk day or night. Its stimulant properties would draw friends and aficionados together on "fox-hopping" quests for the perfect blend.

The sub-commander arrived a bit early, ordered, and found a table.

The head of Vimegan Intelligence arrived shortly afterward, ordered, and was prepared to leave when he *noticed* Vre, who waved to his friend to come over. There were the perfunctory greetings and queries about families and such.

Eventually, the head of Vimegan Intelligence sat down at Sub-Commander Vre's table, using a chair next to his friend rather than sitting across the table.

Using whispers and the cover of nearby conversations, the friends engaged in a deeper conversation ....

Sub-commander Vre spoke softly, pretending to sip his drink. "Draxis is targeting Earth as the first critical step. His sleeper agents will be awakened within the month and encounters among humans will be provoked."

The head of Vimegan Intelligence maintained a casual expression, nodding a bit. "Yes. We have identified three agents, but we know there are more."

"We can't tell Commander Vaaruv of the spy's existence," suggested Vre.

"Agreed."

"Our sabotage of Draxis's plans needs the help of the humans. We must continue Vince and Paul's involvement," continued Vre.

"I can divert extra energy supplies to Vince and Paul. They won't know the source, nor will they care.

"How about the rebels?" asked Vre. "At the moment, their opposition is more of an asset than a liability. We can use their passions and organization to undercut Draxis."

"Agreed," responded the head of Intelligence. "Once we sabotage Draxis, we can deal with the rebels later. For now, our objectives are aligned."

"One other thing. It is critical that the human Nick disrupts the Callum-Pearce Savage entanglement before the end of the month. This human is stubborn and headstrong. His plan is to execute his vengeance against Savage's henchmen before going after Savage. We need to provide Nick with help locating Tubby Vaughn so he can get to Savage sooner."

"That still leaves the problem of how to attack the other sleeper agents. They live in different countries. The three humans do not have access to those foreign agents."

"I believe this issue is where our efforts align with the rebels."

"Yes. Their plan is dangerous. They will need our assistance."

Ending their *accidental* encounter, each wished the other well. They let their voices be heard.

"My old friend, it was so good seeing you here," said Sub commander Vre. "Give my best to your family. Tell your young ones I owe them a day flying the updrafts of Mount Treml."

"Oh, they will love hearing that, old friend. Maybe our families could spend a couple days together. The adults will relax. You can watch over the kids." The two laughed at the joke.

These were serious men, but families always brought forth a softer side of their nature. Six hundred-plus years of friendship added to its steadfastness.

The head of Intelligence rose, gave his friend a smile, then turned to his security detail. The features of his face instantly reshaped as he reentered his stern and ever-vigilant life.

Exiting the Foxcovvy shop, the head of Vimegan Intelligence and his hand-picked confidantes flew off into the Ephemeral day. The synchronous buzz of their phalanx confirmed their status.

25

*Soap took off the grime, but the demons of Nick's mind
made him feel like he was irreversibly tattooed with a deeper stain.*

On Earth, driving north toward Denver, Sylvia drove fast as usual, pushing the limits of what a police officer would accept. Along the way, Tony had found reasonable hotel accommodations. No haunted rooms were mentioned.

For whatever reason, Paul had not intruded since their departure from Blake's Cafe. Tony was tempted to call upon Paul, but resisted. The silence was golden.

Upon their arrival into Denver, they checked in at their hotel, located a nearby liquor store, then found a bar to kill time.

Nick was an hour behind. He had stayed in the Salina area while he checked online for questions that he needed answering. Later, upon entering Denver, Nick veered from the interstate and coasted his car slowly down a few back streets. He made a couple loops around an unpoliced area he thought looked promising.

At the head of one alley, a man approached Nick's car. Nick lowered the window slightly.

"Looking to get a buzz, man?"

"Yeah. That would be good," responded Nick. "Looking for some speed, preferably Addys, some weed, and one exotic item."

"No problem. How much you lookin' for? I got all sorts of exotics, too."

"Ten 20mg Addys, and a half-ounce of weed. But you'll need to do some digging for the exotic. I'll make it worth your while."

The dealer sized up Nick, and calculated the higher profit from the unspoken exotic.

"Two hundred for the Addys and weed. It's primo weed, mon, and a better price than the dispensary."

Nick checked the dealer's drugs. The tablets were imprinted with the markings "AD" and "20." He opened the bag of pot, smelled it, felt it, and took a small sample to chew on. It was primo, like the guy promised, and it implied the dealer had solid contacts.

Nick pulled out a cash roll and gave the guy $200.

"What's your special exotic?"

"Do you know any chemists? I need a substance called thallium. It needs to be handled carefully."

"Thallium? Never heard of the shit. You smoke it or inject it?"

Nick gave out a small laugh. "No offense. It's not that kind of thing. Just find a chemist that could use some extra cash. I'll give you a hundred bucks just to hook me up. It'll be all profit for you."

"Three hundred," responded the dealer.

"I'll give you two hundred, but only at the hookup if he confirms he can get it," responded Nick.

The dealer sized him up. "Okay, two hundred. Come by tomorrow night. You said thallium, right?"

"Yeah. Tomorrow night, then." Nick drove off, telling himself he should soon get a different car. He headed for the hotel.

At the hotel desk, a key was waiting. Tony had set him up.

Tony and Sylvia had 206, and Nick was in room 204. He appreciated the flashback touch. Right now he wanted a shower and some rest.

In his room, he noticed an ice bucket full of ice and three cold beers sticking out. Nick knew this was not that kind of hotel, so figured it was Sylvia's handiwork. He opened one bottle, downed half, shed his clothes, and started the shower. The hot water felt invigorating and he let it run hard over his neck and chest. Soap took off the grime, but the demons of Nick's mind made him feel like he was irreversibly tattooed with a deeper stain.

He knew he would forever see the dying images of Pearce Savage's henchmen. Their death were justified but that knowledge wasn't enough to erase the memories.

Exiting the shower, he examined himself in the mirror. Red welts gave witness to the former bullet wounds. Looking now in the mirror, a tough, middle-aged, walking-dead man stared back from the mirror.

Nick grabbed a second beer and guzzled most of it in a quick set of gulps. He propped himself on the bed and texted Tony and Sylvia that he was going to catch a few winks. Tony and Sylvia decided to go to dinner and let Nick sleep.

He laid down, still wrapped in the towel. He pulled a corner of the bedding over his shoulders and quickly fell into a deep slumber.

Sometime later, when the hotel room's phone rang, Nick was so deeply asleep that the noise was confusing. Barely half-awake, he was trying to answer the harsh ringing, but his arm seemed paralyzed from grabbing it. Finally fighting his way out of the dream's layers, he woke enough to grasp his surroundings.

Almost dropping the phone's handset, he cursed the device and groggily told his brother he was fine and would be over to their room shortly. He struggled to his feet, spotted his cell phone on a nearby table and picked it up. The battery was dead, which explained why Tony had called on the hotel phone.

When Nick knocked on the door for room 206, Sylvia opened the door, holding her phone to her ear while talking. She gave Nick a big smile and an air-kiss while beckoning him in.

Nick caught part of her conversation. Sylvia was promising an extra-large gratuity to schedule a last-minute appointment for a facial, hair styling, and nails.

She completed her phone call. "Well, boys, you'll need to be on your own today. I'm going shopping for clothes. You need to do the same. Make sure it's high-end attire."

"Sure, honey. We got it covered."

Sylvia opened a small bag that was lying on a nearby table. "Do you guys need any of these?" she asked, pulling out a handful of pre-paid cash cards.

Nick laughed.

"I learned a few tricks working for Pearce Savage," explained Sylvia.

"We also have some hidden bank accounts," added Tony. "Sylvia was the mastermind of that idea. Honey, I've got cards."

"All right then. I'll see you boys later. I have some major shopping to do." She smooched a couple more air-kisses and quickly exited.

Shelton Robertson's charity event was a high-end cocktail extravaganza for 500 dear, fawning friends who would be there to consort with each other and show themselves off. Being in the shadow of billionaire Shelton Robertson made them feel more special. They would say his name with a touch of awe and hoped he would shower their lives with his favor.

Sylvia never could fathom how so much power had congregated into this one person. Had he wrought abuses on others? She had little doubt.

In a few days' time, she would meet him as the woman she had become. Unbowed. Stunning. Strong.

Sylvia didn't know if today would be one of her last days alive. She didn't know if she would have the strength to face down her rapist. But at this moment, believing she could stand up to the fear was liberating.

She was proud of how she had learned a few criminal tricks to steal money for herself. It was going to provide her with a big shopping day. After visiting three stores, she chose an A-line V-neck asymmetrical chiffon cocktail dress with ruffled lace in the color of a stormy summer sky. She added a bejeweled evening clutch purse to match.

For footwear, she selected high-heeled, gold, gladiator-style sandals that accentuated her long, slender legs. Carting the new clothing helped keep her mind off reimagining her uncle entering her teenage room. Walking by a jewelry shop, its temptations beckoned. She ducked in and bought a pair of blue sapphire and diamond linear drop earrings. For a bracelet, she chose an 18K gold and diamond-studded bracelet. Her goal was to stun her uncle, showing that she had emerged from his darkness. It was certainly not meant as a value-conscious purchase.

Tomorrow, Sylvia would round out her transformation with her scheduled beauty services.

Carting the loot of an exhilarated shopping day, Sylvia spotted a Spanish restaurant's outside table. When seated, she ordered a mojito and mixed-platter of tapas. Her countenance hid the emotions and memories flooding her thoughts.

It had been a long time since Sylvia had let her childhood memories surface. She knew she was scarred. She had mostly kept the memories of her uncle's assaults buried deep. It wasn't that she wanted to forget but thinking about her uncle only reawakened the pain, almost like he was raping her again. In three short days, the chance to turn that pain back on him would be in her grasp. She closed her eyes as she let the sun spread its warmth.

She let herself imagine jabbing a knife into his heart or unloading a clip of ammo into her uncle. He would be dead. She would be alive even if she ended up imprisoned but wondered if that outcome would be a new imprisonment caused by her uncle. In the end she told herself imprisoning herself by her own hands and being imprisoned by her uncle would be two very different imprisonments. Sylvia ordered a second mojito. She only ate half of the tapas platter.

Upon returning to the hotel, Sylvia found Tony and Nick together in room 206. They had completed their shopping hours ago, buying suits, socks, shoes, watches, and even got haircuts. Tony had a neatly trimmed beard. Nick was clean-shaven. They were amused by Sylvia's arms full of loot. But Sylvia was the most amused by the men in the hotel room.

The two redheaded twins looked dashing despite their casual attire. The guys were wearing their new shiny shoes with thick white socks. In stark contrast, their lounge-around pants and shirts were disheveled. The TV was tuned to a sporting event. The boys were drinking beer.

"You guys look like jerks," she said with a laugh. They took the joke in stride, clicked their bottles together as if to say *plan accomplished.*

"Want one?" asked Tony raising up his bottle as a temptation.

"Definitely."

He reached over to the cooler and lifted an ice-cold beer, dripping with condensation. He took off the top and handed it to her. She plopped down beside him, taking a healthy guzzle.

"What's with the white socks?"

"Putting them on and walking around helps to break in new shoes," explained Nick.

"Seriously?

"Seriously, you should try it."

"I know these shoes will kill me first time out." Tony threw her a pair of white cotton socks. "Okay, what the hell. I'll give it a try."

She laughed but slipped on the white socks and then the high-heeled golden gladiator sandals. She pranced about the room, swaying to a little dance in her head. She plopped down next to Tony, draping a leg over his.

"You look like you enjoyed your day," said Tony.

"I did. It was cathartic." She took another swig. "At least I'll go out with flare," she said stoically.

"That won't happen," said Nick. "We're going to take Robertson down. And the three of us will walk away. Count on it."

"Last we discussed this plan, nothing was really settled," noted Sylvia. "Isn't there a chance I might end up poisoning myself with thallium at the same time I am trying to poison my uncle? Do you have an update to *that* plan?"

"I do. We're still going to poison him, but you won't need to get near the stuff. We're going to squirt it into his car with a syringe. When he leaves the event, it will contact his skin and be absorbed. He'll experience all the symptoms on his way home."

"Shit, Nick. That is diabolical." Sylvia pursed her lips.

"Tony will create a little distraction in the parking lot. I'll take care of the rest."

Sylvia took a long draw of her beer. All the decades of pains she had lived with seemed ready to be assuaged. Stabbing her uncle through the heart would have been deserved, but this thallium plan felt like justice.

"Have either of you heard from our Ephemeral friends?" inquired Sylvia.

"Nothing," answered Nick. "It's rather surprising. Since we're in Denver like they wanted, I assumed they would be trying to give us detailed guidance, if you know what I mean."

"It seemed like they didn't have much of a plan, either," stated Tony. "I would have expected more from someone who can leapfrog across the universe."

"Have you ever wondered what their world is like?" asked Sylvia.

"Vince told me Ephemerons are a religious people. They select their monarchy every 1,000 years and they have the sex life of a pollenating plant," responded Nick.

"We know they want to dominate our planet," added Tony. "In fact, they want to dominate all the other species of the universe."

"What I question," posed Sylvia, "is whether their entanglements are because *they need to*, or whether it's because they simply *want to*."

"Does it fucking matter?" said Nick. "Either way, humanity gets the short end of the stick."

Considering, Sylvia took a long draw on her beer. "I don't know. It might matter."

*For the rebels, their choices were shaping up
like a complicated chess board.*

That evening Nick returned to the alley to meet the drug
dealer.

He cruised by, but no one approached his car. Maybe the guy was
sizing him up, so Nick took the car around the block to make another
pass. This time, the guy emerged from the alley. Nick stopped and
partially lowered the passenger side's window.

"Hey, mon," said the dealer. "I found your chemist."

"All right. Where is he?"

"Where's my money?"

Nick pulled out two one-hundred-dollar bills and fanned them
open so the dealer could see. "You get this after I know I can get my
product," said Nick.

"Pull into the garage up ahead. We'll meet on the top floor."

Nick had to wait a few minutes before the dealer and chemist
appeared, but he spotted them in his side mirror. He put on a pair of
disposable gloves before he exited the car, sizing it all up. The scene
looked good. As the chemist and dealer approached, Nick could see the
nervousness on the chemist's face. That was another good sign.

Nick spoke first to establish control over the moment. "You're the chemist?"

"Yes."

"Do you have the thallium?"

"Yes. I brought a vial. This stuff is dangerous. You know that?" The chemist pulled out a small vial. His stress was obvious.

"I know. How much?"

"A thousand dollars."

Nick laughed. "I may want the stuff, but I can find someone else. I'm not in that much of a hurry."

"It's 5N concentration."

"Six hundred," responded Nick. He pulled out a wad of bills and counted out six Benjamins. The chemist paused. Nick was a foreboding man. The chemist wasn't used to this kind of thing.

"Should we test a drop?" asked Nick seriously.

"NO!" exclaimed the chemist with his eyes registering fear. "Okay, six hundred," and shakily handed the vial to Nick.

Nick gave him the cash and handed the two-hundred-dollar finder's fee to the dealer.

"You know where to find me if you got any more special requests," offered the dealer.

"Yeah," said Nick.

The dealer and chemist disappeared into the shadows. Nick carefully placed the vial into a tight-closing plastic box. There was padding inside. He snapped the lid closed. This was a package that needed to be treated with respect.

The next day, Nick had Tony take him to a used car lot. Nick used the same old string-him-along approach until he walked out with a new used car. It was a silver 2012 Corolla, with a little over 57,000 miles on it. Given the car model's history of durability, it was practically a youngster. He had paid cash.

Nick reminded himself to check on his remaining false IDs. The cars, especially, were a weak link. Plates had to be tampered with. He usually used a razor knife to remove a current year tag from some car's plate sitting in a parking garage. It wasn't that difficult to glue it to his own vehicle. It would last long enough and make the plate look proper. He figured he would dump the Honda on a dark street. If it got stripped or jacked, it didn't matter too much.

Six henchmen had been on Nick's target list plus Pearce Savage. Five henchmen were dead, leaving one to deal with before Savage. But the retribution was being pulled sideways by this Robertson affair. When authorities or some medical examiner finally realized Robertson's death was murder, a lot of heat would be unleashed.

However deep Nick peered down the tunnel of future days, there was no light ahead. He told himself he had to keep moving forward, trust in his skills, and show as much bravery as he could muster. Nick knew the unstoppable train of law enforcement was approaching from behind, squeezing out the remaining time for him to reach the end of his mission.

He knew enough from his war experience that a soldier went ahead each day, not knowing if he would be given the luck to make it to the finish.

Nick and Tony had reconnected after too many lost years. Sylvia had become family. Maybe none would see his or her way all the way through, but somehow, at this moment, even failure was worth it. Nick told himself that they were fighting the good fight.

On Ephemeron, Mr. Coco had been casually approached by a messenger clandestinely sent by the head of Vimegan Intelligence.

The messenger stopped in front of Mr. Coco and shuffled the packages in his arms, but one fell at their feet. Graciously, Mr. Coco leaned over and picked up the fallen package. As the package was being returned to the messenger, a piece of paper was stealthily placed into Mr. Coco's hand. Mr. Coco didn't know what it was but slipped it into a pocket to view later.

He was surprised to see, when he had time to examine the paper, it identified three additional Ephemeral sleeper agents, the names of the entangled humans, and their Earthly locations.

For the rebels, their choices were shaping up like a complicated chess board. With the identification of three more Draxis sleeper agents and their human hosts, one option was to try to again disrupt the E-station entanglements, similar to the trap they set for the Shelton Robertson entanglement. Yet, all the newly-identified sleeper agents were overseas in foreign lands where Nick and company would have no opportunity to intervene.

Most importantly, nothing could be implemented until after Shelton Robertson was dealt with. It had taken over six months of subterfuge and a bit of luck to access the E-station that supported Shelton Robertson's entanglement. If killed or severely damaged, his entangled Ephemeral, Maxxerna, sister to Overlord Draxis, would need to find a new host. The rebel's alteration of E-station software safety coding would reduce Maxxerna's VIP entanglement status to low priority and add a pause-cycle before searching for a replacement entanglement. Breaching Shelton Robertson's entanglement would likely be a one-off strike. Afterward, the remaining sleeper agents would be on guard and additional security would surely be put in place.

There were a lot of things that could go wrong. In the face of the many difficulties to again penetrate the VIP E-station security system, a second option had been circulating among the rebels—an insane option.

But as insane as the second option was, it had remained on the table, never being completely dismissed: Use E-stations to reveal to humans their entanglements with Ephemerals.

For the average Ephemeral, it had been nice and easy sitting within the safe confines of an E-station while casually reaching out across the universe to milk someone else's emotions, maybe even intentionally stirring up emotions as well. Though quantum entanglements were bidirectional by nature, Ephemeral scientists had discovered mechanisms to cloak the entanglements from the "recipient" species. Only Ephemerals were aware of the entanglements. Revealing the entanglement to humans was insane because it would be leaking details to humans of the existence of entanglements. It would give humans a frightening new technology.

The rebels' reasoning behind this madness would be to intentionally send Ephemeron into a worldwide panic that would torpedo Draxis's mad plans by stoking Ephemerals' fear of themselves being manipulated.

The downside? It would put all of Ephemeron at risk. Humans, not a peaceful species, would want to execute vengeance against Ephemeron. It would surely bring home great horrors.

Such a scenario would force the rebels to roll a dangerous pair of dice, threatening their own planet and families on the hope that Draxis's plans would be sabotaged, and the resulting chaos could be adequately contained.

Mr. Coco sent out a call for a meeting of the rebel leaders.

27

A puzzled look crossed Mr. Coco's face.
His mandibles clapped open and shut nervously.
"Ms. Bovemont, what are you saying?"

On Ephemeron, it was a weekend evening. A cacophony of buzzing Ephemerals filled the city's markets, restaurants, and skies. At a restaurant's outside table, tucked away in the back, five rebel leaders congregated together, pretending as best they could to remain relaxed and calm.

Mr. Coco told them of the recent message he had received revealing the identity of three more sleeper agent Ephemerals and the humans they inhabited.

"Could it be a trap to force us into the open?" asked Mr. Traxx.

"Maybe it is a trap. It didn't feel like it," responded Mr. Coco. "Curiously, Vince and Paul's E-stations have unexpectedly been allocated extra energy packets. I don't know if that really answers the question, but the coincidence is notable."

"We don't have time to *cautiously* penetrate the sleeper agents' E-stations," said Mr. Yelty. "It was extremely difficult to penetrate the E-station security system to sabotage the Robertson entanglement. The risk is too high to set up an attack against three more. They are high-status Ephemerals."

"What about the reverse-entanglement option?" asked Mr. Coco.

Mr. Coco's question was the unfathomable idea that somehow remained under consideration. A long silence followed.

"Revealing the reverse-entanglement channel is strictly prohibited. Wouldn't that set off all sorts of alarms?" objected Mr. Traxx.

"The reverse-entanglement alarm systems have been neglected for thousands of years," countered Mr. Coco. "There's never been a reverse-entanglement failure over many millennia. No maintenance funds are even spent keeping those alarms systems current. It could well be that our technicians can breach those systems."

"Even if we could uncloak the reverse-channels, who here has any experience managing such a thing?" asked Mr. Yelty.

"I quake at the thought of us even succeeding," said Mr. Traxx. "Trying to implement the technique without experience seems haphazard for a variety of reasons. Who would we plan on entangling into Ephemeron from Earth? At this point we only have two real choices —Nick and Tony. Without preparation, anybody else that we randomly grabbed would likely go insane. It almost happened to Tony."

"That is exactly the shock that is needed," blurted Mr. Yelty, seemingly unconcerned by Mr. Traxx's misgivings. "Except for the VIP Ephemerals, most E-station entanglements are quite generic and use only basic security features. Do we know how many entanglements there are with humans? Many, many thousands, at least. Can you picture it? Thousands of Ephemerals suddenly realizing that the humans they have been playing with can now interfere with their Ephemeral lives."

"There may be many thousands of entanglements with humans, but it is doubtful we have the time to compromise that many stations," observed Mr. Coco. "We can probably penetrate a thousand at most."

"It will be enough," persisted Mr. Yelty. "Picture it—a thousand Ephemerals suddenly driven to the edge of madness. It will be an unimaginable terror for Ephemerals and humans. Emergency E-station protocols will kick in, severing the entanglements. Suddenly, scores of Ephemerals will have only hours to live as the systems desperately searches for new entanglements. The Draxis plan to make puppets out of the entangled humans will be shattered."

"Mr. Yelty, I can't believe I'm hearing the words you speak," challenged Mr. Traxx. "Ephemerals are our people. Many might die or go insane. Is this what we have become? Dealers of death by psychosis?"

"If we fail to derail Draxis," responded Mr. Yelty, "the trauma that you worry about will not be limited to just humans but will be unleashed across the universe's multitudes."

"Let us be clear what we're talking about," insisted Mr. Traxx. "Such a plan gives humans knowledge they've never had before. It will cause psychological trauma for both humans and Ephemerals, and finally, we risk the potential death of many Ephemerals because they cannot find new entanglements. Ephemeron blood will drip from our hands."

"And what happens if we do nothing?" persisted Mr. Yelty. "Or, what happens if we merely try to break into the systems supporting Draxis's agents that we know about, but we fail? We know repeating such VIP E-station penetrations will be next to impossible.

"If Draxis wins the Selection vote, his clan will Ascend to govern the world's monarchy and Overlord Draxis will become King Draxis. His clan will rule over Ephemeron for the next 1,000 years. Humans and other life-forms across the universe will be playthings for a sadistic monster. Think of those deaths."

The rebels fell into a somber quiet, an incongruence to the revelry swirling around them. Their silence was as obvious as a river's white-water evidence announcing hidden boulders—an anomaly that was catching the attention of the Watchers.

"Mr. Hyde and Ms. Bovemont, you have not said a word," observed Mr. Coco. "Do you have anything to add?"

"I have nothing to add," said Mr. Hyde.

"What of the two Earthlings?" asked Ms. Bovemont. "They may not be able to reach the other sleeper agents on Earth, but maybe they could strike against them here on Ephemeron."

A puzzled look crossed Mr. Coco's face. His mandibles clapped open and shut nervously. "Ms. Bovemont, what are you saying?"

"The Earthlings, Nick and Tony, are aware of our existence. They have ... *accommodated* to us. Well, maybe that is a liberal interpretation, but at least they have learned to carry on with their lives. And we know they hate us. What wouldn't they do to get us out of their heads and to free the rest of Earth's inhabited humans?"

"What would you think they could do on Ephemeron?" asked Mr. Hyde. His antennae vigorously rubbed against each other. His red eyes darted quickly toward The Watchers.

"Kill Draxis's Ephemeral sleeper agents," answered Ms. Bovemont coldly.

"On Ephemeron? That's outlandish," exclaimed Mr. Yelty.

"Is it? Hear me out. Nick and Tony are entangled with Vince and Paul. We know E-stations have the capacity to extend entanglements, essentially entangling more than one object at a time. Yes? And crucially, Vince and Paul are willing to stand against Draxis's plan."

Ms. Bovemont took a sip of her cocktail before continuing. "Using Vince and Paul's E-stations as conduits, we extend the entanglements to a couple of our drogs. With Nick and Tony entangled through Vince and Paul's E-station with drogs, they then will use the drogs to kill the sleeper agents here on Ephemeron. If the drogs are from Ephemeron's stables, no one will suspect the deception until it's too late."

Mr. Coco finished his drink with a robust slurp and raised an appendage to an onlooking waiter and drew a circle in the air to tell the waiter to bring a new round for all.

The rebels sat in silence, impatiently waiting for their drinks while the notions of drog-inhabited humans roaming about Ephemeron haunted their thoughts. When the waiter brought the rebels their new round, Mr. Traxx was tempted to tell the waiter to immediately bring another but stayed silent.

"Drogs are not allowed to roam freely," noted Mr. Yelty. "They would need handlers inside the city. And there is the problem of the third sleeper agent. We only have two humans we could use, Nick and Tony."

Ms. Bovemont took her time to answer. She used one of her appendages to waft the drink's fragrance across her olfactory sensors and took a long sip of the Ephemeron restaurant's psychedelic-infused cocktail. She could immediately feel the mild hallucinogenic effect.

"We will invite Sylvia to be inhabited. We will entangle her with one of the drogs."

Mr. Traxx almost spit out his drink. "That will never happen. The Earth woman would never agree. Ms. Bovemont, the idea is outlandish."

"Is it more insane than opening up the quantum entanglements between a thousand Ephemerals and Earthlings? I think Sylvia will stand by Nick and Tony. If they would be willing to help us here on Ephemeron, she won't abandon them. She will say yes."

"Why would Nick and Tony agree to such an idea?" asked Mr. Coco.

"We will offer to disentangle all Ephemerals from humans. To promise to leave humans alone."

"We don't have the authority to promise that," objected Mr. Coco.

"Maybe not at the moment, but the upcoming Selection will select a new monarch. King Boolong is too old to continue. His heir apparent is Paul. We know he is against Draxis's and Vaaruv's ideas of conquest and domination. Wouldn't he offer that promise? Wouldn't Nick and Tony take the gamble to rid themselves of the Ephemerals in their heads, let alone save the rest of humanity?"

"I definitely need another one of these," said Mr. Traxx, raising an appendage toward the waiter.

"An assassination of a Draxis agent by an Ephemeral would create a firestorm," said Mr. Hyde. "With the upcoming Selection so near, it could flip the Ephemerals' vote."

"Exactly," continued Ms. Bovemont. "Which is why the attack must look like an accidental drog attack."

"Entangling with drogs might be too much for the Earthlings to manage," said Mr. Yelty. "Drogs are fearsome creatures, even those housed in Ephemeron stables."

"Are we giving up on opening up our entanglements with humans?" quizzed Mr. Yelty.

"Not at all," continued Ms. Bovemont. "Uncloaking the reverse entanglements across a thousand humans and Ephemerals will provide cover for the drog attack."

"And how will we get the human-inhabited drogs next to the Draxis agents?" asked Mr. Hyde.

"The annual Crystal Moon Hunt is upcoming. It is common for the hunters to bring back their collections and parade them in front of the king, each clan's royalty, and the Ephemeral citizenry. If we open up the reverse entanglement channels at that time, bedlam will break out. The attack of the drogs will seem like an accident."

"No one can find out that the drogs were manipulated by humans," cautioned Mr. Coco.

"Will it matter?" responded Ms. Bovemont. "The entire affair will be blamed on the rebels. On us. The authorities will hunt us down with even more intensity, but the deed will have been done. Ephemerals will recoil at Draxis's plan, and at the same time, three of his key agents will have been killed."

Ms. Bovemont sucked down the rest of her psychedelic cocktail which caused her wings to shimmer with hues that hopscotched across the color spectrum.

"I will reach out to Vince and Paul," said Mr. Coco. "They will need to present this to the humans. Regardless of whether the three humans agree to this madness or not, we can still go forward with opening up of the reverse entanglements. It is time for us to vote.

"There are three options: One, do nothing for now. We wait. Two, we attempt to break into the Draxis agents' E-stations. Or three, proceed with a plan to reconfigure 1,000 E-stations to open up reverse entanglement channels with humans. And maybe with luck, we pull off the drog option. What say you?"

The Ephemeral rebel leaders answered Mr. Coco with unanimous beetle-like chirping sounds and acknowledging nods. Soon thereafter, they dispersed into the swirling crowd of their fellow insect citizenry.

During the next day's lunch break from their E-station work, Vince and Paul discussed Mr. Coco's pitch.

"Just thinking about the idea of having Tony rummaging around inside my head makes me feel like I'm being invaded," said Paul.

"I suppose that's how the humans feel," answered Vince. "We know what Nick is like. He has told me many times he wants to wring my neck. This would certainly be his chance. How can we trust them?"

"Tony feels the same, but can you see another way?"

"Not at the moment," said Vince. "For all the days and hours that I've prayed to our gods, I'm faced with the hollowness of my words. In the safety of my life, the prayers are easy to say. Our beliefs are easy to believe. Now, I am asked to put my life in the hands of a human that wants to kill me. This tests my faith."

"Your faith? Or your faith in a particular human?" prodded Paul.

"I think both. It's been easy being brave living behind our protective entanglements. What about you, Paul? You are royalty."

"I ask myself what I want for Ephemerals if I was king. I've searched for a new answer. Something that is unique, but each time I come back to the simplest of answers: peace. Yet, for all the beauty that lies within that word, it fails to give me the answers that I need.

"Will Ephemeron's citizens have the wisdom to spurn the Overlord's ideas of conquest? If Tony murders an Ephemeral sleeper agent, but it is done with my assistance, will this bring the peace I seek? Even though we work with the rebels to defeat the Overlord, how much can we trust them? Will I be next on their list? Will my nights be filled with dreams of blood that cannot be washed away? It seems there is no peaceful path to peace itself."

"The idea of extending their entanglements through our E-stations to inhabit drogs is wild."

"Do you think Nick and Tony will agree?" questioned Paul.

"It is a flip of a coin, as the Earthlings would say. And, there is the other question: what about Sylvia?"

"Isn't it more a question of what Sylvia wants to choose for herself? We know who three of the sleeper agents are. If Sylvia would agree to be entangled, she could get to the third agent."

"Who would she be entangled with?" queried Vince.

"Mr. Coco has promised a solution. That's all he said."

"The question is still before us. Do we put our fates in the hands of the three humans?"

"I will tell Mr. Coco we have agreed," said Paul. "Then we must speak to Nick and Tony."

28

Their eyes spoke in words
that would be inadequate to say.

On Earth, it was late afternoon of the Shelton Robertson charity extravaganza.

Tony pulled on a pair of variegated, medium blue calf-high socks, then donned a crisp pale light-blue cotton shirt. His suit was a trim dark blue, tight-woven lightweight wool. A pair of modern medium-brown oxfords and a Breitling Navitimer watch completed the rich, fashionable look. Looking in the mirror, a man of muscular physique and neatly trimmed beard stared back. He felt like his old self—confident. Waiting for Sylvia to finish her last touch-ups, he poured himself a shot of liquid courage with steady hands.

In room 204, Nick pulled on a pair of evergreen-colored socks. His two-piece light-weight woolen suit was almost black, but sported a hint of olive color. Wide-spaced checker-boarding accentuated the rich look of the fabric. He wore a crisp white shirt with a medium-width tie. Its expensive sheen hinted at green but was more boldly in the deep navy family with small polka dot accents.

His $400 two-toned oxfords sported a chiaro-green suede front vamp area and a palette of deep chestnut though the body of the shoe. He put on an 18-carat gold alligator-banded watch.

Nick transferred the vial of thallium to a compact container, which he put in his left suit pocket. He placed a syringe and needle in its case, then tucked the case in his breast pocket. He, too, took a shot of liquid courage and made his way to room 206.

At his knock, Sylvia opened the door of the room, looking stunning. She did a little twirl to show off her long chiffon dress and beamed a wonderful smile, then made a show of examining handsome Nick from head to toe. She leaned in and gave him a big hug. Tony stood behind her. They were ready.

Tony and Sylvia left a several minutes before Nick, careful to ensure a separate arrival. They made their way inside Mile High Stadium, accepting a canapé and a drink.

Nick drove to the event in the old Honda, fulfilling its last mission. He told the valet he would like to park his own car to have time to catch a smoke and stretch his legs a bit. The valet seemed thankful for the pass; a Bentley was next in line.

After a smoke, Nick started walking back. Shelton Robertson had just arrived, driving up in an Arancio orange Lamborghini STO Huracán sporting 631 horsepower of raw power. He parked in a reserved slot near the front of the parking area. Exiting the Lamborghini, Shelton Robertson was engulfed by attendants and those nearby wanting to be part of the growing entourage.

Nick stood back, surveying the scene. It had unfolded better than he expected. He had planned to use Tony as a distraction to get to Robertson's car, but the moment offered its own opportunity.

Slipping on a pair of disposable gloves, he lifted the small box from his left pocket and unveiled the thallium-laden bottle. He pulled the syringe and needle from its case, stuck it into the vial and suctioned the maximum amount the syringe could hold.

He walked forward, stopped at the car's side panel on the driver's side, shoved the syringe through the rubber weather stripping around the window, knowing such a miniscule penetration would not set off the security system, and squirted the liquid contents over the steering wheel and seat area.

With Robertson drawing all the attention, Nick walked toward the convention building and dumped the vial, syringe, and gloves into a trash receptacle.

Tony and Sylvia were inside, mingling without really mingling. Repeatedly, Tony was checking his phone for a text from his brother.

"Nothing?" asked Sylvia.

"No. He should be here by now. Maybe I should call him."

"Bad idea, Tony. Give him his space. He knows what he's doing."

As Robertson entered the building, the focus of the room changed. People's bodies and eyes shifted toward the billionaire. Their voices softened. A small security detail formed a protective circle around the billionaire, judiciously moving patrons from their boss's path.

In the billionaire's wake, Nick entered the building. He texted his brother: "I'm here. Where are you?"

Tony provided their location as Sylvia waved down a server.

She grabbed two drinks from a waiter and made the waiter pause, telling Tony these two were for her and if he wanted one, now's the time. Tony laughed, accompanied by an encouraging smile from the waiter, and then took a glass for himself.

"Quite the elegant affair," observed Nick. Tony and Sylvia turned, startled, not realizing he was near. Nick had approached them like a quiet whisper.

"Jesus, Nick. You creep up like a cat," said Tony. "Robertson is here. When do we make our move?"

"No need," said Nick. "It's already been done."

"Seriously, brother? You left me out?"

"It wasn't intentional. I was walking back from my car. Robertson drove up on his own. When he got out, people focused on him. The car was parked, wide open, in a reserved space in the lot. I walked up and did the deed."

"What about me?" asked Sylvia, also feeling left out.

"No change for you, my dear Sylvia," said Nick. "Whether you confronted him before I spiked his car or after makes no difference. In fact, isn't this better? You know the trap has already been set. You should confront him as you planned."

Sylvia finished off glass number one of the two she was holding, she placed the empty glass on a passing waiter's plate.

"Sylvia," said Nick. His voice was draped in care. "How are you planned to confront him? You never said exactly what you were going to do."

Sylvia had pictured many versions of this moment, but in truth, she had never fully resolved the question to herself.

In one version, she had seen herself loudly calling him out and reciting his travesties. In another version, she had seen herself simply appearing out from the crowd and standing strong in front of him, relishing the facial recognition that would contort across his face as her cold penetrating stare would surely let him know the devil and hell were waiting.

In a third version, she would stab him through the heart.

"We're here for a reason," said Tony. "It's not just to kill the man, but to let him know there is no escape from his past. Sylvia, we're here for you." Sylvia reached out and squeezed Tony's arm.

"Thanks, Tony." Taking a deep breath, she tossed her head and squared her shoulders. "It is time," slipped softly from her lips.

Despite all the doubts and fears swirling inside, Sylvia wasted little time.

She stepped forward into the crowd and through her past's pains, edging closer to her abuser until she was only ten feet from him. As the center of attention, her uncle was occupied by fawning adulations. There was a smile on Shelton Robertson's face that exuded great confidence.

Calmness fell over Sylvia. Patiently she waited, until that moment when his eyes hit upon hers. Recognition flared.

His eyes locked on her. *Sylvia? Young, little Sylvia?*

Their eyes spoke in words that would be inadequate to say.

Yes, it's me, you bastard.

Do you want me, my dear little Sylvia? You said you hated me. Have you come home to your Uncle Sheltie?

Sylvia's smile was colder than the Arctic. *Fuck you. I survived. You have no idea, Uncle, that this is your last day. Enjoy your empty moments. Curses upon you. You will see my face peering down on you during your last agonies. It will be my gift to you, you piece of shit.*

Sylvia raised her hand and gave him the middle finger and a knowing smile of his impending death. "Hell is waiting for you, Uncle."

Robertson laughed.

She turned and walked away, joining Tony and Nick. She told herself to stay calm, but she was shaking.

Nick had said he had sprayed thallium into her uncle's car, but doubts taunted her. Would thallium really cause him to suffer like he deserved? Maybe she should have stabbed him. Had she failed herself?

"He will die today, won't he?" asked Sylvia of Nick, her voice slightly trembling.

"Death today, I don't know. But agonizing pain, most surely," he reassured her.

"As long as he sees me in his mind in his final agonies."

Exiting the building, Nick told Tony to follow him. Sylvia was to drive the Jeep back to the hotel. Meanwhile, Nick and Tony drove to a section of the city with little lighting. Nick performed a cursory wipe of the steering wheel and surrounding area. He left the old Honda unlocked and keys on the seat. He took the old plates off the car to reuse, knowing it wasn't the best solution, but it would have to suffice. Tony drove them back to the hotel in Nick's Toyota.

The next morning, Nick checked out first, heading north in his newly obtained silver Toyota followed sometime later by Tony and Sylvia.

Normally, Nick would push the speed limit bubble, but today set his cruise control to only five miles over. It was going to take days to get to St. Paul. He hoped Tubby Vaughn was still in the city by the time he arrived.

"Vince, you around?" said Nick, somewhat missing his frenemy.

"I'm here."

"Don't you owe me something?" asked Nick.

"Sorry, but I don't know what you mean."

"A thank-you would be nice. I put Robertson out of commission. Tell me again who the Ephemeral was that inhabited him. Was that Ephemeral important?"

"We appreciate the help, Nick. Thank you. Sincerely."

"Somebody needs to teach you some manners."

"Nick, we're aliens. What the hell. That's what aliens do."

Nick chuckled. He kind of liked Vince's insolent humor.

"But to answer your question, the Ephemeral's name was Maxxerna. She was a favored sister to Draxis. At least, she *was* the favored sister.

Oddly, there was a malfunction as she tried escaping the dying Robertson. Last I heard, there was trouble establishing a new entanglement. It doesn't really matter. For Draxis, the key was keeping Maxxerna inside Robertson and using Maxxerna to stir up Robertson as necessary. With that option tied off and Robertson in serious shape, Draxis's day is turning sour."

"My, my," said Nick with heavy sarcasm, "that is very bad luck. You say Robertson is doing poorly?"

"They didn't find him until this morning. On his way home, he ran off the road. They found him outside his car balled up in pain."

Nick tried imagining what Robertson was experiencing. He would not know the details until later. News reports told of massive organ failure and numerous puzzled doctors.

It would take five days for Shelton Robertson to finally die: five days of brutal pain and agony. In his last moments, his mind would be filled with an image of Sylvia standing over him in her A-line, V-neck asymmetrical chiffon cocktail dress in the color of a stormy summer sky, wearing blue sapphire and diamond linear drop earrings, bejeweled with an 18K gold and diamond-studded bracelet … and giving him the middle finger. Her words, having been said in front of Robertson's adoring crowd, would echo in his mind: *Hell is waiting for you, Uncle.*

Vince's voice interrupted his thoughts. "Nick, three more Draxis sleeper agents have been identified that are inhabiting humans. The problem is that they are overseas and you don't speak the language there, among a variety of other complications."

"Good to hear. I've done my part. When will you and Paul be leaving … actually be leaving our bodies? It's time for you two and all your Ephemeral compatriots to go back to where you came from."

"Well, yes, about that …."

"Stop, Vince. I don't want to hear your avoidance and evasion. It's time for you people to leave."

"Nick, it doesn't work that way. Ephemerals have spent thousands of years building their outposts. Humanity is one. There are many others. Ephemeron monarchy and Management will not simply pack up and leave."

"What right do you have? Humans have never been a threat to Ephemerals. Despite all our technology, we didn't know you existed. You are millions of light-years away. You say you *passively* sit inside life-forms, merely harvesting our emotions. It is a lie you keep telling yourselves. You admit that many Ephemerals have tweaked the emotional outpourings of those they inhabit. Isn't Callum a perfect example? The bad-boy Ephemeral, of a privileged class, causing all sorts of disruptions and pranks, but is allowed to continue anyway. He endures a few naughty-boy reprimands, and all is forgotten."

"Wouldn't humans do the same? Have you ever been able to restrain your desires?"

"Fuck you, Vince."

"You may not like what I'm saying, but I'm telling you the same truth back at you. Maybe you're lying to yourself, too."

"This conversation isn't getting us anywhere. Let's just keep our thoughts to ourselves."

"Actually, you should hear what I have to say. I agree with you. Ephemerals should abandon outpost-humanity. I'll admit it's for different reasons than why you want it to happen, but it's the same outcome."

"I'm listening."

"Do you remember what you read about quantum entanglement? The part about what happens to one element instantly affects the other. It can happen in either direction. It's not a one-way street."

In his mind, Nick turned images over, visualizing the implications. If humans were entangled with Ephemerals, that would mean humans could shake up the lives of Ephemerals.

"Why haven't humans known we were entangled? Why haven't we caused problems for Ephemerals?"

"I don't want to get too technical, but as we began harnessing the power of QE, we discovered we could add a protective channel. In essence, it hides the existence of entanglement from the life-forms we inhabit. So, even though the entanglement goes both ways, if you are unaware that it's in place, you have no cause to manipulate the entanglement for your own service. The technology of our E-stations adds additional protection by restricting your possible impacts on us."

"You said you agree that Ephemerals should abandon their outpost on Earth. What did you mean by that?" asked Nick.

"I've told you that Overlord Draxis wants to use humanity as his demonstration project to show Ephemerals that actively manipulating other life-forms is the Ephemeral destiny and a gods-given right. Some on Ephemeron are opposed to this. They see monstrous consequences, but those voices are drowned out by the populist enthusiasm for conquest."

"Speaking of a sour day, that's how mine just turned. Why do you tell me this? I can't do anything about it. What can humanity do about it?"

"If the protective channel is removed, humans would be able to disrupt Ephemerals' lives. You could be the first humans to travel across the universe; at least your quantum projection. Just think. There might be a feature role in the offering for you. Same for Tony and Sylvia."

"You want to be more specific, Vince?"

"What if your self could be projected to Ephemeron by a reverse entanglement? All that rage you feel for us. All the times that you've wanted to wring my neck. It would be a chance for you to serve up those emotions directly upon Ephemeron. Same for Tony and Sylvia."

Schemes of payback ran through Nick's mind. "How would that happen? Us traveling to Ephemeron is insane. You realize that don't you? And why do you mention Sylvia? She's not entangled."

"We will talk later. Much is happening on Ephemeron that I must attend to."

"Wait!" But Vince did not answer. "Damn you, Vince."

29

"You will be born in strife, you will live in strife,
and you will die in strife."

Heading Northeast out of Denver on I-76 and miles behind Nick, Tony and Sylvia followed.

Tony was driving. He, too, had set cruise control to five miles over the speed limit.

Sylvia had pulled out the sapphire and diamond earrings from her purse. She fondled them almost as if they were prayer beads helping her work through the many memories of her life, some being the dark painful abusive times her uncle had forced himself upon her, other memories of the long road fighting for herself against a harsh world, and her uplifting memories of meeting Tony, his brother Nick, the whirlwind of recent weeks, and the stark justice served on her uncle in hell.

"Why do we have to go to St. Paul?" asked Sylvia.

"You know the answer to that. Tubby Vaughn is there. He is one of the henchmen that shot Nick. We're going to help Nick hunt him down. It's straightforward. Why do you ask?"

"I don't know. I feel spent. Worn down. I've been living my life with nightmares because of my uncle. I thought his death would help cleanse me. But in truth, the years I've spent with Pearce Savage was surrounding myself with the same brutality. As I've struggled against my pains, I think I have made things worse for myself. I'm tired, Tony; I want a new life. I know Tubby Vaughn was one of the shooters, but at this point, I don't know if I care. Why not just go after Pearce Savage? He's the monster that we should slay and then be done with it."

"I know it's messed up, honey, but Nick won't back off. He's going for Tubby."

"Tony, I love your brother. I would do anything for him, but he's risking too much. What does all this killing mean if he can't get to Savage? Once Savage is taken out, all the rest of his henchmen will scramble like rats or tear themselves apart trying to take his position."

"Nick won't change his mind. He's going after Tubby."

"Do you agree with me? Go after Savage now," pressed Sylvia.

"I hear what you're saying. It makes sense, but those six guys are the ones that shot Nick. He won't put that aside. He's made one detour. For him, that's showing a lot of flexibility."

"The Ephemerals would love us becoming their hired killers, though they never pay any price. Are you trying to put any of this on me because of Uncle Shelton? Curse his black soul."

"No. Of course not. Nick wouldn't have gone after Shelton if he didn't want to. He's grown attached to you, too. I know how he thinks; well, at least I used to. We are twins, and he is very focused."

"You two are so different. You look alike, but your personalities are from different mothers."

"Hey. Careful," responded Tony with a feigned furrow of his brow.

"I think it's the Ephemerals' fault. Vince was the one mostly dwelling inside you. He played with your emotions. That's what drove you two apart."

"Sylvia, I made my decisions, as bad as they may have been. Not all twins end up exactly the same at the end of life. Just because we're different isn't because an Ephemeral was controlling me."

"Maybe not control, but Vince admits while he dwelled inside you, he pushed your emotional buttons. They've admitted they do that kind of thing. They say it helps them harvest more energy, whatever the hell that means exactly. It seems desperate to me that they have to reap energy from the emotions of other life-forms. They're hiding something."

"Vince saved Nick. That must count for something."

"Sure, it does, Tony, but why did they go through all this effort for one entanglement? Yes, yes, I know. Something about an Ephemeral Management intervention because Paul is a potential heir. Or wait … was it because Vince and Paul wanted to prolong the fun of switching between twins? Truthfully, I think half of it is bullshit. Now, we find ourselves drawn into some Ephemeral scheme that will either doom humanity or free us from our Ephemeral chains. They're not telling us something."

Paul's voice leaped into Tony's head, "Tony."

"Damn it, Paul," exclaimed Tony, jumping in his seat. The car swerved, owing to Tony's startled response.

"Do you want to fill me in?" said Paul, more as a statement than a question.

Tony turned to Sylvia to speak. "Paul wants me to fill him in on what you said."

Sylvia flashed a middle finger. Tony knew it was meant for Paul.

"I think that's private between us," responded Tony.

"Tony, I have been open with you. I'm one of the good guys. Overlord Draxis is humanity's enemy. We need to work together to defeat him."

"What are you not telling us, Paul?"

Sylvia demanded Tony give her a point-by-point narrative of Paul's side of the conversation causing Tony to repeat everything for her:

Paul: I don't know what you mean. You three know more about Ephemeron than any other human. That includes Pearce Savage and the embedded Draxis's sleeper agents.

After the conversational relay, Sylvia shook her head. "He's hiding something."

Tony: Paul, what's wrong with your world? You're obviously an intelligent species. You can certainly tap your sun's energy or wind energy, and a dozen other sources. Nick told us that Vince said emotional energy has a special taste. Is that the fucking reason that you inhabit millions of us and want to control more? Because the energy tastes better? It makes no sense.

No answer from Paul.

Tony: Paul? What gives?

Paul, finally: It's not just the taste of the energy. When we say energy, we mean … food.

Tony: FUCK!

Sylvia, after the translation: FUCK! I knew it. I knew there was something.

Tony: You can't grow your own food?! It's your second planet. You could have picked a place where you could grow food. Jesus.

Paul: You misunderstand. It was evolution that caused the problem. Initially, when we were able to harness QE, it was like a drug. It still is. Everybody wanted a taste. It was innocent. It didn't hurt anybody. We were content to simply reap another life-form's emotions. Millions and billions of little jolts of pureness. You have your cocaine. Rats will choose it over food or sleep. Humans, too. Or you have your casinos.

Pulling the levers or watching the spin of the wheel. Drops of dopamine. There is never enough to satisfy. So, it was with the energy we get from others' emotions.

Tony: That's a sick analogy. Nick said you people were addicts. What does this have to do with evolution?

Paul: The desire for more quantum energy infusions changed our species and our society. You're right about regular energy sources. We have what we need to power the mechanics of our planet. But over many millennia, Ephemeral minds and bodies changed. They evolved to want, need, and live off those QE bursts. Our bodies transformed. The kings of Ephemeron and its businesses gave the people what they craved. There was no stopping the enticement. The evolution of our species was pushed further and further, until the emotional energy of others became the primary food that our bodies process. Now, we will die without it.

Tony: Explain why humans are so important to you. Vince told Nick there are many life-forms across the universe.

Paul: You're not going to like the answer: humanity was simply unlucky. You are an emotional species. We can manipulate you without you catching on. You can't detect us. You have a social media that spews conspiracies. Ephemeral scientists ran their computer analyses and they made a cold assessment. Which planet could provide the best place to start? Which planet would best provide for our needs? Humanity rose right to the top.

Using those research results, it was easy for Overlord Draxis to select humanity as the guinea pig. He has promised extra energy doses for everyone. The thought of more emotional cocaine has captured

Ephemerals' minds and desires. Your planet will descend into worldwide chaos and self-destruction, the likes you have rarely seen. Draxis intends to establish a long-lasting control of humanity. You will be born in strife, you will live in strife, and you will die in strife. If Draxis's plan succeeds on Earth, the same model will be deployed against other life-forms.

Tony: Why was it so important to keep my brother alive?

Paul: It was the king's decision. I guess he believes Vince and my inhabitation with humans is in the monarchy's best interests. One thing I know about him—my father is very calculating. Ephemerals underestimate him. He is always thinking many steps in advance. He can see the ramifications of Draxis's plan.

Tony: That Draxis's plan will be cataclysmic for Ephemeron?

Paul: That's what's being fought over. Remember, Ephemerals are addicts. Draxis is offering them a vast new, cheap drug supply. Why would they say no to that? Humans are simply a means to an end.

Sylvia: Are you an addict?

Tony translated her question to Paul.

Paul: I am. As is every other Ephemeral. Some of us are fighting our way back. I don't know to what. Non-addiction? I don't know if we can hope for that much. For myself, I see it as a personal rebellion. I know the addiction has me, but I want to fight back in the only way I can. Perhaps at the end of the day, it is only a fight within myself, for myself. Maybe it will mean nothing to anyone else. I am trying. Vince is trying. Others are trying.

We pray the upcoming Fusion will provide a new opportunity. Seventy percent of Ephemeral seeds are addicted at birth, though doctors say those children could be weaned to a different food. The cycle could be broken. The rebels are fighting for this. Vince and I are fighting for this. Humanity could help save Ephemeron and could save itself. You will need to take a leap of faith, as you might say.

Tony: What does that mean?

Paul: The entanglement that allows us to live inside you is bidirectional. Technically, you are inhabiting us as we inhabit you. It is only because of our E-stations that you are not aware of the entanglement and have minimal impact on us. If an E-station was modified, you could wreak quite a bit of damage on Ephemeron.

Tony: Paul, what are you suggesting!? That we travel to Ephemeron?

Paul: No. Not travel. It would be like a projection. Physically, you would still be on Earth.

Tony: How much of this does Nick know?

But only silence greeted Tony's question. Back on Ephemeron, Paul's body was being resuscitated. He had talked too long.

After Tony's conveyance of Paul's words, Tony and Sylvia exchanged stunned glances.

Sylvia spoke. "They're desperate. Their world is on the edge of tearing itself apart and they don't even know it. We can figure Vince pitched this same idea to Nick. There is so much wrong with this idea, I don't even know where to start. Tonight is going to be an interesting conversation."

"Damn it!" exclaimed Tony as the wheels of the Jeep lurched toward the side of the road and triggered an abrasive rumble-strip warning.

30

*"I want to let go and float on the world's currents
for days on end, unburdened by the gravity
of day-to-day toils."*

On **Ephemeron,** the Xermegan High Priestess and her personal assistant, the Vimegan spy, clung tightly to thin, ornate, black metal poles bolted to the upper balcony. Their wispy appendages wrapped around the poles which kept them from being swept away by Ephemeron's gusting winds.

"Meerlex, I love this world," the High Priestess exhaled. "I love the Ephemeral people. We are a magnificent species. I have read the sacred texts brought from Old Ephemeron, where our ancestors' muscular bodies built the first civilizations of New Ephemeron. You have visited these old sites with me. Even today, many thousands of years later, we preserve their ancient ruins and hold our most precious ceremonies there.

"It seems impossible that our people are so different now. With the mastery of entanglement, our energy needs were provided by other species, and over tens of thousands of years, our bodies evolved into beings of air. On this balcony, I watch our citizens dash across the skies toward their next moments in life. Ephemeron's majestic swirling gusts pull on my very soul. I want to let go and float on the world's currents for days on end, unburdened by the gravity of day-to-day toils. Meerlex, I want to let go this very moment."

"High Priestess, I would cast myself on the winds to be with you and serve you," replied Meerlex.

Their thin appendages struggled against the blustering winds. Ephemeral's evening skies often displayed a pastel palette of colors, but when high winds blew, the sky's colors would intermingle and toy with the clouds.

Meerlex breathed deeply, hoping to capture a waft of the colorized air. Ephemerals believed that health, luck, and love could be acquired if one breathed in enough streams of Ephemeral's ethereal blue winds.

"Were you trying to breathe in the blue wisps?" asked the High Priestess. "Blue is love."

Meerlex felt sheepish, not realizing the High Priestess was observing her that closely. She wondered if the High Priestess thought poorly of her, quickly closing her mouth, even though her blue-air inhalation already had stirred feelings deeply inside her.

The High Priestess laughed gently. "Oh, my dear Meerlex, you are the tenderest Ephemeral I know. I think it is beautiful that you breathe in the blue winds. Are you attracted to someone?"

Meerlex giggled, trying to hide her growing embarrassment. "Isn't that what we all want? To feel loved. But I have no one that loves me. My dedication is to you, High Priestess."

"Meerlex, when we're alone like this, please call me Artemesia," said the High Priestess.

"I'm afraid I can't do that," replied Meerlex.

"I never hear my name. It's as if power has erased me. I'm asking you to call me by my name—Artemesia. It would make me happy."

From Meerlex's mandibles, the word escaped: "*Artemesia ....*"

As the High Priestess's name escaped Meerlex's whisper, complicated memories of pain and joy echoed inside Meerlex's mind. The winds sweeping across the high balcony should have swept away the spoken name of the High Priestess, but instead, somehow held it with a gentle hand that let the word dance in the moment.

Artemesia ....

"Our people are at peace," said Meerlex. "But I think Ephemerals, deep down, are frightened."

"Why do you say that?"

"Their lives have been carefree. If we manipulate other worlds and they see the pains we cause others, will they be able to remain at peace with themselves? How long can one stand by watching others suffer for what one does?"

"It's a deep question, Meerlex."

"Artemesia, I care so much for you. I worry about you. Selection and Fusion are almost upon us. Much will be expected of you."

"I will gladly fulfill my role. Our gods will give me the strength that I need."

In the distance, a bell rang, announcing the Temple's evening invocation. Artemesia and Meerlex fluttered down to the lower, protected area of the balcony and entered the Temple.

"I care for you, too, Meerlex," said Artemesia, as their bodies bumped lightly against each other.

In the courtyard below, two Ephemerals debated ....

"Do you not feel that our house is being torn asunder?" asked the Xermegan man. "What right do we have to dismiss the beliefs and customs that have been with us for thousands of years?"

"My friend, how long have we known each other?" responded the Vimegan man. "Why do you interpret our clan's differences as a threat to our gods? We've known each other all our lives. We shared our childhoods. But the Xermegan clan has deviated. When you use the words 'our gods,' it seems like you're really saying—your gods."

"Your words wound me," responded the Xermegan man. "Our clan has spent much time praying and discussing Ephemeron's gods, just like your clan. Can't religion be a living thing, able to change? Shouldn't it change? How is it that Ephemerals of thousands of years ago somehow knew more about religion than today's Ephemerals?"

"I don't mean to hurt you," offered the Vimegan man. "But how can it be a religion if each generation can redefine what they want to believe? Isn't the foundation the essence of a religion?"

"Let me propose thinking of the matter in a different way," offered the Xermegan man. "We would all agree that Ephemerals have certain inalienable worth and rights, but by self-effort, luck, or special ordination, we don't treat all Ephemerals equally. Our monarchy rules over Ephemeron. We treat the king with greater recognition and respect. A king, by his nature, has greater power and stands above all Ephemerals. Likewise, Ephemeron has its many gods. None of the clans think all are equal. Some gods stand above others. It is this logic that the Xermegan clan is willing to speak about publicly. That is why we single out the god, Alborix. For speaking the truth, our clan is disparaged … yet you say we have abandoned Ephemeron's gods."

"Although the gods are not all equal, that's not the essence of my concern," countered the Vimegan man. "The differences between the gods are being exploited by Ephemerals who seek power. That path is a temptation. Our people seem to have forgotten the pains of our warring history. The ease of our current lives tricks us with treacherous promises."

"Or, perhaps things are not so treacherous. Perhaps the success of our species and our entanglements across the universe is confirmation of our righteous path."

"So, we disagree."

"As usual, my friend," responded the Xermegan.

"Will you be attending the Crystal Moon festivities? It honors all the gods and I hear it will be especially extravagant because of the upcoming Confluence. Perhaps we can meet."

"I would like that," replied the Xermegan.

Across the city, near a large carved stone fountain, five rebels were playing a fast and simple card game while others were fascinated by an 8x8 strategy board game of a kingdom's moving pieces called Chasqua.

Nearby, Ephemeral citizens sat around a fountain's base, enjoying the aquatic spray and the company of their friends. Watchers wandered among the citizens, hoping to pick up tidbits of information that could be spun with meaning to catch the attention of their supervisors.

Mr. Coco inquired, "How many E-stations can we compromise?"

"It looks promising. We should be able to modify a thousand stations, or close to it," replied one of the rebels. "It will certainly be enough to create panic."

"Are we really going to go through with this?" interrupted Mr. Traxx.

"We all voted on this the last time we met. You said you could support the vote," replied Mr. Coco.

"I know, but what we're doing frightens me. We know the history of the first entanglements with other beings. There were no protective channels. Both the Ephemerons and their entangled hosts were driven to the edge of insanity. Our advanced E-stations dampen the interactions between species and hide the existence of entanglement from those hosts we inhabit. Stripping away the protective channel from our entanglements will have the same consequences that we will not be able to control."

"Mr. Traxx, we will not be debating this matter again," said Mr. Coco. "Vince and Paul have already reached out to Nick and Tony. The die has been cast."

*"You will be inside the heads of drogs.
You should know that they are ill-tempered
and vicious creatures."*

Rolling into Omaha, Nebraska, Nick picked a run-of-the-mill chain hotel that included the same simple breakfast repeated across the nation at every other mid level hotel. A while later Tony and Sylvia rolled in.

That evening, sitting in Nick's room, slim pale-green auras pulsed from around Nick and Tony. Like the double entanglement at the Daphne Hotel, the two auras throbbed at different tempos. The auras' intensity ebbed and flowed. Inside each aura, streams of multitudinous colors randomly emerged. The auras altered again and again until the two auras throbbed in perfect rhythm. The merged aura expanded, finally engulfing Sylvia, too.

A flash overwhelmed the room. A colorless, but evident distortion of the air encircled them. The distortion pulsed slowly, like the inhalation and exhalation of deep breaths.

"I'm telling you. I'm selling my story to the tabloids," commented Sylvia. "I can't say I'm getting used to being encircled by pulsing auras, but it is impressive."

Tony took a swig from his beer.

"How badly do you want to get rid of us?" started Vince.

The three humans exchanged looks that said a thousand words.

"What's the catch?" asked Nick.

"We've identified three of Overlord Draxis's sleeper agents that are entangled with humans. We know there are more. When they are activated, Earth will pay a heavy price. You have shown you have *special skills*. These agents are out of your reach on Earth. Their entangled humans live very far from you, but if you had access to Ephemeron, the agents would be reachable."

"Special skills?" chided Nick. "Why don't you say what you mean? That we're killers. Why bring us to Ephemeron to do your dirty work? Why not do it yourselves?" He took a long draw on his beer as he waited patiently for the pathetic answer he was sure to come. Disgust churned in the pit of his stomach.

"The Confluence approaches. We cannot be seen as involved."

"Then hire the job to be done by another Ephemeral."

"Ephemerals don't murder Ephemerals."

Sylvia and Nick let out howls. Tony spit out some of his beer. "But you're willing to sow mayhem across the universe as you twist your computer dials. You murder all the time, but you do it sitting safely at your E-stations."

"The Draxis agents will be well-protected," continued Vince. "Rival Ephemerals would not be able to get close to them."

"What of the rebels?" asked Sylvia. "Certainly, some of them are from the Draxis clan."

"If any Ephemeral is caught trying to kill Draxis's agents, it could upend the Selection. Ephemerals would believe it is a great conspiracy. Draxis could end up ruling Ephemeron for the next 1,000 years. Planets across the universe will suffer, not just Earth."

"You people are fucking sick," swore Nick. "Your planet is sick."

"Do you want to get rid of us or not?" interrupted Paul.

"Are we going to be inside your heads?" asked Tony, as he tried to grasp the Ephemerals' plan.

"Vince and I will remain as the main entangled conduits for you and your brother. But once we open the reverse entanglement channels, you will be inside our heads as we are in yours."

"Sweet!" exclaimed Tony. "Let's do it now. I won't give you a second of peace."

Without falling into an emotional argument with Tony, Paul continued. "After we open up the conduits between us, we will use the E-stations to extend the entanglements. You will be inside the heads of drogs. You should know that they are ill-tempered and vicious creatures, but are of great use for our forays into Ephemeron's jungles. When you are entangled with the drogs, you will use them to kill the Draxis agents. Since the agents will die on Ephemeron, the entanglements they have with humans will be broken."

"What about me?" asked Sylvia.

"That's for you to choose," responded Paul.

"No. I'm not volunteering for that," snapped Sylvia. "I want to keep Ephemerals outside of my head. Outside of me. Find another way."

"I won't let you take her," warned Tony, though he had no idea how to stop them.

"We don't see another way," pressed Vince. "Sylvia, if we don't sabotage Overlord Draxis's plans, you will be entangled, whether you want it or not. It will be with someone that is loyal to Draxis. It will be like we described for Nick and Tony. An entanglement will be created between you and a drog. Using the drog, you will hunt down the third sleeper agent and kill it."

"How does killing three Draxis agents turn your people against him?" questioned Sylvia. "If we kill his agents, won't it be simply an inconvenience for him? Your people probably won't even hear about the deaths. Even if they do, it'll only be a passing news item."

"It is not just the killing of the three agents. The rebels have a plan to open the protective channels between a thousand humans and their entangled Ephemerals," explained Paul. "It will be like taking away the guardrails between our two worlds.

"Ephemerals will be faced with the stark horror of someone living inside of them, causing chaos in their minds. Ephemerals will no longer be able to live as distant puppeteers of others' lives. Ephemerals will feel what it is like to be turned into a plaything. We believe the resulting turmoil will be enough to turn the people's sentiment against Overlord Draxis before the upcoming Selection. In the mayhem, it will provide cover for your actions. The Overlord's plans will be undermined by your and the rebel's actions."

Nick burst into satirical laughter. "Fuck you, Paul. You tell yourselves you are a peaceful species. And, *oh no, you never murder.* You pray your prayers of devotion, yet, you play frivolously with millions of lives across the universe. You want us to kill for you. One day, you should listen to yourselves and look in the mirror."

Nick stood, walked to a nearby table and poured himself a bourbon. If he was honest with himself, he would admit to a certain pleasure taking advantage of the reverse entanglement, inhabiting a drog—whatever that was—and ripping the heart out of an Ephemeral. It sounded like a pretty good payback. It would be a farfetched story his army buddies would make fun of but listen to with interest.

That is, if he lived.

"What happens to our bodies while we're entangled?" asked Tony. "You said our projections will be entangled. We don't have any E-Stations on Earth. How do we go about our lives in this world while we are controlling drogs in your world?"

"You'll need to find a place where you can hide out," explained Paul. "Consider it like being at a retreat. You'll stay quiet with minimal outside interactions. That will allow you to focus on your projections into Ephemeron. If you focus on your Earthly selves, you can control what you do physically. If you focus on the drog, that's what you'll control. Our E-stations will moderate the connection of your projections into the drogs."

"When will this happen?" asked Tony.

"Soon. The annual Crystal Moon Hunt is upcoming in three days. It is when Searchers go out to collect rare plants and crystals in the jungles of Ephemeron. It is a dangerous hunt because of the wild beasts. Drogs are used for both protection and using their sense of smell to help locate the plants. After the caravan returns, it is tradition that the hunters and drogs parade through the capital city. This year, Overlord Draxis has planned a grand celebration to coincide with the hunt. He wants to elevate himself in the minds of Ephemerals prior to the Selection.

"We know it's a lot for you to think about," said Paul. "But we have to leave now. Our energy is running out. Call out to us if you have questions. We won't be far away."

"Yeah, we know," snarled Nick.

And with that, the enveloping aura flashed into nothingness.

Tony paced the room. Sylvia started talking to herself, barely able to control her anger. Nick pulled his handgun from its holster. His hand shook. Not a good sign. The gun felt foreign to him, though it had been by his side for years.

Nick wondered if his projection into Ephemeron would carry a gun. Everything about the Ephemerals' plan made him nervous.

What was a fucking drog? How was he supposed to control it? How does one kill an Ephemeral? Do they have hearts? Where is it located? Could he trust Vince and Paul, let alone a bunch of rebels that were supposed to be *helping*?

If everything went perfectly and they killed the sleeper agents, would the Ephemerals allow them to return? Maybe the Ephemerals would turn on them. They said they don't kill fellow Ephemerals, but they didn't say anything about humans romping around in their world. Nick's list of questions seemed endless.

"What if we refuse?" blurted Sylvia. "Think about it. How much havoc can just three people cause?"

"Your uncle secretly financed a terrorist organization," responded Nick. "A few powerful people can create a lot of trouble for the world. We have to assume Draxis has carefully chosen the humans his sleeper agents inhabit."

Tony reached out his hand to lay on her shoulder. "Sylvia, it's Nick and I that are entangled. This is not your fight."

Sylvia brusquely brushed his hand away. "Tony, you can be such an idiot. This is just as much my fight as yours. I'm not running away."

"In the car, you said we should give up on finding Tubby Vaughn."

"For now, yes. I think we should go after Pearce Savage first and get Tubby later."

"Maybe you two don't have to go," said Nick, thinking out loud. "Maybe I can get to the three sleeper agents."

"You can't do this alone, Nick," asserted Sylvia. "We're in this together. All the way."

"Sylvia, we can't ask you to entangle yourself with an Ephemeral, let alone a drog." Nick looked searchingly into her dark brown eyes. Her resolve stared back at him.

He glanced over at Tony, who was taking slow deep breaths. That was a good sign, thought Nick.

"You're not asking me. I'm volunteering."

"You don't know what it's like," warned Nick.

"Hell, I think I know enough. I've been on the road with you and Tony for weeks. I've been living in this crazy alien shitshow, too. I've seen up close Tony's ups-and-downs. I still am in love with him. I've even fallen for you, Nick, you big brute. Nobody is twisting my arm. I know what I'm signing up for."

"You won't know who you will be entangled with," cautioned Tony.

"Neither did either of you. One day, you discovered they were dwelling inside you. Listen, there are three sleeper agents that need to be killed. There are three of us. If we don't make it through, it'll have been a hell of a way to go out of this world."

"You should write your alien-possession tabloid story in advance and send it before we are projected across the universe," quipped Tony.

Sylvia and Nick burst into guffaws. "That's seriously funny, honey. And not too bad of an idea. I suppose I may need to send it in anonymously and change the names of the guilty."

Nick looked back down at his Glock. He pulled it out and re-holstered it. It felt like his old friend again. He reached over for the bottle of bourbon and held it up as an offering.

Sylvia and Tony shared the pour.

Nick raised his glass. "This is one hell of a toast and it's certainly not a celebration. How about … *to bravery and courage*." They echoed the salute, clinked glasses, and downed their shots.

"Should we tell Vince and Paul that the three of us have agreed to go?" asked Tony.

"Let's wait," responded Nick. "When we're on the road tomorrow, we should pepper them with questions. Act like we need to know more before we make any decision."

"Then we need to spend some time tonight figuring out what we want to ask them," suggested Sylvia. "Since we'll be in different cars, we should ask different questions. Get as much information as we can."

The next morning, Nick, Tony, and Sylvia headed for St. Paul.

Millions of light-years away in the Grand Xermegan temple, the Xermegan High Priestess Artemesia convened her retinue of Xermegan priests. Her trusted assistant, Meerlex, the Vimegan spy, stood beside her.

The subordinate priests had traveled from the far ends of Ephemeron: from Ru, the holy crystalline city; from Paj, the largest of the oceanic cities; from Zilf, the city of "healing flowers"; from the rural areas of Ephemeron; from the ice cities of the polar regions; from Ephemeron's mountains and deserts.

Along the temple's walls were side altars and nooks that bestowed homage to the hundreds of Ephemeron gods. Within the confines of each altar, specific sacred writings and talismans accompanied each god's image.

In the grand hallway, six large stone columns ran down one side of the temple and six others on the other side. Stone beams rested on the top of the pillars that supported a heavy arched roof of intricately carved metal plates and wooden timbers that arched like spines overhead. Punctuating some of the metal plates, carved crystal sheets had been inserted, allowing for the sun's rays to create dancing streams of colors along the floor and sides of the temple. In the front of the temple sat the altar. By Earth measurements it was almost fourteen feet long, five feet wide and was made entirely of various rare crystals carefully bonded together by the most expert of craftsmen.

Within this inner sanctum of the Xermegan temple was the prominent display of the god Alborix. It was this god that Overlord Draxis had spoken with and who the Xermegan clan was holding above all others for adoration and prayer.

The High Priestess Artemesia stood in the temple's high altar to address her priests.

"Our people face the most important Confluence in Ephemeron's history. The Omegan clan has dominated our world for 5,000 years. Their beliefs have made a terrible bargain with the devil, accepting anyone who simply says they believe in Ephemeron's gods, but requiring no proof of conviction and donation of service. Our Xermegan clan's religious scholars have devoted the longest hours to studying the old texts of Ephemeron One. It is this wisdom that the Xermegan clan understands, that permits—no, *requires* us to take the necessary stand for our Supreme God, Alborix. Each of you chose to devote your lives to the Xermegan clan. Now, Alborix beckons you to show actions to prove the words you have often professed.

"During the upcoming festivities hosted by Overlord Draxis, each of you will be given a flame born of the Sacred Fire that burned on Ephemeron One. It is the flame that has been kept alive for over 40,000 years. During the upcoming celebrations, you are to carry the sacred flame. Next to the flame, a figure of Alborix should always be displayed. This will remind Ephemerons of the presence and power of Alborix."

In unison, the priests exclaimed their approval of the High Priestess's words and their devotion to Alborix. Then, in a single file, each lit a torch from the temple's sacred flame to bring to their distant cities and lands.

Left alone in the Temple's sacred flame room, Artemesia and Meerlex stood next to each other as they gazed into the flame.

"Have you ever wanted to be entangled?" asked Meerlex.

"I am the High Priestess. I'm not allowed to be entangled, as you are also prohibited."

"But have you ever wanted to be entangled? Ephemerals say it can be a wonderous experience. It depends on who one is entangled with."

"When I was young, I was entangled with a Zoomite. It was a terrible experience. The Zoomite was full of rage and black thoughts. Overlord Draxis saw how fragile I was and took pity on me. I don't know why, as I was born of a different clan. When he took me into his household, he weaned me off the drug effect of entanglement. I never again want to be entangled."

"Scientists say Ephemerals will die without the energy from entanglement; that we will starve to death."

"Meerlex, you and I are both alive, are we not? We are not entangled."

"I worry about our people. They think they have no other choice. The words of Overlord Draxis carry great weight."

At that moment, Artemesia's and Meerlex's wings tenderly touched. The sacred flame danced. "The Overlord has changed since I first met him. He has become harder. He is enamored with the thought that Alborix has spoken to him directly."

"I would be overwhelmed if a god spoke directly to me."

"As would I, Meerlex, as would I."

Artemesia's response surprised Meerlex. "Artemesia, do you doubt Alborix has spoken directly to the Overlord?"

"I worry about our people, Meerlex. Ephemerals are beautiful beings. They deserve to live a peaceful life."

Meerlex understood not to repeat her question about the Overlord, but also understood the High Priestess was struggling with her thoughts. The wings of the High Priestess extended and brushed across Meerlex's backside.

"I will see you tomorrow, Meerlex. It is time for me to retire. There will be much to do for the festivities and the upcoming Selection."

That same evening, Mr. Coco sat at his regular card game. He drank his usual psychedelic-infused Foxcovvy. A rebel, seemingly in a hurry, joined those at the table. As she sat, she apologized for her "*tardiness,*" a code word others at the table understood to mean she would later be providing the group with a special update.

The Watchers watched, suspecting that these regulars had learned to play the clandestine game: to not speak boisterously; to change the subject when Watchers approached; to distrust newcomers and hangers-on. Nevertheless, in most of their reports to their superiors, the Watchers had deemed Mr. Coco and his games-playing friends as relatively innocuous.

One Ephemeral provided occasional entertainment to the Watchers.

Mr. Om, when dealing cards, liked to send them spinning and skimming across the table top. Occasionally, with one too many drinks impairing his coordination or the intrusion of an unexpected wind gust, a spinning card would take flight, flipping up to expose its underside, drawing heckles of friendly derision, and forcing a new deal.

What the Watchers never guessed was that some of those misdealt cards were a signal.

On this night, the signaling pertained to the clandestine modification of the E-stations to support reverse entanglement.

If the first card was dealt errantly, it signaled that twenty percent of the E-stations had been modified. If the second card was dealt errantly, then forty percent of the E-stations were modified, and so on for the five cards to be dealt.

However, if a truly errant deal was due to Mr. Om's inebriation or the atmospheric fates, a specific curse would leave his lips. Then, all at the table would know it was not a signal, just a random misdeal.

For the Watchers, it provided entertainment as they laid their bets amongst themselves as to how often or when Mr. Om would misdeal.

Another rebel, Ms. Bovemont, had the coquettish habit of brushing one of her wings across the Ephemeral sitting next to her. They were rapid light flaps that would inadvertently touch one of the neighboring Ephemeral's sensitive areas. She breathed feigned apologies: "oh, excuse me" and "so sorry."

This was another event the Watchers bet on as they wished that Ms. Bovemont would spend a moment of her attention on them.

If her wing touched the rebel to her right, it signaled that the preparations to entangle the humans with drogs was progressing on schedule and no significant problems. But if her wing caressed the card player on her left, it signaled a complication existed. This evening's right-wing touch was a reason for the table's participants to breathe easier.

There was a lot to coordinate. Much had to be deftly accomplished: reprogram 1,000 E-stations reverse entanglement channels that would suddenly thrust humans into the consciousness of 1,000 Ephemerons; secretly track the three Xermegan sleeper agents without triggering computer safety monitoring systems; and prepare three drogs for entanglement with humans, without being able to actually test whether the entanglements would be successful. Drog tests were by computer modeling only. It was usually an effective methodology, but failures were not unknown.

Finally, the *tardy rebel* added her bit of information.

"The Xermegan High Priestess called her acolytes from the far reaches of Ephemeron to the Xermegan temple. We have learned that each priest will carry a flaming ember from the Sacred Flame that will be transported back to each priest's city or town. These embers will represent an unbroken link to the Sacred Flame. As they are carried to the far reaches of Ephemeron, they will be used to light thousands of candles and torches.

"The Xermegan High Priestess has also provided fire crystals to her priests. Each evening the crystals will be placed within the sacred flame. This will bathe the citizens with the redeeming light from the crystals. The Xermegan High Priestess has instructed her priests to carry an image of Alborix ahead of the other gods."

"Sacrilege!" interrupted another rebel. "The fire crystals are the domain of Pheuero, the God of Fire, not Alborix."

"The High Priestess is following Overlord Draxis's orders."

"The Overlord is fanatical. He sees the gods as his tools and casts himself as their special confidant. It terrifies me," said Mr. Traxx.

"The people are drawn to him because he speaks to their desires. He promises them riches and energy. Once our scientists developed ways to use QE for the service of Ephemeron, we have taken from others and have given back nothing. He makes them feel there is nothing to fear. The Overlord says the gods have ordained it as Ephemerals' divine right. Who is brave enough to stand up and question him?"

"Is it not us?" questioned Ms. Bovemont.

"I pray it will be enough," said Mr. Traxx.

"Am I being blasphemous to wonder if prayer is enough? We see evil rising before us. We say 'we believe' that our gods will save us, so we pray, sincerely and devoutly … and wait for the gods' intercession. But what if their intercession was to be us? That we need to act against evil. Where is courage found, but within one's self? Maybe the gods are merely mirrors of our hopes and wishes."

Mr. Om, flustered by the irreverence, misdealt the cards. He cursed. It was the third misdeal of the evening. The Watchers, always on the lookout for a convoluted conspiracy, had exchanged wagered coins at the occurrence of the first two misdeals, but now took heightened notice. Notations were recorded. Suppositions were added. They circled closer.

"You are drunk," accused a rebel to cover over the fuss. He snatched the cards away from Mr. Om.

"I'm tired," lied another. "I'll see you next time." He stood, lifted his wings, and rose into the evening's darkness. A thin ray of light, reflecting off Ephemeron's crystalline moon, danced prismatically across the rebel's chromatic wings.

The rebel who had snatched away the playing cards raised them up, folded them backward so there was tension, then sprayed them forward, pummeling Mr. Om. The Watchers laughed.

Beneath the high jinks, the offensive words had been temporarily buried, but each rebel would think about it later. Were their prayers only reflections of their hopes? The gods existed; could there be any doubt?

But were the gods listening? Certainly, the gods wanted Ephemerons to pray. How else could the gods know the dearest needs of their hearts? What purpose would it serve a god if it was unwilling to listen?

As each rebel would pray for deliverance from the Overlord's hubris, many a common Ephemeral prayed for greater riches and the success of the Overlord to become the next monarch. It was left to be seen if the gods played a numbers game.

"What of the Earthlings?" asked Mr. Coco. "Have they decided? Will they accept their task on Ephemeron?"

Messengers from Vince and Paul gave shrugs, indicating they did not know. With one of their playing partners having just flown off, the night late, and the status of E-stations and the humans' decision in flux, the rebels decided to put an end to the evening. They buzzed into the air.

The Watchers settled their bets.

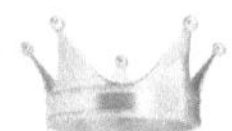

The next afternoon, Vince and Paul met in the luncheon courtyard.

"It is hard enough to earn a drog's loyalty," mused Paul. "Even the stabled drogs remain fearsome. Neither of us have entangled with a drog. How can we prepare humans? Entangling drogs with human killers borders on insanity."

"What has Sylvia decided?" asked Vince.

"I'm told she cursed a lot, basically damning every Ephemeral to an eternity of torturous hell. But her loyalty to Tony and Nick is strong. It is hard to believe she will let them go it alone."

"Your father is king. He knows the Overlord is growing in popularity. Why has he not intervened against Draxis?"

"Do not underestimate him. As he lets his opponents fly higher, the harder they will fall."

"He is playing a dangerous game."

"He has ruled Ephemeron for almost 1,000 years. That counts for something."

"And what about you, Paul? The king is old. If the Omegan clan is to again be Selected to rule over Ephemeron, a deft and powerful successor must come forward. The king may favor you for Succession, yet in this perilous time, you must prove your worth. As the favored prince, you have been able to luxuriate under his protection. As your friend, I, too, have benefited, but we are now called to take a stand."

"We have taken a stand. We have assisted the Earthlings and the rebels."

"Our acts have been in the shadows. Only a few know of our involvement. A king must be seen outside, under the heat of sun and battle. How else will you be able to lead?"

"Vince, what more do you want from me?"

"The Overlord is enchanting Ephemerals with his words of conquest. He supports grand celebrations that raise him up in Ephemerals' eyes. It is no longer enough for you to move behind the scenes. You must find a way to be seen prominently in front of our citizenry. They must see you in their minds as the next king. You must lead them on a different path forward."

Paul's wings stretched out behind him. His antennae rubbed together, and his eyes mutated to a deep reddish-brown.

His friend's words were true.

But the answer that Vince's words didn't provide was … *how*.

"To harvest the rare flowers and crystals,
Ephemerals must deal with Crimson Bears
and Mammoth Snakes."

The next morning on Earth, Nick, Tony, and Sylvia left on their final stretch to St. Paul. As Tony drove, Sylvia spent the time looking for a place they could rent, preferably with few questions asked. She had her fake IDs and cash.

The Ephemerals had said the three of them would need to stay out of sight on Earth while they were entangled with the drogs. An advertisement for a short-term rental caught her attention. She called the number and talked to the landlord.

The place had come open recently. The landlord had evicted the tenant for nonpayment, so most of the landlord's concerns centered around getting paid. She told him she was with her fiancé and his brother, and needed a place for a month or two. When Sylvia said she could pay cash, she heard the eagerness in his voice.

Arranging for all of them to meet late in the afternoon, she texted Nick the details and forwarded the GPS location. During the day's drive, Paul visited Tony and Sylvia. Vince visited Nick.

Late in the afternoon, Tony and Sylvia arrived at the rental. It was about a thirty-minute drive from downtown St. Paul. Sylvia set up the rental for a month, with an option for another month. She paid cash plus deposit.

The landlord noticed she had more cash. He sized them up; they didn't appear drugged-up. He hoped they wanted to stay longer. It wasn't a fancy place, but utilities worked; and except for a *small* mouse problem, the house was perfect for their needs. It was somewhat isolated, yet near enough to local necessities. The landlord gave her the rundown on nearby merchants.

Later in the evening Nick rolled in after taking time to check out a few areas of interest where Tubby Vaughn might frequent.

The house had a modest deck at the back. An old propane grill tempted a future meal. Tony checked the tank, but it was empty. He told himself he'd get it refilled tomorrow.

In a shed out back, he found some sandpaper. He used it to remove rust from the ignition points. The hoses looked acceptable. With a little luck, they could grill tomorrow night's dinner. It would be a respite from interstate restaurants. Sylvia made a run to a local quick-service store to stock up on a few breakfast items and beer. Nick showed up with bags of burgers and fries for the night's dinner.

The clear night sky framed a generous number of stars. Venus and Mars shone down upon them. They scavenged three mismatched chairs and hauled them over to the deck. There was peace to the spartan setting.

"Did you two learn anything more from Paul during the day's drive?" asked Nick.

"Yeah. Quite a bit," answered Sylvia. "We pressed him about the drogs. They are nasty creatures that mostly live and hunt in packs. Over time Ephemerals were able to develop a relationship with the drogs … well, sort of. Paul told us that Ephemeron has special stables for breeding and raising drogs. Even so, the drogs remain vicious and require specially trained handlers to work with them. These stable-raised drogs will accompany 'hunts' or 'caravans' to go into the jungles for rare flowers and crystals. Ephemerals use drogs as defenses against the planet's wild beasts.

"To harvest the rare flowers and crystals, Ephemerals must deal with Crimson Bears and Mammoth Snakes. Paul says the bears have a head like an Earth's grizzly bear's head but that their bodies are like a bison. They are carnivorous and extremely ill-tempered. They can top 1,200 pounds and when they stand on their hind legs, they are over 10 feet tall. A pack of drogs and Mammoth Snakes are the only things Crimson Bears fear."

Tony added to the storytelling. "Mammoth Snakes can grow to fifty feet in length and weigh over a ton. A snake will wrap itself around a bear, suffocating it, then swallow the bear whole. Damn! Picture it. A fifty-foot snake swallowing a 1,200-pound bear. We asked why, with all their technology, they didn't simply kill off these monsters. Paul said it was part of their culture. It didn't make a lot of sense to us, but it would have made no sense to argue the point.

"He said the drogs will sometimes wait till a snake starts swallowing its prey, then while the snake is busy swallowing its victim, they will fly in and chomp through the back of its head, killing it. The drog pack will then consume both snake and prey. Other times, a couple drogs will pretend to be injured, acting like bait for the snake. As the snake approaches, the rest of the pack will descend on it, severing its head.

"Ephemerals prize the snake's skin and its glands. Something about using it for creating an elixir. Then, they feed the snake meat to the drogs. The drogs love it. It's like a reward. Nick, what did you learn from Vince?"

"Vince also told me about Ephemeron's jungles. He said Ephemerals believe that keeping these wild areas pristine is a bond with their gods. A fifty-foot-long snake that weighs a ton sounds damn terrifying to me.

Why take the chance of encountering such a beast on a stroll to pick flowers? They are a strange culture.

"But what I found even more interesting was the backstory of how Ephemerals and drogs developed any bond at all. Strangely, it was because of the Mammoth Snakes. Did Paul tell you the story?"

"No," answered Tony.

"There is a plant, a flowering bush, known as The Serpent Mother. It was given this name because it is critical to the reproductive process of Mammoth Snakes. The Serpent Mother mostly grows near underground hot springs, and its roots extend several feet into the air before uniting at the base of the trunk. These *air roots* capture the warmth of the nearby springs and channel it up through the roots to the top of the bush.

"Pregnant Mammoth Snakes seek out The Serpent Mother to lay their eggs in the warm, moist ground. The warmth of the underground spring serves as an egg incubator, while the roots excrete nutrients that the parchment-like eggshells absorb.

"When the baby snakes hatch, they are attracted to the tops of the bushes where they exude juices from their glands that stimulate the bushes to blossom. Vince said it is a 'frightening' sight to see hundreds of small snakes slithering up and down the bushes, sometimes falling to the ground like devilish drippings.

"Early Ephemeron settlers, frightened by The Serpent Mother plant's capability to propagate the Mammoth Snake, sought to destroy the bush and thereby eliminate the Mammoth Snake's population, but an observant horticulturist noticed that the wild drogs never attacked the baby snakes until the bush flowered. It is only then the drogs would attack the snakes. He understood that the flower of the Serpent Mother bush was prized by drogs.

"The horticulturist, a respected Ephemeral who had long served the monarchy, presented a radical idea to the king. Save the Serpent Mother bush. Harvest its flowers for their extrusions and use the golden nectar to create a bond with the drogs.

"When the horticulturist initially presented his idea, those in the palace hall scoffed at him. The king smirked as well, but tried to be gentle with one of his favored subjects by reminding the horticulturist that drogs and Ephemerals were natural enemies. Yet intrigued, the king challenged him to prove his idea.

"The horticulturist had an assistant bring in a caged, wild drog. The kingdom's hall fell silent except for the drog's screeching and its attempt to break from its confinement. Then the horticulturist pulled out a box that contained nectar harvested from the Serpent Mother bush. Without hesitation, he swabbed the nectar on a couple fingers and stuck them into the cage. The wild drog carefully licked off the nectar, then laid down quietly.

"The kingdom's hall fell silent. The king, as amazed as any, approved the horticulturist's idea. Ephemerals would use the plant's nectar to try to establish a bond with the drogs. The king decreed that The Serpent Mother bush would no longer be destroyed. Ephemerals would train to harvest the nectar. Eventually, the Serpent Mother bush became the link that helped create the symbiosis between Ephemerals and drogs.

"Did Paul tell you about the giant Megaflies? It's another dangerous creature of Ephemeron and a natural predator of drogs and Ephemerals."

"We heard," said Sylvia.

Tony went on to explain. "Paul's voice fell into hushed tones when he started talking about Megaflies. A Megafly is normally a singular creature and a natural predator of both drogs and Ephemerals. Its translucent quality makes it almost invisible to the naked eye. A Megafly's favorite method of attack is to strike its prey with the blinding sun streaming into the eyes of its prey, or strike in the darkest part of the night.

"But what really seemed to scare Paul was Megafly swarms. Under certain conditions, a curse of nature will induce a chemical change that causes Megafly bodies to grow larger, more powerful, and will harden their exoskeletons. Their normal solitary behavior succumbs to a group psychosis, leaving them with no sense of fear. Their reproductive cycle transforms, reducing by half the time it takes for new Megaflies to be born and stimulating their growth into voracious adults. Millions of these ravenous creatures will then set forth, flying, eating, and rampaging across hundreds of miles. Even the protective energy pods that ring the perimeter of the cities are insufficient to hold back the swarm of these creatures.

"Ephemeral cities are protected by energy fields that extended 100 feet high, which is far higher than a Megafly can normally fly. However, during a swarm, some of these enhanced Megaflies are able to fly over the barriers. More frightening is the swarming Megaflies that fly directly into the energy fields. Those on the borders of the swarm are killed, becoming sacrificial shields for the others to breach a city's defenses. Any food out in the open is devoured. Animals or Ephemerals caught in the open rarely survive. In a time of a great swarm, there is little option but to hide in a well-protected shelter, fervently praying the deranged beasts will soon move on. Then, as perplexingly, nature will eventually trigger the swarm's mass death."

"And though they have the technology, they let these beasts live and thrive," observed Nick.

"They say it is part of their customs," said Tony.

"Ephemeral religion is another thing I have a hard time understanding," added Nick. "It is fundamental to how they think about their world and those they inhabit. I try to understand it from the religions we have on Earth, but nothing seems to compare. It is like a bit of this and a bit of that mixed with other ideas. The three Ephemeral clans profess their belief in all their gods. There's like 500 of them. The gods are named in the sacred books that Ephemerals brought from their old planet, Ephemeron One.

"Yet, the clans perceive and honor the gods in different ways. Some think a statue of a god is an actual receptacle for a living god. It is hard for me to understand how a god can live within the many replicas of itself. Then another clan thinks statues are only conduits to the gods. This I can understand. And the third clan seems to embrace both these things. Again, another contradiction that makes little sense. One would think their society would have torn itself apart with its differences. But, somehow, they have held onto their 1,000-year Selection process that picks the planet's ruling monarchy and they've done it for many, many thousands of years."

Sylvia pulled a beer from the ice chest. Cold waters of condensation streamed down the bottle, dripping onto the deck. The moonlight framed her sipping the golden liquid.

"What they have also held onto is their lies to themselves," she sniped. "They face no real hardship. They have created a world of contradictions that they do not have to face. They tell themselves they are peaceful and bury conflict under their addiction to the energy they reap from others. Paul said that their oracles frequently look for signs from the gods above. I wonder if the signs will foretell of three humans who will be invading their world and upending their lives."

"What of Tubby Vaughn?" interrupted Tony. "How important is your vengeance? If tomorrow you found the location of Tubby Vaughn, would you take the time to kill him and let Sylvia and I go to Ephemeron on our own? Paul and Vince, who we say we hate, now offer us an alliance and a chance to free ourselves and the rest of humanity."

"Tony, though I curse the aliens within us and want to escape their hold on us, those who shot me can't be forgiven. It is the fate of the matter. And lately, fate has not been kind. It has listened only to itself."

"Paul said a strange thing," interjected Sylvia. "I didn't think much of it at the time. He said that '*the deaths of soldiers do not end the thirst of a wicked god.*' As I think about it, it seemed he was implying that killing the Draxis agents would not end our task."

"We will need to prepare ourselves," warned Nick. "Our entanglement with the drogs is only a few days away. We will be at the mercy of the Ephemerals. They say we will still have control over our physical selves, that we can withdraw back into our human selves. But they have lied so many times before. They control the E-stations. Perhaps we will become *captives trapped in a worse entanglement.*

"Sylvia, do you still want to be choose … to be entangled? None of us knows what being inside a drog will be like."

"Sometimes, none of us can escape fate," said Sylvia without hesitation. "I won't abandon you two, nor would I want to be left behind either. I've made my choice. We will do this together."

On Ephemeron, the rebels were preparing three assassin drogs. Calculations were made to optimize the upcoming reverse-entanglement channels with the humans.

For the entanglements using Paul and Vince as conduits, the rebels felt confident that two of the selected drogs would be successful recipients. The technicians were less certain of establishing a new drog entanglement for Sylvia, whose situation was unique. She had not yet been entangled with an Ephemeral, nor could the rebels risk a random entanglement since such an Ephemeral might not be on their side.

It was concluded that the *Sylvia situation* would require a direct entanglement between her and a drog. Her modified E-station would manage the entanglement channel so the drog would not be able to control Sylvia. But establishing a direct entanglement with a drog would be many times more intense than the secondary entanglements of Nick and Tony passing through Vince and Paul's E-stations to control their drogs.

The rebel technician looked again at the results of their predictive analysis. The results showed that the best entanglement match for Sylvia was with the alpha female drog. The match was concerning for a variety of reasons. The drog was relatively young, only recently having risen to alpha status. Perhaps because of her new status, she sometimes exhibited rash intemperance. She trusted only one Ephemeral handler on expeditions into Ephemeron's wild areas. Despite her difficult behaviors, the other drogs willingly followed her. It had made for effective and fruitful forays gathering the rare wildflowers and crystals of Ephemeron.

"How far along are you with the E-station reprogramming for the 1,000 Earthlings?" asked one of the rebel team leaders.

"We need another week or so. We are going through our final checks. May the gods bless and protect us. When we do this, it will create a firestorm."

"The gods will see that we fight for them. Let me know when all is completed. The final approval of leadership is pending."

In a quickly arranged conversation between Mr. Coco, Paul, Vince, and the E-station IT expert, the timing of the humans' entanglement with the drogs was discussed.

"My concern is that the humans will need time to acclimate to their entanglements with the drogs and time to become familiar with Ephemeron," pondered Mr. Coco.

"And how about us?" noted Paul, not really asking it as a question. "Neither Vince nor I have been entangled with drogs. Creating a three-way entanglement between ourselves, the humans, and the drogs will be as new for us as it will be for Nick and Tony. We'll need time to acclimate, too."

"A three-way entanglement is complex," cautioned the IT expert. "But one thing in our favor is that it only uses three E-stations. When we ramp up our efforts for the extra thousand humans, we will be at far higher risk. My recommendation is to bring the three Earthlings over as soon as possible and let them adapt and we hold off on the reverse entanglement of the other 1,000 humans. It's too much to manage all at once."

"We can't hold off very long," responded Mr. Coco. "Everything must coordinate with the Crystal Moon Hunt and Overlord Draxis's festivities. There will only be a short window to get to his Ephemeral agents and kill them. Selection is only weeks away. It is now or never. The 1,000 E-stations must be ready. Nick and his friends will only get a couple days to acclimate. Plus, we have to mask our efforts from The Watchers." Mr. Coco slurped down his Foxcovvy beverage and flagged the waiter for another.

"Humans, Ephemerals, and drogs will all be sharing consciousness at once," said Vince, with uncertainties swirling in his mind.

"Well, Vince, Nick has said he has wanted to wring your neck," said Paul morbidly. "I guess this may be his chance to get back at you."

"Enough," demanded Mr. Coco. "Paul. Vince. Reach out to the three humans. Get confirmation that they're still willing to do this. As soon as they say yes, let's move forward. See if you can reach them today. It is still early evening on Earth. They should be awake."

On Earth, Nick and Tony simultaneously felt a warning tingle. "I have a visitor," announced Nick.

"Me, too," echoed Tony.

"What do you two want?" snapped Nick harshly. "Sylvia is here. If you want to talk to us, you'll need to set up a double entanglement."

"Sure, Nick. Give us moment."

Soon, the familiar pulse of Vince and Paul's energy fields engulfed the group. The humans were outside on the deck since nobody had thought about taking the matter inside where they might stay unseen.

With luck they would escape detection, but their carelessness foretold of the many ways the coming days could succumb to disaster.

"The drogs are ready," stated Paul. "We are ready. Every day we wait, there is greater risk for us all."

Sylvia pulled a long draw on her beer as did Tony. Nick wished he could bring his Glock and wondered if humanity's gods had designed an elaborate ill-humored ruse to snatch the deaths of Tubby Vaughn and Pearce Savage from his vengeance.

"I'm ready," said Nick coldly.

Sylvia and Tony locked eyes. Sylvia raised her bottle for a toast, "To the drogs."

"To the drogs," declared Nick and Tony, clinking their bottles with hers.

"When does this happen?" asked Tony nervously. His hands twitched. His body felt cold though it was a warm summer night.

"Tomorrow," answered Paul. "A few reminders. Go out early tomorrow morning and buy some canned food. Nothing that will spoil. Technically, you will still be able to control your physical bodies, but the truth is that most of your effort will be spent within the consciousness of the drogs you inhabit.

"Nick and Tony, your consciousnesses will be intermingled with Vince and I through our E-stations. We will provide guidance to you as best we can, but the entanglement with drogs will be new for us, too. There are likely to be times when you'll be on your own to make the best choice you can. May the gods keep you in their favor.

"Sylvia, your situation will be the most daring and the most fraught with danger. You will be directly entangled with a drog. You have no experience with entanglement. It could be overwhelming."

"How long will all of this last?" asked Sylvia.

"We don't know," answered Paul. "The annual Crystal Moon Hunt will kick off soon. It usually lasts about a week. Overlord Draxis has arranged for festivities to coincide with the hunt. Our sources say that Draxis will use the festivities to begin his assault on Earth by triggering the sleeper agents."

Vince spoke. "We're bringing you in now, so you have a chance to adapt. We know this is a lot for you."

"And your promise to us—to Earth—is that you will leave our planet," prodded Nick for confirmation.

Paul answered. "The promise is that if I become king, then Ephemeron will sever all ties with Earth. All our entanglements with you will be broken. If we can successfully turn Ephemeron's populace against the Overlord, and if the Omegan clan is Selected for the next monarchy, I will uphold that promise."

"A promise shouldn't be dependent on more than one 'if,'" stated Sylvia. "I counted at least two."

"And you say the humans that the sleeper agents inhabit are so powerful that they can affect the world?" pressed Tony.

"You remember Shelton Robertson, the billionaire who was funding terrorist cells around the world? One of the other agents is a country's leader that is threatening an 'incursion' into a neighboring country's territory. It will be more than an incursion; it will become a war. Another sleeper agent is a notorious illegal arms dealer that is ready to supply a large volume of powerful weapons into the hands of a group that will upend a continent's fragile political boundaries. The third provides clandestine capabilities that pushes the illegal development and distribution of nuclear weapons."

Sylvia and Tony looked over at Nick, hoping he had some wise words to say. He had none.

They had volunteered for this nightmare. Now, they would have to live through it … or die by it.

33

*It was bliss and terror and new and overwhelming
and wonderful, all at the same time.*

The next morning, the humans unloaded their grocery store collection of canned cuisine: various pastas, vegetables, canned meats, a repertoire of junk snacks, packaged cheeses, instant coffee, bottled juice, a hodgepodge of other packaged foods, and two fresh items—two gallons of fresh milk and a dozen eggs. Sylvia insisted they would be a treasured choices. And if not needed, they could throw the items away.

Tony, for no logical reason, filled up the BBQ grill's propane tank.

How does one prepare for an interstellar trip across the universe while one's body stays back at a rented house? Tony unproductively searched the internet for interstellar travel answers. He found mostly conjectures and wacko first-person accounts.

Sylvia continued her background search on Tubby Vaughn.

Nick checked and fidgeted with his gun. Their drog entanglement was to begin at noon.

As their reverse entanglement moment approached, a slight tingle coursed through their bodies. Two phones and a gun dropped from their hands. A tornadic-like pull swept their consciousness through a psychedelic tunnel of sights, sounds, and visuals. But it was all over in a brief moment.

Their consciousness remembered what they had been doing back on Earth, yet there was nothing familiar with what they were perceiving. In Nick's and Tony's mind, the subconscious voices of Vince and Paul told them everything was working properly. Everything was fine. It was good to hear the words, even if every sight, sound, and smell was different.

For Sylvia, there was no familiar soothing voice. She was conscious of her Earthly self, but another consciousness dominated her mind. It churned like a deep raging violence.

As Sylvia struggled to adapt to the moment, she saw what the drog saw. She felt what the drog felt. Vince and Paul had told her to try to stay calm; to let it wash over her. She tried to make their words her guide. She told herself to breathe deeply. She closed her mind's eye to the visuals, but the consciousness of the drog was strong.

Sylvia's mind was inside a raging beast. As she struggled to orient herself, she realized the Ephemerals had lied once again. The entanglement was more than a simple emotional entanglement. It was also a connection of consciousness.

Her mind called out to Tony and Nick.

There was no response.

What she saw through the drog's eyes was a world of insect-like creatures. A tall, silver-winged insect with multichromatic eyes stood below, emitting a discordant buzz.

Was it friend or foe? It was difficult to translate the buzz into human words, but her merged consciousness with the drog made her think the silver-winged insect was trying to calm her drog. Sylvia guessed that the sudden appearance of her human consciousness had startled the drog because it also didn't understand its new feelings.

Sylvia again closed her mind's eye, trying her best to exude calmness, hoping this would calm the drog. It seemed to work. She could feel the drog settle on its perch.

Daring to open her consciousness to see through the drog's eyes, Sylvia observed ghastly-looking insects approach her, seeming with reverence, bending their heads down as they touched Sylvia's drog with their antennae. Others regurgitated chewed food like an offering.

If these insects were what she looked like, then she had six legs, and an exoskeleton like an arthropod. Her legs were hairy, like a fly's, and the body a slightly flattened oval.

Most of the drog creatures surrounding her were about three feet long. Stiff hairs like short spines stuck out from each body. Their mouths were shaped like an Earthly insect's mandibles, though she saw that these creatures were outfitted with razor teeth. Some had two wings, while others had four. The wings were a mix of iridescent yellows, purples, and greens. Their large yellow and black compound convex eyes were rimmed by turquoise sockets.

A multitude of these creatures surrounded Sylvia. She had to momentarily close her mind's eye. They were terrifying. She fought to breathe slowly.

Her senses were on overload. The drogs and the nearby Ephemeral handlers, emitted a constant buzzing. Smells of vomited chewed foliage and strong-smelling meat permeated the air. Other smells wafted into her consciousness, discerned by the drog's keen olfactory senses.

These other fainter smells triggered an image of a distant temple surrounded by a jungle. Somehow, she knew its location without ever having been there.

While the sounds and smells of Ephemeron were particularly harsh, it was the drog's vision that was the most disorienting. Looking through a drog's compound, multiprismatic eyes was like being sur-rounded by hundreds of miniature television screens.

Initially, she tried to concentrate on a single small image, then concentrate on another, but this technique proved tedious and far more disorienting. Sylvia found her best option was to let the drog understand what it was seeing, then simply try to read the drog's mind.

Sylvia felt a tingling in her core. It reminded her of the feeling she had experienced just prior to being entangled with the drog. Were the Ephemerals going to pull her out of her entanglement? Had it already been a failure?

Instead, she heard a gentle voice, though not one she recognized.

"Sylvia. My name is Mr. Coco. We are monitoring your condition. We realize everything seems out of control, but you are actually doing quite well. I'm sure you noticed that the drog you're inside of was startled by your arrival. I think it has calmed a bit now. That's a testament to you. Nick and Tony are enduring a similar adjustment."

Though Sylvia had heard the descriptions of what it was going to be like to have an Ephemeral inside her mind, it was weirder than she had imagined. Mr. Coco's voice was clear as someone speaking standing very close to her, but the voice emanated from directly inside her mind.

She spoke back to him from her mind. "Vince and Paul lied to us. Entanglement is more than an emotional attachment. I can feel what the drog feels. I see what it sees. I smell what it smells. Yet, I can feel myself sitting in the room back on Earth. I think I'm going to be sick."

"How could you expect us to tell you everything at once?" replied Mr. Coco. "I don't know everything Vince and Paul said. Perhaps they minimized a few details. Ephemerals have been entangled with many life-forms for thousands of years. Our E-stations manage the connections and the levels of consciousness that Ephemerals experience. Your reverse entanglement may be different. Give it some time. I have every confidence that you will adjust to your drog."

Sylvia closed her eyes, trying to steady herself. She could feel her human body nervously twitching back on Earth.

What had she signed up for? She worried about Tony. She worried about Nick.

"Sylvia? Sylvia, can you hear me?" It was Tony's voice in her head.

"Yes! I can hear you. Where are you? Are you two okay?"

"Yes. Both of us are okay, but my mind is reeling. I feel like I'm on a crazy drug trip. It's even stranger than Paul talking inside my head. Sylvia, what about you? Nick and I have Vince and Paul as guides. Do you have anyone?"

"I'm not sure. An Ephemeral named Mr. Coco said I was being monitored. I miss you. I wish you were with me."

"Sylvia, we are. Our drogs are standing in front of you."

Sylvia opened her mind, letting herself peer through the drog's prismatic eyes. Two drogs stood inches from her. They were as horrible-looking as every other drog, but she sensed a difference in them.

Her mind told her drog to raise up one of its appendages and hold it forward, as her mind spoke to Tony. "If it's you, Tony, touch my hand."

Tony's drog reached out and touched her drog's appendage. "Nick is to my right. He is reaching out to you, too."

She saw the other nearby drog holding out its appendage. She touched it. Nick's voice entered her head.

"Sylvia, it's me. The Ephemerals put you inside the alpha drog. It's just like you."

Sylvia almost laughed. It was so Nick.

"I see you both. What have we got ourselves into? I'm struggling to understand it all. If I think about myself back in the rented house, then I can sense everything around me there. If I think about myself inside this drog, I can sense what it's sensing."

"Paul said the E-stations will help us manage the sensations," said Tony. "It's why we can flip our consciousness back and forth across our human forms and the drogs."

"What are the thin, wispy-like insects? They seem to be monitoring the drogs. Are they the Ephemerals?"

"Yes," answered Nick. "Would you ever have imagined it? This is not what I pictured aliens would be."

Breaking through their conversation, a loud screech punctured the air, earning the attention of drogs and Ephemerals. The entangled humans felt the drogs instinctively stiffen in response and the drogs' heartbeats sped up.

"The Ephemeral who made that screech is the Hunt Master," explained Mr. Coco's voice.

The Hunt Master stood on a high perch that overlooked a hundred-plus creatures, a mix of Ephemerals, drogs, and other beasts. The Hunt Master exhaled another screech. This one was long and warbling.

The indiscriminate mingling of drogs and Ephemerals surrounded them.

Mr. Coco's voice continued his explanation. "A hunting caravan is being assembled. It is the Crystal Moon Hunt. The caravan ventures into Ephemeron's jungles to gather rare flowers and crystals."

He pointed Sylvia's attention to the different participants.

"The brownish-green Ephemerals closest to the city gate's exit are Ephemeral scouts. Their job is to go ahead of the caravan to determine if there are signs of wild creatures in the area."

Sylvia noticed that the scouts' wings were larger and their bodies longer than other Ephemerals. Each wore a chest rig that held what looked like two guns and associated ammo.

Mr. Coco explained the guns and ammo.

"The first gun is called a Stinger. It holds a clip of 12 shots and has a range of 50-60 yards. Their purpose is to defend against attacking Megaflies. The ammo is designed to explode like a small grenade that throws out a destructive pulse designed to kill a Megafly within a

20-yard radius. The second gun the Scouts carry is called a Bolt, which is a pulse laser weapon. By tradition, Scouts use the Bolt against Mammoth Snakes. Also, by tradition, we try not to injure Crimson Bears. We use drogs to scare them off. It is wild drogs and Mammoth Snakes that the Crimson Bears must fear. Only, if necessary, would a Bolt be used.

Noting Sylvia's attention to another group of Ephemeral hunters, Mr. Coco explained.

"Behind the drog handlers are schleppers with their Zalmas. The schleppers check the harnesses and storage bags that are slung over the Zalmas. They carry the treasure of flowers and crystals that are so important to Ephemeron.

"Zalmas are social creatures that have adapted easily to Ephemerals. Their sense of smell and hearing are acute, and you'll notice that their four ears are in a constant state of searching. The schleppers keep a close eye on the Zalmas' ears. When the ears stop twitching and point in a direction, it is a concerning sign. When they exude low grumbles, it means danger is close. Although Zalmas are hardy pack animals, their tendency in the presence of danger is to flee. An important responsibility of a schlepper was to keep a Zalma calm when danger is nearby."

Sylvia guessed Zalmas were about six feet tall, from the ground to the head. The animals looked sturdy and sure-footed. Their feet were cloven, and their thick mottled-green hide appeared as if it would be a natural jungle camouflage.

Mr. Coco directed Sylvia's attention to another group.

"There are two types of *pickers*. One way to tell them apart is by the emblems they wear. Flower picker emblems are silver with an embossed design of a flowering Serpent Mother bush. Crystal picker emblems are gold with embossed red lava spewing from a volcano.

"Early on, settlers discovered that certain plants provided unique substances and effects, but the settlers lacked knowledge of proper cultivation techniques, leading to excessive damage to the plants. However, over time, we have learned how to extract the rare substances while preserving a plant's health and vitality. Ephemeron's rare flowers are essential to the social, religious, and economics of Ephemeron. Mastery of this trade takes years of training. The pickers of rare flowers are some of the most respected citizens and are provided many privileges and benefits.

"The Crystal pickers have one of the most dangerous jobs. We lose two or three a year. Ephemeron is blessed with two active crystal-forming veins, but to access those areas the crystal pickers have to cross high-heat areas. Each carries a bag that contains specialized clothing that protects them from the heat. Some crystals form deep underground and then are expulsed into the air by hot water geysers. Other crystals form by the evaporation of pooled areas of super-saturated liquids. Crystals are an essential item for Ephemerals. They are used in our E-stations, for religious activities, and for personal adornments."

Sylvia sensed the alpha drog's eagerness. In a fit of impatience and annoyance, her drog leaped into the air, flying forward against two drogs that were sniping at each other, putting them in their place. A couple Ephemeral handlers shared an appreciative glance. Though the high-domed paddock kept the drogs from flying off prematurely, it was clear that the current gathering of huntsmen and beasts was exciting the drogs.

Though Sylvia was not normally squeamish, the idea of being inside a three-foot-long insect and surrounded by an ever-growing number and variety of other insects, heightened her discomfort.

Around the fence line of the staging area, Ephemeral youngsters peeked through the barrier as they retold each other tales they had heard from adults. The stories were often embellished by adding extra numbers of Crimson Bears that had attacked a caravan or by exaggerating the size of a Mammoth Snake such as telling of how some snakes are more than a hundred feet long.

The stories set the youngest Ephemerals' wings flapping in a mixture of fear and anticipation. Some would hide behind their older siblings. The brave ones explained how, when they are older, they will go out on hunts to bring back the great riches of Ephemeron's jungles. Other youngsters boasted how they would become drog handlers that would lead the pack to kill Mammoth Snakes and guard against Crimson Bears.

It was these stories of bravado and fables that were woven into Ephemeron's zeitgeist from the earliest of ages. And now, excited by stories of bravery and horror, the youngsters waited anxiously, knowing what was to soon happen—the final call of the Hunt Master.

The Hunt Master checked the data readouts generated by distant Ephemeral monitoring devices. The conditions for a Megafly swarm were low. Nevertheless, a protective blessing would be needed before the caravan started. After all, they were gods-fearing insects.

The Hunt Master shrieked, piercing the air, and commanding the attention of the caravan's hunters. His opal and silver staff glowed with iridescent blue, green, and red colors. As he lifted the precious staff, a deep warbling sound echoed across the paddocked area. The young alpha drog buzzed with carnivorous eagerness. The city's iron gate creaked open, revealing a well-worn path that led into the dense wilderness beyond. The scouts flew out first. The drogs and their handlers were next to depart, then the remainder of the caravan.

A screech from the Hunt Master guided the caravan. The drogs flew ahead, ready to attack any jungle beast a scout might stumble upon. The young alpha drog easily took the lead. It had learned quickly. Both of its parents had previously led hunts. The slower Zalmas and their attendant schleppers did their best to keep pace. They were accompanied by the flower and crystal pickers who had little to do until the harvesting sites were reached.

Raw emotions of hunger, power, domination, excitement, and craving surged through the alpha drog. The animalistic emotions swept unrestrained through Sylvia, whose consciousness was merging more and more with the drog. She closed her mind's eye as she had done before. She grasped for a small island of peace, yet there was little as the nearby drogs' insect screams engulfed her. She felt the drog horde bumping against her. In the tumult, Sylvia became aware of another consciousness intruding itself. The drogs were linking together as a hive mind. Their individuality—even the alpha drog's—was succumbing to a horde psychosis.

The handlers were becoming overwhelmed. Their drogs were failing to obey their commands. A signal went up to the Hunt Master who surged forward of the drog pack. He lifted up his staff, emitting a great flash of light and exploding sound. The drogs were knocked back from their flight and the hive mind collapsed. The drogs fell back under the control of their handlers.

The Hunt Master ordered the drogs to be spread apart. There would be a future and more appropriate time to ignite the hive's madness.

The Hunt Master flew high above the caravan, sometimes positioning himself toward the front, other times staying in the rear. As the inevitable stumbles and troubles occurred amongst its participants, the Hunt Master had no hesitation in making a personal intervention. Repeat Ephemeral offenders were unlikely to be part of the next caravan.

Drogs were always the hardest to control. They routinely pushed forward without concern of whether the Zalmas could maintain pace. Drogs were untethered so it seemed that they flew about in a random frenzy. It was only the personal bond between a drog and its handler that restrained a drog from flying unabashedly ahead. Drog handlers would say they had the hardest job.

Though Sylvia could have easily let herself be swept along by the drog's free spirit, she also found comfort in Mr. Coco's words. As the drogs circled ahead of the caravan, Mr. Coco explained that their hunting custom was to shun the use of radio transmissions. Signaling across the different groups in the caravan was performed by visual signals or vocal calls. He said that the custom was a show of reverence to their traditions. Their religion identified many gods associated with the living and nonliving elements of Ephemeron. The wild areas, especially, were home to some of the most powerful and important gods.

"Sylvia," called Tony's voice. "Are you all right? We've been calling out to you. Why aren't you responding?"

"Tony. Oh, my God … yes, I'm fine. I'm sorry. I didn't hear you. It's the drog. Its feelings and urges are so strong. It was like I was swept away. Are you and Nick okay?"

"Yes, but it's more than I expected. A drog's mind is so … so untamed. Being inside a drog feels like being thrust into a churning sea. I can't imagine how it is for you."

"Mr. Coco's voice has helped. I don't know who he is. I'm not entangled with him, but he is able to talk to me. Has Paul told you what's going to happen next?"

"He said the hunting caravan is on its way to a temple that lies deep in the jungle. From there flower pickers will go off to their gardens.

And the crystal pickers will head to the volcanic springs. Half the drogs will protect one group of pickers and half will protect the other group.

"The temple honors an ancient Ephemeral mythology. Two of their gods, Fire and Water, gave birth to two offspring on New Ephemeron. They were named Jong and Zao, precious flower and precious stone. Jong Fused with a descendant of the sun. Zao Fused with a descendant of the land. Their Fusion birthed Ephemeron's bounties of rare flowers and crystals that grace the planet."

"So that's the image I have been seeing," said Sylvia. "I couldn't understand the image in the drog's mind; it was that temple. It seems like it is important for the drogs as well as the Ephemerals. Do you know where Nick is? I hope our drogs aren't sent in different directions."

"A scout found evidence of a Mammoth Snake in the area. Nick's drog was sent ahead to look for it."

"And if they find it, then what?"

"The drogs will kill it or drive it away."

"Tony, I don't see how I will be able to control this drog like the Ephemerals want me to. I feel overwhelmed by its urges and passions; the drog is a wild creature."

"Paul keeps telling me to be patient. That we will accommodate, but I could hear the tension in his voice. I think he is more *hoping* that everything will turn out."

The Hunt Master uttered a warbling shriek that cut across the jungle.

Sylvia's and Tony's drogs halted and hovered, waiting for their instruction. The Hunt Master pointed his staff into the distance. Sylvia's and Tony's drogs raced forward. In little time, they had caught up with Nick's drog. A great commotion was unfolding in the jungle below. Trees and bushes unnaturally bent and swayed. It was then that

Sylvia's drog spotted the gargantuan snake. It was hissing loudly and seemed very angry.

Nick's drog was ahead and above the snake, taunting it. Another drog was circling behind the snake, trying to set up a position from which to attack, but the foliage was thick.

Sylvia's and Tony's drogs responded without hesitation as they, too, took up positions behind the snake. Nick's drog suddenly sprung toward the snake's head, tearing at the snake with its claws, then abruptly pulled away out of its reach.

The snake lunged and missed. Its hisses grew louder. Nick's drog pivoted away, then alighted on the pathway ahead of the snake, offering itself as bait to the fearsome creature.

The Mammoth snake, hissing with great fury, reared up its body, allowing it to peer down on Nick's drog. As its muscles tensed for its killing lunge, the other drogs attacked from behind. Sylvia's drog clamped its mandibles into the snake's spine. The snake, screaming, exerted a vicious lunge, but Nick's drog sprang out of the way.

The snake's head, severed, fell to the ground. Its headless body thrashed convulsively. Tony estimated its head to be almost two feet long.

"Nick, you dumb ass!" yelled Sylvia, not really knowing if he heard her. "You could have gotten yourself killed."

"I was mostly along for the ride," Nick retorted. Sylvia could hear the suppressed excitement in his voice. "A helluva ride, I might add."

"Have you been able to control your drog at all?" questioned Sylvia. "I think the biggest impact I have on my drog is to make it nervous. I know it feels my presence."

"Sometimes I think it listens to my directions, but maybe it is just random coincidence. Vince says it will take time ... as if he has any experience managing these creatures. I can't wait to meet him in person."

"Still want to wring his neck?" asked Sylvia.

"Of course."

"Yeah, me too," added Tony. "But I think I'm having a bit of success with my drog. It's little stuff. Left turn here, right turn there, hover, go forward. It's not perfect but it is progress."

"Well, *little* brother, looks like we'll be tagging along on your coattails."

"Two minutes, Nick. Two minutes."

Nobody could see, but Nick was smiling with his tease. Nick was the elder twin by two minutes.

With the jungle's pathway cleared of the Mammoth Snake, the caravan continued on its journey.

Inside the alpha drog, Sylvia could feel its heart pound and its strong inhalations and exhalations as it flew across the top of the thick green jungle canopy. It was bliss and terror and new and overwhelming and wonderful, all at the same time.

It was a freedom Sylvia had never experienced.

She stopped fighting her instincts to force her control over the drog.

34

"They sit behind walls of self-righteousness . . . .
How can we even hope to talk to them, to tell them our story,
to think that they will listen to our pains and
the pains of so many others across the universe?"

After the encounter with the Mammoth Snake, it was two uneventful days before the hunting caravan reached its destination, a large stone temple deep in the heart of an Ephemeron jungle. The temple rose fifty feet tall and was surrounded by four stonework pathways laid out in intricate chevron patterns. The pathways extended out from the temple following a compass's cardinal directions. Having been untended since last year's Crystal Moon Hunt, the jungle's overgrowth had spread itself through the temple's openings, entwining and wrapping its deep green tentacles like a protective blanket.

Over the next few days, vegetation was cut back, pathways were opened. Pickers were dispatched to the royal flower gardens accompanied by schleppers, Zalmas, and their guardian drogs. Crystal pickers and their supporting entourage were sent to enter the volcanic fires of Ephemeron. Later in the day, one crystal picker would die when a *burp* of lava would be jettisoned in the air and then fall upon him, momentarily entombing him before incinerating him.

The three humans, having become entangled with the drogs and then thrust into their roles as intimate members to the caravan's orchestration, became tuned to Ephemeron's subconscious pulse.

Homages to Ephemeron's gods were everywhere and were embedded in everything Ephemerals did. By following ancient traditions, the Crystal Moon caravan paid homage to the purity of the world Ephemerals inhabited and treasured. And this respect of their customs was how they showed their appreciation for the bounties of rare flowers and crystals provided by their gods and the Ephemeron jungles. Ephemerals believed that their inhabitation of others was their manifest destiny. Adherence to the Ephemeron caravan's traditions was self-sanctifying.

Ephemerals had successfully launched themselves across the universe using a colonizing technology that had unintendedly insulated Ephemerals from understanding or seeing the disruptions caused by their entanglements.

It was this growing understanding of the Ephemeral world that solidified the three humans' awareness that their drog entanglements were no longer a simple transaction to kill three of Draxis's agents.

It was an existential fight for the survival of humanity.

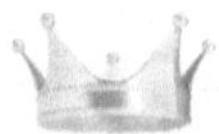

During one of the nights at the temple, the three humans shifted their consciousness back to Earth and their physical bodies. Their bodies had barely moved since they had spent their time on Ephemeron.

Sylvia was the first to speak. "Can persons be good when their actions are bad? Is there an inner self that is separate from one's actions?"

"What are you trying to say, honey?" inquired Tony. "That Ephemerals are merely misunderstood?"

"Their technological superiority has turned into a rationale for conquest. Yet, most spend their days trying to live good lives and be devout. They think of themselves as blessed.

"They sit behind walls of self-righteousness," continued Sylvia. "How can we even hope to talk to them, to tell them our story, to think that they will listen to our pains and the pains of so many others across the universe? They rape us without even knowing what they do."

"Can we talk about this later?" asked Nick. "I'm not dismissing what you're saying. I'm hungry. My drog eats regurgitated foodstuffs of a composition I don't want to imagine. Oddly, while my consciousness is aligned with the drog, then I feel satiated, too. But now, back here on Earth, I'm hungry as hell. What do we have to eat?"

Sylvia gave a look of exasperation. "Am I the only one that's seeing this?"

Chastised, Nick blushed. His red hair and scraggly beard accentuated his embarrassment. "I'm sorry, Sylvia."

"It's okay, Nick. I'm venting. The more I know about Ephemerals, the angrier I become."

"Vince and Paul are helping us take down Draxis," interjected Tony.

"You're defending them? Those two have sucked off your emotional tits for God knows how long."

"Sylvia, that's not fair. I have an Ephemeral living inside me. I'm the one that got the short end of the stick with Vince playing around inside my head. But ask yourself: who is helping us? It's Vince and Paul and your Mr. Coco and a handful of rebels. We're on the same side."

"Oh, Tony … now I feel ashamed. It's just that the whole thing makes me so mad." She put her arm around him and drew him close. "I love you, Tony."

"I love you, too."

Sylvia smiled broadly. "Well, if truth be told, I'm famished, too. How does canned meat, canned pasta, and a couple bags of chips sound?"

"Like a king's banquet, honey."

"Can we hang out here for a few days?" asked Tony after their feast. "We'll let the drogs do what they do. When the caravan finishes its foray into the jungle, they can call us back. We'll reenter the monsters and take down the Draxis bastards."

"Won't you miss your drog buddy?" pressed Nick. "So far, you're the drog superstar. Won't it feel abandoned? Where's your loyalty?" Nick downed a healthy swig of beer.

"Do you really think I'm a superstar?" asked Tony gratuitously.

Sylvia and Nick burst into laughter. It felt good to laugh.

"Tony, you are my superstar," said Sylvia suggestively as she lifted a bottle of beer to her lips.

"I haven't felt this powerless in a long time," reflected Nick, holding his Glock. "Being inside the drog is like being a babe in the woods. I have little control and I'm at the mercy of its whims."

"Don't try controlling it," suggested Tony. "When I tried to control my drog, it never worked. It's more like desiring or wanting an experience. If I think I want to fly high because it will feel good, the drog responds. If I share my desires emotionally, the drog responds. The drog responds to feelings more than forcing control over it. It has to trust you."

"Sharing my feelings was never my strong suit," responded Nick. "How am I supposed to do that all of a sudden?"

"Well, it's true you rarely talk about your feelings, brother, but that doesn't mean you don't have feelings. The drog can sense those feelings; that's what you need to use."

"How about you, Sylvia?" wondered Nick.

"To be honest, I've spent most of my time inside the drog trying to remain calm. Entanglement with an alien insect has been rather unsettling. Mr. Coco said to be patient and that my bond with the drog will grow. Being inside the alpha drog is like riding a wild stallion. But I think Tony's onto something. I feel like it is aware of me. At times, I feel like it is being responsive to me, to my feelings, to my thoughts."

"We don't have a lot of time left to spend with them, anyway," said Nick. "In a few days, the Crystal Moon Hunt will end and we'll return to Ephemeron's capital."

"I know."

"Being entangled with the drogs and being surrounded by Ephemerals is worse than my entanglement with Paul," said Tony. "Inside the drog it is like being stuck inside an unending nightmare. At least with Paul, he sometimes had to leave me alone to replenish himself."

"He could be listening right now."

"So what. What is he going to do? Disentangle me? They need us. Paul and Vince know exactly how crazy their world is becoming. Draxis and his Earth-agents are just the beginning of the insanity. You know what I'm talking about. It's only because there are no consequences."

Seeing the spirited fire in Tony's eyes, Nick lifted his beer bottle in a salute. "Welcome back, brother."

Tony sipped from his beer. He knew he had been the weak link lately, even though he was doing his best to fight back.

Discovering Paul, an alien, inside his head had cartwheeled Tony into a dark abyss. But he had people to fight for, people he cared about. Sure, it was important to help save the Earth, to save humanity, but he needed to be there for Sylvia and Nick.

Blood is thicker, as the saying goes.

"Ephemerals are weak," continued Tony, almost muttering "They don't know it. They wouldn't know what to do if they were faced with someone who stood up to them. Sylvia, you've been the best thing that has ever happened to me. But right now, I would give it all up to bring down those bastards."

Sylvia and Nick exchanged looks. Yup, Tony was back.

"I have a story to tell," said Sylvia, opening another bottle of beer and munching on more junk food. Hearing no objections, she told the story.

"An evil man was sent to hell. The Devil greeted him and said the man could pick his punishment. The man thought this was quite lucky. So, the first punishment the Devil offered was that the man would be subjected to 24 hours a day of loud thrash metal music for eternity. The man, a classical musician by trade, thought that one minute of such music was too horrible of a torture so asked what the second choice was. The Devil took him to a landscape, which, if the man chose to enter, would curse him with an eternity of poxes, infections, boils, and consumptions, but there was beautiful sun and clouds and temperate breezes that covered the landscape. The sinner looked over the sinners of this landscape and saw they all had gone insane from the pains and afflictions that they could never escape. The sinner asked what his third choice was. The Devil took him to a room where damned naked men and women stood neck deep in the foulest smelling room of shit. 'This is your third eternity,' said the Devil. 'What choice do you make?'

"After a brief reflection the sinner said, 'I will stand in the room of shit for all eternity.' The Devil smiled and said, 'So it shall be. Now get in there.' Gagging and vomiting from the wrenching smell, the sinner man waded naked into the room until he too stood standing neck deep in shit … for all eternity. Then a gong struck, and the Devil said, 'Time's up. Back on your heads!'"

Sylvia quaffed a hefty swig of her beer.

Tony's and Nick's eyes bulged with the story's ending.

"The point of the story, my dear ones, is that it's time for us to return to Ephemeron and our drogs. Hopefully, one day, heaven's high mercy will pull us out of the shit we are in."

35

With loops, figure eights, and twists,
Nick's and Sylvia's drogs carved across the sky,
leaving their drog handlers as receding distant specks.

Back on Ephemeron and inside his drog, Nick cursed his fate, the drog, Vince, Overlord Draxis, Ephemerals in general, and himself. But in that moment of anger, Nick discovered the truth to Tony's words. The drog responded to Nick's feelings.

Nick wasn't sure how to interpret the drog's unexpected responsiveness. It was as if Nick's anger had earned the drog's respect. It was as if his and the drog's entanglement had deepened.

There was something else Nick had begun to realize over the last days. The drog seemed to carry a great emptiness. Nick had tried to put his finger on it, but it wasn't until this moment when the drog responded to Nick's rage that Nick understood.

The drog was a creature, *formerly wild,* but now tamed by its Ephemeral masters. Its spirit had been dimmed by the lure of hand-fed nectars of the Serpent Mother bush and the electric canes of obedience that the drog masters carried.

Somehow Nick's fury had reawakened the drog's spirit.

Maybe it was the simple joy of regaining its long-lost spirit or maybe it was a sign of thanks, but whatever it was, the drog was now responding to Nick's wishes. And with the drog's loyalty at his emotional fingertips, Nick willed the drog to fly high, to fly far and wide over the Ephemeral jungle, to fly unencumbered like it had been born to do.

In the jungle below, the drog handlers were in an uproar. They could not understand why Nick's drog had gone AWOL. Of course, if they had known a raging human was inside the drog, they could have put two and two together. But they didn't. And even though Ephemerals could fly, none could fly as high as a drog and, to be honest, the Ephemeral drog handlers were scared. They had seen those occasions, thankfully rare, when a drog went insane and lashed out at nearby Ephemerals. It always ended badly, with a few Ephemerals dying before the drog could be *euthanized*.

The drog handlers also feared calling the Hunt Master for help. Their failure to control the drog would be black marks on their performance sheets and likely to have serious ramifications.

"Send the alpha drog," blurted one of the handlers. "Maybe the alpha drog can bring back that drog."

"Yes. Yes," several answered in chorus.

And so, the alpha drog, with Sylvia inside, was sent to reclaim the errant drog.

Through the eyes of the drog, Nick could see the fast approach of another drog, not knowing it was Sylvia's drog. Well, he thought to himself, let's see if it can catch me. And so, Nick sent his drog racing farther into the distance. The crisply pummeling wind was liberating. The sun's warming rays seemed to beckon Nick and his drog higher.

Eventually, Sylvia's drog closed the gap, but strangely, never struck the escaped drog. Instead, the alpha drog entered into a mirror of flight moves, dancing in synchronicity across the skies.

With loops, figure eights, and twists, Nick's and Sylvia's drogs carved across the sky, leaving their drog handlers as receding distant specks.

For Nick, he felt like he was on a wild steed running untethered. His drog's wings pulled like mighty oars, sending him higher and higher.

The Ephemeral sun beamed down its warming approval. Sylvia's alpha drog urged Nick's drog onward, to fly free.

To Sylvia, it seemed her drog enjoyed the breakout as much. This was the life of drogs before Ephemerals.

"Nick, what are you doing?" It was Vince's voice. "Sylvia is in the drog behind you. You have to return to the handlers. If you don't return, they will kill your drog. All will be lost."

Nick muttered a curse, deeply tempted to ignore Vince's warning, but then willed the drog to stop and hover. Sylvia's alpha drog, catching up, hovered in front of Nick's rebellious drog while chattering half-hearted admonitions.

Sylvia's voice pierced the moment. "Nick, you crazy bastard."

"Sorry, Sylvia. I had to. The drog was finally obeying my thoughts, doing what I wanted it to do. It felt good flying off, both for me and the drog. Tell me, why didn't you stop me? Your drog just flew as my drog flew."

"I think the alpha drog enjoyed it as much as your drog. But enough is enough. Time to return home."

"Yes, Mom."

"You must have driven your mom crazy."

Nick laughed, knowing how true it was. "Tony wasn't any easier, so multiply that times two."

As Sylvia's and Nick's drogs turned back to return to the temple, explosions burst into the air off in the distance over the jungle canopy. It was in the area where the flower pickers were located. More bursts shattered the sky. Distant sounds of frenetic insects churned the air.

Instinctively, the alpha drog headed toward the commotion. Nick's drog followed.

More bursts lit the air. Then Nick and Sylvia saw a swarm of several dozen Megaflies attacking the flower pickers. Scouts were firing their guns in defense. Though knocking out several of the Megaflies, the Megafly numbers were too many. It was a mini-swarm. Nick could see dead and dying flower pickers strewn on the ground while others were trying to protect their precious harvest.

Without hesitation, Sylvia and Nick's drogs instinctively dove into the fray, ripping at the Megaflies, then banked around and sped back into the swarm. Again and again the Nick and Sylvia's drogs attacked fearlessly as the explosions of Stinger guns blasted dangerously close. The Megaflies, seemingly hypnotized by the plucked flowers and their sweet nectars, were undeterred. Unflinchingly, they attacked the flower pickers and the cargo-laden Zalmas.

On one dive into the swarm, Nick's drog screeched in painful agony as a Megafly took a chomp out of the drog's side. Feelings of retribution surged through Nick, which seemed to embolden the drog even more. So, again it returned to the fray, taking on two Megaflies face-to-face. Sylvia's drog was squaring off against three of the violent creatures. The swarm was winning. A day's collection of nectar was being stolen. The situation looked hopeless.

Sylvia's could feel the rapid beating of the alpha drog's heart and its deep breaths. Her drog seemed unfazed by the loss of one of its limbs. She observed that one of the three Megaflies was seriously injured, barely able to hover. A wing was damaged, and a large open wound stretched across the length of its body. With Sylvia and the alpha drog entangled, the drog instantly noticed the same weakened Megafly. With lighting quick acceleration, the drog attacked and killed the Megafly, but the attack left the alpha drog in a precarious position with one Megafly in front and one behind.

A wave of drog screeches reached Sylvia and her drog.

Then, chaos struck, as a pack of drog reinforcements entered the fray. Sylvia could hear Tony's voice screaming some sort of war cry. The reinforcements mercilessly tore through the Megaflies, sending them all to their deaths, leaving some of the dismembered bodies reflexively lurching and bouncing on the ground.

It was late in the day before the flower pickers and the accompanying Zalmas returned to the temple. Nick, Sylvia, and Tony perched their drogs together. The Ephemeral drog handlers were huddled in animated conversation. A few times, a couple of the drog attendants pointed at Nick's drog. But then others would point toward where the fight with the Megaflies had occurred.

"They were going to kill your drog for being disobedient," said Vince. "But your drog's bravery has earned it a reprieve."

"Where the hell have you been, Vince? I could have used some help."

"What could I have done, Nick? You were starting to connect with the drog when you took off. Was I supposed to stop the bonding? Then what was I supposed to do when you were in the middle of the fight? Was I supposed to tell you how to fight? You and your drog's reactions took over. There really was nothing I could do. And if I had tried, I'm sure it would have ended badly. I had to let it play out. Besides, you're one with the drog now. The plan couldn't have come together any better."

"I still want to wring your neck, Vince."

"I know, Nick, but not today."

The voice of Mr. Coco similarly explained to Sylvia his non-interference, as did Paul for Tony.

"What about my drog's missing limb?" asked Sylvia of Mr. Coco, her tone full of concern.

"Drog limbs regenerate. By the time we return to the capital, it should be mostly healed. In any case, it will be seen as a mark of stature and bravery."

"I'm exhausted and so is my drog."

"Get some sleep, Sylvia. Rest up on Earth. We'll call you back when the time is close."

"Will Nick and Tony be joining me?"

"Of course. You've all done well."

36

*"He tells them Ephemerals are the superior race
of the universe and we deserve the riches of the universe.
It is a powerful message."*

Artemesia, the Xermegan High Priestess, and her attendant, Meerlex, the Vimegan spy, were awakened by the morning's streaming sunlight.

Disentangling themselves from the prior night's respite, Artemesia spoke. "The Crystal Moon caravan will be returning soon. Overlord Draxis will stand on the receiving podium with King Boolong and Vimegan Commander Vaaruv. He wants the people to see him as the new king."

"Many Ephemerals believe in his ideas," responded Meerlex. "He tells them Ephemerals are the superior race of the universe and we deserve the riches of the universe. It is a powerful message."

"The ancient texts have never taught that we should have dominion over the universe. That is the idea and interpretation of Overlord Draxis."

"Overlord Draxis has said that Alborix has spoken to him directly."

"I am the High Priestess of the Xermegan clan. I have spent my life speaking to all our gods. They do not converse like you and I speak. When they speak, they speak through actions and mysterious ways."

"Maybe Alborix sees the Overlord as special. Can we truly say they have not spoken together?"

"Meerlex, how many years have you been at my side? You know the Overlord. You've seen what happens to Ephemerals who have criticized him. Do you think he is driven by compassion? Do you think that if he becomes king of Ephemeron that he will be benevolent?"

Meerlex's mouth dropped open, but no words came out. She was confused by the High Priestess's candid words. Meerlex didn't know if she was supposed to respond to the High Priestess … and if she was supposed to respond, what could she say?

Seeing Meerlex's perplexity, Artemesia let out a short Ephemeral chuckle.

"Meerlex, I don't expect you to answer, but we both know the answer."

"Artemesia, you have arranged The Overlord's festivities. The return of the Crystal Moon caravan will be their start. Ephemerals will see the splendor and attribute it to him."

"I serve the Overlord. I also serve the gods of Ephemeron."

Meerlex waited for the High Priestess to finish her thought, but again only silence filled the air.

A long, weighty silence.

A ringing bell announced the call for morning prayers. Responding to the summons, the High Priestess and her attendant glided through the temple's corridors. Nearby Ephemerals bowed in reverence at the approach of the High Priestess. Entering the inner sanctum, the High Priestess seated herself behind the altar, as she waited to see if Overlord Draxis would be joining the congregation. Meerlex positioned herself in the rear of the temple's chamber as usual.

After waiting for a dutiful time and no appearance by the Overlord, the High Priestess approached close to the altar. She began to sing. The congregation's choir joined in. The service had begun.

In the Overlord's chambers, his attendant cleaned and polished the overlord's limbs, stroked his antennae, and removed small bits of leftover foodstuffs from the overlord's mandibles. The Overlord needed to look his best; he would be walking the streets today and he wanted to be seen and honored. The scheduling of his festivities at the time of the Crystal Moon caravan's return had created much public anticipation. Not one to shy away from the limelight, Overlord Draxis would embrace the spotlight and publicity he had stirred.

A device on his desk rang and an announcement appeared on a screen announcing the incoming callers. With a small trill-sound, images of three Ephemerals were displayed.

"I have been informed that the Crystal Moon caravan will be returning in two days," said the Overlord. "I will be with King Boolong on the receiving platform. I want you three to station yourselves down, in front of the king's podium. You are to wear the Xermegan clan's ceremonial attire. You will greet and honor the hunters. To nearby Ephemerals, you will laud them with extra gifts and energy packets. Your job is to remind the populous of the Xermegan clan's generosity and how we honor Ephemeron culture.

"Now give me an update of the Earthlings that you entangle."

Upon hearing their reports, a smile that looked more like predatory enthusiasm, crossed the Overlord's face. He let loose a rough-like insect squeal and raised himself to full length. His wings beat fiercely. He was hungry.

The nearby attendant stood reverently, a tempting nearby morsel.

Instead, the Overlord breathed deeply and decided to let the attendant live as he reached for a plateful of flipping-and-flopping crunchy ZoZos.

Across the city, a handful of rebel leaders met for the morning's stimulating cups of Foxcovvy. Today there was no card-dealing to signal the reprogramming progress of the 1,000 E-stations. No Watchers were in obvious sight. Still, undercover Watchers might be around so sensitive conversation needed to be conducted carefully.

"Our E-station progress?" asked Mr. Coco in a whisper. "In two days, the Crystal Moon caravan will return."

"We are ready," informed one rebel. "Upon your signal, the protective channels will be dropped. The consciousness of 1,000 humans and 1,000 Ephemerals will be combined. Each will be fully aware of each other within themselves. There will be chaos."

Mr. Traxx fidgeted nervously. He had reluctantly agreed to the plan, but its impending reality was stoking his fears.

"Is there no other way?" pleaded Mr. Traxx. "Many could go insane and some might die. Most will be innocents."

Mr. Coco, patiently but with authority, responded. "Without the cover of the disruption, there is little chance that the drogs will be able to successfully attack the Overlord's agents."

"Every day I pray for the forgiveness of our gods."

"But you know that if we do nothing, far greater horrors will happen," said Mr. Yelty.

"It doesn't make it any easier."

"Mr. Coco, what of the three humans and their entanglement with the drogs?" asked Ms. Bovemont. "What can you tell us?"

"Initially, it was difficult for both the humans and the drogs, but eventually the humans were able to synch with the drogs. Amazing, really, it is all that we had hoped for. The Earthlings are resting on Earth as we speak. Their consciousness with the drogs is still intact, but it is in a muted state. The E-stations are managing the entanglements. The humans will resume their drog entanglements before the caravan returns to the city."

"Watchers," warned Mr. Traxx. "Two just entered."

Mr. Yelty downed his Foxcovvy and said his goodbyes. Slowly, each of the other rebels also dispersed.

Nick, Tony, and Sylvia, upon reentry of their consciousness back to Earth, gobbled down a mishmash of foodstuffs. While inside the drogs, they had felt satiated, but their human bodies were now famished. The milk Sylvia had bought was still fresh. Milk had never tasted so good. Tony cracked a dozen eggs and served them scrambled. Then, each of them slept for almost fourteen hours.

"Tony, wake up," slurred Sylvia still half asleep. "Tony, wake up," she repeated shaking him.

"Leave me alone," he pushed back. "I could sleep for another day." He rolled over, hoping that would help him escape from Sylvia's attention.

Sylvia tossed a plastic package of beef jerky toward Nick, which bounced off his head.

"Damn it," blurted Nick sourly. "Who did that? Tony?"

Sylvia returned her nudging efforts toward Tony, unceremoniously jostling him again and again.

"Okay. Okay. Stop it. I'm awake."

Nick was sitting on the bed, scratching his chest. He looked like hell. His tousled red hair would have made him look like a wild Irish warrior, except for his half-sleepy countenance.

"Damn those drogs," cursed Nick. "It was like living inside a furnace. Sylvia, how are you doing? It was the first time you experienced entanglement. The alpha drog, no less."

"I'm as spent as you two. At first it was overwhelming. I think the prismatic eyesight was what threw me the most. I had to shut my eyes a lot. It was a lot to deal with. You're right, the drogs are savage. And how can my muscles feel sore? I wasn't doing anything physical, just mentally entangled with a drog. Now I understand why Vince and Paul were always running off to recuperate." She arched her back, stretching.

"When do we have to go back?" asked Tony, not having arisen, but had only rolled over to face his friends. His scraggly red mop of hair matched his brother's. His formerly neatly trimmed beard had turned into a scruffy outcrop.

"Mr. Coco said we had a couple days before we had to return."

"Yeah, but what day is it now?"

Sylvia and Nick exchanged glances, each searching for an answer to the question. Then, they burst out laughing. "We have no fucking idea, honey," answered Sylvia between chuckles.

Nick got up from his bed and walked over to a window. He gazed out at nothing in particular, nor was there anything of particular interest to focus on.

Tony struggled to his feet and joined his brother at the window. "What are you thinking about? You're right, the drogs are savage."

"Killing Tubby Vaughn doesn't seem as important as it used to."

"It's because of the drogs, right?"

"Yeah. It was full-time rage, every day."

"But Tubby was one of the guys who shot you."

"He's just a low-life that will end up dead by someone else's hands."

"And Pearce Savage? What about him? He was the mastermind of it all."

"That, I don't think I can let go."

"Perhaps we could borrow a drog and send it his way."

"He would certainly deserve that, but it seems too easy and the fact my drog is billions of light-years from here creates a certain impediment."

"It sounds like you're getting attached to the critter."

"Me? Tony, you bonded with your drog way before Sylvia or I did. You're the drog-whisperer."

A smile crossed Tony's lips. The same smile crossed Nick's. The twins felt closer than they had in a long time.

At that moment, the three humans each heard an Ephemeral voice inside their heads.

"I just heard Mr. Coco's voice," exclaimed Sylvia.

"You're still entangled with the drog," said Mr. Coco. "So, the communication channel is still open between us. We want to set up a special entanglement so all of us can talk together. We need to finalize plans for your drog attacks."

Sylvia looked over at Nick and Tony, who were giving their nodding approval.

A moment later, the room was filled with three different pulsating waves, one wave around each human. Around Sylvia, the waves were blue. Around Tony, green. Around Nick, red. As the pulsing colors intersected, white light became visible. Around each human, the pulses vibrated faster and wider until they finally merged and engulfed the room in a dazzling white pulsing light.

"You've all done well," said Paul. "It is as much as we could have hoped for. The drogs have connected with you. They listen to you."

Nick replied, his tone wary. "What of your promise to break the entanglement with us and leave us in peace? Is that still your promise?"

"If I become king, then yes."

"When do we have to return to the drogs?" asked Tony.

"By Earth time, noon tomorrow."

"How will we know who the Draxis agents are?" asked Sylvia. "How do we get close to them?"

Mr. Coco answered. "The Overlord has directed his closest confidants to stand in front of the receiving platform. When the Crystal Moon caravan returns, its bounties will be displayed to King Boolong, Overlord Draxis, and Commander Vaaruv. As you pass by the platform, you will strike out against his agents who will be standing at street level. They will be wearing the same colors as Overlord Draxis. You will see."

"Won't our drogs be killed for their treachery?" asked Sylvia. "I think I've become attached to mine."

"There's another thing that you must know," said Mr. Coco in a voice that seemed a little too calm.

It immediately raised Nick's wariness. "What do you mean by another thing?"

"The rebels have reprogrammed 1,000 E-stations," explained Vince. "The protective channels will be dropped. The consciousness of a thousand humans and Ephemerals will be suddenly merged. It will be like the first moments that you heard our voices inside your heads, but it will be happening to both humans and Ephemerals at the same time."

"Are you people fucking crazy?" blurted Nick. "I don't give a damn about your Ephemerals, but who are the humans you are targeting?"

"We're not targeting anyone in particular. It will be random."

"Random?! Seriously? The rebels are picking a thousand humans randomly for their plan? Most will be innocents, won't they?"

"There is no other way, Nick."

"When can I wring your neck, Vince? My desire burns brighter."

"You say it's the rebels, but that sounds like a flimsy cover," interrupted Sylvia. "You three are just as much a part of the planning as these … *rebels* … as you call them. And what of you, Mr. Coco? Up until a few days ago, we had never heard of you. But suddenly, you show up and are quite knowledgeable of everything. Are you one of the rebels?"

The pulsing white entanglement light pulsed more forcefully, bringing emphasis to the ensuing long silence.

"I am," finally admitted Mr. Coco. "Merging the consciousness of a 1,000 Ephemerals and humans was to be a cover for your attack of Draxis agents. Without the mayhem, it would look like the Xermegan clan was being specifically targeted. We fear that Ephemerals will revolt and vote for the Xermegan clan to rule Ephemeron, propelling Overlord Draxis into the monarchy. All of humanity will then be in danger, as will many other planets across the universe. You will be colonized and subjugated without any ability to fight back. A thousand humans and their entangled Ephemerals seems to be a reasonable sacrifice."

"There has to be another way," pressed Tony.

"We don't see any. Present us with an option," responded Mr. Coco.

"When is Selection?" asked Tony.

"Two weeks."

"And that determines your planet's monarchy for the next thousand years?" continued Tony.

"Yes. If it's any comfort to hear, Ephemerals will experience the worst of it. Our entanglements feed us. We live by our entanglements. When the disruption occurs, Ephemerals will be thrown out of their entanglements and need to find new hosts. In such an unexpected event, many will likely not find hosts and will die. Humans do not need entanglement. Yes, their lives will be disrupted, but they won't die. They will have the chance to put their lives back together."

"You might think of us as scum," interrupted Vince, "but we are the ones that are fighting against Overlord Draxis. We are the ones fighting for your Earth and humans and the many other intelligent species across the universe. If you don't like our methods, offer us an alternative."

"Time is short," interjected Mr. Coco. "Tomorrow morning, we will visit you again. You will then return to your drogs—or not. We will not force you. Now, we must go. As you have become aware, active entanglements are exhausting."

Without waiting for a response from the humans, the encompassing white light of entanglement vanished.

37

And with a powerful flap of her wings,
Artemesia, the High Priestess, flew out of the temple
and across the cityscape with Meerlex
devoutly following alongside her.

Overlord Draxis had called the High Priestess into his **Chambers.** Neither his attendant nor Meerlex was present.

"The king's emissary visited me this morning," said the High Priestess. "This is the note he handed me."

The Overlord read the king's message. "Why is the king calling together Ephemeron's religious scholars? There was a convocation of scholars earlier this year. What is he up to?"

"It is hard to say. Certainly, the gathering is unexpected. Selection will be soon. The king is old. Perhaps he is thinking of his heir or how Ephemeron will be ruled."

"The note says each clan can be represented by five scholars. Have you thought of who you will bring with you?

"Yes, Overlord. I took the liberty of drawing up this list. I can also bring an attendant. I was intending to bring Meerlex."

"I know these scholars. I approve of your choices. But I caution you; the king is devious. We need to know what he is up to. The Crystal Moon caravan should be returning in a couple days, and I hear they have collected many riches. The start of Xermegan's festivities will coincide with the caravan's return. Everything must go according to plan."

"Overlord, all has been arranged. The great pageantry will shine brightly on the Xermegan clan and your generosity. You will outshine the king himself."

The Overlord's antennae rubbed together in self-stimulating enjoyment. His mandibles opened and shut, clacking together with thoughts of becoming king.

"High Priestess, that is very good to hear. You may go now."

With an ever-respectful bow, the High Priestess exited.

Meerlex was waiting in the grand hallway.

She thought that her mistress looked disturbed, so waited for the High Priestess to speak.

"Our Overlord sees himself as the next king."

"That is no different than yesterday. He has thought of himself that way for some time."

"For tens of thousands of years, the ruler of our world has been decided by Ephemeral citizens, not by self-appointment."

"High Priestess, the people are enamored of him. Should he turn away from the adulation?"

"I have served him for more than a hundred years. I have built him up, helped him navigate the political shoals."

"How could you do less? That was your responsibility and duty."

"So is my duty to our people."

"What is it that he said that has so upset you?"

"He cares not for any, but himself. If he could, he would raise himself to be a god. How could I have been so blind?"

"My dear High Priestess. Actions have been taken. Decisions have been made. How can the course be turned back?"

"Come with me, Meerlex. There are things I must do." And with a powerful flap of her wings, Artemesia, the High Priestess, flew out of the temple and across the cityscape with Meerlex devoutly following alongside her. The sun's rays glinted magnificently off Ephemeron's crystalline moon, rays that reflected and refracted, creating a dazzling sky.

On the far side of the city, a small home sat at the edge of the city's protected perimeter. A small clearing, extended from the backside of the wood-hewn house, separating the city's limits from Ephemeron's jungles.

At the far side of the clearing, laser towers guarded against intrusions by Megaflies and Mammoth snakes. At the edge of the clearing, next to the edge of the jungle, a formidable crisscross of steel fencing guarded against the entry of wandering Crimson Bears.

Seemingly unconcerned by the potential danger represented by the clearing, a short, older Ephemeral tended a garden on the backside of the house.

It was an odd garden, with one part devoted to a variety of common but especially tasty vegetations that any self-respecting Ephemeral would truly appreciate. Another part of the garden was devoted to growing exotic mind-altering flowers prized by most Ephemerals.

The last part of the garden, an enclosed section, was devoted to the growth of thousands of various small insects that would eventually serve as protein bites for the old Ephemeral's meals and to sell to a limited circle of friends. If one were to enter this third section of the garden, one would be met by a cacophony of buzzes, trills, chirps, squeaks, and, if one listened closely … slitherings.

It was this short old Ephemeral that the High Priestess was flying to visit. She and her attendant landed at the edge of the front yard to the house, not crossing over onto the property. Meerlex wondered why the High Priestess did not approach the house; then she saw off in the corner of the yard, hidden in the thick shade of bramble bushes, a large drog staring at them.

"If we don't enter the yard, the drog will only watch," explained the High Priestess.

Then she called out in a loud trilling voice, "Mr. Coco. Mr. Coco. Are you home?"

They waited and when there was no answer, the High Priestess called again. Eventually, Mr. Coco appeared from around the corner of his home. He gave a short wave and a little smile. His chromatic eyes bulged larger, and his antennae wiggled.

"High Priestess, this is a pleasant surprise." Mr. Coco shot a look at his guard drog and gave it a motion of a limb to indicate all was fine. The drog dropped his head back on the ground and closed its eyes.

"It has been a long time, Mr. Coco. It is good to see you."

"What brings you this way, High Priestess? Would you like to come in?"

"Yes, certainly. Mr. Coco, this is my trusted attendant Meerlex. She has been with me for many years."

Mr. Coco nodded his acknowledgment and led them into his wood-hewed house.

"May I offer you a little something to eat? I have worms, ZoZos, and kakoches. They are fresh out of my garden. How about something to drink? Foxcovvy, perhaps?"

"Much appreciated, Mr. Coco. Perhaps next time."

"Well then, what can I do for you, High Priestess?"

"I'm sure you're aware that Overlord Draxis has arranged for three days of Festivities timed with the return of the Crystal Moon caravan. His intent is to put him and the Xermegan clan forefront in the minds of Ephemerals."

"Yes, I am aware."

"The Overlord cannot become king of Ephemeron."

Mr. Coco locked eyes with the High Priestess, then glanced at Meerlex. "High Priestess, surely you jest, and it is a poor jest at that. You are the Overlord's closest confidant. Why do you say these words?"

"I have known you longer."

"That is true, Artemesia. That is true. But still, tell me why you say these words about the Overlord? There is nothing I can do. I am old. Even with a Fusion close at hand, it would not be surprising to see me left unfused. I am happy to live out my days tending my garden."

"The Overlord is heartless. He cares not for Ephemeron. He uses our gods to serve his desire for power. And I know you are not as helpless as you want people to believe. I see the Watchers' reports. They mostly report you and your friends engage in harmless activities. But your friends are a tight-knit group and engage in many quiet conversations."

"Artemesia, you speak of power, but isn't that what drove you into his arms? You abandoned the Omegan clan to gain the Overlord's favor. You have risen to be their High Priestess, second only to the Overlord himself."

"Father, you are right. I wanted the power, but becoming the High Priestess has also brought me closer to Ephemeron's gods and our traditions." Tears flowed down the High Priestess's face. "Can you forgive me? I know I have sinned. Can you believe in me again?"

"Artemesia, you are my child. You admit your sin and you ask for forgiveness. As your father, it is my duty to forgive and welcome you back, but I can do nothing to stop the Overlord."

"Father, I know you are the leader of the rebel group. I know who Mr. Yelty is. I know who Mr. Traxx is. I know who Ms. Bovemont is. I know that Paul and Vince are helping the humans. I know you are helping the humans."

Meerlex sat stunned and wondered if the High Priestess also knew of her Vimegan loyalties.

"Father, I tell you this so you will believe me. You know that if my loyalties were still with the Overlord, then all I'd have to do is to mention my suspicions to him and he would have you and your friends killed. I have protected you."

"Why, child?"

"For many years, I thought the activities of you and your friends were harmless. That you posed no danger to the Overlord. I believed in the Overlord. I kept hoping he would change, but he never did except to become an even worse monster. By then, I felt like I was in too deep, and I could see no way to stop him. If I stood up against him, I would be killed and I would be replaced. So, I let you and your rebels continue. Where I could, I favored your group with protection and fortuitous benefits. I thought that my only hope was if your group became strong."

Artemesia's father rose from his chair and pulled his daughter close. "My child, welcome home." They wept together.

As Artemesia stepped back from her father's embrace, she looked over to Meerlex.

"Meerlex, what do you think of me now? Have I sinned against you, too?"

Meerlex buried her head into her forelimbs, exhaling deep sobs.

In an instant her clandestine world had shattered. All her sacrifices suddenly became vindicated. She was no longer alone. The love that had been in her heart for the High Priestess had exploded into a confusing mix of shock, fulfillment, an even greater love, and hope for the future. Images of her parents' scorn flashed in Meerlex's mind. Would they now welcome her back into the family? She wanted to fly through the cities and lands of Ephemeron, crying out her vindication.

Lost in her deep sobs, Meerlex had not noticed that the High Priestess had approached close, not even noticing that Artemesia's limbs tenderly embraced her.

"Can you forgive me, Meerlex?"

Meerlex, in Artemesia's embrace, raised her head to peer into the High Priestess's eyes.

"High Priestess. I have a confession as well. It is also one of treachery. I am a Vimegan spy. I've made this sacrifice to bring down the Overlord. But over these years serving you, I have fallen in love with you. I would give my life for you. Artemesia, can you forgive me?"

Meerlex had never felt so vulnerable. She had confessed her two deepest secrets. Would the High Priestess now explode into anger?

Artemesia did not release Meerlex from her comforting embrace.

"Meerlex, who would I be to ask forgiveness and then not give forgiveness?" Artemesia released her embrace and kissed her antennae against Meerlex's.

Looking up to her father, Artemesia asked, "What are we to do now?"

Artemesia's father smiled. "Wasn't it you who came to me? What was it that you were going to ask of me?"

Through her remaining tears, Artemesia sniffled back a small laugh. "I don't know, Father. I only knew I was going to ask you for help. It was quite silly of me."

Mr. Coco's gaze met theirs. "What is our greatest fear?"

"Overlord Draxis becoming the next king," answered Artemesia.

"Then it is time for my confession."

"That you will be merging the consciousness of a thousand Ephemerals and humans?" interrupted Artemesia.

"Oh, for the love of our gods, you know of that, too?" exclaimed Mr. Coco, who collapsed onto a nearby chair, stunned by his daughter's knowledge. "We see of no other way."

"You are merging the consciousness of humans and Ephemerals. Why?"

"To create confusion. The overlord's special agents will be at the festivities honoring the completion of the Crystal Moon Hunt. We intend to kill them, but it must look like an accident. We cannot risk creating sympathy for the Xermegan clan that elevates Overlord Draxis to the monarchy."

"But if Draxis dies, too, he cannot be king."

"What are you saying, child?"

"We let the killing of the Draxis agents proceed and we kill Overlord Draxis, too. We let our people see it all, but we don't merge Ephemerals and humans. They are innocents."

"And what of the upcoming Selection for Ephemeron's next ruling clan? Won't that create sympathy for the Xermegan clan?"

"Yes, there will be turmoil, but we let Ephemerals decide their fate, without Draxis."

"Who will kill the Overlord? He will be on the podium with the king and be well-protected."

"Meerlex and I will be on the podium. I will kill Draxis."

"*No!*" exclaimed Meerlex. "I will do it. I have nothing to lose. This is what I have sacrificed for."

Seeing hesitation in Mr. Coco's and the High Priestess's faces, Meerlex forcefully continued her plea. "I've earned this right. If you love me, Artemesia, you will let me do this task."

"It saves the thousand Ephemerals and humans," acknowledged Mr. Coco.

"Father, there is something that I don't understand. What is the plan to kill Draxis's special agents?"

A smile crossed Mr. Coco's face. "You don't know about the three humans entangled with drogs?"

"No. When did this happen?"

"A few days ago. You heard about the apparent attack on Omegan's crown prince, Paul?"

"Of course. Paul and Vince were playing around, switching between human twins. There are various speculations—plots against the current monarchy or maybe it was just an accident. King Boolong ordered an investigation. How are drogs involved?"

"Overlord Draxis's special agents are entangled with powerful and dangerous humans. He is going to use them to create chaos in the human world and thereby reap a huge increase of energy. It will prove his idea of actively manipulating those we inhabit. You know this."

"Yes."

"There are only three humans that know of Ephemeral entanglements. They killed Sheldon Robertson; that action disentangled the Overlord's sister, who ended up dying. Paul has promised to free all humans from their entanglement with Ephemerals if he becomes king. For this favor, the humans have volunteered to become entangled with drogs of the Crystal Moon Hunt. At the return of the caravan, they will pass by Draxis's special agents and then use the entangled drogs to kill them."

"Father, that is an impressive plan. Obviously, my spies didn't find out everything about your group."

"But I will still be the one who kills the Overlord," stated Meerlex.

"Then, that is our plan," said the High Priestess. She did not add— if Meerlex failed the attack on the Overlord, Artemesia would do it.

"I will let the humans know," said Mr. Coco. "They are brave. If their drogs are killed in the milieu, they will simply return to their human selves to live their lives. But there is a problem."

"And what is that?"

"The humans want their freedom. Paul has promised if he becomes king, he will remove all Ephemeral entanglements from the humans.

But he can't guarantee that the Omegan clan will be Selected as the next ruling clan."

"We will have to think on that."

"High Priestess," said Meerlex. "According to Xermegan customs, if Overlord Draxis dies, you could be selected as the Xermegan's next ruler."

"I doubt I'd have much of a chance if either you or I were involved in his assassination."

"There is little to be gained puzzling out which promises may or may not be kept," observed Mr. Coco. "The most important thing is Overlord Draxis dies and his special agents are thrown out of entanglement. The humans will soon be reentering the drogs' consciousnesses. I must be off."

"Goodbye, Father. I love you."

"I love you too, child. May the gods bless us and look over us." Then turning to his daughter's attendant, he continued, "Meerlex, trust that your bravery will be rewarded."

With a last hug, the High Priestess felt like a new hope for Ephemeron's future had sprung forth. "Let us go, Meerlex."

As they flew off, Mr. Coco's front yard drog opened an eye, but then returned to its slumber.

38

"I must admit I'm glad I stayed around.
Think about it. By fate or chance,
we have turned into king-makers."

On **Earth,** the impromptu call for a meeting from Mr. Coco raised the hairs on the back of Nick's neck. Weren't they supposed to be left alone until tomorrow? Why this sudden meeting in the middle of the night?

With Vince and Paul joining, the group entanglement was imposed, again surrounding all in a pulsating white light.

"We may not have to sacrifice the thousand humans," began Mr. Coco. "There have been new developments."

"You have our attention, Mr. Coco," said Nick.

"The original plan was for you three to kill three of Overlord Draxis's agents. These agents are entangled in humans who are extremely wealthy and in positions who can cause immense havoc on Earth. The reverse entanglements of a thousand humans was a strategy to cover the agents' assassinations."

"Yes, Mr. Coco, we know," said Nick impatiently. "What are you proposing?"

"In your attack on the agents, could you also try to kill Overlord Draxis? He will be standing only a few feet away on the podium with the king."

"That seems like a *big* ask," said Nick.

"Is it? How is that any different than attacking his agents? The Overlord and the agents will all be right there for the taking. Overlord Draxis is the one who is pushing for dominion over earth."

"Won't he be guarded?" asked Tony.

"Yes, all those on the podium will be guarded, but no one will expect a frontal assault from Crystal Moon caravan drogs."

Mr. Coco explained some of what had transpired between himself and the High Priestess, telling of how the High Priestess had grown disillusioned with the Overlord's mad ego and it was only because of this that she had let the rebel group to continue to exist. He said nothing of the High Priestess being his daughter, nor that Meerlex or Artemesia planned to kill the Overlord themselves.

"Mr. Coco," exclaimed Paul, "all of this time, the High Priestess has known about our rebel activities?"

"Most of it. If she wanted to, she could have had us all killed. But I fear our group is living on borrowed time. She may not be able to protect us much longer."

"There are only three of us," said Sylvia. "The Overlord is a fourth Ephemeral."

"If we can kill the Overlord, that will be even better than our original plan. Do the best you can against the agents."

The idea of going after the Overlord made sense, thought Nick, but the idea of making a last-minute change of plans raised unresolved concerns.

"Paul," called Tony, "how about you? Will you keep to your promise? How will you feel if your clan is not Selected?"

"If I become king, I will keep my promise."

"There is one other thing," said Mr. Coco. "I can't make any promises, but if the Overlord dies, the Xermegan clan can choose the High Priestess as their next ruler."

"You're playing with us, Mr. Coco," said Sylvia. "*If* the Overlord is killed, and *if* the High Priestess becomes her clan's next ruler and *if* that clan is Selected as the next Ephemeron monarchy, then maybe the High Priestess will promise to set all humans free of entanglements. Promises shouldn't be dependent on more than one *if*."

"I said I can't make any promises."

"But you tease us with the idea."

"The death of Overlord Draxis gives you the best chance of freeing yourselves."

Nick, Tony, and Sylvia exchanged looks. "All right, Mr. Coco, we're in," said Nick. "We'll go after Draxis."

"In a few hours you will be reinserted with your drogs," said Mr. Coco. "Catch what sleep you can."

On Ephemeron, the hand-picked religious scholars of each clan were meeting inside King Boolong's palace. A chaotic series of debates tore through the participants' exchanges, causing many to stridently belittle the views of others and piously elevate their own views.

Into this swamp of discord, the king entered the great hall, muting all but a few.

The king, noting the insolent jeering of a few of the scholars, called to his guards and had the miscreants thrown from the palace.

With the gathering of scholars chastened and deferentially attentive, the king began. "We will have disagreements, but we will show respect for others. Those who cannot follow this simple principle will also be removed. I hope you will all understand and take me seriously."

Having already set a precedent, the king knew there would be no further transgressions.

"I have called you here for a singular debate. What is the role of our god Alborix? The Xermegan clan has pronounced him a god above all other gods. The Vimegan clan honors Alborix, but honors him as one of our many gods, not supreme over the other gods. And as the spokesperson for the Omegan clan, we have tried to accommodate the passions of the Xermegan and Vimegan clans. Thus, we are here today to find a path forward by which each Ephemeral can believe what is important, but which allows for the passions and beliefs of fellow Ephemerals who differ in their beliefs.

"Our society has survived for tens of thousands of years. We have survived moving to a new planet and the hewing out of a new life against the challenges of Ephemeron's wild jungles and beasts. We have respected this world and cared for it. For tens of thousands of years, we have respected each other and have accomplished great things. But our world hangs in the balance. Will we tear ourselves apart or find a different path forward?

"This is why I have called you here. I charge you to find a way forward that mends our world. This is your task. And as the most senior religious scholars of our planet, it is your duty to chart that path."

In the wake of the king's words, many scholars jumped in with their well-rehearsed views.

The king observed the discord and felt great sadness. He had tried his best to encourage their adherence to high principals, but instead, saw feigned allegiance and duplicitous conversations. The king wondered if his Selection had been the last free vote of his people. The king had thought bringing each clans' scholars together would be a way to keep Ephemeron together, but now he realized that his hopes might have been folly. It seemed there was little reason for the clans to work together.

Having said his words, the king exited off to the side of the temple's altar space. Artemesia, the High Priestess of the Xermegan clan, stood in wait.

"High Priestess, your clan's Overlord has been very willful. His weighty promises and proclamations are alluring."

"Your Highness, I do not speak his words."

"But you support him."

"As is my duty."

"High Priestess, your highest duty is to Ephemeron, not to the Overlord."

"King, that is my sworn loyalty."

On Earth, morning had arrived. It was time for Nick, Sylvia, and Tony's consciousness to be reactivated inside the drogs.

At the time of each insertion, each drog jumped from their perches. Their drog handlers cussed at the commotion while puzzling about the cause of the upheaval. But in a few short minutes, each drog, having resynced with a familiar human consciousness, quieted down.

The Crystal Moon Hunt Master took a position overlooking the riches-ladened caravan. It was time to return to the city and present their gatherings to the king. Lifting his opal and silver staff, it glowed with iridescent colors. A deep warbling sound echoed across the temple's grounds and into the depths of the surrounding jungle.

As before, he sent out scouts and their drogs first. An encounter with any of the jungle's wild creatures could prove disastrous. They had already lost precious cargo due to the recent Megafly swarm. The caravan was evidently anxious. The Zalmas pulled at the schleppers' reins. Pickers milled close by as if that would ensure extra safety for all of the Ephemerals' hard work of gathering rare crystals and flowers.

Receiving notice from the scouts that the first part of the route back to the city was free of danger, the Hunt Master unleashed the all-clear sound for the caravan to head out.

"Sylvia, how do you feel today?" asked Mr. Coco.

"It feels like the alpha drog and I are in sync, but the true test is yet to come."

"I'm hearing the same reports from Vince and Paul."

The alpha drog belted out an annoyed set of rapid clicks at the drog that had bumped into her. Sylvia heard Nick's laugh at the intentional collision.

Sylvia, through the drog's eyes, could see Tony's drog approach. "Tony, don't bash into my drog. She'll probably snip off one of your limbs."

"I thought you liked me."

"Yeah, but I'm not so sure my drog has the same hots for your drog."

"Has anybody thought about what we're going to do if we get out of this mess?" asked Tony.

"Which mess are you talking about?" responded Nick. "The mess of being in these drogs and our assassination task, or the mess of what needs to be done back on Earth?"

"I thought you had decided to let Tubby Vaughn off the hook," said Tony. "That would only leave Pearce Savage."

"I haven't thought that far ahead. Just getting back to Earth safely and getting these damn Ephemerals out of my head would be welcomed."

"As close as I came to committing suicide with Paul's voice in my head, I must admit I'm glad I stayed around. Think about it. By fate or chance, we have turned into king-makers. How about you, Sylvia? What do you want if we get out of this mess?"

"Marry you, you dummy, and have a long, relaxing honeymoon."

"That seems worth fighting for," said Tony.

A harsh blast from the Hunt Master's staff pierced the air.

"What's going on?" asked Nick to Vince.

"Hell Pigs have been spotted in the area. We need to avoid a confrontation."

The Hunt Master would push the caravan at double-time to get back to the safety of the city. He didn't need any more incidents.

39

*In the distance, the Hunt Master's staff emitted warbling sounds
and brilliant prismatic streaks of light,
announcing the caravan's approach.*

Anticipating the return of the Crystal Moon caravan, Ephemeron's capital city was transformed by the work of many. Stories of bravery and death, accompanied by embellishments and rumors, had arrived ahead of the returning caravan. Ephemerals from the countryside did what they could to find lodging in the city. For those who could not attend, the caravan's arrival would be live-streamed.

A grand entrance to the city was planned. King Boolong, Overlord Draxis, and Commander Vaaruv would be seated on the Crystal Moon platform, an elegant stage carved out of rare crystals bedecked with the wafting psychedelic scents of Ephemeron's wild flowers. Behind them stood the most important VIPs of each clan.

The return of the annual Crystal Moon caravan always motivated the city to present a wonderful celebratory welcome. A kaleidoscope of colors and cultures converged to create an atmosphere of wonder and unity. Families from all clans gathered under the wispy colors of Ephemeron's sky, sharing the rich tapestry of Ephemeron's traditions.

Youngsters wearing traditional clan garments ran around, their faces painted with excitement. Parents proudly showcased their clan heritage through intricately designed attire and colorful crystal adornments. On multiple stages scattered across the city, dance troupes from Ephemeron's countryside and distant cities showcased their exotic talents, the most spectacular involving flying above, around, and through torches of fire that leaped hungrily at the Ephemeral dancers' insect wings. A mesmerizing fusion of traditional and contemporary styles enthralled the crowds. Spectators were invited to join in, forming impromptu dance circles to learn and share dance steps.

Aromas of exotic cuisines wafted through the air. Vendors of food stalls called out to passersby, tempting them with morsels of free food. The togetherness of communal tables accentuated the deep bonds of Ephemerals, pulling those of different clans together, sharing stories of family and hopes for the future. The young Ephemerals easily made new dear friends.

Music venues dotted the city, each pulsating with distinct rhythms. Traditional music intertwined with modern sounds, creating an eclectic panorama of sound. Young and old swayed together, accentuating the powerful beats. Musicians invited the crowds to join with them. Those musicians, especially imaginative and daring, might ask for song ideas and then create a spontaneous verse.

Yet amidst these great festivities, the religious pageantry of Overlord Draxis's ambition was intermixed.

Two Ephemeral friends stood among the enthusiastic crowd, waiting for the caravan's arrival.

"The Crystal Moon Hunt is a day of celebration for all Ephemerals, regardless of clan. Why is Overlord Draxis putting on Xermegan religious festivities on the same day?"

"The gifts and benefits that Draxis is giving out are available to all clans. He is simply honoring the bravery of the hunt's participants."

"It feels like a snub to the king and to our people."

"Not at all. See! Look there. The Overlord's agents and priests are giving away free energy tokens. The tokens are given to all clans."

"They carry staffs honoring the god Alborix and torches of the eternal flame. The Crystal Moon Hunt is supposed to be a time of universality and honoring all our gods."

"The Xermegan clan shares those common ideals. Are not many people wearing the garments and colors of their clans? You accept that diversity. Carrying the eternal flame honors all."

"I fear for our world. It seems there are too many divisions."

"My friend, I think you are reading in things that are not there. King Boolong is old. The Selection is near. A new king must emerge. Overlord Draxis is not the only one who has placed themselves in the public's eye. The next 1,000 years will bolster Ephemeron's role across the universe."

In the distance, the Hunt Master's staff emitted warbling sounds and brilliant prismatic streaks of light, announcing the caravan's approach.

On the royal grand stage in the center of the city, King Boolong and the most powerful families of Ephemeron waited. Standing with Overlord Draxis on one side and Commander Vaaruv on the other, the king spoke so both could hear.

"Overlord, the return of a Crystal Moon caravan is something that should be rejoiced by all Ephemerals, don't you agree?"

"Of course, Your Majesty."

"But you have planned your religious festivities to overlap."

"Your Majesty, the festivities of the Xermegan clan are meant to accentuate and honor the caravan's return. Our festivities are open to all."

"Yet your acolytes ask Ephemeral citizens to make a special pledge to Alborix."

"Your Majesty, it is true that the Xermegan clan has a special devotion to Alborix, but we honor all the Ephemeral gods. It is our belief Alborix is of special power and authority amongst the Ephemeron gods."

"Overlord, have you not heard?"

"I'm sorry, Your Majesty. I don't know what you are referring to."

"This afternoon, the convocation of the clans' religious hierarchy has released a special edict that clarifies that all Ephemeron gods are of equal stature. Though each may manifest special natures, none are above any other."

An almost ashen countenance descended across the Overlord's face.

A special glee seemed to cross Commander Vaaruv's face.

"My priests would never have agreed to such a decree," blurted the Overlord.

"But they did, Overlord. They did. Unanimously. You have always sworn yourself to such edicts. You will abide, will you not?"

"Your Majesty …" stuttered the Overlord. But before more could be said, the blaring of the Hunt Master's staff and the citizenry's celebrating cheers drowned out his blubbering words.

Entering the city through its heavy iron gate, the Crystal Moon caravan was greeted by many thousands of individual insect buzzes that morphed into a wave of synchronous sound that rhythmically oscillated into crests and troughs of appreciation. The news of the caravan's great hardships had spread. Ephemerals were eager to express their gratitude and admiration for the participants' bravery. The Hunt Master hovered above, beaming with pride.

The weary hunters maintained a steadfast formation. The sea of anxious citizens parted. The dead and severely injured were carried in front, followed by scouts, then drogs and their handlers, flower and crystal pickers, and lastly by the richly-laden Zalmas and their schleppers. Special cheers arose as the wounded alpha-drog passed by.

Overlord Draxis, seething with anger but having to publicly hold himself with the stature of a future monarch, could do nothing but accept his humiliation with false waves to the crowd and feigned cheers for the caravan's return.

On the ground in front of the regal crystal platform stood the three Draxis agents, unaware of their master's distress. As instructed, they were freely giving out high-priced gifts to the nearby citizenry in the name of Overlord Draxis and the Xermegan clan.

Stopping in front of the king's podium, the Crystal Moon hunters turned and bowed in deference. The drogs hovered above, but also bowed to the king.

Sylvia and her alpha drog, missing part of an appendage and still showing partially healed slash marks from her battles, held her position only a few feet away from Overlord Draxis.

Commander Vaaruv spoke. "Overlord, it is good luck to pet the alpha drog upon its return. It seems to be eyeing you."

"The drog is filthy. It needs a wash."

Whether the alpha drog exactly understood the Overlord's words or only sensed their tone, it had the same result.

Sylvia, by this time perfectly tuned to the drog's emotions, thought of charging forward and decapitating Overlord Draxis, which is what the alpha drog rapidly executed without hesitation.

Nick and Tony's drogs easily decapitated the three Draxis agents, with Tony taking out two. Screams erupted everywhere.

Hoping to give their drogs a chance to escape, Sylvia, Nick, and Tony spurred their drogs off into the crystalline sky. Giant viewing screens and live-streaming captured it all. The king's foot *accidentally* sent the head of Overlord Draxis rolling off the podium to be subsequently trampled in the melee.

In that brief moment of escape, the human-entangled drogs had never felt freer. It was a wildness they had been long owed and that Sylvia, Nick, and Tony shared.

Silently King Boolong wished they would escape, though he knew it could not be.

A shattering, multi-toned blast exited from the Hunt Master's staff, raced across the crystalline-colored sky and blew apart the three drogs. Antennae, limbs, mandibles, and insect blood filled the sky, temporarily creating an ooze-filled cloud.

Moments later on Earth, Sylvia, Nick, and Tony were sprawled across the sofa and floor having been safely released from their entanglements with the drogs. It was some minutes before anyone caught their bearings.

"Damn!" said Tony. "We did it! Nick and I got the Draxis agents." They looked over at Sylvia.

"Overlord, decapitated," she said matter-of-factly, though not being able to completely hide a hint of enthusiasm. "I assume his evil ass is still twitching about."

"Then our deed is done. We are free," exclaimed Tony.

"Sorry, brother, we're not," said Nick. "There are still the entanglements with Vince and Paul."

"Fuck."

"Well done, Nick." It was Vince's voice.

"What happens now," asked Nick out loud and causing confused looks on Tony and Sylvia's faces. "Vince is talking to me," explained Nick pointing to his head.

"You did good, Tony," congratulated Paul.

"Damn, now Paul's talking to me."

"No one's talking to me," Sylvia boasted.

"Hi, Sylvia," came Mr. Coco's voice. "You're still connected to the E-station that was synching your consciousness. Don't worry, we won't be able to keep the channel open very long, then you'll be free of me."

Sylvia, now with a sour look on her face, pointed to her head. "I spoke too soon. Mr. Coco is still in my head."

In short order, the humans realized they could do nothing but wait for Ephemeron's Selection to occur to find out what their fate would be.

Sylvia said they should find a restaurant so they could eat a real meal.

Tony promised to fire up the BBQ in the coming days.

Nick was already thinking about Pearce Savage.

All of them badly needed a shower.

40

"There's one other item that needs mentioning," said Paul.
Oh-here-we-go-again looks crossed the faces
of Nick, Tony, and Sylvia.

On **Ephemeron,** the Crystal Moon calamity was what everyone talked about. Two days after the event, King Boolong went before his people with a streamed address.

"The recent drog attacks at the Crystal Moon celebration have been deeply disturbing to me as I know it has been for you. Regardless of one's clan allegiance, this is a sorrowful chapter for Ephemeron.

"But my dear Ephemerals, it appears the gods have intervened for a reason us mortals could not see. Upon investigation of the incident, it has come to light that Overlord Draxis was engaged in a devious plot to manipulate your passions to be Selected as the next monarch and anoint himself as a new god.

"The gods knew of his evil plans, and it was our gods who directed the drogs to kill Overlord Draxis and his complicit agents. It was our gods who once again stepped in to save us and our world.

"Further, our investigation shows that High Priestess Artemesia is innocent of the Overlord's scheme. As second in hierarchy of the Xermegan clan, I give her my blessing to run as the Xermegan clan's leader and to be properly considered in the upcoming Selection for Ephemeron's next monarch. May the gods continue to bless us and care for us. Goodnight, Ephemeron."

Three weeks later, Ephemerals went to their voting stations. Betting parlors had predicted another reelection of the Omegan clan, but in an upset, the Xermegan clan was chosen to be the next ruling clan over Ephemeron for the next 1,000 years. And in a sign of her favor with the Xermegan clan, the High Priestess was chosen to be the ruling monarch.

One week later, Queen Artemesia had decreed the removal of all entanglements with humans and had decreed that the remaining entanglements across the universe would follow a strict code of noninterference. Meerlex was elevated to the position of Xermegan High Priestess.

On Earth inside the rented house, enveloped by a pulsing white double entanglement, Vince and Paul were saying their goodbyes.

"Did anybody learn anything from this?" asked Sylvia.

"Ephemerals are ugly," offered Nick.

An awkward silence permeated the room, then a set of five chortles burst forth.

"The same could be said about humans," responded Vince, keeping to the theme.

"Perhaps Ephemerals and humans are more similar than we imagined," observed Paul.

"Do you really think so?" questioned Nick.

"Yes, Nick, I do. Except for our technical capability using quantum entanglement, each species is just as flawed. We each want power. We lie. We're devious. We kill."

"I though you said Ephemerals don't kill," responded Tony.

"We might have lied about that, too," revealed Paul.

"So, we really didn't need to be entangled with the drogs?" blurted Sylvia.

"That was real. We really did need your help. We didn't see any other way to get to Draxis and his agents."

"What about the future of humanity?" questioned Tony. "Are Ephemerals really going to leave us alone?"

"At least while Queen Artemesia reigns. She should live another 800 years or more."

"What happens to your rebellion?" asked Nick.

"Overlord Draxis is dead," answered Vince. "The idea of actively controlling other life-forms will never be allowed by the queen. There is no need for a rebellion. The rebels have disbanded. You helped bring that about. We are in your debt."

"Finally, some sort of thank-you," muttered Nick.

"Do you still want to strangle me?" asked Vince.

Nick let out a long exhale. "I guess not, Vince, but a firm throttling still seems appropriate."

Annoying insect laughter filled the room.

"There's one other item that needs mentioning," said Paul.

Oh-here-we-go-again looks crossed the faces of Nick, Tony, and Sylvia.

Sensing the humans' sudden anxiety, Paul spoke up quickly.

"It's not anything bad," he continued, "just something you should know. Even though we will no longer inhabit you, there is still an infinitely small quantum connection that exists between us. It is a leftover from when the universe first burst into existence. You may not understand the value, but leaving those ancient subatomic connections in place will one day benefit humanity when you want to cross the vast distances of space."

"So, Nick and I are still connected with you?" inquired Tony. "Won't we be long dead before our scientists develop that kind of technology?"

"No doubt, you will be, but the remains of your body will be recycled into your planet. Someday a worm may eat that particle, and the worm will be eaten by a bird, which will be eaten by something else and on and on that particle will be recycled. Preserving those ancient entanglements will someday serve your species."

"What about me?" asked Sylvia. "I was entangled with a drog."

"Yes, and now you have become part of the quantum web."

"I'm not sure I understand," said Sylvia. "You're saying the three of us are still quantumly connected to Ephemeron at some subatomic level, even though you are no longer inhabiting us. Is that right?"

"That's basically it," answered Paul.

"Then one day we could all meet again?"

"Theoretically, yes. But Queen Artemesia has set you free so that scenario is empty speculation. We assume you would never want that to happen. And if it makes a difference, we wouldn't want you inside our heads, either. Experiencing your presence was very unsettling."

"I need a drink," observed Nick. "I know Tony and I can't wait for you to be out of our heads." There was hesitation in Nick's voice. "But it's almost hard to say goodbye."

"Then we'll do it for you," said Vince. "Bye, Nick."

"Bye, Vince."

"Bye, Tony," said Paul.

"Bye, Paul."

And with that, the double entanglement vanished, leaving Nick, Tony, Sylvia—and humanity—free.

A month later, the time of the great Fusion spread across Ephemeron. Following tradition, Queen Artemesia decided the fusions of the most senior royals for each clan.

Paul and Vince were fused by their wishes.

Queen Artemesia and Meerlex were fused, setting a new precedent.

Callum, having been entangled with Pearce Savage and having been lobbying for entanglement with Sylvia, was harshly disappointed as he was left unfused and reentangled inside an especially revolting, slothful, and long-lived Reevin reptile.

In her final edict, Queen Artemesia ordered that all newborn Ephemeral young would no longer be weaned on energy harvested from E-stations. It was time to break the addictive cycle.

A month later, Pearce Savage was found in an alley with a razor-sharp, broadhead-tipped arrow through his heart.

Tubby Vaughn had been given his reprieve from Nick's vengeance, though as Nick had predicted, Tubby eventually got into an argument with another criminal that ended Tubby's life.

Six months later, Nick and Tony were fly-fishing in Montana. For tomorrow's supper, Tony promised to barbecue a brisket.

In town, a popular new bar and restaurant, called Sylvia's, had opened.

Though police found most of the dead henchmen that Nick had dispatched, the men's rap sheets were long and notorious. It wasn't to say the police didn't care, but there was the assessment that a modicum of justice had been served.

An inquiry into billionaire Shelton Robertson's death unearthed his support of terrorists. His name was trashed, his ill-gotten wealth was seized, and his reputation was buried in ignominy. People thought he got what he deserved.

Tending his garden, Mr. Coco popped a crunchy ZoZo into his mouth. He inhaled deeply trying to catch the blue wisps of Ephemeron's atmosphere that were especially prominent on this day. He thought he heard the tintinnabulation of faint bells ringing in the distance.

"Blue wisps are love," said the beautiful young Ephemeral, grasping one of Mr. Coco's appendages.

"That they are, my dear. That they are."

"I have something to tell you. Our Fusion was successful. Our seed lives."

Discussion Scenarios and Questions
He Died Two Days Ago

Ephemerals

What were your thoughts about the Ephemerals? Their society? Their beliefs and customs?

What were your thoughts about Ephemerals' belief that they were *peacefully* reaping energy from other species' emotions?

What did you think about Overlord Draxis's rationale for the Manifest Destiny of Ephemerals?

Do you see any similarities between Overlord Draxis and human figures?

What were your thoughts about the religious variations within Ephemeral society?

How did you see the relationship between Artemesia and Meerlex?

How did you see the relationship between Artemesia and Overlord Draxis?

To sabotage Overlord Draxis's plans, the rebels voted to remove the E-station barriers between a thousand humans and Ephemerals, likely driving both groups insane. Did you see this as justifiable? How did you vote?

What were your thoughts about Vince and Paul?

Humans

What were your thoughts on the violence that the humans implemented?

How did you see Nick? Do you feel Nick's personality evolved?

Thoughts about Tony?

What were your thoughts about Tony and Nick's lives possibly being different because of which Ephemeral they were entangled with (most of time)?

Sylvia

What were your feelings when you found out that Sylvia might become entangled against her will?

What did you think of Sylvia's choice to become entangled with the drog?

What were your thoughts when Sylvia confronted Uncle Shelton at the charity event?

Was it sufficient *how* Sylvia confronted Shelton while Nick laced Shelton's car with thallium?

In Gratitude

With sincere appreciation, I wish to thank my developmental editor *Barb Wilson.* In this second novel working together, Barb's gentle, but challenging suggestions again pushed me.

And despite great care to present a novel with few grammatical and typographical errors, my proof editor, *Peggie Ireland* demonstrated her cold-eye expertise. (How does she find all those errors?!)

The cover and internal design were the masterful work of *Rebecca Finkel.* We tore our hair out working out the concept. One would think a picture of a dead person on the cover should have been appropriate. So much for preconceived notions.

My journey of developing this novel could not have happened without the discussions, impressions, suggestions, and love provided to me by dear friend *Nellie Peña* and my sister *Jane Parsons.*

Finally, this novel would not have happened without the amazing expertise and efforts of *The Book Shepherd, Judith Briles.* Truly, Judith is the tough-love book publishing expert any novelist would want in their corner. Thank you, Judith.

Dear Reader—Thank you for your interest. Enjoy the journey.

About John Posner

For John Posner, the captivating thing about Sci-Fi/ Fantasy is that it encourages the reader to step back from everyday lives and be a kid again that wonders —*what if?* With imagination, a universe of human and social worlds is exposed. Impossible technological marvels become harbingers of reality.

Before becoming a full-time writer, he was an IT Project Manager for more than 40 years with an extensive technical writing background.

Since the age of six, he has had a fascination with science and science fiction. Novels that captured his imagination included: Time *Machine, Stranger in a Strange Land, Fahrenheit 451, The Invisible* Man, the psycho-thrillers of Stephen King, and so many comic books: Spider Man, Green Lantern, Thing, and Fantastic Four.

TV shows and movies that influenced his imagination and writing: *Twilight Zone, Outer Limits, Star Trek, 2001: A Space Odyssey, Terminator, Alien,* and *Star Wars.*

John invites you to **Dive into the Fantasy** of Science Fiction's thematic journeys within and beyond.

He calls Maryland home. In his spare time, you'll find him honing his BBQ skills.

Other Books by John

Sci-Fi/Fantasy **Forever is Too Long** envisions a future technology revealed by the confession of Jake, a human who crosses over to being a Mindar. Jake is now forced to wrestle with the Unintended Consequences created and the internal demons that he must face. Noah is a young boy whose human DNA is altered causing genetic mutations. As he fights for his self-identity, he discovers his untapped powers.

Jake, Noah, and others are willing to take a stand for the soul of humanity. It speculates about the technological consequences humans are not prepared for.